The Legend of Flying Horses

Sarah Vail

Title of Book: The Legend of Flying Horses

Copyright © by Sarah Vail 2025

Published by Bitterroot Mountain Publishing House LLC
P.O. Box 3508, Hayden, ID 83835

Visit our website at www.BMPHmedia.com

Interior and cover design by Jera Publishing
Photographs: All images in author's collection
Illustrations: Horses by Judy Parker; Airplanes by John Stahr
Editor: Sue Eller and Suzanne Holland

Library of Congress Cataloguing in Publication Data

ISBN: 978-1-960059-39-0 Hardcover
ISBN: 978-1-960059-38-3 Softcover
ISBN: 978-1-960059-37-6 eBook

Printed in the United States of America

10 9 8 7 6 5 4 3 2 1

Acknowledgements

I would like to thank my editors, Sue Eller and Suzanne Holland for their hard work in helping me produce this book.

Also I'd like to thank my writer's Zoom critique group for their great suggestions for improvements in my story.

I'd like to thank my artist friends; Judy Parker for her wonderful horse drawings and John Stahr for the Stuka Dive Bomber and B17 Flying Fortress drawings that enhance the story.

Chapter One

"HA! ONE HORSE SHY OF being the crazy horse lady? Granny Annaleah *WAS the crazy horse lady!* I'm not going!" Seventeen-year-old Karena Bradshaw stomped into the living room, hands dripping with dishwater. Her mother followed tight to her heels.

"Dad! Dad, can't I stay with you? She doesn't need me!" Karena turned abruptly, and her long blonde braid whipped in the air, settling on her left shoulder. Maybe she wouldn't feel so desperate if it were a different time. She glared at her mom and dried her hands on the towel her mother tossed her way.

"It's not fair! This is my last summer with Sam," she whined. He was off to Princeton in the fall, and she still had one more year of high school. Already, their relationship cracked under the weight of the ton of bricks stacked against it. She knew it would be a miracle if it survived, even if she didn't have to go with Mom.

Sam had already tested his freedom and checked out other bikini-clad girls hanging out at the beach when he thought Karena wasn't looking. He'd definitely dump her if she went away for the last two weeks before school started again.

Karena wasn't sure if she even cared. Sam was comfortable, not exciting. They'd been together since the first day she started her freshman year. She'd never dated anyone else. They'd become a high school fixture: Karena and

Sam, prom king and queen; Karena and Sam together in every yearbook picture; Karena cheering Sam on at every football and basketball game—they were such a mind-numbing cliché. But she wasn't sure she wanted to change it.

"Your mother wants you to go. You're going." Dad glared at her. He sat forward in his brown leather recliner, bumping the footrest shut. He folded the evening newspaper with a rustle down onto his lap. His green eyes sparked with anger. "She asks very little of you. You can give your mother two weeks."

Two weeks might as well be two years.

"But you said Granny A was nuts," Karena protested.

Two days ago, Grandmother Annaleah Baker's attorney called, informed Mom her stepmother had passed, and asked Mom to come for the funeral and reading of the will. They'd been fighting about it since. By forcing Karena to go with her, Mom blew up her end-of-summer plans as if with a brick of C-4.

The whole family dreaded visits to Granny A's when she was alive—all she talked about was horses. Mom listened to her boring stories about her champions with their unpronounceable Polish and Arabian names; this one is from the Koheilian strain, this one from the Seglawi, this one desert bred—whatever that meant. And who cared? Only other horse crazies, that's who.

Sure, Karena was sorry the old loon had passed. But they were never close. She understood Granny A died rich, and Mom stood to inherit something, but she wasn't alone. Her brothers stood to gain, too, along with her cousins. Now, all the relatives who had ignored the old woman in life were converging on her estate like vultures circling carrion.

Mom insisted she go because she needed an ally.

Dad said he would go but couldn't get away from work. So, the next two weeks would be a living hell while Mom and the relatives fought over some dusty old furniture and horses no one cared about or even wanted.

"Now finish packing. I don't want to hear another word." Karena's father straightened the paper with a dramatic snap and started to read. He momentarily paused and looked at her over the top edge. "You know I love you, but your mother needs you."

"I know." Karena slumped her shoulders, conceding to her parents' wishes. What could she do about it anyway? Run away? She was angry but not stupid. Unlike some friends, she knew she wasn't prepared for an independent life. Not yet, anyway. Always the pragmatic one, she wanted the college education her parents promised to provide. She worked hard to keep her grade point average high to get into UCLA.

Karena took the stairs to her second-floor bedroom and slammed the door, ensuring Dad realized she went under protest. She would miss out on everything, especially the big end-of-summer beach party.

Besides, the late August surf was at its best before school started again. Typhoons churning their way across the Pacific sent wind-driven waves back to the coast in a South swell. But lucky her, instead of surfing, she was going to Idaho, fricking Athol, Idaho, population six-hundred ninety-five. In frustration, Karena flopped face-first onto her bed.

After the five-hour flight from Los Angeles to Spokane, the depressing funeral, and the drive to Athol finally ended, Karena and her mother sat at the long, twelve-person table in Granny A's farmhouse dining room, sipping hot coffee. The cheapo red-eye flight landed at seven this morning, and the funeral was over at ten. Karena was in no mood to be here, let alone around her annoying relatives.

It seemed everyone here felt just as she did. Her favorite, Uncle Ray, shot daggers across the table at pinched-faced and prissy Aunt Helen. Shy Uncle Willie sat pensively, looking into his coffee cup. If he could jump in and disappear, Karena was sure he would have.

The bully in the crowd, Aunt Eveline, was uncharacteristically silent, her ruddy cheeks more flushed than usual. Clearly, with considerable effort, she held back her barbed tongue. On the sly, she dumped brandy from a silver flask into her coffee and peeked around as if pretending no one noticed. Uncle Martin, usually the happy guy in the group, looked like the serial killer Jeffrey Dahmer in full clown makeup. His kinky red hair stood out from his head like a wig. Everyone at the polished cherry table glared at each other. Karena would be surprised if these fun-filled two weeks didn't end in someone's murder.

Soon enough, it would come down to a battle over who got this table, and the lawyers hadn't even read Granny A's 'Last Will and Testament' yet. That event was scheduled for the end of their two-week stay. She groaned. No wonder her mom wanted her to come.

Before they'd even walked through the door and could get suitcases settled in their rooms, Mom's two brothers, Martin, the oldest, and Ray, the youngest, bent her ear and tried to convince her to throw in with them and sell the farm. Karena rolled her eyes. *Duh! As if Mom had a reason to keep it!*

The relatives had broken into several warring factions: keep the 250-acre farm, sell it, divide it into single-family housing lots—as if anyone wanted to live in this one-horse town. Well, that was a lie. Granny A had close to thirty horses. So, it was a thirty-horse town. At least horses liked living here.

Karena needed to get out of the stuffy room. She picked up her mug of coffee and wandered out to the wrap-around porch surrounding the front and sides of the big craftsman-style farmhouse. After walking to the edge of the deck, she leaned against the turned wood railings.

The house sat on a knoll above the expanse of green pastures and hayfields. *What a view!* The scent of newly cut grass fragranced the air with a sneeze-teasing freshness. In the furthest field, a big, green-and-yellow John Deere mowed the second hay cutting into neat windrows. Each time the tractor made a pass, the weanling foals in the adjoining pasture dashed away, bucking, snorting, and racing each other. It was a game. They kept returning to challenge the mechanized beast to play with them. But, at least on the warm August afternoon, there was peace away from the contentiousness over Granny A's belongings.

Beyond the pastures, the Bitterroots rose skyward, their flanks covered with Douglas Fir and Ponderosa Pine. It was a beautiful change from California's parched, brown, grass-covered hills. The thought of California brought Sam to mind. She tried to call him for the third time. He'd said he wanted to know when she arrived, but he wasn't answering his phone. She looked up the forecasted wave heights on her iPhone's Surfs-Up App. The predicted six-foot curls would keep Sam out in the water all day. She missed the surfing, but not necessarily Sam.

She took a sip of her coffee. Karena didn't like coffee unless the bitterness was adjusted with a sufficient amount of sugar and cream. But she didn't know how she'd stay awake today without it.

Karena was in the odd and lonely position of being too young to stay around the adults and too old to hang with her younger cousins. She'd heard the three girls, Marsha, Lizbeth, and Sharon, were already in the sixty-foot barn saddling up horses, planning to ride in the covered arena. And twenty-year-old Kevin Baker, the oldest male cousin and a born sexist, had taken the three younger boys, Kenny, Matt, and Sherm, to Silverwood Theme Park. She was glad she hadn't been roped into that adventure. She was too grumpy to put up with Kevin's disparaging remarks about women—a subject he knew nothing about.

Maybe later in the week, she'd suggest the theme park to the little girl cousins if she needed to break the monotony. *What else am I going to do for two weeks?* She'd forgotten to bring a novel.

Karena recognized her mother's footsteps on the wood-planked deck but didn't turn. She wanted to make her point. She was unhappy and needed to remind her mom of it.

"Thank you, Darling, for coming with me," Mom started to lay down her gentle reprimand. "It's going to be difficult. As you can see, everyone has their own idea about what should be done. I'm so glad you're here." When Karena looked over at her mother, her frown had melted away, and a weightless gaze filled her eyes as if she were savoring a piece of dark chocolate. "It's so beautiful here. So peaceful." She took a deep breath.

"Well, you're the only happy one." Karena tilted her head and continued to stare at her mother's profile. Mom's guilt trip was a one-hundred percent success.

"I know I ask a lot of you. Leaving Sam and all."

"It's fine, Mom. Sam and I are going to break up anyway. He'll be back east. I'll be in California even after I graduate. We are doomed. I know it; he knows it, and now, you know it," Karena sighed.

"Is that what you want?" She set her hand on Karena's arm in sympathy.

"Sometimes. Am I old enough to know what I want where boys are concerned? Besides, I haven't even dated anyone else. And don't tell me about you and Dad. I've heard your story a million times." Her parents met in high school and had been together for twenty-five years.

Karena's mom rocked back in laughter. "You're more mature than I was at your age. I thought having a boyfriend was everything—the only thing."

"I want to be a doctor and join Uncle Ray's practice. If Sam's still around and the lawyer he says he's going to be, then we can talk," Karena said.

"Granny A would be so proud of you. Your dad and I are so proud of you."

Karena turned when the deck boards creaked as if under a heavy weight.

"All right, here's what we have decided." Karena recognized Uncle Ray's deep baritone. For a doctor, he was terribly overweight. "We're each going through a room. Sort out what's valuable from what's not and get organized for the estate auctioneers." Ray stood authoritatively; his hands planted firmly on his hips.

"You've gotten Eveline to agree?" Mom asked.

"Finally, Renae, but it took some doing. So don't argue." He smiled, looking like the gentle doctor Karena admired so much. He and Mom were the closest of her siblings. Uncle Ray was only eighteen months older than her mother. Growing up, Mom said they were almost like twins. They didn't look like it. Karena's mom was still beautiful at forty-two, and Uncle Ray hadn't aged well.

"Where do you want me?" Mom asked.

"It would be great if you would take Granny A's bedroom. Eveline is afraid Helen will pinch the jewelry," he answered, rolling his eyes.

"And me?" Karena asked, expecting to be assigned with her mother.

"The attic."

Karena groaned. "But there are spiders ...."

"Not in Granny A's attic," Mom said.

"Shall we get started?" Uncle Ray asked, motioning for them to return inside.

The staircase to the attic was narrow but pleasant and well-lit. Karena had expected a creepy, old, rickety ladder.

Here goes nothing! She took out the color-coded keys on the ring Uncle Ray had given her, found the proper key, and turned it in the lock. The door opened quietly as if on oiled hinges. She flipped the light switch and stepped inside.

This wasn't an attic but a shrine. Glass display cases filled with polished silver trophies, bright red, blue, and gold championship ribbons, and full garlands of red silk roses lined the far wall. Above the cases, original paintings with a brass nameplate in each frame's center bottom memorialized one of Granny A's champion horses.

Karena walked forward into the room. Two wingback chairs with a side table in between occupied the space in front of a bay window overlooking the pastures below. For only a flash, Karena thought she saw a young woman and man sitting there. They held hands across the table and looked lovingly into each other's eyes. She shook off the vision and briefly thought she should be frightened. After all, she wasn't prepared for ghosts. But instead, the whole room was suddenly infused with a feeling of warmth and devotion. If there were apparitions here, they were benign ones.

In the corner of the long attic, stacked against the wall, were three large trunks. They were easily three feet wide by six feet long and inlaid with expensive hardwoods in a Parque design. There wasn't even a speck of dust anywhere in the room. Perhaps the spirits cleaned up after themselves. She laughed.

Karena sat on the floor in front of the first trunk. Looking over the keys on the ring, she chose an ornate one matching the polished brass lock connecting the lid to the trunk's base.

For some reason, she felt excitement rushing through her. Opening this first trunk was like opening a secret treasure. Karena felt like a little kid playing a game. Would she find gold, silver, and precious jewels inside? She inserted the key into the lock. It fit perfectly. She sat back on her heels, rubbed her hands together, palm to palm, and then turned the key. She lifted the lid, and the clean, wood-spice scent of cedar filled the whole room.

Chapter Two

THE TRUNK'S CONTENTS WERE NEATLY organized as if waiting for Karena to find them. On one side, journals were stacked neatly, one cloth-covered book on the other. Next, letters bound up in a blue satin ribbon, picture albums, newspaper articles precisely taped in scrapbooks, and leatherbound volumes on veterinary medicine written in a foreign language were arranged in date order. And finally, underneath it all, she found a typewritten manuscript. The title page read: *The Legend of Flying Horses, A novel by Annaleah Sabrosky Baker.* It was as if Granny A expected and maybe wanted someone to go through her history. Karena sat back and pulled out the picture album from the top of the stack.

She knew the Baker clan, her mother's family, hadn't liked Granny A. The gossip was that Annaleah and George Baker met on a ship bringing home troops and some captured horses from Germany to the American remount stations at the end of World War II. After working together for many years, they married. Granny A didn't have her own children but raised George's three kids by his first wife.

Karena heard there was a sordid affair. But, the truth was more straightforward. George's first wife died a year before George even left for the war and met Annaleah. So, Granny A was innocent of the vicious rumor, at least.

The Bakers assumed Granny A was a Nazi; she didn't lose her foreign accent even after living here for years. That gossip should be put to rest, too.

Her accent was Polish, not German. Karena learned in one of her history classes the Nazis hated the Polish people almost as much as they hated the Jews. So, if anything, Granny A was a victim of the war and not a perpetrator.

Karena sank onto one of the wingback chairs, wriggled into the seat for comfort, and focused completely on the album's first page.

The first picture was a shock. When Karena met her grandmother, the woman was in her seventies. She was attractive for a woman of her age, but time always takes its toll. This picture of Granny A at a much younger age was stunning. The photo was black and white, but Annaleah seemed to come through in living color. She was as beautiful as one of the 1940s movie stars, Veronica Lake, perhaps—blue-eyed and blonde, near-perfect nose, luscious lips, and an engaging, traffic-stopping smile. No wonder Grandpa George fell in love and married her.

In the photo, she stood in the center with one young man on either side. They were all in uniform, even Granny Annaleah, and each held the reins to a bridled horse standing behind them. The explanation under the picture, written in English, said August 31, 1939, Janow Podlaski, Podchorazy (student officer) Nabozny, Podchorazy Wazdoda, and Annaleah Sabrosky. The friends' last happy day together.

Karena stared at the picture and felt almost as if she had entered their world. She closed her eyes and could hear horses in the background calling to each other and feel the end of summer warmth on her face. When she opened her eyes, she scrambled to the trunk and grabbed the dog-eared, typed manuscript from the bottom of the stack of scrapbooks. Opening the binder's padded cover, she read the short paragraph on the first page as she returned to her seat. Karena sank into her chair and set the picture album on the table. She turned to the beginning of the manuscript and began to read:

Preface:

"I created this novel by combining the thoughts in my journals and diaries and those of Janow's German Veterinarian, Dr. Erik, as we struggled through the years of World War II. It is my greatest hope you will learn the futility of war and the devastation and ruin it brings to all.

We humans are created in the image of God and loved by Him. Any hatred because of race is not of God. There is only one race—the human race. We must yield to God's will if we are to survive."

Karena contemplated her words for a moment. Her parents weren't religious, and she hadn't gone to church except when invited by friends. She shared her grandmother's comment about race. She turned her attention back to the book.

September 1, 1939, World War II began for Poland and the stud farm at Janow Podlaski.

The sky outside Annaleah's window was rain-washed blue—a color only appearing after the thunderstorms like those they'd experienced last night. She slipped out of bed and quietly dressed. Annaleah wanted to get to the stud farm early to oversee the morning feeding. The yearling colts grew like garden weeds and needed a little extra grain. Magnar Lesnik, the farm's veterinarian, had asked her to help this morning.

She carried her boots down the stairs and tip-toed in sock feet through the convent orphanage's long stone hallway. As she passed the chapel, she cautiously peeked in. Usually, Mother Superior and at least one or two sisters were at prayer by six-thirty in the morning. *Odd—the chapel was empty.* Maybe it was earlier than she thought. The clock at the end of the corridor hadn't yet chimed out the half-hour toll.

As she approached the large kitchen, the scent of freshly brewed coffee filled the air. She heard Father Jerzak's hoarse voice whispering excitedly. She stopped in her tracks, pressed her body against the cool stone wall, and listened.

Annaleah only heard a few words, enough to send a chill through her bones.

"...war...eminent...prepare...refugees...lost children...."

She didn't want to hear anymore. War! She didn't want to believe it. What about the horses at Janow? Dread cloaked her like a fog. She slipped by the opening, and once past, she sprinted to the outer doors and shouldered her way through.

She only slowed long enough to step into her riding boots. Once she'd wrestled them on, hopping on one foot at a time, she climbed the fence between the convent's property and the stud farm's pastures.

Still wet from rain and morning dew, she left a trail of bright green footprints behind her, where she'd knocked silver water droplets from the blades of grass. The scent of wild herbs and grasses crushed underfoot wafted in the air. She shrugged, knowing her early morning visit to the farm would no longer be a secret.

She'd been in trouble so often for sneaking off to the stud farm that Mother Superior had given up on discipline. Finally, the Nun threw up her hands and said God made Annaleah a horse-crazy girl, so He must have a purpose for her. Annaleah was grateful she'd no longer be such a disappointment.

The farm's Veterinarian, Dr. Lesnik, had come to her defense and told the sisters Annaleah was as valuable as gold regarding her work with the horses. It wasn't exactly a lie; she was certain he'd told it to keep the peace. She did love the horses.

Since the 1600s, Janow Podlaski has bred some of the finest Arabian horses in the world. So, she wasn't the only horse lover. All the children from the surrounding farms gravitated to the stud farm. The magnificent horses were a source of pride, and luckily for the children, the farm's director allowed them to come to the farm after school and in summer as long as they agreed to work. There were rules. Each child must be twelve years old, have a guardian's consent, and pitch in with the stall cleaning and grooming chores. It quickly weeded out the true horse lovers from the others.

If Annaleah could, she'd live at the farm. The horses made her happy and alive. She did as many extra chores at the orphanage as possible so Mother Superior would let her continue to see the horses. Secretly, she'd attended every foaling since her twelfth birthday by sneaking out each night during the foaling season while everyone else slept. She knew and loved every horse at the farm, and they knew and loved her.

She could hear the commotion long before she crossed the last half mile to the farm. The horses called to each other. Men shouted orders, metal clanged against metal, wood against wood, and a cacophony of panicked noise echoed off the barn walls. *Was war really coming?* Anxiety squeezed at her stomach.

When she arrived at the barn, soldiers in full uniform packed trucks with hay and grain. Horses old enough to be ridden were saddled and ready to go.

Dr. Lesnik counted bottles in one of the medicine trunks and motioned to a soldier to pack it onto the truck. He looked up and noticed her. Usually, he had a smile for her, but not this morning. It confirmed her fear, and she trembled inside. She'd been born in 1921, and now, at eighteen years old, the adults around her often talked about the Great War and the horrors it brought.

"Oh, Annaleah," he started, slipping from the white coat covering his tan uniform shirt. "You must go home. Go back to the convent. Go now. The Nazis have crossed the border and are bombing Warsaw. We must evacuate the horses east." He motioned to a young soldier to load up another medical kit.

"The horses—will they kill the horses?" she stammered. Suddenly, the old stories the nuns told of the Bolsheviks crossing the border during the Great War filled her thoughts. They slaughtered the horses and hung their decaying bodies in Janow's courtyard. As a warning, they painted the word "arystrokracja" (aristocracy) in horse blood on the white walls. Tears pooled in her eyes. *What did horses know of human politics and governments?*

The communists had decimated Janow's priceless herd. It had taken almost twenty years to restore, and some bloodlines were lost forever. Dr. Lesnik's face was grim. It was clear he didn't know what the Germans would do.

"Where will you go?" she asked. "I can help. I can go with you." She knew they would never let her go. For a moment, she considered stowing away, but doing so would just add to their burden.

"We must go east. We plan to cross the Bug River at Wlodawa, stay in the forests by day, and travel the roads by night," Dr. Lesnik explained.

At Wlodawa, the river's banks were wide apart, and the water shallow. It had been used as a ford for thousands of years. It would be much safer there than the closer bridge at Brest-Litovsk. But Wlodawa was fifty kilometers away.

"We are dividing the herd into groups. Pregnant mares and mares with foals at their sides will go first. Then an hour later, the stallions, and finally the yearlings, separated into groups of colts and fillies," Dr. Lesnik said.

"I can help. I really can."

"No. Annaleah. You must go home. Our army will mount a defense. I promise to send word when we've repelled the enemy and it's safe to return." He took both her hands in his, a gesture she knew was a desperate plea. "Now, go, child."

She wandered helplessly through the barns, needing and wanting to help. The young soldiers ignored her as they hustled in all directions, preparing to evacuate. Through the din of shouts, she heard the Germans attacked by air and tanks they called panzer divisions crossed the border. Janow's soldiers changed to peasant garb in hopes the Luftwaffe wouldn't strafe farmers leading horses to safety.

Would they bomb the barns? Annaleah entered the arched passageway to the yearling barn. Except for the sound of horses munching their breakfast hay, it was quiet here. The soldiers hadn't started to prepare the young colts to evacuate yet. Looking into each stall as she passed by, she etched each lovely face into her mind.

She stopped at Lotnik's box. The rose-gray colt looked up from his ration and nickered softly, his gentle nature radiating from big dark eyes. He came forward to her, putting his head through the opening at the door. Customarily, she brought apples from the fruit cellar or carrots from the convent's garden. But when she heard the word 'war' this morning, she forgot everything else. The colt searched her hands with his velvety muzzle, looking for treats. He didn't leave even after he knew she had none. Instead, he lowered his head as if letting her rub his face would calm whatever bothered her.

"It's war, Lotnik," she explained to the colt, who had as much concept of its meaning as she did. Annaleah scratched his withers, and he pushed his top lip forward in delight and searched along her shoulder for a good place to reciprocate the gesture. They stood together in a horse hug for a long time, parting when two soldiers entered the barn.

Jan Nabozny and Nelek Wazdoda discussed what they would do in a fight with the Germans, imitating a sword fight. Annaleah wanted to believe their boasts.

"Annaleah, what are you doing here?" Jan scolded, a deep frown furrowing his brow.

"I will take good care of your Lotnik," Nelek reassured her as he took the colt's halter from the hook on the outside wall of the stall. She stepped aside to let him enter. "He's my charge for the evacuation." Annaleah had gone all through school with Jan and Nelek. She knew they would do their best—still, her heart filled with dread. Would their best be enough?

She followed the young men leading the rambunctious colts out of the yearling barn. They had their hands full. Excited and full of play, the colts pranced and danced down the dusty road as if on an exhilarating adventure.

Finally, she stopped at the end of the pasture fence and watched them go, wondering if she would ever see her friends and horses again.

Chapter Three

September 17, 1939

THESE TERRIBLE DAYS, IT HAD become Annaleah's habit to hover unnoticed outside of the convent's kitchen in the early mornings and listen as the sisters tuned in to the news from Radio Warsaw. So far, only bad news filled the airwaves. Though the Polish soldiers made a brave defense, what good were bicycle brigades and horse-mounted cavalry against German Panzer Divisions? Though Britain and France had declared war when Hitler invaded, they had not offered any solid support. Hopes faded, and now, the worst report possible--the Russians had entered the war, and troops advanced on Poland from the East.

Rumors still circulated of Russian horrors. When Stalin collectivized the wheat farms of the Ukraine, he burdened the farmers with grain quotas higher than their land's yield. The Russian overlords then raided private stores for the *collective good*, and the Ukrainian people—millions of them—starved to death.

Annaleah couldn't help but imagine famished and wasting hordes pouring over the border and slaughtering Janow's precious horses for food. If the Russians were victorious, what would be their fate?

The sisters tried to keep the full scope of the terror facing the convent and orphanage from the children, but could no longer. Though the nuns kept a cheery front, wisps of worry slipped out on tiptoes under their smiles. Annaleah was old enough to understand and sworn to secrecy so the younger children wouldn't be frightened, but to no avail. Each time the German warplanes approached from the west, they had to quickly collect the children and take cover in the convent's basement or the fruit cellar.

Soon, Annaleah became fully aware of the nightmare following the sound of their approach. First, a low rumble and a shadow appeared on the distant horizon like a cloud of locusts. Then, there was a consistent louder droning and humming sound of evil with wings. The children protected their ears from the dreaded high-pitched wail of the Stukas as they nose-dived to attack their targets like ghastly birds of prey.

Annaleah remembered the day Benit, a nine-year-old boy and unruly brat, hid outside as the dive bombers approached. She remembered racing to find him in the woods by the creek. They crouched in the underbrush until the Stukas passed overhead on their way to dive-bomb Brest. She shuddered. They could've lost their lives that day.

After she helped put the younger ones to bed at night, Father Jerzak would tell the sisters and older children the Luftwaffe strafed neighboring farmers as they brought in their hay from the fields. Winter would be bleak this year, no matter what the war's outcome. The men of the nearby village of Biala met in the church at night to form and plan a resistance movement. Her heart was heavy with fear. She was alive, but how could the Polish people survive with enemies on either side? Poland was squeezed in a vice.

Each morning, as the sun rose, a haze of blue smoke filled the air from the bombing raids on Warsaw, Lublin, and Brest. Annaleah hoped the horses and soldiers would come home. She ran through the farm's pastures to find Janow still stood untouched by German bombs but vacant and bare.

Alone and overwhelmed with fear, she walked through the barn aisles, amazed at the emptiness. Nothing was left here, not even the buzz of a pesky fly--only the sweet smell of clean straw. She picked up a handful, crushed it in her palm, and remembered the happy times. The birth of a new foal, the delight of seeing the beautiful, spirited animals at play, and racing to the barns with friends after school, hoping to be allowed to ride.

Her memory was filled with those thoughts like welcome ghosts. Even the drudgery of the daily chores, the things she dreaded and complained about, were a joy to her now. She needed those carefree days to return.

For two weeks, they received no news about the men and horses of Janow. Each morning now, Father Jerzak included her in the adult conversation held with Mother Superior and the sisters. Annaleah guessed the war had made her a grown-up long before she wanted to be.

On September 19, 1939, the Russian forces reached Janow. From the cover of a copse of trees, Annaleah watched the soldiers saunter happily along the road, laughing and singing as they marched behind the olive-green tanks headed for Warsaw. Young men, most no older than her eighteen years, seemed caught up in something terrible they clearly did not understand. The Russian soldiers passed by, showing no interest in the stud farm or the convent. She was grateful. The sisters had warned her of the brutality of some soldiers, so she stayed hidden until long after they'd gone. Wondering who would rule over Poland, the Russians or the Germans, she walked through the empty barns.

Annaleah took her usual stroll through the quiet aisleways, remembering the past. She drifted back to when she and her classmates hurried to clean on summer mornings so their afternoons could be spent riding Janow's magnificent horses. She plopped down on a bale of straw and daydreamed, remembering everything—the deep, rich smell of oiled leather, the scent of horse sweat mixed with citronella and lemongrass.

She reclined on the straw, pulling a shaft to chew and allowing her mind to wander into a daydream. One day, she and the colt, Lotnik, would bring home Olympic Gold for Poland and the equestrian team. In the fantasy, she and Lotnik performed a dressage pattern she recalled from one of Dr. Lesnik's books on horsemanship.

She imagined Lotnik as a magnificent grown-up stallion, his sleek coat gleaming white and shimmering under the arena lights like wedding satin. She envisioned her hands light on the reins, establishing subtle contact, encouraging collection. Pressing her legs softly against his sides, she urged him to rebalance his weight onto his powerful haunches. His forehand became light and airy in her fantasy as he picked up an elegant, elevated Passage as if they danced in the clouds. *In the daydream, she touched his left side with subtle but steady pressure at the halfway point in the arena, causing him to bend his body. With an almost imperceptible touch of her right leg behind the girth, she could almost feel his body surge forward as he instantly picked up the three-beat canter. Horse and rider became one, like dance partners in a magnificent ballroom.*

Of course, she knew the Olympics would never happen for her. The horses at Janow were military horses, and the maneuvers she considered dance: the Passage, the Levade, the Capriole, were, in reality, meant for battle—hand-to-hand combat with a horse as a weapon and partner. She preferred the idea of dance far more.

Before the evacuation, Dr. Lesnik let her work with young Lotnik on the lunge. He understood the words walk, trot, and canter and would pick up the gait on her voice command. He yielded readily to the pressure of her hand on his side, learning to flex his body away from the touch as he would respond to his rider's legs in the future.

If Lotnik returned and wasn't lost to man's murderous desire for power, she could teach him how to accept the bridle and drive him on long lines. He was her favorite, and she vowed to make him the best riding horse on the farm, even if she would never be allowed to perform the rigors of Haute Ecole with him. The honor would be given to one of the cavalry officers.

A week later, once again, she lost herself in the daydream of Olympic Gold, forgetting the Stukas and the tanks, as she made her way to the barn in the stifling heat of a September afternoon. In the distance, a cloud of dust rose from the road in the east. Another Russian battalion, she thought, rushing to hide behind Janow's white stone walls. The first legions to pass by hadn't given the stud farm a second look. But this time, they surely would. She heard the faint call of a horse announcing its arrival at Janow's outermost pastures.

The horses! Her heartbeat quickened, sending a rush of happiness through her body. With Dr. Lesnik in the lead, the soldiers brought Janow's mares home. Annaleah ran to open the doors to the paddocks and the mare barn as the exhausted horses trotted in. They were calling to each other almost as if sharing her joy. They were happy to be home.

More than anything, she wanted to hear the yearling colts would be coming home soon. But so much had to be done. So immediately, side by side with the soldiers, she went to work, loading stall feeders with hay, filling waterers, and fluffing up the straw bedding. Her best friends, Jan Nabozny and Nelek Wazdoda, found her, news about their adventure barely contained behind their grim faces.

"The stallions are not far behind us. We need to get their stalls ready," Jan said, dropping as if exhausted onto a bale of straw. "While we were away, I missed *you*, Annaleah." She knew Jan loved her. They'd shared an on-again-off-again crush since kindergarten. Some of the sisters believed they would one day marry. He was tall, strong, and handsome. She cared for him—she really did—but couldn't say she loved him. At least not how she dreamed love would be when she married. Mother Superior said she read too many novels, and her head was full of foolishness. At eighteen, she supposed it was true. But where were the colts? Where was Lotnik?

"Has Jan told you? The yearling colts panicked during one of the bombing raids and scattered all over the countryside. Starting tomorrow morning, we must go back and try to find them," Nelek said, looking at the ground, lifting his shoulders defensively, and peeking up at her.

"You promised me you'd keep them safe! The Russians will kill them." But she knew once the horses stampeded, there was no stopping them. She knew the Polish farmers would recognize the Janow brand and take good care of the animals.

"Lotnik and Witez are gone," Jan reported, his voice full of desperation.

"Our best colts? Both lost?" she murmured under her breath and sank onto a straw bale beside him.

"No men were lost, though. You should be happy. But you only care about the horses. You're a heartless woman, Annaleah," Jan complained, his face dark and sober.

"Of course, I'm happy about it." She touched Jan's arm, reassuring him she was human. She pouted at him until he smiled. Did she really care more about horses than humans? Was she heartless? Briefly, she thought she would need to pray and go to confession.

"It is better for Polish farmers to possess the horses than to fill Russian cooking pots," Jan said.

He was right. When the Bolsheviks crossed the borders after the Great War, the Polish farmers saved many animals by hiding them in secret stalls, smearing their coats with mud, and turning them out with their livestock. Still, so many irreplaceable horses—once-in-a-lifetime bloodlines—were lost to starving Russians.

"Let's get the stallions' stalls ready," Jan tugged her to her feet.

As they walked along, she whispered a prayer for God to keep the colts safe.

On the morning of September 27, 1939, the mood at the convent was grim. Radio Warsaw's broadcasts were static, no matter how often Father Jerzak carefully turned the tuning dial.

After Annaleah finished her coffee, she walked to the stud farm. The morning was eerily quiet and joyless. The songbirds seemed to have disappeared, though winter's chill was still at least six weeks away. Not even the slightest breeze rustled the leaves in the treetops. Annaleah's legs felt heavy, and her footfalls plodded on the road, each step causing a poof of dust to rise in the air. She stopped to listen for a moment and then continued. She had become wary of everything and anything lately. Fear was a constant companion.

When she entered the mare barn aisleway, the horses, usually excited about their morning feeding, did not greet her. They were hushed and huddled in the back of their stalls as if a dark fog of evil had settled throughout the countryside. Quietly, she loaded her grain cart. None of her compatriots dared whisper even a morning greeting. They felt it, too. After a few moments, she realized what had changed. The drone of aircraft engines, the screams of dive bombers on their runs, the distant explosions, the rumble of tank tracks on the dirt road, and the rhythmic swish and stomp of marching men she had become accustomed to had vanished. The new silence carried a sense of foreboding and danger, and she shivered from its weight.

Doctor Lesnik and The Ranking Polish Officer Krzytalowicz appeared at the west end of the barn aisle, and Krzytalowicz clapped his hands. "May I have your attention? Everyone, quiet, please!"

Stall cleaners came forward to the doorways. Annaleah finished pouring grain into a feeder, and it rained noisily against the metal. Everyone turned and scolded her with their stares. Lifting her shoulders in a shrug of apology, she turned to listen.

"The Polish government has surrendered to Germany," Dr. Lesnik said. His harsh words made trepidation spread through her like the ever-expanding ripples after a stone is dropped in a pond.

"In an agreement with the Russians, the lands to the west of the Bug River belong to Germany—the lands to the east to Russia. Poland is no more."

In unison, as if prompted by a choir director, a gasp rose from the crowd. Here at Janow, they would be ruled by the Germans.

"All our soldiers must get out of uniform and go into hiding to escape arrest, incarceration, or execution. You must go now. Those of you who remain will be expected to take on extra duties until the Germans take over," Krzytalowicz continued. "The takeover may be days, weeks. We just don't know."

Jan jostled through the crowd of workers and slid beside Annaleah, grabbing her hand. When she looked up into his face, resolve tightened his jaw and radiated from his hazel gray eyes. "I will stay to protect you," he whispered. It was unexpected, and she stepped back in surprise.

"You will not! No, Jan, go. I will not be the reason you are imprisoned or killed. To save Poland, you must save yourself!" She knew the men of Biala had developed a plan for this eventuality. They had already formed a resistance and gathered a cache of arms and ammunition. Father Jerzak explained this after morning prayers. Annaleah leaned against Jan's arm and whispered, "You must stay alive."

He turned and stared at her. She hadn't realized how tall and broad-shouldered he'd become, how the roundness of his boyhood face had tightened and squared into a solid and handsome jaw, and how radiant his blue-gray eyes were. His full lips parted softly. "Will you wait for me, Anna? I will go without complaint if you promise to wait for me."

So moved by his plea, she felt her eyes fill with tears. War left all dreams in desperation and ruin. Could she send this beautiful man, full of life and promise, off to danger without knowing she'd be there for him to come home to, even if she wasn't sure and it was a lie? Could she commit, at this moment, to a man she'd grown up with and had known all her life? Even if she wasn't in love with him? The sisters said love grew over time. But how could women who'd never experienced it tell her anything about this kind of love?

"I'll be here when the war is over." It was as close as she could come to saying she'd wait. Jan sighed.

"Anna, can't you humor me? Give me hope?" He shook his head.

Once again, Dr. Lesnik raised his voice over the commotion. "All soldiers must go now. There isn't much time," he warned.

Jan took her hand and pulled her along at a jog out of the barn. He tugged her to the saddling area just outside the riding arena's gate and lifted her to the first step of a mounting block so they were face to face, eye to eye.

"I love you, Anna. I always have," he said. The ravages of war and the specter of death brought out these desperate declarations of love. She looked around and saw several other young couples embracing each other. Jan kissed her awkwardly, their novice lips bumping into each other clumsily. But then his kiss and embrace became strong, assured, and passionate, as if they were saying goodbye forever. So, this is how it would be—her first kiss dampened by fear and hopelessness.

Stunned, she stared into his eyes. "Yes. Jan. I will wait for you," she whispered.

Chapter Four

KARENA SLUMPED DEEP INTO THE upholstered wingback chair and dropped the still-open manuscript to her lap. *Granny A was eighteen and had just experienced her first kiss.* Wow! Karena could hardly believe it. She'd shared her first kiss and more at fifteen. She and Sam had moved on from first base to home run at sixteen. Luckily, her mom was the proactive type. She'd taken her to the doctor to get birth control pills on the suspicion she and Sam might be experimenting. Mom didn't know for sure and didn't ask. On the other hand, Dad believed Karena to be as pure as a first snowfall, and she wanted to leave it that way.

What was it like to live through war? The descriptions of emergency evacuations and divebombing Stukas made her heart race. The thought of buildings turned to piles of rubble, haunted people wandering absently through abandoned streets, and the wail of lost children filled her mind. A shudder raced along her shoulders.

The family members who constantly disparaged Granny A didn't know what it was like to be in a country torn apart by war. They hadn't, as the old saying goes, "walked anywhere in her shoes."

Karena heard a creak on the stairs and realized one of the adults, likely her mother, was coming to check on her progress. Karena scrambled to replace the manuscript in the trunk and dropped the lid.

Quickly, she looked around the attic. After finding an empty box, she began ripping trophy ribbons from one of the walls and placing them inside, push pins and all. As the door opened, she tugged one of the satin championship rosettes from the wall, tearing one of its long tails in two.

"Oh. No!" she exclaimed, looking up to see her mother standing in the doorway.

When Mom looked around the room, an exasperated frown wrinkled her brow. She walked over, examined the contents in the bottom of the box, and placed her hands squarely on her hips. Karena had barely touched the packing.

"This is all you have done? What have *you* been up to all afternoon? Daydreaming?" Mom asked.

"*The attic isn't going to pack itself.*"

Karena caught herself mouthing the words in unison with her mother, sassily bobbing her head side to side.

"Young lady, don't you mock me!"

"Well, I don't know what's important! You tell me what to keep—what should go!" Karena defended. After the words spilled out, she was almost ashamed of her tone. Daydreaming was precisely what she'd been doing.

For some inexplicable reason, she didn't tell her Mom about the memoirs, journals, and especially not about the manuscript. The Baker family didn't appreciate Granny A while she was alive, so they didn't deserve to know about the trunk's contents now. Reading her grandmother's words created a bond between Karena and the old woman. She felt as if Granny A had touched her heart from beyond the grave and placed a treasure inside—a secret she shouldn't share—until the right moment. Would she even know the right moment?

"It's time for dinner. So, come down and get washed up." The angry tone hadn't left Mom's voice. She squinted her eyes and tried to read Karena's mind. She knew something was up, magically, without Karena saying a word. It was uncanny.

Karena decided that after dinner, she would return and take the manuscript to read in her room. She followed her mother down the stairs from the attic.

After washing her hands, letting down her braid, and running a brush over her long blonde hair, she went to join the others. The mood in the parlor was bizarre. Instead of a warm family reunion, bitter rivals stood on opposite sides of the large rustic room, shooting mean glares at each other like rifle salvos. Karena glanced through the open archway to the dining room table. She thought about picking up a place setting and moving it to the kids' table in the kitchen. She'd rather hear about her cousins' horseback riding and their visit to Silverwood Theme Park than suffer through the hostility between the heirs.

"I thought you said dinner was ready." Karena wanted to get back to the attic and Granny A's story.

"Not everyone is here yet," Mom answered.

"Who else is coming to dinner?" she whispered.

"The vet, Rich Wilson, and his assistant. They're doing the vet checks today and tomorrow so we can sell the horses, and it's our duty to feed them after they worked so hard." Mom swept a hand over her brow, brushing away her blonde hair.

"Good. With strangers here, it'll cut down all the bickering," Karena said under her breath to her mother.

"I hear he's quite handsome." A sly smile curved Mom's lips.

"Who's quite handsome?"

"Dr. Wilson's assistant."

"Mom, I'm going with Sam," Karena scolded, shaking her head. "And what can come of it anyway? He's up here, and I live in California."

Karena looked up just as Dr. Wilson and his assistant walked through the door. Sam, considered a good-looking guy by her friends at school, couldn't compare to the vet's helper. He didn't even warrant a close second. A small grin barely tickled across his lips, almost as if he was embarrassed by her reaction. Karena felt a blush race hot into her cheeks.

"He's Russian. An exchange student," Karena's mother whispered as if it would add to his mystique. Success; it did.

The Doc and the young man approached to greet them. *Who cares if he's a Ruskie? He's gorgeous!* Karena thought. He was tall and fit, and his neatly trimmed, blond-streaked hair, which surfers like Sam would die for, perfectly framed his face. Barely able to look away, Karena felt hypnotized by his intense but thoughtful blue eyes. The young man grinned at her as if apologizing for his striking good looks.

"Hi, Renae. I'd like you to meet Gerard Kemperman, my assistant," Dr. Wilson said. "Is this lovely young lady your daughter?"

Gerard Kemperman wasn't a Russian name. Karena expected Uri or Vladimir and a last name ending in "ov" (as in Romanov), or "skia" (as in Valenskia).

"Yes. This is Karena. So nice to meet you, Gerard." Karena was instantly annoyed by the sickening sweetness in her mother's voice. Though she'd never said so, Karena knew her mother disapproved of Sam. Unashamedly, Mom shoved her at this Russian guy. Her mother's stare was pregnant with match-maker overtones, upping Karena's humiliation to over-the-top levels.

Gerard the Gorgeous awkwardly reached out to shake her hand, smiling helplessly, almost as if he wasn't used to attention from women. Karena didn't believe that for a second. *Was his shyness an act?* Well, at least he didn't respond to her mother's underhanded behavior like an experienced lothario and kiss her hand.

"Karena, why don't you get Gerard something to drink? We have wine, beer, water, sodas…."

"A beer would be nice," his speech still held a slight Russian accent. It made this handsome man all the more fascinating.

"Karena?" Mom's voice hinted Karena bordered on being rude, and she quickly snapped out of her trance.

Obviously, her mother had planned this, and she had to decide how to handle this unexpected turn of events. At this point, she wasn't sure whether or not she minded if the robust Russian was her dinner companion. *Oh, hell! What could it hurt? Sam was probably making it with some bikini-clad bimbo already, anyway.* He hadn't called as promised, and she'd left messages.

"Come on. I'll get you a beverage." Karena took his hand and led him toward the small walnut buffet in the corner of the parlor, where her mother had set up a makeshift bar. "What'll you have?"

"Beer, please. That one." He pointed to a craft beer in an amber bottle half-submerged in a metal tub full of ice.

Karena hated beer, but to make Gerard believe she was older than her seventeen years, she poured herself a glass of white wine after handing him the opened bottle. With drinks in hand, they walked to the large picture window and looked at the pastures below.

"So, you want to be a veterinarian?" Karena asked after taking a large swallow of her wine, mostly to bolster her courage.

"Yes. I received a gift scholarship and will attend Washington State University at Pullman this fall. It's not too far from Moscow. Idaho, that is," he laughed. She got the joke and giggled. "In the summer, weekends, and vacations, I'll be working here with Dr. Wilson. And you? Where are you going to college?"

Karena pursed her lips. Briefly, she thought about making something up, making this handsome college boy believe she was older than she was. He'd probably never see her again after these two weeks were over. She could lie like the hand-braided rug under the coffee table. He'd never know. Finally, she decided against it. "I'm still in high school. One more year to go. I'm only seventeen." She sighed, looking down into the wine glass in her hand and rubbing her thumb across the smooth surface of her polished nails.

He grinned at her, showing off his perfectly white and perfectly straight teeth. "Do you like horses?"

"I don't know. I wasn't exposed to horses growing up. Granny A lived all the way up here, and we live in California. We'd visit, but I didn't know her as well as I should've." For some strange reason, as she looked up into the Russian's eyes, she remembered Granny A's sad first kiss. Gerard stared deeply into hers; then his gaze traveled to her lips. Suddenly, she wondered what it would be like to kiss him. After all, Sam hadn't bothered to call her as he'd promised, and it would serve him right if she kissed this new boy.

"Dinner is served," someone shouted. And the family crowd made their way to the dining room like hungry soldiers heading for the chow line.

Karena realized she stood right behind her mother. When her mother turned slightly to face her, she smiled expectantly.

"Is he nice?" Mom whispered.

"Yes. Very. But now, I think you should vote with Uncle Ray and keep this place," Karena said.

Chapter Five

AS SORRY AS SHE WAS to have to part from her new friend, Gerard, Karena could hardly wait to sneak back up to the attic, grab the binder containing the typed manuscript, and immerse herself in Granny A's life again.

"I'm drained. It's been a long day. I need to turn in." Karena forced a yawn.

"Yes. We should go. We have work early in the morning." Gerard hesitated as if he wanted to say something more.

Karena smiled and shook his hand. "Good night. It was nice meeting you." She was impatient to get back to reading.

"May I see you again?" He mumbled the question as if he expected her to turn him down.

Well, finally! It couldn't have been so hard to ask. But, the Russian was very shy. She decided she'd give him some slack and cheerfully said, "Of course. I'll be here for the next two weeks."

"Tomorrow evening? I can take you to dinner—The Athol Diner, or we could go to the Silverwood Theme Park."

She thought about it for a second. "Let's go to Silverwood." At least she could compare her roller-coaster experiences with her cousins. Gerard's face broke open in a toothy grin. She almost had to do a double-take—he was such a hunk. Was this guy for real, or was she watching a movie? He didn't know it, but he tested her loyalty to Sam. In her mind, she checked off the list. Gerard had a career goal; Sam would party through college without direction. The Russian had a summer job. Sam thought his summer 'job' was surfing. Agghh! It was silly to think about it now. She would be going home in two weeks. Come September, she would likely never see either of them again.

"Well, goodnight then," she sighed.

"I'll pick you up at six." He gently took hold of her hand.

"At six," she repeated. He let go, turning back at the door to wave.

Once Gerard and the vet had gone, Karena scanned the relatives for her mother. Engaged in a serious conversation with Uncle Ray, Mom would be awhile. Karena took the opportunity to slip away. As soon as she thought she was out of sight, Karena sprinted up the attic stairs. She tip-toed across the room to the trunk, opened it, and took the cloth binder holding the manuscript.

Karena didn't want to share what she found just yet. The greedy, fighting relatives would consider it unimportant trash, and she knew it wasn't true. She covered the chronicle with her sweater, buttoned it, and crossed her arms in front of her chest to keep it in place. Carefully, noiselessly, she slipped down the stairs, turned off the light, and scampered to her room, locking the door behind her. She took the precaution of stuffing the secret under her pillow while she cleaned up and prepared for bed.

Ready now, she plumped two pillows and stacked one on top of the other so she could sit halfway up. Snuggling into the covers, she got comfortable and prepared to read. She picked up the manuscript and turned to the page she'd last read.

September 30, 1939

As was her custom, Annaleah rose just before sunrise. In the darkness, she dressed quietly, making sure not to disturb the others on her floor. Annaleah's comings and goings had ceased to bother them these days like they had years ago. Now, the nuns and other children slept through them with barely even a groan of protest.

Carrying her boots, Annaleah crept through the hall and down the convent's stone stairway. She could feel the cold seeping through the weave of her socks and knew this morning she'd need a jacket. There was a dampness to the air—a portent of coming rain. They could've used the rain earlier. But the weather was not on their side. The warm, clear skies had helped the Germans with their bombing raids. The dry roads allowed safe passage for tanks and motorized vehicles. And now, they were a conquered people. The thought hurt her heart as she slipped into her boots at the main door.

As Mother Superior said, though, life must continue. Whatever came was supposed to be God's will, even if she couldn't see it or understand it.

Annaleah waited for a moment at the open kitchen door. Father Jerzak was here again this morning. The tone in his voice was urgent, and instead of whispers, his words were commands. Curious, she stepped into the doorway.

"Our phone communications are down. We must act. Take the canned goods and dry goods quickly to the cellar," he instructed. The sisters quickly complied, filling baskets with jars and canisters until they were almost too heavy to carry.

"Annaleah, come help," Sister Rosland begged.

Rushing to help her, Annaleah was clouded with confusion.

"The Russians have started their retreat. By late morning, they will be here," Father said. "They will take everything they can lay their hands on."

Annaleah knew what that meant. With the harvest in and winter on the way, they must hide their stores, or they would starve. Grabbing the handle on one end of Sister Rosland's basket, Annaleah helped her walk down the steps to the below-ground cellar.

"This is not the first war we have had to survive," Rosland sighed. They placed the basket on a rough wooden table at the far end of the cellar. Rosland leaned her weight into the bookcases there, and they slowly moved away, exposing a dark hidden passageway. She took two candles from the front pocket of her vestments and handed Annaleah one. Smiling, she struck a match on the side of the box and lit Annaleah's candle and then her own. A rusted metal door opened to a large, shelved pantry and wine cellar at the end of the narrow corridor. The sisters had organized countless jars of canned meat, vegetables, fruit, and jams on the shelves.

Barrels labeled sugar, rice, oats, and flour lined the walls. Open baskets of this year's apples and pears were stacked in the coolest corner. "Quick, child. We unload this basket and go back upstairs for more. We may need to feed the whole village once the Russians are done with us."

Annaleah placed her candle on the table in the center of the room and hastily unloaded the food. Once it was empty, she dashed up the stairs with the basket, Sister Rosland trailed behind. In the main corridor, she passed Sisters Agnes and Theresa, each pulling one of the boys' red wagons behind them.

Once in the kitchen, Annaleah started to refill the basket.

"Wait." Father Jerzak lifted his palm to stop her. " We must leave some food in the kitchen pantry for the Russians to take, or they will search the whole convent. We can't risk them finding the hidden cellar."

She nodded in agreement. "Should I put these back?"

"No. But hurry, Annaleah. Finish quickly."

Rushing back with her loaded basket to the secret pantry, Annaleah helped Rosland unload the wagons and the remaining baskets. Rosland motioned they were finished. She closed and locked the door and placed the key behind a tan stone in the hallway wall. When she pushed the stone back in place, it fit so tightly it looked as though it had never been moved.

Suddenly, Annaleah heard a distant rumble. "Tanks!" she screamed. Panicked, Agnes and Theresa shoved the bookcase back in place and ran to the stairway.

"Stop!" Annaleah caught up to them and brushed away the dust from their skirts and hems, ensuring no evidence was left on their clothes. She couldn't let the Russians discover their secret. When the women reached the top stair, Father Jerzak hustled them into the chapel sanctuary.

All of the rest of the sisters congregated there. The orphanage's twenty-five children, many still tucking in their shirts and with shoes untied, clamored into the pews. Mother Superior started to sing praises in her beautiful soprano voice. The other sisters joined in harmony. The children were completely still and bowed their heads in prayer. *Did they know?*

Annaleah settled into the pew in the back. The sound of the tank tracks grinding into the road became louder and louder.

"Heavenly Father, make them pass us by," she whispered. Sitting beside her, Little Martina clutched her hand, eyes wide with terror. "Don't cry. Be strong." She puckered her lips, and water welled in her eyes, but Martina didn't utter a sound.

The soldiers began pounding on the convent's main doors, and then they broke through. Father Jerzak and Mother Superior raced past Annaleah's pew and into the hallway.

"This is a house of God," she heard Father Jerzak explain.

Boldly, Annaleah stepped out into the corridor. As soon as she did it, she regretted it. She wasn't sure what she thought she could do.

"There is no god!" the Russian shouted in his face and struck him so hard Father Jerzak fell unconscious to the floor. Annaleah gasped.

The soldier turned toward her, and an evil glower filled his eyes. Fear rushed through every cell in her body, but she forced herself not to tremble. Standing straight and tall, she faced him defiantly. But behind her façade, she prayed.

Annaleah didn't cringe when she heard the soldiers rummaging through the kitchen and the sound of pottery shattering on the stone floor. One man walked out with the big pot of oatmeal, steam still rising from its surface. The cereal was to be the children's breakfast. Another had grabbed armfuls of freshly baked bread, part of a loaf still hanging from his mouth. Father Jerzak had been right; all canned goods were quickly removed from the shelves and carted away.

"We are an orphanage. This food is for the children," Mother Superior cried out, trying to appeal to their sense of mercy. The soldiers brushed her aside, and she stumbled against the wall.

Annaleah started for her, but the man who'd hit Father Jerzak intervened. He grabbed her by her braid and yanked her head forward.

"Is this all there is?" he demanded.

Annaleah wanted to scream but didn't want to give him the satisfaction of knowing her fear. "Yes!" she said, lifting her chin against the pain. He pulled harder on her braid and wanted her to cry out. She bit her bottom lip to keep it in.

He shoved her back against the stone wall. She could smell his sour sweat mixed with the dirt from his clothes and the rancid odor of his breath. She choked back a gag.

"There's more. I know there's more," he growled.

"No. No more. You've been through our village before, and there is nothing left." She shook her head, trying to convince him of her lie. He backhanded her, and she felt the sting and heat racing into her cheek. He grabbed her hands and pinned her wrists above her head with one of his large hands. With the other, he traced down her cheek and across her lips. Annaleah knew what would come next, and prayed for the strength to endure it.

As he started to slide his hand down to her throat, he suddenly stopped when someone yelled, "Attention!"

He dropped her arms and whirled to face in the opposite direction. Annaleah inched her body along the wall, crawling away from him.

"Enough!" his commanding officer shouted. After making eye contact with each soldier one at a time, he bent over and helped Father Jerzak to his feet. Slowly, he walked down the line of men, stopping square in front of Annaleah's assailant. "These are servants of God! Have you no fear or shame?" His glare filled with anger, and without warning, he slapped the soldier across the face so hard the sound echoed off the stone walls.

"Get out. Get out of my sight!" All the soldiers who had invaded the convent scrambled from the building. The commander looked Annaleah up and down. Once he assessed she wasn't badly hurt, he turned his attention back to Father Jerzak.

"Father, I apologize for my men. Their behavior is unforgivable," the leader said with sincerity. He bowed slightly before the priest. Annaleah had heard the Russians were no longer allowed to worship God. This commander disobeyed the order. She scrutinized him, trying to determine if it was from a superstitious fear or from an uncrushable faith. Annaleah knew she had to pray for this enemy.

"Go in peace," Jerzak said, holding tightly to the golden cross hanging on a beaded chain around his neck.

Huddled together, they waited until all the mechanical noise of the tanks and the rhythmic marching of the soldiers waned. Annaleah wanted to run, to run across the pasture and warn Janow. The Director and Dr. Lesnik needed to know the Red Army headed their way. With the phone lines disabled, how else could she warn them? She bolted toward the main door.

"No! You mustn't. Not today." Mother Superior stepped in Annaleah's way and softly touched her arm. "Here you are under God's protection, child. Out there, if the soldiers should find you...." She squeezed her eyes shut and breathed out a heavy sigh.

All night, Annaleah lay awake, hoping and begging God the Russians wouldn't kill and eat the horses. In the early morning, well before dawn, when she could wait no longer, she rose, dressed, and slipped out of the convent. A light rain filled the air, and she pulled her wool knit cap from her jacket pocket and slipped it over her hair. Periodically, she stopped and listened for the sound of the Russian troops. Were they still bivouacked near the stud farm? Except for the chirp of crickets and the croak of frogs, silence hung on the predawn mist.

The buildings were eerily dark. Annaleah was almost afraid to go closer. But her love for the horses drove her on. She entered the mare barn through the open door. Sliding with her back to the wall, she stopped to listen. Certain she was alone, she removed the lantern from its hook on the wall and lit the wick. Carrying it out ahead of her, she illuminated the aisleway.

Each stall door was open. Bales of straw, strings broken, were scattered haphazardly all over the floor. A barrel of oats had fallen on its side, and the white grain spilled from under the lid. Through the main door leading to the mare pasture, she could see old Raina and Marena huddled together against the fence. But where were the other mares? Oh, no! Oh, no! she repeated over and over as she dashed to the stallion barn. Empty.

Annaleah circled to the yearling barn, dreading what she would find. Tears clouded her vision, but she saw several fillies milling around aimlessly in a paddock as if their home was instead a strange, new, dangerous place. They called out to her.

She climbed the fence, and they came to her, seeking reassurance. Surrounded by their warmth, Annaleah felt velvety muzzles exploring her back, arms, and hands. She knew each one of these girls. When they were born, she'd attended their births. She was part of their family, their herd, and it comforted her.

With the fillies, she was able to face the stark and depressing reality: The Russians had stolen the mature breeding stock. The prize stallion, Ofir, and the beautiful mare Frederika, were gone.

For the first time since the horses had returned from the evacuation, she took solace in the fact the yearling colts had bolted in the Stuka raids and were lost in the Polish countryside. At least they would be cared for by Polish farmers and not destined for a Russian cooking pot.

Chapter Six

KARENA SQUIRMED DEEPER DOWN INTO the covers. Granny A's life was terrifying, full of fear from one day to the next. She had to worry about what would happen to change her world and how to survive. Karena tried to imagine what it would be like and couldn't. Everything in her life was comfortable and easy. At this point, she didn't have to worry whether or not hostile troops would steal her food or hurt her. But could it happen? She swallowed the tightness that clawed at her throat.

She tossed the manuscript beside her on the bed and stared at it. She wanted to quit reading and sleep, but she couldn't. Instead, she picked it back up. In the preface, Granny A noted she had translated this from German. She remembered her dad defending Granny A when some other relatives accused her of being stupid. Granny A spoke five languages. The education she'd been given at the convent could easily put theirs to shame.

The point of view shifted in this part of the book, translated from the memories of a man Granny A called Dr. Erik. Karena couldn't help wondering who this man was and why her grandmother included him in her story. She guessed she was about to find out and opened the first page.

September 30, 1939

Erik Kemperman turned when he heard the big hiss of steam. Clouds of white billowed from the undercarriage of the sleek black and red train engine, adding an ominous atmosphere to the early morning fog at Berlin Station. Red, black, and white Nazi flags attached to the engineer's compartment fluttered in the blast of condensation. After confirming this was the troop train headed for Poland, he acknowledged the porter's salute with a nod and passed off his gray-green duffle bag in exchange for a claim ticket.

With his University graduation certificate barely in hand, Erik had been served his conscription papers. His choice was simple. Join the Wehrmacht (German Defense Power) or join the ranks of the men considered traitors in the concentration camps. He decided on the former.

Erik's friend and mentor, Professor Godfried, went to the Heer Board and argued on his behalf. Surely, a young veterinarian would be more beneficial to the Reich using his hard-earned veterinary certificate in the cavalry rather than on the front lines. So, Erik became an officer candidate, emerging from training with the rank of Rittmeister (Cavalry Captain) of the Veterinary Corps. He was one of the lucky ones. His degree in veterinary medicine earned him a ticket to the stud farm at Janow Podlaski in Poland. They had both a dairy operation and a horse breeding station located there. Though he'd learned about every animal he was likely to encounter in a veterinary practice, Erik had specialized in dairy cattle. Their breeding, calving, milk production, and cures were his forte. He learned that instead of the dairy operation, he'd been enlisted to be in charge of Janow's horses. The bureaucracy, in its infinite wisdom, decided that.

Originally, he'd planned to set up a practice in the village just a few miles south of his family's dairy. The town and the surrounding farms desperately needed a vet. They often lost valuable cattle waiting for help, and he wanted to change the odds—but the war intervened.

While at the university, Erik wasn't involved in politics. He'd left the marches and book burnings to others. Initially, he'd used Liselle, his former love, as an excuse. Everyone in his village and all his friends thought they would marry when he finished his studies. But she didn't wait. She married another when he was in his fourth year of study, with four more to go.

His dormitory roommates used the political marches to meet girls and accused Erik of being too shy and heartbroken for encounters with the opposite sex. He let them believe it.

Erik kept his head down and mouth shut. He'd found the euphoria over Herr Hitler difficult and stressful. Had Europeans thrown off the yoke of Monarchy only to replace it with a dictator? The German Weimar Republic failed after surviving for only fifteen years.

Some embraced fascism, some communism, but either way, emotion displaced reason. What used to be topics of civil debate turned into violent disagreements. The persecution of the Jewish citizens and the destruction at Kristallnacht shocked him to his core. Many of his university professors had been Jewish. Those who were able had fled Germany when the Nazis came into power, and those who remained were treated horribly.

He stood before the chrome steps to one of the officer's cars for his trip to Janow. In the dissipating engine steam, Erik watched as the Schutze (regular soldiers) filed up the stairs to their train accommodations. The victory over Poland in the Blitzkrieg had bolstered their confidence, sense of nationality, and pride. Boisterous laughter filtered through open windows, almost as if they were drunk. Erik worried the German people would wake up one day to one hell of a hangover.

"Erik, in here." He turned at the sound of his name. Gunther Bishof yelled through the car's open window in front of him. Bishof was a roommate from school and now was an officer with the Gestapo police services. Like Erik, he was part of the occupation forces managing the Polish people. Bishof did it with delight; Erik dreaded it. He never coveted power over others.

Erik waved hello and took the steps up into the car. He removed his hat, exposing his short-cut blond hair, and found his way to the table where Bishof and two others waited. As he peeled off his overcoat, he noticed the young officers had converted this dining car into a makeshift bierstube (beerhall). They planned to drink for the entire seven-hour trip from Berlin to Warsaw. In his opinion, it was way too early in the day for drinking. After hanging his coat over the back of his chair, Erik sat down.

"Coffee, please," Erik said when the waiter came to take his order. Other than Gunther, the men at the table were SS in black uniforms with death's head insignias on the collars. Erik wore the Waffenfarbe of the veterinary corps on his collar and shoulder epaulets. Both the SS and Gestapo were political 'soldiers.' The thought police. They seemed to dismiss him as inferior. Erik was not intimidated. He was proud of his accomplishments—a scientist, veterinarian, and doctor—and he outranked them all.

"Whiskey all around," Gunther ordered. When the shots arrived, he stood. "To our victory over Poland!"

Everyone in the car cheered and swallowed whatever they'd raised in a toast. Erik sipped his whiskey, which burned and rumbled in his empty stomach.

"Where are you headed?" The SS officer named Klaus asked. He first stared at Erik's mostly full shot glass and then up to his eyes with skepticism bordering on suspicion.

"The stud farm at Janow Podlaski. I am assigned as a veterinarian there. And you?" Erik asked.

"Biala, at the area headquarters with me," Gunther said, cheerful to be associated with the SS.

The second officer, Rudolf, leaned forward across the table as if what he told them was in confidence. "I hear the Polish women are willing—very willing if you know what I mean."

Though he smiled with them, Erik's stomach soured. Though the Poles were defeated, it didn't give the new rulers license to abuse their women. He suddenly wondered how he'd feel if the suffering woman were his mother or younger sister. He knew firsthand the brutality of the SS and Gestapo, so he held his tongue. In 1934, his neighbor, Herr Mikal Von Numger, was delivered to his wife as ashes in a wooden box. His crime? Criticizing the Reich.

Erik was the firstborn in his family of three children and had always been accused of being too serious and sober by his siblings and mature for his age by his parents and teachers. Instinctively, he knew the Polish men would fight to protect their wives and daughters just as fiercely as all the men at this table, in this car, would if the circumstances were flipped. Ruling a conquered nation wouldn't be as easy as they assumed. At his last visit home, just days before boarding the train, he'd heard rumors of a resilient Polish resistance.

"They breed very fine racehorses. The Polish horses are hard to beat," Gunther said.

In their early college days, Gunther liked to bet on horses at the race-track. Erik had been too poor to follow those pursuits for long and bowed out of the betting but made himself available for the track veterinarians. It was a learning experience he was grateful he'd practiced.

"They are German horses, now," Klaus piped up and broke into guffaws of laughter.

After the laughter died down, an air of seriousness or maybe sleepiness overtook the drinkers at the table. In time, Erik found himself alone as the others drank themselves into a stupor and passed out across the table. He wandered back to the officers' seating car and plopped down by the window. He took out the small booklet Professor Godfried had given him from the pocket of his overcoat and began to read about the history of the Polish Arabian Horses.

The three-hour car ride from Warsaw to Janow was as tiring as the train trip. Erik watched the landscape roll by, and as expected, the fur-ther they were from Warsaw, the fewer bombing pockmarks marred the ground. Awash with fall colors, the Polish countryside was a patchwork of cultivated farmlands with dark, rich soil. The leaves had turned bright red, orange, and gold on the trees lining the banks of the small creek tributaries of the Bug River. The scent of fall—the spice of the dying leaves, dust, and the occasional hint of woodsmoke—filled the air. From time to time, they would pass a farmer, still gathering bales of hay from his field. They were met with hate-filled glares as they passed peasants along the dusty road. Erik hadn't expected a ticker-tape parade and wondered what it would be like to be a vanquished people. He hoped never to find out.

Finally, he saw the whitewashed walls of Janow. It was just like the pic-tures he'd seen in the book Professor Godfried had given him. The famous clock tower still stood in front of the slate gray-tile-roofed buildings. Erik was frightened and excited, both at the same time. He wanted this chance to test his skills but was concerned he wouldn't live up to the expectations now resting heavily on his young and inexperienced shoulders.

When the car came to a stop, Erik retrieved his duffle bag from the boot and waved goodbye to his companions, promising to meet up with them in Biala. When he turned to enter the grounds, he was met by a very stern-faced Major Fellgeible.

Erik raised his right arm in a weak Nazi salute as Fellgeible contemplated him. The Major had two assistants, one on each side. They all wore cavalry uniforms with crimson trim and trouser stripes. The Major stood tall—the very essence of a Prussian soldier, clean-shaven, perfectly starched, and pressed. His close-trimmed brown hair was barely visible under his Schirmmütze, the traditional peaked cap.

"First, I don't approve of your companions. We have a job to do here. It requires clear thinking and sobriety," Fellgeible said in a clipped tone. Both the Gestapo and SS had earned reputations for drunkenness and debauchery in the occupation's first weeks. Though Erik had only accepted a ride with them for expedience, he decided it would make him look weak to explain.

"I understand, sir."

"If you must see them, join them in Biala. Don't bring them here."

"Yes, sir," Erik replied. Fellgeible just fed the rumors there was discord between the branches of the Heer.

"Grab your things, and Sergeant Albrecht will show you to your quarters," Major Fellgeible said, a smile finally curving his lips. "You have a choice of accommodations. You may bunk in the main house with the other officers or take the veterinarian's quarters attached to the laboratory, apothecary, and treatment rooms at the front of the mare barn," Fellgeible announced. He started to walk through the clock tower entrance. Erik took hold of his duffle bag strap, slung it over his shoulder, and followed.

"I would prefer the veterinarian's quarters, sir. I can watch the animals and perform the laboratory work without disturbing anyone, should I be needed at night," Erik said. "Foaling usually takes place at night."

"That's very considerate of you, Captain." The Major stopped and scrutinized Erik by staring deep into his eyes. He sized up his new veterinarian. He finally nodded, and Erik felt relief wash over him. "Report to my office in an hour. The Sergeant will show you where it is, and I will take you on a tour of the barns."

"Yes, sir." He had researched the Major before embarking on the train. Fellgeible joined the Wehrmacht straight from military school, and though his older brother was a general in Hitler's inner circle, he'd chosen not to take advantage of the connection and join the favored SS troops. Erik wondered about him; most men he knew had done everything in their power to curry favor with the National Socialist Government.

Fellgeible was an accomplished horseman, celebrated even, so Erik understood why the man wanted to be here—a famous horseman with famous horses. All the same, Erik knew he would need to be extra careful not to show his disdain for dictators in the open. The Nazi Party had already demonstrated its willingness to punish anyone who disagreed with their philosophy, German citizen or not. He adjusted his duffle bag on his shoulder and followed Albrecht.

The laboratory and apothecary, located at the front entrance to the mare barn, were sparkling clean. There was a light scent of antiseptic soap in the air.

"Through here. These are your quarters, sir," Albrecht hustled him through the laboratory too quickly for Erik to explore. He'd have to orient himself and take inventory of his supplies later.

He walked through the door to his quarters. Light poured in from a series of paned windows along the wall opposite him. In anticipation he might choose this space as his own, someone had started a fire in the stone fireplace in the far corner of the room. Its light flickered and danced in reflection on the polished wood floor. On each side of the fireplace, bookshelves filled with volumes of veterinary medicine books lined the walls. Erik would add the ones he'd brought with him to the library. Two overstuffed chairs sat on either side of a matching sofa in front of the fireplace. A small dining table with four spindle-back wooden chairs sat on top of a red oriental rug next to a compact kitchen. Framed photographs and paintings of horses were displayed on the walls.

Albrecht flipped on the light switch and closed the door. Elevated by a step up, a neatly made double bed dressed in a thick quilt in shades of blue and ready for winter filled the space opposite the sitting area. A small closet with several askew coat hangers would serve as a place for his uniforms, coveralls, and lab coats. Erik dropped the duffle bag just inside the closet opening.

Next, Erik inspected the kitchen. Along the window were cooking facilities; a small two-burner electric stove with an oven, a Bosch refrigerator, and double sinks. The window looked out over a small garden. He stopped and stared out for a moment. Erik couldn't help but laugh as he watched several colts racing along the fence line in the large pasture beyond.

At the end of the counter surrounding the sinks, a door opened to a covered deck with a wood box and space for a small table and a couple of chairs. Erik imagined drinking his morning coffee on this deck. Though he wasn't sure what his life would really be like.

Finally, Albrecht pulled back a curtain, screening off a small bathroom facility with a sink, water closet, and a clawfoot tub fitted with an overhead shower.

"Shall we go meet up with the Major?" Erik asked as he pulled the curtain closed. It was a nice apartment, homey and comfortable, and he needed nothing more for the time being.

"Yes, sir."

"I'd like to examine the horses, evaluate their condition, and feed," he said.

Albrecht stepped back, whipping his gaze up into Erik's eyes. "Sir, the Major has already done that." He huffed as if Erik had just insinuated the Major was incompetent. Erik cringed inside.

"I understand. I want to know what we are feeding so I can carry on." Erik smiled until Albrecht returned one to him. He certainly didn't want to start his tour with contentiousness. His choice of companions bringing him to the farm had already placed a black checkmark by his name. He didn't need any more.

Erik and Albrecht joined the Major in front of his office at the other end of the mare barn.

"Is your apartment acceptable?" The Major asked, but Erik knew it had to be. Though he'd said he chose the apartment so he wouldn't inconvenience others in the officers' housing, which was true enough, the real reason was he didn't want to give up his privacy. It would be much easier to retire to his own quiet place when he needed to study up on a treatment or cure.

"It is," Erik answered.

"Shall we?" The Major gestured toward a sliding doorway opening into the mare barn. They slowly walked down the rough, finished concrete aisleway, with the Major telling him each horse's name as they stopped for a second to look inside the stall.

Erik had never seen more opulent horse barns. The complex was designed in a large U shape. On one side were twenty-four twelve by twenty-four-foot stalls for the stallions. The bottom of the U was double the size of the stallion quarters, which were fifty-twelve by twelve stalls for the weanlings and yearlings. The final side housed fifty large stalls for the mares. At the end of the mare barn was the apothecary, laboratory, and, at the very end, Erik's new apartment. At the center was a 120- by 100-foot covered riding arena.

All the stalls were constructed of stone. The ceiling height was at least twenty feet. The interior partition walls were five feet tall, with wrought iron bars and elegant scrollwork. The iron had two uses: to maintain a beautiful appearance and to keep the horses from fighting over food. The stall fronts were hinged half-doors constructed of polished hardwoods. The top half consisted of wrought iron bars, with a drop-down center allowing the horses to hang their heads into the aisleway. Erik knew it was important for the horses to see each other—cementing their relationships as members of a herd.

"When the Russians retreated, they pilfered much of the mature breeding stock. Many horses had escaped along the way and straggled back over the last few days. Countless others were lost in the initial Polish evacuation. We have a reward system in place. Five hundred zlotys for the return of Janow's horses, no questions asked," Major Fellgeible explained.

Surprised, Erik lifted both eyebrows. "That's good."

"We have kept the barn's civilian employees as well. Once we replenish the herd, we will continue with the Polish breeding program. Why change what was working? The less disruption, the better," Fellgeible continued. "The Polish people will be treated with respect." He leveled an accusatory glare into Erik's eyes.

"I understand," Erik nodded. This was the opposite position Gunther Bishof and the two SS officers expressed on their trip to the farm. They'd made a number of unsavory suggestions Erik immediately dismissed. Maybe the Major's lecture warned he had best not take a brutal view of the occupation unless he wanted to be reassigned. Erik felt a kinship with the Major. If Poland were now part of Germany, they would need to extend the hand of peace.

Erik turned sideways to let the two women sweeping the aisleway pass by before following after Fellgeible. Both young girls glanced at him quickly and then dropped their gazes to the floor, almost in a gesture of submission. Erik didn't like it. He strained to hear their whispers but couldn't make out the words that eventually erupting into giggles.

Major Fellgeible stood waiting in front of an open stall door. "You'll need an assistant," Fellgeible said. "This is Annaleah Sabrosky. She is good with the horses and will help you. Anna, this is Rittmeister Dr. Erik Kemperman, our new veterinarian."

A young woman, dressed in dark brown riding breeches, tall boots, and a crisp white blouse covered by a hand-embroidered wool vest, turned to face him. She took his breath away. She was a small woman, and he immediately wondered how she would feel in his arms. Her face and body had incredible symmetry. A golden braid hung down her back and over her left shoulder. Her turquoise eyes matched some of the colored threads in her vest, and her full lips almost begged to be kissed. Erik momentarily lost his emotional balance. It was as if the war, the Major, and Sergeant Albrecht faded away, and he alone stood face to face with this lovely young woman. He knew he stared but didn't want to stop. Couldn't stop. Speechless, he awkwardly reached forward to shake her hand. Though her expression was as cold as stone, the mare she'd been brushing betrayed her. The horse nuzzled her hands as if asking for more attention. Only a gentle, loving touch brought such a response from animals. Erik knew well from his own experiences when training to become a veterinarian. Animals were better at sizing up people than people were.

"Miss Sabrosky, it is good to meet you," Erik finally said.

Chapter Seven

THE SOUND OF MORNING BIRD songs filtered into Karena's dreams. She pulled the covers up around her shoulders. The plop and rattle of paper pages startled her, and she realized Granny A's manuscript had dropped to the floor. She stretched and thought about retrieving it, but she was so warm and comfortable under the star-patterned quilt she snuggled down further into the bed covers instead.

She turned on her side and faced the bedroom window. Outside, early dawn's gray light brightened moment by moment. First, the sky turned a soft pink as if painted by a master artist with watercolors. As the sun rose, the clouds turned brilliant red and orange, almost like the sky was on fire. A rainstorm was coming—it revealed itself in the cool breeze, whispering through her open window.

Last night's reading began to flood back into her mind. She'd learned Janow's new young veterinarian was smitten by Granny A, but she wondered if her grandmother returned his fascination. Too cozy to reach for the binder holding the manuscript, she closed her eyes and tried to imagine the scene. But finally, overwhelmed by curiosity, she threw off the blankets, grabbed Granny A's tome from the floor, and dove back under the covers, finding the warm spot where she'd earlier been. Karena opened the page marked by a scrap of stationary she'd torn from a tablet she'd found in the bedside nightstand's drawer.

September 30, 1939

How could they replace Dr. Lesnik? Annaleah thought, her stomach contracting with anger as she turned to face the new German veterinarian. She wanted to hate him, but his blue eyes glinted with an easy-going nature, and her bitterness and loathing melted like butter on fresh-out-of-the-oven bread. She guessed he wasn't too much older than she. Maybe twenty. She'd developed an image from the gossipy whispers racing around the barn among the female employees, and he fit it. He was tall and broad-shouldered from hard work, like the young farm boys she'd grown up with. His blond hair, strong jawline, and even features made him the very image of the Nazi Ideal—a true Aryan. He even made the hated Wehrmacht uniform look nice. Unlike many soldiers encamped around the farm, his demeanor wasn't pretentious and cruel. His eyes held a gentleness and empathy she expected from veterinarians and animal lovers. No matter. He represented the occupation army, and she the conquered people. She shuddered. She remembered Jan, Nelek, and all her male school friends who had to flee and hide, moving from one place to the next, never in the same place twice, just to stay alive. She nodded a greeting to the new vet, but it was filled with bitterness.

"Has something happened...where is Dr. Lesnik?" she asked. Major Fellgeible had, so far anyway, been good to her, and she searched his face, fearing the worst. Had Dr. Lesnik been sent to one of the rumored labor camps?

The Major smiled. "He's still here working under Dr. Kemperman's direction."

The new vet straightened up, his face open with surprise. Had he not known he was now in charge? Why would the Major put this young man over a veterinarian with years of practical experience? When Fellgeible looked away, Dr. Kemperman shrugged as if baffled. Annaleah tried to mask her suspicion. Did this man intentionally try to endear himself to her? It almost worked—but she couldn't let it show. She jerked her chin up and frowned at him. Handsome or not, he was still the enemy.

Albrecht appeared at the far end of the barn, and the Major acknowledged him with a nod.

"Annaleah, will you show Dr. Kemperman the rest of the farm?" He bowed slightly, excusing himself, and she watched him walk briskly to join Albrecht.

She removed Petrina's halter and turned her loose in the stall. The new vet quickly jumped in to help her close the mare's stall door and ended up standing too close to her. When he stared too long into her eyes, she began to feel an indescribable helplessness she'd never felt before. A new fear coursed through her whole body. It took all her remaining strength to stand tall, stay, and not run away.

Petrina poked her head through the stall door window and separated them. It wasn't a hostile move, but it was almost as if the mare recognized Annaleah's distress and tenderly intervened to keep her safe.

"Ah, you want attention, do you, little miss?" Kemperman asked the mare, stroking her face. She closed her eyes and nuzzled his cheek. He reached under her mane and scratched her neck. "That's a good girl," he cooed.

"Rittmeister...Dr. Kemperman, shall we?" Annaleah clumsily stumbled over his title. She didn't know what to call him.

"Erik," he said, a disarming grin turning up the corners of his mouth. Annaleah knew the dangers of being taken in by charm. Long before the invasion, unwanted babies were left on the orphanage's doorstep. She imagined it would continue, even more so, since the German soldiers thought the Polish people were less than human and took whatever they wanted. Even with a perfect smile, he was still the conquerer, and she the vanquished.

He let the mare continue to search his hands. Petrina stretched her neck and intentionally knocked his hat off with her lips. He caught it midair and stepped away laughing. Petrina bobbed her head and popped her lips together as if enjoying her joke.

"I don't like wearing it either, Missy," he said, replacing it on his head.

"Dr. Kemperman, sir. This way," Annaleah fumbled. She compromised formality as far as possible and tipped her head toward the door. Inside, she cringed. She'd seen another soldier backhand a young woman who'd displeased him.

But, instead, his smile was playful and broad, "Erik," he said again, as if amused.

She stifled her reply, pressing her lips tight together. She wanted to tell him to stop it. They would never be friends. But she wanted to stay more with the horses and her family at the convent. The specter of the labor camps loomed like a dark storm in her thoughts.

Just this morning, Father Jerzak described the brutal treatment of the Jewish citizens and shop owners in Biala he'd witnessed firsthand. Their shops and homes were taken from them, and they were hauled away in the back of a truck. They had always supported the orphanage and helped raise money for the convent's needs by selling the sisters' handmade jams and jellies, canned vegetables from the gardens, and their handmade soaps and fragrant lotions. With winter on the way and no one to sell their goods in the village, keeping her job at the stud farm was imperative. Here, they paid a small wage. Others were forced into slavery.

Annaleah continued the barn tour, mostly in silence. She told Dr. Kemperman each horse's name. He looked into the stall, acknowledged the animal, and jotted down the name and stall number in a small notebook he'd retrieved from his coat pocket. Then, with a nod, he signaled it was time to move on.

After they reached the last stall, he turned to her, all business.

"I would like to evaluate the feed. Can you show that to me?"

"Yes, Dr. Kemperman, sir." Annaleah didn't want to meet his gaze, although his voice held no harshness; her fear made him a monster. She hadn't called him Erik as he'd asked. Would it have consequences?

He took a deep breath and let it out, though he didn't correct her again.

"Then, Miss Sabrosky, we will inventory and re-organize the laboratory and apothecary."

"Yes, sir," she said before correcting herself. "Dr. Erik," She focused on a crack in the concrete floor and mumbled, tucking her arms tight to her sides.

"Ummm." The skin between his brows wrinkled with concern. "Are you afraid of me, Miss Sabrosky? Have you been mistreated here?"

"No, sir. Not mistreated," she answered, finally looking up into his face.

He smiled at her in a way she didn't understand, as if searching for a path into her thoughts. Then he chuckled softly. "You've not been mistreated. Good. But you are afraid of me. I hope, in time, we can change that."

It was true. These men invaded her country and threatened her life and everything she knew. Annaleah was furious for not saying what she thought of him standing in the enemy's uniform and laughing at her. Disheartened and frightened by all that had happened since the war began, she wanted her old life back. At the time of the Russian retreat across the Bug River, she had participated in hiding their food stores. When the Nazis came calling, the supplies were still safe in the secret bunker. But her neighbors in the surrounding farms were raided, their provisions stolen, and men who resisted were beaten, imprisoned, or shot.

Annaleah could barely look at Dr. Erik without being reminded of the horrors he and his soldiers had brought, even if it was against the teachings of Christ. She was supposed to love and pray for her enemies. Ashamed of her lack of charity, she felt a blush warm her cheeks. She'd need to expose this sin at her next confession and repent.

Dr. Erik's smile faded, and he lifted one eyebrow as he sized her up. "The feed? Can you take me there?"

She led him to the storage barn. It took them both to slide open the big wooden doors. The farm had relatively new haying equipment, and hundreds of square 57-kilogram bales were stacked on wooden pallets to keep airflow underneath so they wouldn't mold during winter's ice and snow. The stacks alternated, first orchard grass bales, then alfalfa, like a checkerboard. He investigated the hay, occasionally pulling a handful from a bale, smelling it, and then rubbing it between his palms, checking the moisture content before brushing it away.

Against one wall, tall grain hoppers were filled with oats and barley. He grabbed a bucket, released a sample of each, and carefully inspected the kernels. With effort, Annaleah tamped down any thoughts of giving him credit for checking the hay's sugar and moisture content and the quality of the grains.

She didn't want to like him, but his efficiency and concern for the horses chipped away at her distaste a little.

In the afternoon, he removed his uniform hat and jacket, slipped into veterinary cover-alls, and tossed a pair to her to cover her breeches and blouse. They reorganized the apothecary to his preferred alphabetical arrangement. Side by side, they placed the drugs not needing refrigeration in neat rows in the upper cabinets, the sterile needles and syringes in the drawers beneath. They cleaned the refrigerator, counters, and work areas until they were sparkling. Dr. Erik worked as hard as she did, cleaning and sorting, not once trying to lord over her like the other soldiers had.

Occasionally, when she glanced his way, he would smile as if she'd caught him thinking something he shouldn't.

"Why do you stare at me? Am I doing something wrong, sir?" she asked.

He laughed. "Ah, you caught me. Since we have been assigned to work together, I'd like it if we could be cordial." So, he had read her and felt her animosity. She felt terrible. He reached out to shake her hand. Reluctantly, she took it, holding it with the tips of her fingers like it might be poisonous. Disappointed by her response, he turned away and started to wipe the counter again. "Besides, you are very pretty, Annaleah. You are nice to look at." He lightly chuckled, mostly to himself, but he knew she heard him.

Not knowing how to take his compliment, Annaleah lowered her head and kept working, scrubbing the cabinet face much harder than she needed to.

They finished rearranging the laboratory just as the horses were brought in from pasture for the night. Dr. Erik had her hold each horse by the halter lead while he measured the height and weight with a cloth tape he stored in his pocket. He wrote more notes on his small pad and observed while she fed. When they finished with the mare barn, he took a second spiral-bound notebook from his front pocket and handed it to her.

"Miss Sabrosky, do we have a hay scale?" he asked, giving her the pencil he retrieved from the pocket of his vet coat.

"We have one for weighing the finished bales."

He contemplated her for a moment. "That won't do. Please make a list for me. We will get a smaller one when we are in Warsaw. I'll never remember all the horses' names. We need to purchase something to use as name plaques. Also, I'd like to post their feed rations so nothing is missed. Do you have a suggestion on what we could use?" he asked.

Annaleah guessed he was only trying to engage her and break down her barriers. "Perhaps a child's chalkboard," she offered.

"Good. We need quite a few and may have to order them. We can have them shipped. One for each horse." He smiled.

The thought of going to Warsaw in the company of a German soldier made Annaleah's stomach flop over. Her countrymen couldn't see her in the company of a Nazi. They would label her a sympathizer. The thought made a shudder run through her shoulders.

"I can't go with you, sir," she protested. She would be hated by all sides--hated by the Nazis for being Polish, hated by the Poles for helping the Germans. Quickly, she tried to come up with an excuse. He tipped his head, lifted an eyebrow, and tightened his lips as if she had just crossed the thin line of tolerance he had shown her all day. She felt as if her knees would buckle. Expecting to be punished like she'd seen other soldiers do to those who didn't obey their wishes, she quickly said, "I didn't ride my assigned horses today. I must tomorrow." Her excuse shakily tumbled out.

Dr. Erik's eyes softened. "I didn't realize you were assigned horses to ride, too."

She nodded sheepishly.

"Well, I'll help you catch up on your riding chores when we return from Warsaw."

It wasn't what she wanted to hear. "Yes, sir. Dr. Erik." She had to prepare for the consequences.

Chapter Eight

October 8, 1939

For the day, Dr. Erik and Annaleah worked together congenially. She didn't annoy him or make him exasperated with her. They gave the yearlings their shots, tube-wormed the mares and stallions, and exercised horses in their free hours. They were always together. Annaleah hadn't even a moment to catch up on news of her friends in the resistance from the other barn workers, and she wondered if Jan and Nelek were alive and well.

She dismounted her mare, slid the stirrups into place on the sides of the English saddle, and unbuckled the cinch. Clara, her best friend at the barn, walked up, and helped her, exchanging the bridle for a halter. Annaleah eyed Dr. Erik as he led his mare into the stall next door. He seemed to be keeping her under his watchful eye. Unsuccessfully, she'd been careful not to give him a reason to distrust her. But how she'd acted on their first day together set the stage, and she would have to work to gain his confidence. At least he hadn't brought up going to Warsaw. She hadn't had time to manufacture a solid excuse to get out of it.

Clara slipped into Delphona's stall, and Annaleah handed her the light-weight saddle. After tying the mare to a hitching ring, she picked up the brush she'd left in her stall and started grooming her.

Clara moved close to her, still holding the saddle over her arm. As if they were going to share secrets, she glanced behind her before speaking.

"What's it like to work with him all day?" she whispered, a conspiratorial smile on her face.

Annaleah scowled at her.

"He's so handsome," she giggled.

"Clara! He's German. A Nazi. Do you forget?" She chastised her with a harsh whisper. Erik removed the tack from his horse next door, and she imagined him listening, his ear pressed against the wall. He was nice to look at; Annaleah had eyes. But he was a member of the enemy army, and that fact never left her mind. Though he'd been patient with her, she didn't know if he would turn against her.

"At least he isn't Russian. We'd have no horses if he were," Clara retorted. "But what is it like?"

"The same as working with Dr. Lesnik," Annaleah said, causing Clara to roll her eyes.

"Annaleah! Annaleah! Come quickly. It's Witez—he's back!" A female voice called from the end of the barn aisleway.

What joy! Her heart leaped in her chest. She forgot all about Dr. Erik. The yearling colts were found, and she couldn't wait to see them. They were more than just horses—they were friends. Scrambling from Delphona's stall, she raced past Gizella's stall, forgetting she needed Dr. Erik's permission to go anywhere. Begrudgingly, she returned, impatiently standing in the doorway.

"Witez is back," she said, expecting him to understand. His expression became confused, his stare blank. He didn't know the horses by name. Instead of waiting for his permission, she wheeled away from him and ran toward the yearling barn. She could hear his footsteps behind her, but she didn't look. *If Witez had been found, would Lotnik have been as well?* Hope soared from deep inside like an eagle's flight. In English, *Lotnik* meant 'the flyer.' It brought visions of the mythical Pegasus to her mind.

When she first came to the stud farm, years ago at age six, with the other children from school, Dr. Lesnik spun delightful stories of magical Arabian horses, drinking the wind and racing across the desert sands, their hooves never touching the ground. To a child, their beauty made those stories entirely believable.

Annaleah dashed to the yearling barn and, through the doorway, stopped to watch Major Fellgeible pay the young man holding the colt's halter lead—Five Hundred Zlotys, no questions asked. She didn't recognize the youth, dressed in tattered and dirty peasant clothes, but she could tell the reward was important to him.

"Did you bring Lotnik, too? Another colt, gray?" she asked, trailing the boy as he walked briskly toward the exit. Panicked, he shook her grasp away from his arm.

"No, madam. Let me go. Only this one colt." His expression was desperate. He wanted to flee the barn, fearing the Germans would change their minds. She understood and let him go.

"Anna!" Dr. Erik's voice was stern but not angry. "Help me here."

She hustled back and took the lead rope from him. Witez was thin. His once shiny bay coat was lackluster, and he lowered his head, asking for comfort from an old friend. Annaleah stroked his face and scratched behind his ears, and he pressed forward, resting his muzzle against her arm. Major Fellgeible watched. A slow smile spread across his lips.

"You are very good with the horses, Annaleah," he said. "I will leave him in your capable hands." He motioned to his adjutant and left the building.

As Anna held the colt, she watched Dr. Erik wrestle with the stethoscope hanging around his neck and press the rubber-tipped ends into his ears. He listened to the horse's lungs and heartbeat. He coursed his hands down the colt's back and over his ribcage. Witez stood perfectly still, seeming to know this was his home and the people here cared for him. Erik picked up each hoof and inspected it.

"Well, there's nothing wrong with this colt that time and good feed won't cure." His smile was confident and reassuring. "Give him a double ration of grass hay tonight, and we will slowly get him to his proper weight."

Annaleah followed his command and led the colt to one of the empty stalls. One of the barn helpers quickly filled his hay feeder. Another filled his fifteen-gallon water bucket. Witez buried his muzzle into the feeder, grateful to be back home.

"Before you go tonight, recheck the water," Erik instructed the helper, but he didn't hurry away, even though it was the officers' usual time for dinner. He stayed in the stall, standing on the opposite side of the colt from Anna.

"He knows you. He remembers you," Erik's voice was just a little louder than a whisper.

Dr. Erik was so aggravating. His soft voice and gentle eyes made it impossible for Annaleah to hate him. She tried not to acknowledge him and massaged Witez's shoulders as the colt munched contentedly on his hay.

Dr. Erik stared and leaned across the colt's back, resting his chin on his arms. He grinned at her in his way, leaving her feeling weak, afraid, and her thoughts a muddled mess.

He said, "Anna, no more excuses. You *WILL* go to Warsaw with me."

She glared at him, her eyes wide with a strange mixture of terror and anticipation. She had no choice. She was going to Warsaw.

Annaleah was startled awake by the familiar sound of pebbles tick-ticking against the dormitory window. She couldn't believe it was real at first. *Only a dream*, she thought and closed her eyes. Jan and Nelek were in hiding with the resistance. It had to be a dream. But once again, the tinkle of a small stone hitting and bouncing down the glass roused her from sleep. She threw back the covers and tip-toed to the window.

In the moon shadows reaching long fingers across the convent's court-yard lawn, a tall figure stood, looking up at her. He didn't call her name like he used to do in their school days. Jan only motioned for her to come down to him.

Racing from the window, she grabbed her breeches and put them on. Each button seemed too big for its buttonhole as she struggled to fasten her blouse. She tried to tuck the tails in the waistband but only halfway succeeded before giving up. Even her socks fought her. But, finally, she went to the window and showed Jan her boots, signaling she was on her way.

In stocking feet, she crept down the stone stairway and corridor to the main entry. The wooden door creaked on its hinges as she opened it, and she winced, hoping she didn't awaken the sisters. Listening, she stood in the silence, making sure no one stirred in the convent. She nearly jumped out of her skin, when the soft chime from the hallway clock announced three in the morning.

Anna closed the massive wooden doors with a soft click as the lock's tongue passed over the strike plate and rested in its receptacle.

She stepped into her boots and galloped down the last remaining steps to the gravel in the convent's driveway. In the front garden, dew glistened in rainbow droplets on the evergreen bushes, and the manicured lawn sparkled with a silvery sheen in the moonlight. Annaleah dashed to the stand of trees where she'd last seen Jan waiting.

The oak, ash, and maple trees were nearly bare of their autumn leaves. The fallen leaves rustled underfoot as she entered the growth of trees alongside the small creek bordering the convent's property. A mist rose from the water as it babbled over stones and pebbles on its way to the Bug River. A chill nipped at her cheeks and nose, and she wished she'd brought her jacket as a shiver made goosebumps stand on her skin.

"Jan, where are you?" she called out in a throaty whisper.

"Here." He stepped out from behind a large tree, leaning his rifle within reach against the trunk.

"Whatever are you doing here? It is so dangerous." He took hold of her hand and tugged her forward. The warmth from his body chased away the cold as he enveloped her in his arms.

"I missed you so much. I needed just to see your face." He kissed her cheek like a brother—not with the passion she expected and wanted from a man who was to become her husband. She didn't want to be disappointed, but she was. They'd known each other since childhood, and maybe it cooled off ardor, replacing it with a more mellow love.

Annaleah wanted the love she'd read about in novels, even though the sisters told her those stories weren't real, just someone's imagination. Marriage was hard work, they said. So, maybe this was the way life was supposed to be. It didn't stop her from wanting more. Once again, she thought, *How could women who'd never experienced the love of a man tell how it should be?*

"How is my family?" he asked, intertwining his fingers with hers.

"Surviving. Your whole family was at Mass on Sunday." She squeezed his hand to reassure him. For a moment, she tried to imagine what it would be like to belong to a family. Jan's had always welcomed her. She knew very little about her family. She knew her mother and father had died of influenza. She shook off those thoughts. The Sisters of Mercy were her family now and would always be.

"I took them a basket with flour, sugar, eggs, and butter this week. Your mother grew a wonderful garden, and they hid much of their goods away from all the pillaging armies."

Suddenly, she imagined the German officers dining sumptuously on the food they'd stolen from the farmers, and she wanted them to choke on it. Her sentiment was wrong; hard-hearted and not in the least bit in line with the teachings of the Church. She tried to stifle the feeling, but it simmered inside anyway.

"Is it true the Russians took Ofir and Frederika?" She could tell he wanted her to refute this rumor. Ofir—the son of the magnificent desert-bred Kuhailan-Haifi, was his favorite of all the stallions.

"It's true."

He looked down at the ground and kicked at the dried leaves, sending some skyward. Annaleah could smell autumn's spicy, earthy scent as they settled to the ground. The clouds overhead shrouded the moon and plunged the small woods into blackness. Linking her arm through his, she moved closer to him for protection.

"Witez is back. A farmer brought him in today," she offered as consolation.

"I know. Nelek and I found him pulling a vegetable cart. The farmer wanted to keep him, but the Janow brand gave the colt away. I convinced him it was better to turn the horse in for half the reward than to be reported to the Germans. I hired the boy to take Witez to the barns. I can't be seen, you know." Jan reached into his vest pocket and took out a roll of bills. "This is my part of the reward. Will you give it to my father? Tell my mother you saw me, and I am alive and well. She worries, and I can't go home. The Gestapo watches my house, waiting for my return." He pressed the money into her hand. She stuffed it into a front pocket in her breeches.

Annaleah nodded. "I will. Oh, Jan. You must go. I'm afraid they watch me, too. I can't bear the thought of the Germans arresting you." Every shadow seemed to conceal the enemy in her imagination. She felt fear over her whole body. For a moment, she thought she saw a figure in the shadows. When she looked again, she dismissed the vision as her imagination running amok.

"I won't be found out." Jan was sure and embraced her, holding her gently against his chest. Then he let go and picked up his rifle. With a wave of his hand, he encouraged her deeper into the woods. After looking around to see if the monsters she feared hid behind them, she followed Jan into the dark.

They both turned toward the creek when a whistle like a bird call breached the silence.

"I must go," he said, sorrow in his eyes. They hugged once more. "I love you, Anna."

She nodded, hesitantly. She did love Jan—their friendship was deep, she reasoned. Before he could go, she rocked up to her tip-toes and kissed him full on the mouth, trying to evoke her longed-for passion. Instead, he rebuked her with his stare.

"Not here, Annaleah. This is not the time for kissing. We must wait," he scolded.

Was Jan right? She wasn't sure. There may never be another time. Her heart felt as if burdened by a lead weight. She held his hand as long as he would allow, sliding her fingers along his palm slowly until only their fingertips touched. For a moment, they lingered there until he turned away.

"Be safe," she whispered, and his silhouette faded into the mist.

Annaleah stood for a long time, surrounded by the early morning fog. The chilled air finally made her turn and sneak back into the convent and the dormitory.

After she changed back into her nightgown, she wandered to the window, hoping to glimpse Jan and the resistance soldiers as they vanished into the forest.

Morning at the Stud Farm was busy as usual. The women and girls who delivered the feed and cleaned the stalls and aisleways surrounded Dr. Erik like a flock of chickens at feeding time. *Women could be so silly.* Annaleah thought. She wasn't blind. She could see how attractive he was. But handsome or not, they had to understand the new veterinarian was part of the war machine that took their husbands, sons, and lovers from them. She sighed, disgusted.

"Anna," Dr. Erik called out. He threaded his way through the small group of women, his open lab coat flowing out behind him like a cape. She stopped. Though she wanted to ignore him, she couldn't. The regime had power over her. Resentment flowed through her like a river current.

"Yes, sir?" Her mouth was as tight as the lid on a newly sealed canning jar.

"Good morning." As usual, Dr. Erik's disarming, infectious smile shamed her. Annaleah knew she should see him as an individual instead of categorizing him as a mindless automaton like the other German soldiers around the farm. She'd come to hate their stiff posture and ridiculous salute. Every time she saw it, she bristled. *Thou shalt have no other gods before me.* The Bible verse would flash in her mind. Their *god* was a madman.

Dr. Erik had always been sympathetic toward her. When he caught up, she slowed so he could walk beside her toward Witez's stall. Annaleah took up a brush and reached for the door.

"Ann-ah." He covered her hand with his and removed the brush. When she turned to face him, they were, once again, precariously close. He lifted her chin with his fingertips. She had to look at him. She dreaded looking into his eyes—she seemed to lose her thoughts and suddenly became weak-kneed as if the electrical field around them had somehow changed. Annaleah was frustrated for feeling this way. *I'm just as silly as the other women. No matter how much I don't want to be.* She certainly wasn't going to show it. To make things worse, he laughed softly at her as if he enjoyed inflicting every minute of misery. "Stop for a moment. I need to talk to you."

"I'm sorry, sir." She dropped her gaze to the ground. Her cheeks flushed with heat and color.

"The Major wants to see us before we go to Warsaw tomorrow." He tipped his head in the direction of the commander's office. "Shall we?" He reached for her hand. She gasped. She couldn't let him take her hand—not in front of the feeders. She could imagine the gossip. And if Jan heard about it, even if it were pure fabrication, he'd be heartbroken. She couldn't let it happen. Not while he risked everything to free Poland from the Germans' grasp. She hadn't fabricated a reason not to go with him to Warsaw . How was she going to get out of this?

Dr. Erik shook his head and laughed again. He withdrew his hand and, instead, he dramatically gestured so she would walk in front of him. He opened the door for her when they arrived at Major Fellgeible's office.

This was the first time Annaleah had seen the inside of Major Fellgeible's office. He'd taken it from Director Krzytalowicz when he'd first arrived at the farm. The children were never allowed in there. Since the Major had confiscated it, she never expected to see it. *Was she in trouble?* She tried to imagine what she'd done but couldn't. She hadn't strayed from the usual routine.

The office was huge. A fire crackled behind an ornate brass screen in the floor-to-ceiling stone fireplace, warming the room. Portraits of Polish-bred stallions hung with honor on the walls. She and Dr. Erik stood before the Major's massive carved cherry desk. Two chairs, upholstered in leather, were in front of the desk, but Annaleah didn't dare sit without permission.

"Ah, Captain Kemperman, Anna, good you're here." The Major looked up from the papers in the center of the desk. "Captain Kemperman has very good things to say about you, Anna. He tells me you have an extraordinary relationship with the yearling colts."

"Yes, sir. I attended each of their births. I think they see me as one of their herd," she answered.

He considered her as if weighing her words and said, "We have received information that several of our yearlings are at the Warsaw race track. The man housing them has an unsavory reputation. And even though we have posted our reward for their return at the track, it is rumored he intends to keep some of the colts as if they were his own. Annaleah, would you recognize the horses who belong here?"

"Yes. I know I would. Lotnik? Have you found Lotnik?" Annaleah asked, hope rising in her like a spring. He was her favorite of all the horses. She folded her hands and touched them to her lips, saying a silent prayer.

"We're not sure. But the horses are said to have the Janow brand, and we will get them back. One way or another. Will you help us?" Major Fellgeible asked. Dr. Erik smiled at her.

"Yes. I will help you. What do you need me to do?" After she blurted it out, she was overwhelmed with remorse. *Oh, no. She was the hard-hearted woman Jan had accused her of being.* She had volunteered to help the Germans. If the horses were Janow's, they belonged here, didn't they?

"So, you and Dr. Kempermann will go to the racetrack in Warsaw. We decided you will pretend to be a rich couple, a husband and wife, looking for inside information for betting purposes. Check and see if the horses are the ones we are looking for. If they are Janow's colts, some soldiers will arrest the man for refusing to comply with our orders and bringing the horses home."

Husband and wife? If this got back to Jan and the resistance, she'd be branded a collaborator and hated. But her mind wouldn't stop the counter-argument. *Wasn't it better to recover the horses and have them here at Janow, where they'd receive the best care?*

Chapter Nine

"KARENA, ARE YOU AWAKE?" HER mother's voice filtered through the closed door, together with the softest knock. She heard the lock unlatch and knew her mother had a key. Karena quickly closed the book, stuffed it under her pillow, and pretended to be asleep.

"Karena, I need help fixing breakfast," Mom said as she twisted the knob and opened the door. She sat up as Mom sank to the edge of the bed. Lovingly, like a good mother, she brushed Karena's messy hair away from her cheek.

"Did you sleep okay?" she asked.

"Yes. It's just so cold outside and so warm under the covers, I didn't want to get up," Karena answered. Afraid she'd disappoint her, she hadn't told Mom about Granny A's book. Mom would accuse her of wasting time and avoiding the work they'd come to do. Which, of course, was true. Deep inside, Karena knew Granny A's book was important. Her dad had warned her it was a mistake to ignore the lessons of history.

"Well, no wonder you're cold. The window is wide open." Her mother rose and slid the glass closed across the screen.

"I love fresh air at night," Karena protested.

"It's time to get up, honey. We have so much work to do, and the relatives are beginning to stir. You better get your shower before the hot water runs out," she chuckled. Karena knew Mom thought that would bring her daughter out from under the covers. Karena shook her head. Mom was right.

"There's nothing worse than running out of hot water when you've just finished lathering up," Mom reminded her, with a slight tip of her head toward the bathroom. She wore a smile that was more of a grimace.

Karena threw back the covers and stood. Mom placed her unpacked suitcase on the end of the bed with a thud and bounce. *The book*! Quickly, Karena scrambled to straighten the bed covers. She fluffed both pillows, ensuring they matched each other in shape and size. She hoped Mom wouldn't look under the one hiding her secret.

"Mom," she complained. "You aren't going to choose my outfit this morning, are you? I'm seventeen. I can get dressed," she whined, conceding, but only to herself that her mom had good taste in fashion and good intentions. Then she remembered *Gerard the Gorgeous* would be here today, maybe even for breakfast, and she wanted to be at her best.

Sam hadn't bothered to call her back last night. It had been over twenty-four hours since they'd talked. Karena fought with her feelings of abandonment and anger. He should've broken up with her. Ignoring her was cruel. She suspected he'd be surfing; there was a big South Swell from Hurricane Naomi off the Baja Peninsula. Her Surf's Up App predicted fifteen-foot waves. She hoped a shark hadn't eaten him. She decided to call his sister later if he didn't return her call soon. Though Sam would never know of her flirtation, she still felt satisfaction at getting some sort of revenge.

Mom set a clean pair of blue jeans across the end of the bed, ignoring Karena's complaint. "Dr. Wilson and his veterinary student will be joining us for breakfast. He's such a handsome young man, don't you think?" she asked, lifting a pink pullover sweatshirt from the case and shaking it so the travel wrinkles would fall out. "This color is so pretty on you."

"Thank you, Mom." Taking her mother by her shoulders, she turned her toward the door. "I'll be down in a minute." She snatched the sweatshirt From Mom's hands with a big grin.. They did enjoy teasing each other.

Mom studied Karena before leaving but let her handle her morning routine alone.

After showering, Karena put on the jeans and pink sweatshirt her mother had laid out. It was an easy compromise; she hadn't even thought about what to wear. She added her own flair by donning her leather cowboy boots trimmed with pink accents and tied her hair in a ponytail with a pink ribbon.

Karena stood quietly for a moment at the window, absorbing the view. It was beautiful here, even though it wasn't by the ocean. A breeze tickled the grain heads in the last uncut hayfield, stirring the grasses like ripples across the water. She was reminded of the ocean and thought she should've been homesick. She wasn't.

Karena had always been overwhelmed by the beauty of the West Coast. It's hard to match a sunset over the Pacific when the last rays turn the waves to liquid gold. But last night, the beauty of the August full moon rising over the Bitterroots filled her with awe. Beauty was everywhere if she bothered to look.

After a few moments, she turned and glanced at her image in the dresser mirror and gave herself a nod of approval. She left her room and closed the door. Without giving it serious thought, she danced down the stairs to the main floor much too noisily, expecting all the relatives to be up and milling around.

The living room was empty and dark, except for the sunrise cresting the mountains to the east through the big picture window. The sunlight splintered into shafts radiating through the rainclouds to the mountaintops and valleys, like photos she'd seen in one of her mother's devotional books.

A new, unexplainable emotion welled in her heart as if her grandmother were here with her. She felt warmth coursing through her whole body. *No wonder Granny A loved this place.*

The clanging of pots and pans in the kitchen broke through her reverie. Mom started breakfast without her. She needed to move to help her but was frozen—transfixed by the view.

Finally, she gave in to her inner voice's nagging and pushed through the kitchen's swinging door.

Mom set skillets on the stove's burners and began frying bacon. The delicious smell, mixed with the scent of brewing coffee, would rouse the sleeping relatives.

"Let's set up a buffet," Karena suggested and reached for plates in the cabinet by the sink. Through the over-the-sink window, she watched Dr.

Wilson's white vet truck pull up beside the barn. All her thoughts of Sam disappeared when Gerard stepped from the truck's passenger side. Dressed in blue overalls, with a stethoscope hanging around his neck, he looked perfect as a large animal vet. Karena imagined a thermometer in his top front pocket and horse treats in one of his pants pockets. Unlike Sam, his blond streaked hair was neatly trimmed, and there wasn't even a hint of stubble on his cheeks, so popular with the California boys. Sometimes, she thought kissing Sam was like kissing a square of rough-grained sandpaper. *Clean-cut, polite, hardworking—did Gerard the Gorgeous have any faults?*

Mom moved from the stove and stood beside her, resting her arm over her daughter's shoulders.

"You should go help." She shoved her hip against Karena's. What she wanted wasn't lost. Her mother disapproved of Sam; always had.

"I can handle breakfast. Besides, Aunt Helen and Uncle Ray will come help me once they smell food," she said, chuckling.

"Help them with what? I don't know anything about horses," Karena complained. But it was false. She liked the thought of hanging out with Gerard. It was a better plan than enduring the battling relatives.

"Take Dr. Wilson and Gerard some coffee. There are thermal mugs in the cupboard, and sugar packets and little tubs of cream on top of the fridge." She peaked both eyebrows, hopeful.

Karena stuffed her pockets with sugar packets and tubs of cream and filled two thermal mugs with coffee. After affixing the lids, she turned to her mother. "Here goes nothing," she said with a grin.

Dr. Wilson and Gerard had already entered the barn, so Karena followed. She should've known her young horse-crazy cousins would be up and in the barn. Marsha, Lizbeth, and Sharon pursued the vets, asking a million questions and putting the kibosh on Karena's plan of being with Gerard alone. She caught up to the group.

"I thought you would like some coffee before you started work," Karena offered Dr. Wilson a mug. Gerard turned to her, and a dazzling smile brightened his face. Karena was instantly reminded of Granny A's story and her battle with her feelings for Dr. Erik.

She sensed a giant crush brewing. *Move over, Sam!* she thought at first, but like a schoolgirl crush, she feared her feelings had no basis in reality.

Karena handed the second mug to Gerard. "I have sugar and cream if you need it." Even saying it made her blush. She pulled the condiments from her jeans pockets and offered them to the men.

"Thank you," he said, taking one of the cream tubs.

"Breakfast will be ready in about half an hour if you're hungry," Karena said, walking with Gerard in the aisleway.

"I'm always hungry." He laughed.

The horses began poking their heads through the stall door windows, nickering for their breakfast. Granny A had hired two young women to feed for her, and the cousins joined them as they loaded the hay and grain cart. The girls seemed happy for the help.

Chapter Ten

KARENA FOLLOWED GERARD FROM STALL to stall as he completed a well-check and a blood draw to clear each horse for transport. Even though she feared horses, Karena felt a heaviness inside as she looked at each one. The relatives wanted to schedule the private auction for next month. After reading the first pages of Granny A's Story, she understood how much her grandmother had cared for her horses. Karena couldn't help but think perhaps Granny A had hoped one of the relatives would want to keep the farm and the horses.

The barn was wonderfully appointed and kept spotlessly clean. Ornate wrought iron scrollwork adorned each stall front, reminding her of the description of the stalls at Janow. Had Granny A recreated her barns from her memories of the Polish stud farm?

A sliding door served as the opening and was set on the right side of each 12 by 24-foot rectangular box. Each stall had a door to an outside run that could be closed when the weather turned rainy or wintery. A wooden tack trunk with a padded top, doubling as a seat, was positioned in front of each stall. The trunk held brushes and various grooming items. Karena remembered it all from her childhood visits.

The stall floors were first covered with rubber mats and then piled with at least a foot of clean, fragrant pine shavings. Granny A pampered her prize horses and treated them like children, earning her the title, behind her back, of the *Crazy Horse Lady*. Karena wanted to learn why and longed to get back to the book. But she wanted to learn more about Gerard, too.

The horses liked the young, handsome vet but viewed her cautiously. Some were friendly, others more stand-offish. The friendlier ones frightened her a little. They would readily poke their heads through the opening in their stall doors, eager for attention.

"Let them smell you. They get a sense of you then," Gerard said. He encouraged her by example, letting the horses breathe in his scent and explore his hands and even his face. She watched as one of the mares tousled his hair with her lips.

It took courage, but after a few tries, Karena let the same mare give her the once over. Even on her childhood visits, she'd stayed away from the horses, opting instead to read a novel. They were so big.

"Will she bite me?" she asked, feeling a flutter of fear.

"No. She won't bite. Like this." He laughed and moved close behind her. He took hold of one of her hands and encouraged her to scratch the mare under her mane at her withers. Karena couldn't believe the unexpected rush overwhelming her when Gerard's arm rested along her shoulder and matched the curve of her back. The feeling was stronger than any desire she'd ever had for Sam. A blush warmed her cheeks. *Awkward. Clumsy. Ridiculous.* She scolded herself, trying to gain composure. She glanced over her shoulder, and a timid smile creased his face. She gazed into his eyes, far longer than she should've. Embarrassed, Gerard took one step back and cleared his throat. Somehow, Karena knew it wasn't a reproach but was more an act of self-control. Gerard was attracted to her, too.

"There. See. She won't bite." He stuffed his hands in his overall's pockets. Karena speculated he felt as uncomfortable as she did. After all, they'd only just met last night.

In response to Karena's massage, the mare began returning the favor by rubbing Karena's shoulder with her upper lip. Karena giggled and stifled the impulse to move away. Gerard was so darn cute; she wanted to impress him, no matter how frightened she was. She'd never been one for horses. Even when her family visited while Granny A was alive. She'd stayed well away from the barn, only venturing through the door when forced by her mother. The mare started to nuzzle her cheek. Karena flinched away at first but relaxed when Gerard stood next to her. The horse-kiss wasn't slobbery, and the mare's breath smelled clean and sweet—like new grass. Karena started to relax.

"Horses look at people as part of the herd. They accept us as the herd boss. And since they are on a predator's menu, they believe they have reason to be scared if you are scared," Gerard said confidently. "Staying calm and relaxed is very important. I've always believed horses were empaths. They seem to be able to read minds."

"Will you go back to Russia when your schooling is finished?" Karena asked, following him as he walked to the next stall. The horse in this one was one of the prettiest animals she'd ever seen. The stallion was as white as snow; his big dark eyes stared inquisitively at her. He took a few steps forward, but he stopped when she responded by backing away.

"Yes. I only have a student visa. I thank your grandmother for helping me. If not for her, I wouldn't have this opportunity. I worry my Visa could be withdrawn, and I could be forced to leave any day. I don't want to go back. They will force me into the army to fight Ukraine. I'm very sorry your grandmother is gone and for your loss." He delivered a tight smile—more of a grimace. "She and my grandfather were friends during World War II."

"Dr. Erik? Your grandfather is Dr. Erik?"

"Yes. Dr. Erik Kemperman. Do you know about him? Did she tell you about him?" He grabbed the halter hanging on the blanket bar and opened the stall door. After he haltered the horse, he handed her the lead rope. Hesitantly, she took it.

"He won't bite you either. He's a very nice boy." Gerard talked while he worked. He pressed the stethoscope into his ears and listened to the horse's heart and lungs.

"I found their journals, and a book Granny A wrote about the war," Karena said, and Gerard stopped and turned toward her, pulling the ear-pieces from his ears and letting the stethoscope dangle loosely around his neck. His lips parted, and he breathed in as if he wanted to ask something.

"Do you want to see them?"

Immediately, pain filled his eyes. Karena felt stupid. She'd only read the first pages; she didn't know the whole story. Did Gerard?

"My Grandpapa passed away eight years ago. Will you share them with me?" he whispered, seeming to be choked with emotion. Karena became acutely aware he'd been very close to his relation.

"Yes." It spilled out without a second's hesitation. She wondered why. She'd been unwilling to share the stories with her relatives and mother but would with this young man. What was she thinking?

"We'll be through the rest of the horses by this afternoon. Perhaps we could…"

"We can sit on the porch swing and read them together. I just started to read them yesterday."

"I would like that," he said. He prepared a syringe for a blood draw.

"Oh, no," Karena clapped a hand to her forehead. "I forgot. I was supposed to ask you and Dr. Wilson if you'd join us for breakfast."

Dr. Wilson grinned, leaning into the stall's doorway. "Thank you for your thoughtful invitation. I'm sure we could make time. I'll just help Gerard with the stallion, and we'll meet you at the house."

Chapter Eleven

KARENA BOXED UP GRANNY A'S horse treasures all day while Gerard finished his veterinarian chores. She made certain she did a careful packing job out of her new-found esteem for her grandmother and, of course, to please her mother.

She had agreed to meet Gerard the Gorgeous at five to share the secret manuscript with him. At four-forty-five, she hustled to the kitchen to gather supplies to set up the front porch for her date. In the cabinet above the refrigerator, she found a small bucket and filled it with ice. Rummaging through the fridge, she stocked the pail with several bottles of beer. Before closing the door, she glanced around the kitchen guiltily. She grabbed two bottles of her mother's Mike's Hard Lemonade and buried them deep in the ice. If Mom caught her, she'd be in deep trouble. She found a plastic tray fashioned like it was made of crystal and filled it with cheese and crackers.

Karena carried the drinks and snacks to the porch and looked toward the barn. Amused, she watched Gerard wash his hands and rinse them with the warm water stored in a tank on the vet-truck. He waved to her and headed to the porch.

Gerard plopped down on the white wicker two-person porch swing next to the matching side table. Karena gave him a chilled beer and an iced mug from the bucket. With a grateful smile, he poured the bottle's contents into the glass.

"How was your day?" Karena asked.

"We finished. The horses are ready for auction and transport." He smiled. "Thank you for this." He lifted his foaming mug. "I'm ready for it."

What could be better? Karena lifted her shoulders in a shrug of contentment. She was spending time with a handsome young man on a warm August afternoon.

The house topped a hill with views all around, the ones from the front porch being the most beautiful. The first hints of the coming autumn turned the tips of the leaves to gold. In the farthest pasture, closest to the road, a four-man crew collected the last of the second cutting hay bales. The scent of newly mown grass drifted in the air. To the east, a thunderstorm roiled in the late summer heat, building higher and higher into the blue sky. There would be rain tonight; she could feel it.

Karena crossed in front of Gerard and sat on the swing beside him.

"It's nice to be done for the day," he said as Karena unfurled a knitted throw blanket, exposing the three-ring binder holding her grandmother's manuscript. "Is your grandmother's story a secret?" he asked, raising his eyebrows with the question.

"I haven't told anyone about it but you," she smiled guiltily. "My family didn't respect Granny A. I think they'd just want to throw it away."

"How do you know they didn't respect her? She was a generous and wonderful woman."

Karena wiggled her head from side to side with a pout on her lips. "They called her the crazy horse lady. Heck, I called her that before I started reading her story. They accused her of being a Nazi. She was Polish and a victim of the Nazis instead. I don't think they realized her accent wasn't German." Karena adjusted the binder on her lap. "And they really didn't understand her love of the horses."

Gerard chuckled. "Horses were humans' main source of transportation until around 1912 when Ford invented the assembly line and made cars affordable. They still used horses during the Second World War. The horses at Janow, where your grandmother worked, were used for Poland's mounted cavalry until armies were fully mechanized. And of course as race horses. Leaders and kings throughout history have prized Arabian horses."

"I didn't know," Karena said, looking at Gerard with wonder. Not only was he good-looking—but he was also well-read.

"My Grandpapa always said the Arabian horses were coveted for their beauty, speed, stamina, and friendliness," Gerard concluded.

Karena opened the binder. "When I met Granny A, she was in her sixties and seventies. But look at this picture. Can you believe how beautiful she was?"

Gerard examined the picture and then shifted his gaze to her face. "I see you inherited her beauty." He smiled.

Karena frowned. She wasn't much for accepting compliments, especially about looks. It made her squirm uncomfortably in her seat.

"I didn't inherit any genes from Granny A. She had no children of her own. She raised Grandpa George's children. The family accused her of substituting the need for children by raising horses," Karena slowly sighed and shook her head. "She was so misunderstood. It was sad. Well, anyway, I've already started reading her story," she said, opening the rings. She removed the pages she'd already perused and handed them to Gerard. "Since I'm ahead, I'll give you new pages after I've finished. Sound good?"

He nodded and took the pages. They each began reading.

October 10, 1939

Erik looked up as Annaleah descended the convent steps. She looked elegant in the stylish navy blue suit and high-heeled pumps borrowed from one of the officers' wives. As an orphan from the convent, she had no such fancy attire. He could tell she was uncomfortable out of her riding breeches and boots. And suddenly, he was uncomfortable, too. He adjusted his gray tie and ran his thumbs under the lapels of his dark gray, pinstriped suit, smoothing any wrinkles. Quickly, he opened the door to Fellgeible's Mercedes-Benz G-4 Staff Car for her. Warsaw's racetrack was a three-hour drive west, so he'd ensured the car's soft top was in place.

The original ruse of a rich German couple was in play. It was very likely a rich couple would be paraded around in Major Fellgeible's six-wheel off-road beauty.

The look on her face when she first saw the vehicle was a reward. Awe and surprise mixed in her eyes. Erik couldn't help but notice and hoped she was duly impressed. Since he met her, he'd wanted to give her everything. Even though he knew she didn't feel the same, he was crazy in love with her. Maybe he could change her mind during the trip to Warsaw—especially if they found her favorite horse.

"You look lovely, Annaleah," the Major said, turning in the front seat to watch as she stepped on the running board and sank onto the car's leather back seat. She glanced around, her lips parted in awe. Carefully, she ran her hand over the expensive leather. Erik closed the door, raced to the other side, and took his seat beside her.

"Now, we believe there are seven horses in Otto Gronlochev's possession. Lotnik, a long yearling stallion, Ibn Kowalska, an Ofir daughter…."

Erik could tell Annaleah heard none of the other names after the Major mentioned Lotnik. This magical horse was clearly her favorite. She leaned deeply into the seat and closed her eyes. Erik imagined she thought recovering the colt could change the world back to how it had been before the war.

Erik knew the Major had planned for an overnight stay in Warsaw, but Anna didn't. He'd arranged to meet with his older brother, General Fritz Fellgeible, currently the Heer's General of Signals, a bureau specializing in originating secret codes and breaking the codes of their enemies.

Erik was relieved Major Fellgeible avoided the bombed-out ruins of Warsaw. They drove the roads skirting the city and stayed at an elegant hotel close to the racetrack. He feared that if Annaleah saw what the Luftwaffe had done to her countrymen, she might refuse to play her part in this charade.

Erik intended to escort Annaleah to the track this afternoon to find and identify Janow's horses while the Major met with his brother. In the dark of night, they planned to return with soldiers, trucks, and trailers to collect the horses they found.

Annaleah was like a child in a dreamland when they walked into the racetrack's main observation and betting floor. Erik took her hand. When she tried to pull away, he scolded her with a frown.

"We're supposed to be married," he said quietly, and she reluctantly turned her palm up to take his hand in hers. "When your friends see the horses returned to Janow, they will forgive you, Anna." Erik smiled at her. "Come, look."

He led her through the big, open betting lobby to one of the staircases. The lobby dropped off into tiers of tables on concrete balconies overlooking the brilliant green grass mile-and-a-half oval track. Inside, there was a groomed dirt track for other shorter races. A man on a ladder changed the betting odds—white numbers on a big green tote board in the center of the racing ovals next to the judges' platform. Several men stood with binoculars studying horses, gathering for the next race in the paddock. Two mechanized tractors pulled large rakes behind them, smoothing the dirt into corduroy rows. German soldiers in different uniforms, some grey-green, some black, sat with finely dressed women, drinking and dining at tables covered with white linen cloths. A buzz of conversation and peals of laughter were everywhere. It was as if they weren't near Warsaw's ruins. There was no war outside of their make-believe bubble.

"Let's go walk the barns," Erik said, tugging Annaleah to the stairway.

They descended the wide concrete stairs to track level and followed a dirt path to the barns opposite the racing ovals.

The barns were laid out in long parallel rows, with hot walkers in the open spaces between. A young boy walked with the horses, keeping them steady as they cooled from their earlier exercise. Grooms dashed here and there, preparing horses for the afternoon races.

Groups of German officers wandered down the barn aisles, looking into the stalls and making notes on their racing forms. Erik felt like no one would notice Anna and him making the rounds.

Starting at the barn nearest the paddock and racecourse, they casually looked into each stall. Many of the officers milling about the barns nodded to Erik and smiled with envy as he walked hand in hand with Anna. Though she was Polish, she was the German ideal. Blue-eyed, blonde like a fairytale Nordic princess. She could fool them all.

"If the colts are here, they are in the stalls furthest from the action," Anna said. "They are yearlings, and Lotnik isn't old enough to carry a rider, let alone race."

Erik knew horses in Poland were raced after their bones were set. Though they didn't have the exuberance of younger horses, they had more mature minds and far fewer injuries. He worried the Janow horses wouldn't be here at all.

"Then, let's start with the far stalls first," he said.

"Let's," Anna said, pulling him along briskly. She was anxious to find her colt.

Anna stopped at the end of the furthest barn, and a sigh left her lips. "Lotnik," she whispered, dropping Erik's hand. The gray colt was in the fourth box down the barn row. The young stallion leaned against the open top of the Dutch door with his head and neck fully exposed. When he saw Anna, he danced in place and called to her. Anna ran to him.

Before Erik could stop her, she threw her arms around the colt's neck, and she and the horse stood together like long-lost friends, his head over her shoulder in a horse hug . Erik quickly looked around for the dangerous Otto Gronlochev.

Had Anna, in her exhilaration, blown their cover?

Chapter Twelve

ANNALEAH HURRIED AHEAD OF ERIK along the box stalls in the barn row and discreetly placed a small yellow chalk 'X' in the upper right corner of the stall's Dutch door. Erik made certain he blocked the view. He didn't want Gronlochev tipped off before they could collect the horses. They'd only marked three stalls when a huge lumbering man approached from the North end of the barns. He was flanked on either side by rough-looking bodyguards, and Erik carefully sized them up. He could probably take one of the men down, but not both, if it came to it. No matter, he had Annaleah to protect. Diplomacy was his best option.

"How can I help you?" The large man Erik assumed was Gronlochev asked. Balding and nearly as wide as he was tall, Gronlochev dressed in a light-colored suit, completely inappropriate for the cool October air. The man dabbed the sweat from his brow with a handkerchief. Erik recognized the symptoms—Gronlochev was in congestive heart failure.

Erik stepped forward. "My wife was admiring your horses. Are any for sale?" he asked. "She is especially fond of the young gray colt." He pointed to Lotnik's stall.

Gronlochev's eyes lit up with greed. Erik guessed he weighed whether he would make more money selling the colt or waiting and racing him. The Heer's offer of five hundred zlotys hadn't enticed the fat man in the slightest. Ironically, greed blinded Gronlochev to reality. Posters in the betting lobby and distributed throughout the barns warned the Wehrmacht's offer of a reward for Janow's horses was not to be taken lightly. Forbearance was limited, and there would be consequences for ignoring it.

"He isn't currently for sale, but I might consider it for the right price." Gronlochev's avaricious grin had Annaleah turning away so he wouldn't notice her disgust.

"May we see him?" Erik asked. He grasped Anna's hand, reminding her she had to play her part. She turned back, and a cool smile curved her lips. He slipped his arm around her waist and gently pulled her to his side. She felt perfect there, and for a flash, Erik was distracted by her perfume.

Gronlochev tipped his head, and the man to his right grabbed the colt's halter and lead rope. He aggressively opened the stall door. His forcefulness caused the colt to tense and skitter to the back of the stall.

Erik tried to stop her, but she wrestled away from his grasp.

"Here, let me," she said, hurrying to the door as the man raised the halter to strike the colt. "Let me!"

A smirk crossed his lips, and he lowered his arm. He challenged Anna by tossing the halter to her, and then, with an exaggerated genuflect, he stepped out of her way.

Erik knew the outcome before she started forward. All the tension left the horse's body as Annaleah walked to him, cooing softly.

"You're such a handsome boy. Such a good boy," she said. She slipped the halter over his muzzle and hooked the buckle at the side. With a completely relaxed lead rope, she walked forward into the aisleway, and the colt followed.

Gronlochev and his henchmen exchanged intrigued glances. Erik was afraid it would turn to suspicion. The men might take the horses and flee.

"Isn't my wife great with horses," he quickly said. "She's always been able to calm the beasts."

"Ah, yes," Gronlochev said. He and his men laughed together, sharing guarded glances.

Erik slowly circled the colt. No wonder Anna and Fellgeible wanted this colt back. He was wonderful. As close to perfection as Erik had ever seen. He had a lovely face typical of Arabian horses and big, soft, expressive eyes. His long neck was set high and flowed gracefully into the withers. His shoulders were well-muscled, his back short and strong, and his hips powerful. He stood on well-formed forelegs with square knees and clean bone. Erik ran his hand down his calf. The bone was dense and yet refined. His hind legs were the nicest he'd ever seen. The hocks were well shaped and dropped true and straight as if measured by a plumb line. Even when he moved, they were strong and solid. His feet were round and well-shaped. Lotnik was a very fine horse—an athletic horse—a horseman's horse. Erik thought.

"How much?" he asked, resting his hand on Lotnik's back.

Gronlochev looked carefully at Erik and then said, "Ten thousand zlotys."

Anna gasped. Erik wished she hadn't.

"Do you want him, darling?" he asked.

"I do," she answered. Her eyes widened. She looked at him as if she struggled to imagine so much money. Erik loved her naivety. It endeared her to him more, if it was even possible. And though this was a game they played of husband and wife, in his imagination, he wanted it to come true.

Gronlochev rubbed his hands together, salivating as if he could feel and taste the money. "It's a deal."

"I will have my bank wire in the money. May we meet here tonight?" Erik asked.

"Yes. 10:00 this evening," Gronlochev suggested, rolling his wrist and glancing at his watch. Erik saw conspiracy flash in the fat man's eyes. It was a perfect hour. The racetrack would be empty of patrons, and no one would be around to report the clandestine sale to the authorities.

Erik reached out and shook his hand. They exchanged hotel information to keep in touch.

"10:00 o'clock, then," Erik said. He took Annaleah's hand. Erik hugged her to him and kissed her forehead. They walked back to the main racetrack building.

Once they reached the top of the stairs to the betting lobby, Erik looked deep into Annaleah's eyes. "He intends to rob me," Erik said with a chuckle. "Surprise!"

Annaleah examined the dining area from the entrance of the hotel's foyer. Erik clutched and lightly squeezed her hand, reminding her she still must play her part. He pointed out Major Fellgeible and his brother with a tip of his head. They sat at a four-person table by the window, and Erik led her, weaving through the dining room seating and passing other diners as they enjoyed their meals.

Annaleah felt anxious. Major Fellgeible's brother was a general rumored to be part of Herr Hitler's inner circle. Expecting his hatred, she cringed in her skin, and her breath quickened. She was Polish and their hated enemy. She vowed to keep her mouth shut and her bitter thoughts to herself.

"[...] he won't listen to me, but if we add three, just three more rotors, the Enigma will be indecipherable," General Fellgeible complained under his breath. But his disgust and contempt for the person who wouldn't listen was clear. "And now there are rumblings he plans to attack Russia. The man has no honor."

Erik cleared his throat, signaling they had arrived.

Major Fellgeible glanced up. "Ah, Erik, you're here." The General snapped his gaze to the strangers standing beside his table. Annaleah noticed his eyes soften when he looked at her, making her even more uncomfortable.

The General looked nothing like his brother. He was considerably older and thinner, with a pinched expression as if plagued with worry.

"This is Captain Erik Kemperman, our lead veterinarian, and his assistant, Annaleah Sabrosky. As I explained earlier, we are here to recover some of Janow's horses lost in the Blitzkrieg. Sit. Please sit," Major Fellgeible gestured with his hand across the table. "Erik, Annaleah, this is my brother, General Fritz Fellgeible."

Erik offered a weak salute, unlike the soldiers at the barn, who snapped to attention and rushed to give a dramatic display. Annaleah had never seen Erik salute before. His mouth turned into a frown, almost as if it irked him to use it. Interestingly, the General seemed to feel the same way.

Erik, acting the perfect gentleman, pulled out her chair for her. Annaleah sat, and Erik took the chair beside her. Nervously, Annaleah placed her hands on the table, and Erik covered her right one with his left.

"So, did you find our horses?" the Major asked, lifting a glass of whiskey over ice to his lips.

"Yes," Annaleah said. "All seven of them are there. The farthest barn row from the betting lobby."

"I've made arrangements to meet Gronlochev at ten this evening. Lieutenant Bishof said the Gestapo plans to arrest Gronlochev just before our soldiers move in to load the horses. Gronlochev has two thug bodyguards with him. I'm sure they are armed. They may not surrender peacefully. I noticed the bulge of shoulder holsters under their suitcoats," Erik reported and then, with laughter, added, "I offered to buy the colt Lotnik for Ten Thousand Zlotys." The Fellgeible brothers exchanged surprised glances. "I'm sure he intends to rob me of the money and keep the horse."

"Good. Then, he won't be prepared and will certainly show up," the Major said. "Will you have a cocktail before dinner?" He motioned for the waiter.

Chapter Thirteen

ERIK KNEW ANNALEAH WOULD FIGHT him if he asked her to stay at the hotel while they gathered the horses. He formed his defense and rapped softly on the door to her adjoining room. She yanked open the door with an enthusiasm he hadn't expected. Thrilled to get 'her Lotnik' back, she was alight with happiness, replacing her usual barely masked resentment.

He couldn't blame her. Erik was part of the army upending her life. Expecting her to like it would be ridiculous, but he wanted her friendship and more. If she knew the war had also derailed his dreams for the future, would she despise him any less?

Tonight, the pink flush in her cheeks made her blue eyes sparkle. She'd taken her long blonde hair down from the French Twist she'd worn earlier and tied it in a loose braid hanging over her right shoulder. She had changed from the loaned business suit to her white blouse, embroidered wool vest, riding breeches, and boots but looked just as enchanting.

Like her, Erik had donned his work clothes. Their plan was clear. They would lead the convoy of trucks and trailers to the racetrack barns. In the back of their trailer, six Gestapo agents, led by Lieutenant Gunther Bishof, would hide, waiting to arrest Otto Gronlochev and his bodyguards.

Erik remembered Bishof from University. Gunther Bishof was an all-the-way-to-the-bone Nazi. Erik was not. He hated the war and found

Hitler distasteful. The hardship on people and animals caused a heaviness in his heart. It was a waste of precious lives.

Erik and Anna would proceed to the furthest barn row to meet Gronlochev. When Erik handed over the briefcase full of zlotys, the police would descend on the scene, arresting Gronlochev and his thugs. That was the plan, anyway, and if all went well, they would arrive home to Janow with their prized horses early in the morning before dawn broke in the east. But Erik was a realist. He could separate imagination from reality. Gronlochev's thugs were armed. They would be lucky if they surrendered without incident.

Since Erik had noticed the guns this afternoon, having Anna join him on this adventure made his stomach roll over. Too much could go seriously wrong.

He took both of her hands in his and intentionally softened his voice. "Anna, please wait for us here. There is no need for you to go back to the barns. We can handle it."

The warmth in her eyes quickly drained away, replaced with an icy-blue anger.

"I will not wait here. I'm going with you. The colts will load easier if I'm there. They trust me," she pleaded her case. She was right. Erik had witnessed the horses' responses to her. It was as though she was their trusted shepherd. Anna claimed she was 'the herd boss.'

"All right, Anna. But stay in the truck. There may be gunplay, and the truck is armored and will offer some protection," he said, waiting for her agreement. She smiled but didn't acquiesce. He picked up the briefcase with the zlotys and sighed.

They took the elevator ride to the main lobby in silence. The hotel's driveway was lined with four trucks and horse trailers. Erik held the passenger side door open for Anna. If this horse rescue went as planned, she might soften toward him. He could only hope.

Once Anna was in the truck's cab, Lieutenant Bishof piled in next to her, forcing her to slide closer to Erik. Her face contorted with discomfort as if touching him would kill her. But when she scooted closer to Bishof, it was worse. Bishof ogled her, and a greedy lust shined like onyx from his eyes. It made Erik recoil with anger. He remembered what Bishof and the

SS boys said about Polish women from their train ride. With certainty, he could attest this Polish woman was neither easy nor willing to engage in any unbecoming conduct with Nazis. Quickly, Erik slipped his arm along her back and pulled her closer to his side. The gesture made a wry, almost evil, smile fracture Bishof's face. Anna was nothing like the women who ingratiated themselves with Bishof and his SS buddies in Biala. Erik immediately thought Bishof counted him as one of their crowd—taking advantage and using the conquered women as playthings. Irritation simmered in his core, and then self-hatred. The threat of the Gestapo's unreasonable brutality kept Erik silent. No one was immune. They searched for reasons to harass, arrest, and torture those who disagreed with the Reich. Tonight, though, Erik needed Bishof and his henchmen if they were going to collect Janow's horses. He tenuously walked the line of compromise.

The air was tense as Erik, Anna, and the trailer full of Gestapo agents drove to the race track. Major Fellgeible and the other six trailers lagged by five minutes, hoping Gronlochev would get comfortable with the money exchange before they sprang the trap. He should've heeded the Wehrmacht's offer.

Erik forced himself to focus on the road because each time he glanced at Bishof, he caught him scrutinizing Anna. He could feel her fear: it radiated through her clothes from her skin to his like an electric current, and she moved closer. Erik knew it would only take one wrong move, and she'd be thrust into one of the concentration camps. He wasn't sure Major Fellgeible would stand up for her. Protecting her landed squarely on his shoulders—a duty Erik relished rather than dreaded.

They pulled through the gate to the barns. Erik stopped.

"Gunther, it's time for you to join your men. Any closer and one of Gronlochev's men might see you," Erik said.

Bishof grinned. "I'll see you later, Fräulein." He glowered at her and placed his hand on her thigh. Every muscle in her body stiffened, and Erik could see her jaw tighten as if fighting back a reprimand. He shifted the truck into neutral and applied the parking brake. He rounded the front of the truck just as Bishof stepped out.

"We need to talk," Erik growled. When he was sure Anna couldn't hear them, he continued, "Gunther, Miss Sabrosky is with the sisters. Don't treat her like you treat your Biala women. She's not like them."

Bishof laughed. "You're in love with her." Erik's stare remained threatening. But it was true. He was in love with her, but acknowledged letting Bishof know might spur a competition which could turn out badly for Anna.

"Get in the trailer. Remember, when I hand the briefcase to Gronlochev..."

"We arrest him," Bishof said with a wicked glee.

Suddenly revolted, Erik imagined Bishof planned to torture the man. He needed to put a stop to it. "No one has to get hurt. I will remind him of the Wehrmacht's offer of five hundred zlotys per horse—no questions asked. We want our horses, nothing more. He'll be disappointed, but I'm guessing he'll take the money."

After Bishof climbed into the trailer, Erik returned to the truck's driver's side and stepped up on the running board. Annaleah had scooted to the passenger's side of the cab, hugging tightly to the door. If she could've escaped, she would've. Erik ducked in through the open driver's side door, slid into the seat, and pulled the door closed behind him.

"Anna, we are supposed to be newly married. Can you pretend for a little longer? At least until we get the horses?" He asked softly, tapping the empty bench seat next to him. He understood how hard it was for her to collaborate with the conquerors, even if it was to rescue the beloved horses.

Erik noticed the fleeting smile crossing her lips. She slipped closer, but not to his desired distance. He tipped his head and chuckled.

"Move closer. We look like we are fighting. I'm buying you a horse worth ten thousand zlotys," he patted the seat next to him and skimmed his upper teeth across the bottom lip of his smile.

Annaleah sighed. "You're laughing at me."

"No. But Anna, you know by now I won't hurt you," he said with sincerity. He held her stare until she repositioned herself. Erik breathed in the scent of roses radiating from her skin. As always, it was as intoxicating as strong drink. Anna made him feel things and imagine a life with her by his side. Somehow, he had to overcome the obstacle—the barrier between the conqueror and vanquished.

"It's almost ten. We should go," she said, a strong hint of excitement mixed with anxiety in her voice.

He grinned at her and started the engine. Slowly, he crept forward, tires crunching on the gravel drive, to the rendezvous with Gronlochev.

As they approached the barn row, whisps of fog formed and swirled in the cool October air.. Anna gripped Erik's arm. He liked her touch. But she caught herself, colored with embarrassment, and quickly jerked her hand away, tucking it between her knees.

"Scared?" he asked, slowing the truck by taking his foot off the gas pedal.

"Do you think he'll be here?"

"He'll be here. He wants the money." Erik smiled. The truck's headlights reflected off the increasing ground fog, and he squinted, trying to see ahead.

"Are you ready?" he asked, only moving forward when she nodded.

Gronlochev stepped out from the barn's overhang into the mist and shadows. Erik could barely make out the outlines of the fat man's body-guards, one on each side and slightly behind him in the gloom. Erik's stomach squeezed tight—he suspected the man intended to rob him. Erik touched the holster containing the Walther PPK sidearm he'd been issued as a cav-alry officer. But as a veterinarian, he hadn't had occasion to use it since his initial training. He hoped he wouldn't need it tonight.

For a moment, he feared the horses might not be here, but when he turned into the aisleway, the headlights reflected off the stall fronts, and Anna's favorite, Lotnik, poked his head through the top half of his stall door.

"Wait here," Erik said. But Anna had already opened the passenger side door. He grabbed the briefcase of money and scrambled to keep up. "Anna, wait," he called after her. He couldn't stop her. She ran to the stall and stood there happily stroking the colt's face.

"Women. Who can control them, ey? They do what they want." Gronlochev walked forward. "Do you have the money?"

"Of course," Erik responded, carefully observing the bodyguards. He lifted the briefcase with his left hand, ensuring his right was free if he needed his gun.

"Put the briefcase on the ground in front of you and step back," Gronlochev demanded breathlessly, an oily grin curling his lips. He retrieved a handkerchief from his pocket and mopped the beads of sweat forming on his brow. Once again, Erik wondered if the man was in congestive heart failure. He said nothing.

Erik heard the rumble and rattle of the other trucks and horse trailers approaching the barns.

"You betrayed me!" Gronlochev growled. "You cheat!"

The two bodyguards raced forward, one snatched the briefcase, and for only a second, Erik lost sight of the other. His heart sank when he heard the scuffle next to the barn.

"Dr. Erik, please help me!"

The second bodyguard seized Anna from behind, wrapping his thick arm around her waist. With his right hand, he pressed the barrel of a Luger 9mm pistol against her temple. The bodyguard lifted Anna from the ground and drug her back toward Gronlochev and the briefcase. Cold ran through Erik's veins like icy river rapids. He unholstered his pistol and took a shooter's stance in one smooth movement.

"Let her go. Do it now," he threatened.

Like phantoms in his peripheral vision, Erik noticed shadows closing in from all directions. Janow's soldiers and Bishof's Gestapo policemen surrounded Gronlochev. Suddenly, the colt, Lotnik, shoved his stall door open and bolted full speed into the barn aisle. Chaos reigned. The young stallion charged toward the bodyguard, who stumbled and released Anna as he tried to rebalance. Instantly, she dropped to a crouch.

Erik's sense of time slowed as he watched the colt shift his weight to his hindquarters, his muscles contracting like coiled springs. The young horse leaped over Anna, knocking the bodyguard backward to the ground and struck him with his front legs. The colt scrambled and fell on top of the man. Grunting and groaning, the bodyguard lost his grip on his pistol, and it flew from his hand. The gun skittered and spun on the concrete under the barn's overhang out of reach. Panicked, the colt stood and danced a few steps on the man's chest before dashing to the center aisle. Lotnik stopped and stood with his tail rolled over his back. He held his head high and arched his neck, snorting, blowing, and prancing in a defensive circle.

Several soldiers blocked the only escape route at the far end of the barns.

Anna crawled away from the bodyguard and stood. She wrestled a halter free from a hook near the colt's stall and approached the frightened animal, talking to him quietly.

Bishof and his men encircled Gronlochev and one goon, while soldiers wrenched the other man to his feet and bound him in handcuffs.

Erik lowered his pistol. Looking to his side, he watched as Major Fellgeible strolled into the scene in complete control. Calmly, he collected the briefcase from Gronlochev's hand.

"Mr. Gronlochev, I see you have found several of Janow Podlaski's horses," he began. "You know, of course, there is a reward of five hundred zlotys for each horse returned to the stud farm. No questions asked," The Major said, quoting the flyers nailed to the posts holding up the overhang. " I assume you intended to bring them to us?"

Gronlochev glared at Erik, his dark eyes brimming with hatred. "Indeed. We had every intention of bringing the horses back to their rightful home." He lied with a nervous grin.

Fellgeible walked to the truck cab, set the briefcase on the hood, and opened the snaps. "Five hundred each for seven horses would be three thousand five hundred zlotys, by my calculation. Do you agree, Mr. Gronlochev?" The Major counted out the bills. Gronlochev eyed the zlotys greedily.

"That is very generous of you, sir," Gronlochev groveled, his disappointment clear.

"They are all here and in good health?"

"The best of health, sir."

The Major handed the fat man the money.

The soldiers quickly moved in, haltered the horses, and loaded them in the trailers.

Erik went to Anna. She had easily captured and calmed Lotnik and led him to their assigned truck and trailer. Erik opened the loading doors for her, and she walked the colt in. He buried his nose in the rich hay she'd earlier placed into the feeder. She tied him and backed out. Erik stood beside her, and they watched the colt contentedly munch for a few seconds before closing the doors.

"Anna, are you all right?" he asked, securing the latch bars. He wanted to scold her for not staying in the truck as he'd asked. But more than anything, he wanted to hug her, to hold her close to him.

"I'm good now," she said, sagging against his shoulder. She breathed out a heavy sigh. "Let's go home."

"Yes," he said. He brushed strands of her golden hair away from her face. "Yes. Let's go."

Chapter Fourteen

ERIK GLANCED OVER AT ANNA, sleeping against the passenger side window as he arrived at the arched entrance to the stud farm. The slowed speed and the reduced engine noise caused her to stir from her dreams.

"Are we here already?" she asked, blinking away sleep.

"We're here. But it looks like Lieutenant Bishof beat us." Erik tipped his head toward Bishof's sleek black Mercedes parked inside the courtyard in front of the clock tower. Now that Bishof had met Anna, Erik understood the hungry lust in his eyes and speculated he'd show up as often as possible. The prospect unsettled Erik, and he ground his teeth together.

He could see Bishof waiting for them in his car, and to avoid him, Erik intentionally continued to the main entryway to the colt barn.

Anna jumped from the truck and rushed to unload Lotnik. Erik went to help, but she'd already backed the colt out of the trailer.

Lotnik stopped outside, breathing in the scent of home, and called out. From inside the barn, the answer came from his friends and pasture mates. As Anna walked him into the barn, he pranced down the aisleway to his old familiar stall.

Once in his stall, Anna turned the colt loose and moved to the open doorway. Erik stood beside her, watching the young stallion settle in. Lotnik circled the stall, pawed the ground, and dropped into the clean, deep, sweet-smelling straw. He rolled, and rubbed his face as if fluffing a pillow.

"He's happy to be home," Anna said, satisfied.

"He's probably tired. We should let him sleep. And get some rest ourselves." Erik wanted to slide his arm around her shoulders but stopped himself. She didn't feel the way he did. In his mind, he added *yet*. If he rushed or forced her, she would never care for him.

"Have you put the colt away?" Bishof asked as if the colt were a toy they could close in a box. Insinuating his body between Erik and Anna, he rested his arms along their shoulders like they were old college friends. Anna cringed away from his touch, but Bishof didn't notice or care. "Shall we have a drink to celebrate bringing the horses home?"

"No. Gunther. We need to get some rest. We have work to do first thing in the morning," Erik said. "Some other time."

"Fräulein Anna, may I drive you home?" Bishof offered an alternative.

"I'm driving her home." Erik glared at him. Bishof removed his arms and threw his hands up in a gesture of surrender, meaning anything but. Bishof lifted an eyebrow, and a know-it-all smile creased his face. He'd just picked up the gauntlet. The competition for Anna was on.

"Come, Anna, it's time. I should get you back to the Convent," Erik said, reminding Bishof once again she was with the sisters.

"Until we meet again, Fräulein," Bishof said, taking hold of her hand and lifting it to his lips.

Erik quickly stepped between them, pretending to stumble, slightly unbalancing Bishof before he could complete the kiss. "Oh, I'm sorry, Gunther. Anna, shall we go? I promised to get you home when the horses were unloaded."

Erik feared the sisters hadn't warned her about the secular world of men. And certainly not of the threat of conquering soldiers, who believed they were entitled to take whatever they wanted. Anna's innocence and naivety made Erik's protective instincts climb to the top of the scale.

He jogged to catch up to her, opened the truck's passenger door, and blocked the entrance until she was seated. He pressed the button lock and closed the door. Erik made certain Bishof couldn't get in. Once in the driver's seat, Erik drove to the equipment barn, parked and unhitched the trailer while Anna waited in the cab.

Deep in thought and in complete silence, he drove to the convent, expecting Bishof to be there waiting. But he wasn't. Anna had no understanding of the peril she was in. Danger she had no part in bringing down on herself. Erik looked over at her as they came to a stop.

"Anna, be careful. You have stirred Lieutenant Bishof's attention. He is a treacherous man," Erik said.

She acknowledged him with a nod and looked down at her hands.

"Get word to your friend. He shouldn't come here anymore."

"My friend?" Her eyes widened, and Erik could see the anxiety.

"Your lover, Anna. The young man who tosses pebbles against your window late at night. The one you rush to meet beside the creek."

Erik wanted her to contradict his assessment. He wanted to hear her say the man wasn't her lover. She gasped and covered her mouth with her hand. He knew he had to explain. "Sometimes, I can't sleep, and I walk. Several nights ago, I took a forest trail and ended up here. I saw him and watched. He tossed small pebbles at your window, and you came down to him. If Bishof catches you, he will assume you are resistance spies and arrest you both."

Her anxiety had turned to fear, making her tremble. She tried to hide it by hugging herself.

"I told no one, Anna." He tried to reassure her. She held his gaze as if trying to ascertain if his words were true or lies. She closed her eyes and wrung her hands. A tear sparkled on her cheek like a diamond in the moonlight. Erik wanted to wipe it away and hold her.

"Trust me, Anna. If our roles were reversed, I would be in the resistance. But I warn you now, because I don't want to lose my best assistant," he smiled, trying to lighten up this desperate situation. "Instead, I've committed treason." He covered her hand with his. "If the boy comes to you tonight, don't go out to him. Bishof plans to stay overnight at the farm. Arrive tomorrow as you usually do. I will think of a way to keep you as far away from him as possible."

"Why would you do that for me? For Jan?" Her eyes narrowed with skepticism.

"Jan, his name is Jan?" Jealousy nibbled at his insides. He wanted to say it. To get it out in the open. *I've fallen in love with you.* The thought almost breached his lips. But to say it would cause her to retreat and withdraw even more. He chose not to answer her.

"I'll walk you to the door now. I don't want Bishof to come searching for us."

She looked at him differently—more sympathetically. He climbed from the truck, rounded the hood and opened the passenger's side door for her. They walked side by side up the concrete steps to the convent's large carved wooden doors. Anna gently accepted his hand. Her tenderness surprised him. Under different circumstances, he would've taken her in his arms and kissed her. He wanted to now but kept his desire in check. He opened the door for her.

"Sleep well, Dr. Erik," she said, slipping her hand along his palm until only their fingertips touched. They lingered in the moment. Longing washed over his body in waves, but he couldn't give in. Briefly, he closed his eyes to gain control.

"Good night, Anna."

"You are a good man." She scrutinized his face, turned, and disappeared into the dark stone corridor. Erik watched her until the door closed. She hadn't turned back to give him hope. He needed to win her. What could he do to win her?

Chapter Fifteen

KARENA SAT FORWARD TO THE edge of the white wicker porch swing, her eyes wide with wonder. She looked over at Gerard.

"Our grandparents were in love. Isn't that wild?" she blurted out, laughing.

Gerard dropped the page he was reading into his lap. "Didn't you know?" He grinned at her, and she lost herself in his blue eyes.

"We weren't close," Karena said. She looked down at her hands and smoothed her thumb over each fingernail, one at a time. She'd never even tried to warm up to the woman. "She was married to my Grandpa George. I don't expect she would admit anything to me."

"I wonder...I wonder if she loved him?" Gerard said, his eyes filling with a faraway look. "I admired my Dr. Erik. He was my role model and inspired me to become a vet. He used to call me his little sponge. As a boy, I followed him on his daily rounds."

"Did he talk about his friendship with Granny A?"

"He often talked about going to America to connect with a long-lost friend but never achieved his goal. I thought it was just a dream. The day before he passed away, I guessed this friend might've been more than just a friend. Out of the blue, he told me a woman named Annaleah Baker would take me in if I gave her some letters. He had saved money for me to go to college in the United States. He insisted I must come here. But he also told me never to mention it to anyone, especially my Grandmother. He said it would hurt her, and she was a good woman. She didn't deserve to be hurt." Gerard reached for a bottle of beer and refilled his glass. "Dr. Erik's stories and myths were larger than life. To him, America was a magical land where all dreams come true. I never believed it. I figure you have to work hard and be a good citizen, no matter where you are or where you go," Gerard said. "He made me promise I would come to America. So here I am."

"Are you sorry?" Karena tipped her head toward him.

"Not at all. It's been good working with Dr. Wilson. I've learned so much," he said. His voice rang with gratitude. "Your Grandmother arranged the internship for me. I have a job the day I graduate. Which means I can stay."

"I'm learning so much. I'm sorry I didn't get more time with Granny A. I didn't know how generous and sweet she was," Karena sighed.

"Reading this is like getting more time, isn't it?" He smiled, sipped his beer, and reached for the next page.

Karena laughed and handed him the stack of pages she'd finished, replaced those he'd read in the binder, and took out more for herself.

October 30, 1939:

Annaleah raced through the field to the fence between the convent's property and the stud farm's. The sun had yet to crest the horizon, and the stars still glittered in the dark sky. She was late. Last night, Jan had visited just as the clock announced midnight. The sadness of their argument still covered her emotions like a black fog.

She'd wanted to warn him Lieutenant Bishof set up nightly patrols around the convent and stud farm. Dr. Erik told her Bishof suspected resistance spies exchanged secret information under cover of night. Other than how their families survived, what confidences could nuns and farmhands have? She thought of herself working alongside Dr. Erik, performing their daily veterinary duties. Would the Nazi empire fail if she told someone which of the mares at Janow were pregnant? The Gestapo was a paranoid organization. Paranoia and power created unbelievable evil.

Jan, instead, charged her with being a traitor to her country. He even accused her of being in love with Dr. Erik. It brought tears to her eyes. She'd had no choice but to go along with the Germans when they went to collect Lotnik. Did Jan want her in one of the concentration camps?

She was afraid of Dr. Erik—afraid of the way he looked at her. Afraid of the way he made her feel. Reality always lingered at the edge of her thoughts; Dr. Erik was part of the triumphant army. His kindness toward her could be withdrawn at any moment on a whim.

With indignation, she fought the waterworks, kicking at a fallen branch with her boot. It shattered under her ferocity, surprising her.

After they parted and Jan melted into the woods with his resistance companions, she returned to the dormitory but couldn't sleep. She'd pay for that all day. Annaleah climbed the last fence between her and the barns. The lights inside flickered on just as she jumped to the ground. She dashed for the gate to the courtyard.

Her thoughts still spun wildly. Lately, Dr. Erik slowly gained more and more of her respect. How could she hate the man who started to help the farm's Polish neighbors with their animals and livestock? Dr. Erik helped the Stanislovs with two of their egg-bound chickens, rescued the Tenovsky's dog after an unhappy encounter with a porcupine, and neutered ten of Mrs. Stuberg's feral cats. Was this the behavior of a hardened conquerer?

Annaleah slipped beside her best friend, Clara, in the morning line-up, hoping no one noticed her tardiness. They didn't dare say a word to each other. With notorious efficiency, the Germans took roll call each morning. Major Fellgeible walked the line, tapping his riding crop against his black jackboots, inspecting each laborer as if they were his troops. Dr. Erik stood in a line facing the Polish workers. His gaze landed on Annaleah, and he paused. A smile breezed across his lips for only a moment. She couldn't read it. Was he acknowledging she was late? Her stomach tightened, and she swallowed.

Major Fellgeible saluted. His officers returned the gesture. He barked the command, "Dismissed!" And the farmhands hustled to begin the day's work.

Annaleah noticed Elizabeth Wazdoda, Nelek's nine-year-old sister, speaking in anxious tones with Dr. Erik, though she couldn't decipher the words. When finished, Elizabeth ran out of the courtyard toward home.

"Anna," Erik called out. Annaleah glanced at Clara as if looking at her for support. Clara seemed to need to talk, but she shook her head, warning her off, and went to work. Dr. Erik made his way across the courtyard. "Anna, it looks like our neighbors to the east…"

"The Wazdodas?" she interjected. Nelek's family. Visions of her school friend's arrest began to swim in her mind. She felt her knees weaken and wanted to sink to the ground and cry, but she couldn't let Erik see her.

Erik grinned at her. "Yes. The Wazdodas need our help this morning. They have a young heifer who's having trouble delivering her calf. We may need to pull it. I need you to gather supplies from the apothecary." He wrinkled his brow as if perplexed.

A sigh of relief trembled on her lips. "Yes, sir," she said, unable to meet his eyes.

"The pulling chains are in the farthest drawer under the disinfectants. I'll need a bucket, soap, iodine, long black rubber gloves, a vial of penicillin, syringes and needles. . . Anna? Is something wrong?"

"No, sir," she pressed her arms tight against her sides as if trying to protect herself.

"I'll get the truck and meet you by the entrance gate." He wheeled around and sprinted toward the equipment barn.

Annaleah ran to the apothecary and gathered supplies. She counted each item from his list in her mind—twice. On her way out the door, she grabbed a stack of clean towels and a freshly washed pair of veterinary coveralls and dropped them on top of the bucket. She hurried to the arched entryway and arrived just as Dr. Erik stopped the truck to collect her. He reached across the seat and opened the door. Annaleah set the bucket on the seat between them and climbed in. Erik didn't check to see if she'd assembled all he needed. She realized he trusted her. Luckily, he didn't mention her lateness.

Outside of the barn, Annaleah dumped the soapy water from the bucket and refilled it with their supplies. Mrs. Wazdoda hugged Dr. Erik. Annaleah wondered if Nelek would still hate him after hearing what the German had done for his family. If the calves survived, they would have three heifers to provide them with milk, cream, butter, and cheese—priceless commodities at this time of war.

In silence, she and Dr. Erik returned to the stud farm just as the light gray sky began to drop its snow.

"I'm going to bathe and change. I am supposed to have lunch with Major Fellgeible." Erik shook his head and laughed. "What a morning."

"Does he approve of you helping the farmers?" Annaleah asked.

"You are citizens of the Reich now. We must learn to live together," Erik said. "I feel I should take care of the animals, in any case. What do animals know about who should be the ruling government? Besides, it's good practice." Erik expressed a sentiment she held. When she looked at him, she wasn't surprised.

"I'll clean the equipment. Go get ready for your luncheon." Annaleah practically skipped down the barn aisle to the apothecary. Dr. Erik had saved the day. Two brand new calves lived. She rinsed the stainless-steel bucket, readied the shot needles and glass syringes for the autoclave, and the soiled laundry for washing.

Dr. Erik had impressed her. She contemplated him. Physically, he was a beautiful man, tall and fair, though the Nazi Aryan ideal made her cringe these days. Sometimes, she lost herself in his gentle blue eyes and winsome smile. She knew at first she'd judged him harshly. Quickly, she cleared the thought from her mind. It had been silly to judge him before knowing him.

Annaleah heard Dr. Erik enter the apothecary. She recognized his brisk, purposeful footsteps on the wooden floor and turned to face him. He struggled to button the starched cuffs of his white shirt. He draped his Captain's Uniform coat across the counter.

"Can you help me? These buttons are so small," he smiled with frustration. Somehow, he'd missed a button in the middle of his shirt and seemed perplexed by the fact the buttons didn't match the buttonholes.

She laughed softly, "Here, let me."

Stepping close in front of him, Annaleah began to undo his shirt to start over. He grabbed her hand, pressing it against his chest to stop her. But to her surprise, he held it there. She could feel his heart pounding.

Gazing into her eyes, Erik took a deep breath. "You are so beautiful, Anna," he murmured. She realized her mistake. Dr. Erik was not one of the boys she'd helped dress at the orphanage. He was a grown man with all the urges and feelings the sisters had warned her about.

Annaleah wanted to pull away and run but couldn't seem to move. Erik touched her cheek tenderly and barely, as light and soft as a feather, brushed his thumb along the curve of her lips. It sent shock waves through her whole body, and she sighed. What he felt, she felt, too. He closed his eyes as if trying to contain the need engulfing him.

Erik whispered, "Anna."

He bent forward and took her in his arms. Without realizing it, she yielded. She wanted to feel his lips against hers, even if it was wrong. Even though she'd promised Jan. Even if he was the enemy. In her imagination, she could taste Erik's mouth against hers and feel his warm breath against her skin. So close, almost touching, lingering there, Anna was hungry and longing for the moment desire transformed into a kiss.

"Dr. Erik! Dr. Erik!" Clara's voice filled the far end of the apothecary. The moment was shattered. Erik stepped back.

Color flushed hot into Anna's cheeks. She turned and fussed with some medicine bottles on the counter. Had Clara seen it? Would she tell and expose Annaleah as one of the hated traitors? How would Annaleah go forward now? She had almost betrayed Jan and fully recognized she had betrayed him in her heart. Dr. Erik had almost kissed her, and she'd wanted him to.

"What is it, Clara?" Erik asked, hastily putting on his jacket.

"My sister-in-law has been in labor since last night. Can you help her? Please help her. I think she's dying." Clara's eyes filled, her desperation obvious.

"But, but I'm an animal doctor. You should get a real doctor, a people doctor," he said, shaking his head.

"The Gestapo arrested our village's doctor last week," she answered, her cheeks awash with tears. "He is Jewish."

Annaleah could see the empathy and pity in Dr. Erik's eyes. She knew he had nothing to do with the Nazis' treatment of the villagers and the Jews.

"You are a real doctor. It can't be so different, can it?" Anna interjected, hopeful. She touched his forearm, emphasizing her plea.

Erik examined her and conceded. "No. It's not too different. Just smaller. I'll see what I can do."

Chapter Sixteen

ERIK WAS STRESSED. HE DIDN'T have the drugs for pain relief he needed. He had the nerve-blocking agents Novocaine and Procaine but wasn't sure he could safely make a spinal block or epidural for a human if he needed one. And what if the woman couldn't deliver, and he needed to perform a Cesarian Section?

"Clara, where is the doctor's office from here?" Erik asked. Since the Gestapo had arrested the doctor last week, he envisioned trashed rooms: broken medical vials, overturned cabinets in splinters, surgical implements exposed to the air, and patient records strewn everywhere. The Gestapo, in their stupidity, likely destroyed the place during their hate-filled, racist rage rather than preserving precious resources. Erik hated what the SS soldiers had become. He felt helpless to do anything about it and tried to force it out of his mind.

"In Biala. On the main street," Clara said, her voice breaking with anxiety.

"Biala is no more than five miles away," Annaleah explained. "I can drive. What do you need?"

"I need...." he stopped. It would be better if he went. He knew what to look for. "You and Clara go make—what's your sister-in-law's name?"

"Caterina," Clara answered.

"Anyway, make her as comfortable as you can. I'll see if I can redeem any supplies from the doctor's office. Anna, collect vials of Novocaine, Procaine, and Adrenaline, syringes, and the smallest needles you can find. Sterile scissors, number ten surgical blades, sterile gauze, and silk for stitches." He nervously rubbed his hand over his short blond hair, trying to stimulate thought. He continued, "Clean towels, gloves, clean overalls, antiseptics, and penicillin. I'll meet you there as soon as I can," he barked as he turned to head for the door. "Oh, where's there?"

"It's the farm west of the convent. The drive is just a hundred yards past ours," Annaleah answered. Erik nodded and briskly walked away.

Suspecting a Cesarian Section might be the only way to save mother and child, Erik wanted to see if the police had left a medical encyclopedia behind. They wouldn't take it and would consider it trash. He didn't tell Anna and Clara he had no idea how to deliver a human baby, and he'd only performed C-sections on dogs and cats. He'd read about it at university— there was a cross-over between human and veterinary medicine. But he'd never considered delivering a baby human being in real life. His specialty was large animals, and C-sections weren't done for them.

And what would he do if he failed and mother or baby or both died under his inexperienced hand? Because of Anna, he'd foolishly and impulsively committed to try. He realized she could ask for anything, and he would do it. He pushed the thought out of his mind.

It seemed everything he did these days was to either protect or impress Annaleah. When she placed her hand on his arm, reason took flight. He had no choice but to help.

He ducked into the Major's office and quickly explained why he'd be absent from their luncheon. To his surprise, Major Fellgeible looked up from the papers on his desk and gave his blessing.

On his drive to Biala, Erik's thoughts kept cycling through almost kissing Annaleah. His mind played out the what-ifs like a cinema. If Clara hadn't come into the apothecary, if his lips had touched Anna's... the thought left him breathless. He was no idiot. He knew what would happen to her. She would be hated by her countrymen, disrespected by the Germans, and ostracized. He suspected even the sisters would turn her away. He could never do it again. No matter how much his body fought him. Putting her in danger was never his intention. Loving her, eventually making her his wife, if she'd have him, was.

He arrived at his destination, and thoughts of Anna had to wait.

The doctor's office in Biala was worse off than he'd imagined. Indignities were painted on the exterior's cream-colored bricks. *Christ Killers. Jews are not wanted here.* A Star of David was partially obscured by a red Swastika painted to look like it dripped blood. It made Erik's stomach turn. Before entering through the shattered door, he walked a slow circle, observing the people on the street. He wore a German Captain's uniform, so most people averted their eyes. He had license to do anything he wanted.

He walked inside. Shards of broken glass and papers covered the floor. The sharp smell of medicinal alcohol and iodine still wafted in the air. As he walked from one examination room to the next, he found broken drawers as if they had been pulled from their cabinets and forcefully thrown to the ground. Sterile tools had been tossed, overturned, and rendered inoperative. Exactly as he expected, the Gestapo and SS goons had destroyed rare and much-needed medical equipment. Broken vials of precious medicines were scattered everywhere. They'd be sorry they'd done this as the war wore on and medical shipments became harder to come by. He shook his head in dismay.

He searched through the rubble and found an intact bottle of ether, one of chloroform, Gamgee gauze, and a Schimmel Busch mask. In the middle of the room, he located one undamaged drawer, set it upright, and stacked the usable items in it. If he needed to do a surgical C-section, he could at least put Clara's sister-in-law to sleep.

Impatiently, he investigated the offices, trying to locate the doctor's library. He hurried down a darkened hallway and shoved open the door to the last room on the right. The bookshelves had been overturned. Searching through the books, he quickly found important volumes on disease and medical procedures strewn like trash all over the floor. Erik located the one he needed most. It was face down on the floor of the doctor's office, its pages rumpled and torn. Quickly, he searched the index and found the pages for delivering a baby. He ripped a page out of a notebook he found next to it and marked the place. Erik knew the basics, but his luck had turned to the good side. This book included a step-by-step guide covering difficult deliveries with black-and-white pictures.

Erik grabbed it, briskly jogged to the room where he'd left the drawer full of salvaged items, and added the book to his stash.

He raced out of the office, avoiding the broken glass, and climbed into the car he'd borrowed from the Stud Farm. As he drove past the convent, he hoped he'd arrive to a successfully delivered baby, and Clara was simply panicked. Erik had never considered himself the praying type, but today, as he raced down the dusty road, he imagined himself down on his knees.

Chapter Seventeen

ERIK CLIMBED THE STEPS TO the white plaster-covered cottage belonging to Clara's brother and his pregnant wife. The soft moaning he heard coming from inside dashed his hopes that the baby had arrived in his absence.

Carrying the drawer full of equipment, he shouldered open the door without knocking. He followed the sound of pain, wriggled out of his Captain's Coat, and tossed it across a stuffed chair in the parlor as he passed by. Once he'd entered the bedroom, he set the drawer on the dresser, unbuttoned his cuffs, and rolled up his sleeves.

There were four women in the room. Clara and Anna, he knew. One of the women he assumed was Caterina's mother, her hair, though pulled back into a head scarf, was the same red color. The gray-haired woman he guessed to be the grandmother. She scrutinized him with a look as sharp as a knife.

Anna quickly brought him clean veterinary overalls. Erik nodded his thanks and stepped into them, pulling them up over his clothes.

"Why do you believe this German cares if your daughter lives or dies?" the grandmother growled under her breath to her daughter and Clara. Hatred saturated her words and flashed like lightning across her face. Erik scowled at her briefly but ignored her otherwise. Erik knew he first had to assess the patient's condition.

"Grandmother!" Clara cried, silencing the old woman. "He's come to help."

Erik understood the grandmother's feelings. Her country had been stripped away from her. Why should she trust a German soldier? He had met this skeptical reception before. Even though he'd come to assist. Each time he worked with the stud farm's Polish neighbors, he had to prove himself. Right now, there wasn't time for adversarial sentiments.

He retrieved his stethoscope from around his neck. "Has her water broken?" Directing his question to Annaleah, he carefully pulled back the covers, not waiting for an answer.

"Yes, sir," Annaleah answered.

"Caterina? I'm Erik Kemperman. I'm here to help you," he said softly. She nodded and then grimaced in pain as a contraction racked her body. Erik had seen contractions before, but never in a human. It shook him to his core. To counter his trepidation, he went to work, listening to the woman's heart and lungs when the spasm eased. Her heartbeat was rapid but still in a steady sinus rhythm. She panted, which he knew to be a method of easing the pain. He placed the stethoscope on her pregnant belly. He could hear the racing heart of the infant inside. At least the baby was still alive.

Caterina was no older than Annaleah and Clara's eighteen years. Her reddish-brown hair was pressed to her forehead in sweat-dampened strings. Her green eyes were dull and sunken with pain. Labor had gone on far too long.

"Caterina. I must try to ascertain the position of the baby. I will need to touch your abdomen. It may cause the baby to move and trigger another contraction. I'm sorry, but I must do it. Do you understand?"

A weak dip of her head was her reply.

Annaleah watched with great interest.

Erik gently touched Catarina, closing his eyes and letting his fingers draw a picture in his mind. He turned and grabbed the book, tossed it on the bed within reach, and flipped to the page he'd earlier marked for reference.

He read from the typed pages. *If the baby is in the best position for delivery, the mother's abdomen will feel firm and smooth. This means the baby is head down, and the spine is pressed against the mother's womb in Occiput Anterior position.* There was a drawing in black and white, but it wasn't the picture his fingers had conjured. He swallowed hard.

"What Doctor has to read a book to deliver a baby?" The old woman complained, louder this time. Erik didn't look at her.

Though she was right, he ignored her bitterness. *If the mother's abdomen is soft and slightly sunken, the baby could be in the Occiput Posterior position.* Erik sucked in a breath, hoping more oxygen would fortify his courage. The baby was Occiput Posterior, lovingly called 'Sunny-side up.' This explained Caterina's lengthy and painful labor. Erik's fears of having to perform C-section surgery had just become very real. Her water had broken, and the time for delivery was here. Hesitation only meant things could get worse.

Was there a way to turn the baby? Erik read on. If the baby's head was past the pelvic rim, there was nothing he could do but wait. Babies often turned themselves as they maneuvered through the birth canal. He looked at his hands. They were big and strong for wrestling a calf or a foal into position, but too large to handle a delicate baby. He glanced at Annaleah. Could he guide her through turning the baby? She handed him the clean pair of gloves. She trusted him. It was written all over her face. An encouraging smile beamed from her eyes, and she spread a receiving blanket across her arms, expectant.

Erik wiped his left hand across his jaw. He slipped his hands into the gloves.

Chapter Eighteen

ERIK PREPARED AND WAS READY to give Caterina his hastily concocted Epidural injection. Her pain had become so intense Erik feared her heart would give out. He resigned himself to the fact that he would have to do surgery. He turned to administer the shot when he noticed the baby had crowned. Erik dropped the shot to the bed and prepared. The baby came headfirst and fell into Erik's hands once the shoulders were delivered. Breathing out in relief, Erik laid the infant on the clean blanket Anna had spread out at the end of the bed. She pressed a clamp into his palm before he'd even asked for it. With the sterile scissors Anna handed him, Erik cut the umbilical cord.

Anna reached for the child, and Erik gratefully lifted the baby and placed him into the clean blanket she held for him. The other women followed her and began to coo and fuss over the infant, who began to cry as Anna carried him to the changing table they had earlier prepared to wash away all the remnants of birth.

Erik pressed tenderly on Caterina's abdomen, encouraging the delivery of the afterbirth. As he did with the animals, he laid the placenta out on a blanket, inspecting it for tears and missing pieces that could cause an infection if left in the uterus. It was completely intact.

Thank you, God. He whispered in his thoughts. Erik had just assisted in the delivery of his first human baby. Caterina had done all the work. He laughed nervously to himself.

"We should change the bedding and get the mother comfortable," Erik said, returning to his task after catching another glare from the grandmother. There would be time later to review what he'd done right or wrong.

"You're lucky, young man. Very lucky," The old woman muttered, grabbing fresh linens from a small night table beside the bed.

"I know, ma'am. Believe me, I know," Erik answered her with a humble smile. He recognized he would need to stay for another hour or two if anything went wrong. With the book's help, he could figure out what to do.

Clara helped her grandmother strip away the soiled sheets and put on new ones, ensuring they didn't cause Caterina any more distress. He'd seen nurses at the university hospital do it this way. The new mother needed to be treated with care. She smiled at him weakly, and it was reward enough.

He stepped out of the way, retreating to a corner. Unless he was needed, the women in attendance would care for Caterina from here. He steadied himself as withdrawal from the adrenaline dump left him shaken. The stress hormone had helped him get through the birth, making his mind sharp, his hands steady, and bolstering his courage. He rubbed his temples with trembling hands and was glad the women were busy. He didn't want them to know he'd been terrified. He had just helped deliver his first human baby. And the mother and child were doing fine. He pressed his back against the wall for support.

Annaleah carefully set the freshly washed baby in the arms of his exhausted mother. When Caterina saw the baby's face, all the hours of labor were replaced by overwhelming love. Erik noted this was no different than the reaction he'd seen in animals. A mother's love, whether human or animal, was a miracle.

Annaleah joined him in the corner and slipped a comforting hand on his arm. It was unexpected but welcome. Besides delivering the child, impressing Anna had been one of his goals.

"You're a good man, Dr. Erik," she said softly, removing her hand and dropping it to her side. At least, it seemed he'd accomplished his goal.

Now, another unsavory task weighed on his mind. Earlier, as he drove to the doctor's clinic in Biala, Erik promised himself he would never try to kiss Annaleah again. He understood the consequences and the danger he would put her in.

Snow began to fall in big, lacy flakes as Erik and Annaleah climbed into the car.

"I'll drive you home. You don't need to feed this evening. The other girls can take care of it," Erik said. By the time he pulled the car into the gravel circle in front of the Convent, snow dusted the ground white, like powdered sugar on an apple strudel. "I think we've both had enough work for the day." Though he smiled at her, he knew he avoided saying what must be said.

Once he stopped the car, he walked around to open the door for her and reached for the handle as she opened the door for herself. He walked with her to the portico overhanging the large wooden double doors. Ice crystals glittered on the stone steps in the light from the lanterns on either side, giving the entry a heavenly quality.

"Thank you for helping Caterina today," Annaleah said, brushing the snow from her shoulders and shaking it from her hair. The adoring smile he'd seen earlier rose like a sunrise across her beautiful face. As ever, it left him speechless.

Erik's mind wasn't on the delivery, and he dismissed it. "Yes, of course." He paused, took in a deep breath, and licked his lips. "Anna, I must talk to you," he said, waiting for her to acknowledge him. He cleared his throat. When she didn't focus on him but dropped her gaze down to the stone steps, he picked up both of her hands. "Please look at me, Anna."

She timidly glanced at him, her cheeks flushed with color. She trembled as if she couldn't meet his eyes. It was his fault—he had put an uncomfortable wedge between them.

"You're shivering. I'll let you go in, and we can talk tomorrow," he said.

"It's not from the cold. Please tell me. Please say what you must say."

He straightened, knowing he had to set things right. "I need to apologize for what happened in the apothecary today. I'm sorry about it. I don't know what came over me to behave so badly." He dropped his shoulders, ashamed. He kept her hands in his. "I promise you, it will never happen again. I promise," he whispered.

Finally, she explored his face and nodded. He couldn't read her then, and he couldn't read her now. Her expression confused him. *Was she sorry?*

Had she wanted him to kiss her? Her contempt, he understood. That she might care for him bewildered him but filled him with hope.

She rotated her hands to get free, but he didn't let go.

"Forgive me?"

Annaleah met his gaze. With tenderness, she said, "There's nothing to forgive. Nothing happened." She smiled softly. "Rest, and I'll see you in the morning. Goodnight, Dr. Erik." He released his grip, yet she left her hands in his for longer than expected. It took every ounce of restraint he could rally to keep from taking her in his arms and kissing her.

"Good night, Anna." The fear he usually saw in her eyes returned. After opening the convent's massive carved doors, she disappeared down the stone hallway. Slowly, Erik walked to the car and climbed inside. Contemplating her, he shook his head, rolled his eyes, and sighed. He realized he wanted her now more than ever. *I'm never going to be able to keep that promise.*

Annaleah ran past the chapel where the sisters were holding Vespers. It wasn't the first time she'd missed evening prayers. She glimpsed Mother Superior standing by the partially open door, waiting for her. Her soothing expression reminded Annaleah she'd, once again, disappointed her. There would be a gentle interrogation and reprimand. She couldn't sort out her feelings or describe them to anyone else. Once inside her room, she leaned against the door, softly closing it.

Annaleah wanted to hurry to the barn, to Lotnik's stall, and to wrap her arms around the colt's neck. She could tell him anything, and he wouldn't judge her. He would reciprocate her attention with affection, though he didn't understand her words; his comforting nuzzles always soothed her confusion.

She sank to the patchwork quilt covering her small bed. Running her fingers over the pattern, she escaped to the memory of the sisters teaching her how to sew, but the moment didn't last.

Jan accused her of something she didn't do, and Dr. Erik stirred up the passion she had always dreamed of feeling. She replayed his *almost* kiss in her mind. She traced an index finger along her lips. It left her wondering what it would be like and wanting more—something Jan's kisses had yet to accomplish.

She heard the soft knock and complaint from the hinges as her door opened.

"Annaleah? Annaleah, dear, what's bothering you? You know you can tell me anything," Mother Superior said, standing in the doorway. She seemed to float into the room, the skirts of her habit flowing around her as if she didn't touch the floor. Annaleah had always considered her an ethereal being, not really of this earth.

She couldn't hold back the tears. Mother sat beside her on the bed. "What is it, dear? The war? God will see us through this horrible time."

Annaleah wanted to tell her, but Dr. Erik had made his promise, so it was pointless. She knew how Mother Superior felt about soldiers. She had warned her, and Annaleah wasn't ready for her lecture. Besides, she had expected Erik's reaction. And she hadn't expected her own. "Yes. It's the war. The war has brought all this upon us."

Dr. Erik wouldn't be here if it weren't for the war. She wouldn't be confused. Her path would be clear. She would marry Jan, have children, work the family farm, and continue to help with Janow's horses. But how could she marry Jan now when her uninvited thoughts drifted constantly to Dr. Erik?

Mother Superior wrapped her arms around her. "God has a plan for you and your life, child. Trust Him." She encouraged Annaleah to her knees and knelt beside her. Taking her hand, Mother Superior whispered a prayer.

Chapter Nineteen

GERARD HAD CAUGHT UP READING and shared the pages Karena held for them with his arm resting along the back of the porch swing. Karena enjoyed the feeling of his strong arm behind her.

"Here you two are. We've been looking for you," Karena's mother's voice sliced through the silence. Gerard stood as if caught doing something wrong, embarrassment flooding his cheeks. "What are you two up to?" Mom asked, intrigued, looking from Karena's face to Gerard's and back again.

"Mother. You scared me," Karena said, slapping the binder shut and shoving it into Gerard's hands. She didn't want to explain Granny A's manuscript yet. "We were looking over some of Gerard's veterinary notes."

Gerard's mouth dropped open as if surprised by her lie. Grateful he didn't betray her, Karena touched his arm. It didn't change his disapproval.

"It's nice to see you're making new friends and learning something." Mom delivered Karena a skeptical frown. "Gerard, would you like to stay for dinner? Dr. Wilson is ready to go, but Karena can drive you home after if you want to stay."

"Thank you, Mrs. Bradshaw. It's very nice of you." He looked at Dr. Wilson for approval.

"Fine with me," Dr. Wilson grinned.

Gerard glanced at Karena, hugging the binder to his chest. "Do you want me to stay?"

"Yes. Of course," Karena widened her eyes, hoping they signaled her desire to keep reading the book with him after dinner. "You can show me more about horses."

Gerard tipped his head toward her and frowned. *So, he was displeased with her cover-up. She'd tell him why the subterfuge later.* Karena's Mom was watching their every move. Karena suspected Mom hoped she'd given up on Sam and started fresh with the handsome Russian. Karena thought about doing just that. Sam hadn't called her. When Mom wasn't looking, Karena took the binder, set it on the porch swing's seat, and casually covered it with the knitted throw blanket.

She linked her arm with Gerard's and walked with him into the house. He leaned toward Karena. "Why aren't we telling your mother about the manuscript?" he asked, whispering.

"She'll take it away from us. You want to keep reading, don't you?" Karena replied, studying the room to ensure no one eavesdropped on their conversation.

"What are you two whispering about?" Mom asked. A sly smile radiated from her eyes as if she wanted to be part of the game.

"We were trying to decide if we wanted to go to the Silverwood Theme Park after dinner," Karena replied, earning another surprised scowl from Gerard. But he played along, becoming just as guilty of the deception as she was. Karena felt a twinge of shame. It was easy to bully a guy who hadn't had time to make friends and who only wanted to hang out with a girl close to his age. Besides, Karena knew how pretty she was. She ruthlessly made him her unwilling partner in crime. But keeping the manuscript secret wasn't all bad. Karena reminded herself most of the relatives despised Granny A. Most were here for their share of her money. They would probably want to burn the manuscript or throw it away.

"Sounds fun. You should go," Mom said. "Uncle Ray and I can sort through the items for auction . . ."

"Not the Attic. Gerard wants to help me with those things," Karena blurted out. Her mind dashed to the trunk and its pictures and memorabilia about the war. "We can do it tonight and go to Silverwood tomorrow," she announced, distorting her smile. Thoroughly disgusted with herself, Karena could see Gerard's mind racing a million miles an hour. For the third time, she'd lied. He probably thought she was a terrible person.

Mom scowled at her. Karena knew Mom realized she was up to something. "Whatever you decide, the auctioneers won't be here until Friday to evaluate." Mom turned and addressed Gerard, "We've set up dinner as a buffet. Fill your plate and sit wherever you like. Karena, show Gerard to the dining room, okay?" She patted him on the shoulder, dropped her chin in warning at Karena, and walked away.

"I think your mom is suspicious of you," Gerard said so only she could hear.

"I hope you don't think I'm a big fat liar. The Bakers never liked Granny Annaleah. Grandpa George adored her, so they couldn't say anything while he was alive. But I remember them whispering about her with contempt. I'm pretty sure they thought she was a Nazi ."

"My Grandpapa was persecuted, too. He was German, so everyone assumed he was a Nazi. But he told me he never believed in it. It was a brutal dictatorship. He was conscripted into the Heer, under threat of imprisonment, and only survived the war because he was sent to Janow to become their veterinarian. Otherwise, he said he wouldn't be alive, and I wouldn't be either," Gerard said.

They walked into the dining room and were overwhelmed by the delicious smell of fried chicken. Karena hadn't thought about food for hours, but now her tummy rumbled with hunger. The dining table was loaded with platters of her mom's special fried chicken, bowls of steaming vegetables, and colorful salads, reminding her of a restaurant buffet. Her mother and cousins had worked on it all day. Karena felt guilty for not helping, but in her mind, it confirmed her mother's desire for her to dump Sam. She'd let her spend the afternoon on the porch with Gerard without interruptions.

When the relatives started discussing whether or not to sell Granny A's farm, and the talk between Uncle Ray and Aunt Helen got heated, Karena motioned to Gerard to take his plate and follow her. They walked through the dining room as if going back for seconds. After waiting for a moment to ensure no one watched them, Karena led Gerard through the farmhouse kitchen to the back stairs and the attic.

Karena unlocked the door. Gerard stood quietly in the center of the room, seeming to be amazed at the ribbons, trophies, and silk rose garlands Karena hadn't yet packed. He turned in a slow circle.

"Are these from racing?" he asked.

"No. Granny A had show horses and breeding stock. As I understand it, she was a very accomplished equestrian in her younger years." Karena went to the two chairs in front of the window overlooking the pastures. After glancing at the full boxes stacked in the room's corners, Gerard joined her, taking the chair on the other side of the small table. They started to eat the fare from the buffet.

"I'll show you the scrapbooks in the trunks," Karena said before taking a bite of chicken. Gerard nodded. Like many others before him, she could tell he was hungry and found out what a good cook her mom was.

"This is great chicken. Do you make it this way, too?" he asked.

"I've never made it on my own, but Mom has promised to give me all her recipes when I go away to college."

"Have you chosen a school?"

"I am hoping to get into UCLA. But I've got to keep my grades up."

"You should come to Pullman and join me." He grinned.

"So, I can cook for you? Ha! Nice try, though." She laughed. "So, it is true then the way to a man's heart is through his stomach."

"Knowing how to cook doesn't hurt." His lips parted in a big smile. "Especially if you cook like your mom."

"I want to become a doctor, like my Uncle Ray." She set her empty plate on the window ledge, anxious to show Gerard the contents of the trunks. "Come, here's where I found the manuscript. There's lots of interesting things in here." Karena sat on the hardwood floor, using her momentum to slide to a stop in front of the trunk. She lifted the lid, and the familiar scent of cedar fragranced the air.

Gerard set his plate beside hers on the window ledge and joined her.

"My mother interrupted me, so I didn't get through this photo album." She pulled the padded white book from inside and offered it to Gerard. Using his jeans as a napkin, he wiped his hands down his thighs before handling it. He made himself comfortable on the clean hardwood floor and investigated the pages.

"Wasn't Granny A beautiful?"

"Wow. Yes. I can see why Grandpapa was so attracted to her."

Karena scooted next to him, matching him by using the trunk as a backrest.

"Comfortable?" he asked.

"Yes."

He stretched out his legs, and she did the same. Karena thought about Sam the moment they touched, but she didn't withdraw. She wrestled her phone from her pocket. *Sam hadn't called.* She placed her phone on the floor beside the trunk. Gerard put his arm around her, and she settled against him. He opened the album, sharing it across their legs.

"Is he your grandfather?" Karena asked, pointing to the picture of the tall, handsome German soldier standing in front of Janow's white clock tower.

"Yes," Gerard answered. "And look at this picture. Our grandparents are together as if getting ready for a morning ride." The black and white photo showed them standing with Arabian horses tacked up as if ready to go.

"If they had time to ride horses, maybe the War wasn't as awful as I imagined," Karena said, dropping her hands onto the plastic-protected page and staring at Gerard's profile.

He shook his head. "It was their job to ride horses. Grandpapa said it was a dark time—a very bad time. Men were inhumane to each other in ways we cannot imagine, let alone understand. The German brutality inspired horrors in revenge. He said the Russians, my people, visited vengeance on the women and children as they conquered Poland, Hungary, Czechoslovakia, and Germany. Everyone seemed to lose sight of the value of human life," Gerard answered.

"I'm going to go get the book." Karena stood. "I need to learn more. I can hardly wait to get back to their story. Can you?"

Gerard turned and rose to his feet. "Shouldn't we pack up this room? That's what you said we would do and what your mother expects us to do."

"I can pack tomorrow. She thinks we're organizing and won't check," Karena explained. "It won't take much time. I did most of it yesterday." She pointed to the boxes.

Gerard tightened his lips together. Karena knew he wasn't happy with her deception but liked Karena enough to go along.

"Your mom won't confront me if I go get the book. She thinks it's my veterinary notes."

"Good idea. I'll pack some more stuff while you're gone. Then I won't be so far behind tomorrow."

Karena dug around in the trunk while waiting for Gerard to return. She figured they had a good three hours before Mom would come snooping. They could get a lot of reading done in three hours.

The overhead light glimmered on a pale blue bow deep in the back corner of the trunk. Karena moved some books aside and reached for the satin. Old letters—opened but returned to their envelopes—were bundled and tied together. Karena could see the return address was written in a foreign language. *Were these letters from Dr. Erik? Oh, boy!* The relatives would hate Granny A more than ever if they thought she received and hid letters from her German lover while married to Grandpa Baker. Depending, of course, on whether or not they were lovers. Now she wanted Gerard to hurry to find out!

She crept to the attic door and peeked down the empty staircase. Hearing her mother's and Gerard's voices, she quickly searched for something to pack and began stuffing ribbons and winner's plaques into a new box.

She quickly turned to find more trophies when she heard far too many footsteps on the stairs to be Gerard's alone. Karena's mother entered through the door first, followed by a chagrined Gerard. He'd been caught. He held the binder containing the manuscript, still wrapped in the throw blanket, close to his chest. Granny A's book was safe for the moment.

"Gerard said you found a trunk full of photo albums. I wanted to see," Mom said, her eyes wide with curiosity.

Karena glanced at the table by the window where she'd left the bundle of letters. Granny A would become the evil stepmother if Mom found those.

"Yes. They are in the trunk in the corner." When her mother passed by, Karena rushed over to the table and snatched the letters. She quickly stuffed them under the throw blanket with the manuscript, nearly knocking Gerard off balance.

"What's. . . ?"

She shook her head, hoping he wouldn't finish his question.

He started to look, but she pulled the blanket back over the bundle. Gerard lifted his eyebrows and mouthed, "Oh, okay." He slipped past Karena, sank into one of the chairs by the window, hurriedly adjusted the secret documents so they wouldn't be seen, then beamed.

Karena stared at him and realized he enjoyed their covert game. She probably made it worse than it was. She wanted to finish reading the manuscript before her relatives found out about it. They'd want the money if she published it.

Karena watched her mom rummage through the trunk and pull out the album with the World War II pictures.

"Oh, my. This is great. I'm going to share it with the relatives. They will get a kick out of these old pictures," she said as she quickly thumbed through the pages.

"I want them, though," Karena insisted. "No one gets to take any pictures."

"I didn't know you cared so much for Granny A," Karena's mother said, surprise tinting her voice.

"I just want to keep everything together so we can all share it. I can print the photos for everyone who wants them," Karena said.

"That's very generous of you. I'll put you in charge of doing it." Mom smiled. She took the photo album and went to the stairs. Karena followed. "Darling, you are growing up. I'm so glad you want to preserve your grandmother's legacy."

Karena accepted her praise and her hug. *Boy. Did she ever feel guilty!* She closed the door after Mom was down the stairs and turned back to Gerard.

"Can you read German?" Gerard asked. He'd removed the bundle of letters from their hiding place.

"No. Can you?" She tipped her head slightly, hoping.

"Yes. I can translate these for us," he offered. "I have a couple of hours left before I should go. I don't want Dr. Wilson waiting up for me."

"Take them with you. Translate when you can," Karena said, moving to the other chair next to the window. "Let's read some more. I'm dying to discover if Dr. Erik and Granny A were lovers."

Gerard grinned and rubbed his hands together, palm to palm.

Chapter Twenty

DR. ERIK UNDID HIS UNIFORM jacket, loosened his tie, and unbuttoned the top few buttons of his white shirt. The barn was quiet except for the horses contentedly munching their evening hay. The day's chores were complete, and Erik realized he was bone tired. He smiled to himself. Only two hours ago, he had delivered his first human baby. He sank onto a bale of straw the workers had set out for the morning cleaning.

The barn aisles were swept; nothing was out of place. He had to get ready for Major Fellgeible's inspection. Erik hadn't eaten all day, and his stomach rumbled. He tried to remember if he had anything in his small refrigerator to eat.

When he heard footsteps on the cobblestones on the walkway to the barn, he reluctantly rebuttoned his shirt, straightened his tie, and closed his uniform coat. The sliding doors to the mare barn opened, and Erik stood at attention.

The Major and a small entourage walked into the barn, stopping and glancing into each stall along their way, chatting happily and casually, though he couldn't make out their words.

"Captain," Major Fellgeible greeted him. "We missed you at dinner. I understand you had extra work this afternoon." Fellgeible let a small smile curve his lips. He approved of Erik delivering a Polish farmer's baby, but the others in his party probably would not. "Your friend Lieutenant Bishof joined us. He came looking for you." Fellgeible scowled. He wasn't pleased. He'd made his stand clear on Erik's first day at the stud farm. Erik was not to invite the Gestapo or SS officers to Janow.

"I'm sorry, sir. I didn't know he'd come to see me," Erik said, turning and walking with the Major.

"He joined us and is still with us."

Erik winced. He searched the group of officers and caught sight of Bishof. The man had brought two lady friends with him, and the young officers fussed over them, obviously starved for female company. Dread crept over Erik. He was too tired to deal with Bishof and his debauchery tonight. He'd avoided it so far, making excuses each time Bishof invited him to join him and his SS friends.

Bishof helped when Erik went to collect the yearlings from the racetrack. He'd known sooner or later Bishof expected him to return the favor, even if it was joining him for drinks.

"Lieutenant Bishof has asked if he might take riding lessons from Annaleah Sabrosky. I told him I'd see if you could part with her. I suggested he might join the cavalrymen in their morning practice. Annaleah leads the practice, and he wouldn't take her away from her duties or interrupt our operations." Fellgeible breathed out as if expelling annoyance. It was clear he had no patience for Bishof's interference. The Gestapo wielded too much power. Fellgeible disapproved of their treatment of the Poles.

Erik knew when he'd researched his commanding officer, the Major, and his older brother, who had been born and raised in Poznan when Poland was part of the Prussian Empire. Erik heard the rumors that the Major was assigned to Janow because he knew horses and had command of the language and customs of the Polish people. Fellgeible didn't share Führer's assessment of the Polish people as second-class citizens. Neither did Erik, but he did understand the Reich's desire for cheap labor.

He didn't think of anyone as second-class or less than human. Even though Eugenics was the popular theory of the day, Erik couldn't reconcile it with his Catholic upbringing. In his view, Adam and Eve were the father and mother of the whole human race. How, logically, could one nationality be less than any other when they were all brothers and sisters? Erik kept his mouth shut about this belief. Openly expressing opposition to the Reich meant imprisonment or death.

"Yes, sir. I understand," Erik said. "I don't believe I can part with her." Erik knew he said the words from his instinctive desire to protect her. He hoped the Major didn't notice. He'd just made work for himself; he'd have to think up things for them to do to fill the time.

Fellgeible grunted.

"Erik, we missed you at dinner," Lieutenant Bishof said as he caught up. The women he'd brought with him clung to him, one on each side. "Meet Zena and Katia. We wondered if you'd like to join us for drinks in Biala."

Erik noticed Major Fellgeible narrow his eyes. Erik might swallow a shot of whiskey in his private quarters but had no desire to join Bishof and his women.

"Lieutenant Bishof, look what we found hiding in one of the horse stalls."

Erik turned when he heard the struggle behind him. Two of Bishof's agents thrust Annaleah forward into view.

Erik reacted without thinking. He launched forward. With everything he had, Erik shoved the man to her left away from her. Before the man on her right could react, he landed a solid blow to his jaw, sending him stumbling in retreat. Erik grabbed Anna's arm and pulled her behind him, positioning his body between her and the men.

"Call off your attack dogs!" Erik yelled, glaring back at Bishof. "She's my assistant! Call them off!"

"She broke the curfew. She should be home at this hour," One of the agents retorted, rubbing his jaw. The second man pulled a Ruger from his waistband and pointed it at Erik's chest. Guiding Anna backward, keeping her behind him, Erik withdrew a step. His heart raced, and adrenaline surged. He had no gun, but they weren't going to take her. Not while he had breath in his body.

"I asked her to stay and help me with the colts," Erik growled. "She's my helper. You leave her alone."

Bishof raised his hand. "Enough! Let her go!" he shouted, and both of his agents reluctantly backed away. Their angry stares charged the air like lightning. Even the mares felt it and fled to the rear of their stalls, calling out anxiously to each other.

"If she's here past curfew, she can be arrested," Bishof said, his eyes narrowing and glimmering with a barely contained maliciousness. Erik knew what would happen to Anna if Bishof got his lecherous hands on her. He shuddered at the thought.

Major Fellgeible bolted forward into the fray, tapping his ever-present riding crop against his tall boots. His whole demeanor exuded power and authority. Bishof's agents would take out Erik at their peril. They recognized immediately that they and their boss would be sent to the front lines before they could get a second shot off.

"Do you challenge my authority? I say when it's curfew, and who can stay past it in my barn," Fellgeible warned, anger causing his left eyelid to twitch.

"I enforce the laws of the Reich," Bishof sneered.

"And I outrank you, Lieutenant. I make the law in this barn. If my head veterinarian needs Miss Sabrosky to help him after hours, he will have his assistant help him after hours. Are we clear?" The Major's threat resounded against the stone walls. The standoff was instantly diffused.

"Dr. Erik, will you see Miss Sabrosky safely home? If I must, Lieutenant Bishof, I will post a guard at the convent," Major Fellgeible threatened.

Bishof was intimidated. He showed his deference with a tense bow and a salute. Erik was sure he knew Fellgeible's brother was a general and a member of Hitler's inner circle. If the Major reported this unpleasantness, at the very least, Bishof could lose his position and rank or worse.

Erik could feel Annaleah slump against his back. A barely perceptible sob reached his ears, and he wanted to turn and take her in his arms.

"Lieutenant Bishof, you and your agents are dismissed. Captain Kemperman, please see Miss Sabrosky home. And Lieutenant, I trust there will be no further incidents with the employees of this barn," Major Fellgeible lowered his glare, his jaw tight with anger.

"Of course, sir. I can drive Miss Sabrosky home in my car to make amends," Bishof said. His tone was slimy with evil. Erik felt alarmed and looked to the Major for help.

"Captain Kemperman will go with you." Major Fellgeible offered the compromise, delivering Bishof a blistering smile. He strolled out of the barn.

"Shall we go?" Bishof grumbled, turned on his heel, and stomped out of the barn, motioning to his agents and women to follow. He'd been humiliated in front of them. Erik suspected the petty little man wouldn't be happy until he got retribution. He was a coward and would exact it against Anna because she was powerless. Unless reassigned to a new post, Bishof would be a constant danger to Anna. Erik worried for her. He worried for himself. But he had to ensure her safety.

When Bishof and his troop were outside, and he and Anna were alone, Erik pivoted and put his arm around her shoulder. She rested her head against his chest. "Oh, Anna, why did you come here?" he asked quietly. "I gave you the night off. Why did you come back?"

"I wanted to see—I wanted to see Lotnik," she murmured.

Not me? He thought. He sighed and tipped her chin so she looked at his face. "Oh, Anna. The old days of freedom are gone. These are perilous times. For you and for me. You must listen to me. You must listen to what I tell you. Bishof is a dangerous man. For your safety, you must listen to me." He waited until she nodded her agreement. "Come on. I'll get you home."

"I'm sorry I'm so much trouble." She looked down at the floor, withdrawing into herself as if she expected him to strike her.

He could never hit her. It wasn't in his nature. They slowly strolled down the barn aisleway and out the door.

In the courtyard, Bishof waited with his car engine running. The windshield wipers could barely keep up with the volume of snow drifting down from the sky. Erik knew to keep the peace, he needed to let Bishof drive Anna home. He quickly removed his greatcoat and covered their heads as they dashed for the car.

The two women—one in the front passenger's seat and one in the back—looked at the pair, anxious to understand what had just happened. They had turned to face each other, their eyes big with curiosity. Bishof's two agents were in a separate car, and he waved them off. Erik watched until they drove away. He helped Anna in the back seat next to Zena, shook the snowflakes from his coat, and climbed in beside her. He took hold of Anna's hand, reassuring her. When they arrived at the convent, Erik walked Anna to the door. They stood for a moment face to face but without words.

He stifled his desire to scold her again. She was frightened enough. He touched her cheek with the back of his fingers.

For the second time tonight, he watched her until she climbed the stone stairs at the end of the long corridor. He waited until the large wooden door closed, and he could no longer see her. Then he returned to the vehicle and climbed into the back seat next to Zena. He realized Bishof had brought Zena along for him. Erik detested Bishof for taking advantage of these young women. They sold themselves in exchange for food and protection, even though it wasn't guaranteed. Fear and starvation were horrible masters. Erik hated the war. It had ruined everyone's dreams.

Erik glanced over at Zena. She was a pretty girl. Her brown hair was styled in the latest fashion, and her blue eyes were warm and friendly. They held a promise he wanted—but not from her. He wanted Anna. He wanted what he shouldn't and couldn't have. Marriage to women Hitler considered foreign and lesser was forbidden.

"Let's go get a drink!" Bishof said cheerfully.

"No. I'm too tired. Drop me at the entrance to the stud farm. I've had an exhausting day," Erik said.

"I heard. Delivering babies for Polish farmers," Bishof snorted. "I say let them deliver their own." His tone was merciless. When he arrested the doctor, Bishof had to have known he'd left the villagers and surrounding farmers without medical help.

Erik felt a heaviness in his heart. Cruelty wasn't in his nature. None of God's creatures should needlessly suffer. Gunther Bishof had let a little power turn him into a monster.

"You aren't going to let Zena down, are you, Erik? I've told her all about you. She's been waiting to meet you all day," Bishof grinned.

"I'm sorry, Zena. I think I'd be useless to you. I had a busy day. And tomorrow isn't going to be any better. Another time?" he asked, without the slightest intention of carrying through.

"We have a bottle. We could go to your quarters," Bishof suggested.

"I won't get the rest I need then, will I?" Erik countered with a chuckle. "No. Another time. I didn't expect you today."

"You're in love with Miss Sabrosky. That's what this is about," Bishof said, looking into the rearview mirror at him. Erik glared back.

Zena leaned against him and whispered, "Are you in love with her?" She seemed genuinely concerned.

Erik took a deep breath. He slumped against the seat. "Yes." His quiet answer was meant only for her.

"Then why don't you just take her? If she were given to me, I do it. We are the master race. We are the conquerors. We can take what we want," Bishof said boldly.

Zena stared at him. Erik read pity in her eyes. He didn't want her pity. "Could you force a woman who didn't want you?" she asked.

Erik shook his head. "No."

She smiled and reached for him, placing her hand on his thigh. "Don't listen to him. He's just being 'Bishof the Terrible.'"

Bishof guffawed almost as if he were proud of the moniker .

Lieutenant Bishof stopped the car in front of Janow's clock tower. Erik noticed the malicious expression in the man's eyes, analyzing him in the rearview mirror. He knew he'd be watched from now on and reported for the slightest perceived infraction.

"Another time. Okay, Zena?" Erik opened the door and climbed out, not waiting for her answer.

Chapter Twenty-One

MORNING ARRIVED, AND ANNALEAH ROSE early. Sitting up in bed, she rubbed the sleep from her eyes. The earth outside her window had transformed into a wonderland of white. She grabbed the quilt from her bed and wrapped it around her shoulders. Outside her window, just breaking the horizon, the sun spread shafts of golden light into the sky and refracted rainbows through the icicles hanging off the roof, fences, and tree branches. The new drifts of snow sparkled as if jewels were cast across the surface. Winter was a beautiful season. It would be clear and cold today.

She wanted to get to the barn and finish her chores. Excited by her plan to start Lotnik's training, she dreamed of making him a perfect riding horse. She tossed her quilt across her bed. From her small wooden dresser in the corner of the room, she collected long underwear, clean wool breeches, socks, a fresh shirt, and her thickest wool sweater.

Annaleah dashed to the bathroom down the hall, knowing she'd be first to shower in the warm water that had accumulated overnight. But then, last night's encounter with Lieutenant Bishof's men overwhelmed her happy thoughts. She was certain she'd managed to alienate her only German friend. Dr. Erik was so disappointed in her. She groaned. He'd warned her Bishof had nightly patrols, and she'd been watchful when she crossed the pastures to the yearling stable. She hadn't expected Bishof and his men to be *inside* the barn.

Maybe Dr. Erik went out drinking and dancing with one of the girls Bishof had brought for him and was in a better mood. She remembered Zena and Katia from school before the war. They were only two years older than she. They looked so pretty in their stylish new clothes, silk stockings, and bright red lipstick. But deep down, she knew how they obtained those things and their real role. She shuddered at the thought.

Hopefully, Dr. Erik had forgotten she hadn't listened to him and had no common sense. She'd always run to the horses when she felt sad, lonely, or heartbroken. Just being in their company cheered her. It was hard to get used to the idea the Nazis controlled everything, watched everything, and punished ruthlessly for anything they chose. Their rules were arbitrary and sometimes insane. She wanted this war to end and life to return as it was before.

Unbidden, Dr. Erik's almost kiss reappeared in her thoughts and replayed. She wondered what it would feel like. She closed her eyes and brushed her index finger across her lips. *Ahhgg! Such foolishness.* He'd promised it would never happen again, so she would never find out. She shouldn't be thinking these things since she'd promised Jan she'd wait for him. She set her clean clothes on the bench next to the shower and turned on the water. Once again, she'd need to go to confession and pray about her terrible thoughts. She hated being an inconstant woman!

Clean and dressed, Annaleah carefully ran a comb through the wet tangles in her long blonde hair. She decided to dry it in front of the radiator by the window in her bedroom since snow covered the ground and the icy air might cause her to catch a chill. It meant she'd have to sit for at least a half hour, but it was early, and everyone else still snuggled under the covers of their beds. She could use the quiet time to think and pray.

Her thoughts ran through her list of plans for the day. The joy of training Lotnik took center stage. She decided she'd encourage him to take the bit by placing small pieces of apple on top of it in her open palm. She'd used this trick before, and it eliminated the fight. It became a positive experience for horse and horseman rather than a battle. After a few times, the horse would reach for the bit rather than give her trouble. Today, she'd ask him to carry a training bridle with a smooth copper snaffle under his lunging halter.

After her morning barn chores, she would have to see what else Dr. Erik ....Dr. Erik. What was she going to do about her confused feelings for Dr. Erik? Should she go to Major Fellgeible and ask to be relieved of her duties as his assistant? Would they then send her to one of the labor camps? Or worse? Would she be forced to become like Zena and Katia—concubines to the German Officers?

Jan hadn't visited her since they fought about Dr. Erik's warning about Bishof and his nightly patrols. She longed to change Jan's mind by telling him the vet had delivered his sister, Caterina's baby. And he'd saved Nelek's favorite heifer by pulling her twin calves. Annaleah remembered Jan's scolding when she and Dr. Erik returned from collecting Lotnik and the lost yearlings. Jan needed to understand Dr. Erik's life had been upended by this war, too. His dreams were on hold, just like Jan's. Surely, Jan could see Dr. Erik in a different light.

Suddenly, there was a commotion on the floor below. Unfamiliar noises filled the chapel as if the candelabras had fallen over. *Benit!* she thought. The ten-year-old boy was always playing too rough where he shouldn't and getting into trouble. She dropped her hairbrush, stood, and raced to the top of the stairs.

The main corridor was filled with soldiers in black. They tore down the tapestries in the hallway and hung huge black, red, and white Nazi flags in their place. Father Jerzak and Mother Superior quickly followed, rolling up the priceless artifacts and carrying them to the main office for safety.

Annaleah wilted against the wall, wanting to disappear into the stone. She remembered the Russian soldier's touch on the day of their withdrawal, and her stomach roiled with fear. *Coward! You coward!* Her thoughts screamed at her. She gulped in a breath and straightened. "Lord Jesus, give me courage," she whispered.

"What are you doing?" she shouted from the top of the stairs. Chin lowered like a charging bull, she descended. "Stop it! This is God's house!" She grabbed the framed picture of Christ from a soldier's hands.

He shoved her back, laughed, and ripped down a medieval embroidery of knights on fine horses dating back to the Crusades. She gasped.

Lieutenant Bishof appeared at the Chapel doorway. His self-satisfied grin was vile, like the devil himself stood there instead.

Annaleah asked him directly. "Why are you doing this?"

"Berlin has ordered all churches to conform to the laws of the Reich," he announced, his expression daring her to question him. He picked up a framed reproduction of a painting of Hitler and hung it where the picture of Jesus had been. She followed Bishof as he marched down the center aisle to the altar. "Mein Kampf will replace your Jewish Bible," he said, enjoying her agony. He scraped the table with his arm, sending the Chapel's Bible to the floor. Annaleah crossed herself.

She wanted to charge him and scratch his eyes out. Her anger was ready to boil over. Father Jerzak grabbed her, his arm around her waist, coaxing her away from the Gestapo chief. But her glower met Bishof's, and her fierceness forced him to look away. She had heard the church was persecuted everywhere the Germans had conquered. Was there no one to stop this evil? Tears began to form in her eyes. The soldiers toppled a brass crucifix to the floor and draped the Nazi flag behind the pulpit.

Father Jerzak pulled Annaleah into a second-row pew and held her with his arms around her shoulders. At first, she struggled to get free.

"Anna, no. Don't fight them. They will send you away. Remember, God is always in control," Father Jerzak said softly. She realized he protected her from her impulsiveness.

Annaleah was shocked back into reality. Any charitable thoughts she held for Dr. Erik, Major Fellgeible, and the whole Nazi regime changed in an instant. She reminded herself they were enemies. She would do everything in her power to defeat and destroy them.

Chapter Twenty-Two

AFTER BISHOF GAVE THE ORDER, the soldiers noisily climbed the stairs to the dormitory rooms. She could hear their heavy boots clomping on the wooden floor above her head. Several sisters raced up after them to protect the children. Annaleah could barely control her emotions as she turned in her pew to face Bishof.

"Are there any Jewish children here?" Gunter Bishof demanded.

Mother Superior shook her head, "No."

"Are there?" he growled again, yanking Annaleah to her feet, away from Father Jerzak's protection. Bishof narrowed his eyes with suspicion.

"No," Annaleah said, fear and hatred making her whole body tremble. He squeezed her arms and shook her.

"Don't lie to me."

Anger filled her with a cold resolve, and strength radiated from her eyes. Bishof let her go and stepped back almost as if he'd touched an electric fence. She sensed underneath his overplayed bravado, he was a cowardly weakling.

"We are a Catholic Order, sir. Jews would not come here," she said boldly. It was a lie. Only three days ago, four Jewish boys, escapees from the carnage in Krakow, had arrived at the convent—filthy, freezing, exhausted, and starving. They had given them food and water, a hot shower, warm clothes, and shelter overnight. Father Jerzak burned their old clothes and any connection to Krakow in the basement incinerator.

In the morning, Father Jerzak had walked them down the secret path through the forest, passing them to resistance fighters, who would give them forged papers. The resistance would secure passage for the boys on a fishing boat in the Baltic Sea. If all went as planned, the children would be transported to free Jewish families in Sweden, Holland, and Norway.

Annaleah could tell Bishof didn't believe her but was afraid to push her any further. Bishof walked into the main office where the records were kept. He would account for each child here, matching it to Mother Superior's logbook. With the book under his arm, he climbed the stairs. Annaleah could hear the little ones crying, but two soldiers blocked her path up the stairs.

They had left carnage in the chapel, main dining room, corridor, and classrooms for her and the sisters to clean. The wrought iron prayer candle stand had been overturned. Shattered glass mixed with hot wax stuck to the stone floor. By God's grace, the wax had doused the flames but solidified on the cold floor and would have to be painstakingly scraped up. They hadn't set fire to the orphanage and chapel as they had to the Jewish synagogue in Biala. Annaleah was thankful. She heard from her fellow barn laborers the Nazis had locked women and children in barns and churches and burned them alive inside. The soldiers had thrown the carved wooden crucifixes in the main corridor to the floor, and some splintered into pieces. Mother Superior swept them up, her eyes brimming with tears. It was the desecration of the sacred in Annaleah's mind. She went to Mother and put her arms around her. For the first time in her life, she was the comforter. Annaleah guessed she was truly a grown-up now.

Dr. Erik walked down the yearling colts' barn aisle, looking for Annaleah. She missed roll call this morning, her second time late this week. He shook his head. Was Annaleah using him for special favors? She hadn't given him any indication she returned his affection. But he admitted: *I am a fool in love.* Inside, he laughed at himself.

He slid the barn door open, and Benit, one of the orphan boys from the convent, raced through, crashing into him like a charging ram. Erik stumbled back, regaining his balance.

"Dr. Erik, come quick. The soldiers—destroy—everything—the convent. Come now!" The boy cried breathlessly, grabbed his hand, and tugged him through the opening. Erik remembered the boy was only ten years old.

"What? Slow down, boy." Erik's mind tried to make sense of his words. "Who is destroying the convent?"

"Come. Now. The soldiers . . . ." Benit choked on the words, as if fighting tears.

Erik felt a chill race through his body. *Bishof.* He exacted his revenge earlier than Erik expected. At a run, he dashed to Major Fellgeible's office. Without knocking, he burst through the door, surprising everyone inside.

"Bishof is at the Convent with SS Soldiers!"

Fellgeible's eyes widened with surprise, then narrowed with anger. He picked up his phone and demanded the operator connect him to his brother.

"Rolf, get a small transport ready and my car." He paused until the call was transferred. "Fritz, Hans here. [...] Yes. It's cold here, too. Listen, the Gestapo is destroying the convent and orphanage next to the farm. [...] I need the Führer's authority to stop them. [...] No. All the Jews were sent to Warsaw weeks ago. [...] There is no one left to harbor."

The Major listened intently and slowly hung up, his face expressing confusion and alarm. "They promised religious freedom," he mumbled, as if talking to himself.

He stood from his chair, snatched up his riding crop, and motioned for Erik to lead to the equipment shed. The Major's two adjutants stumbled along behind him.

"Sir, sir?" Albrecht called after him. "We can't interfere with Gestapo actions. Sir!"

"It's an orphanage. It's helpless women and children," Fellgeible replied and then barked orders to several cavalry soldiers, who had quickly come to attention. "Come with me!" They took up their rifles and loaded quickly into the transport trucks. Erik helped Benit into the back with the soldiers and climbed in last so he could disembark first.

Remembering the doctor's office, Erik groaned in disbelief as the truck rumbled down the snow-covered road to the convent. He imagined the destruction. In a majority Catholic Country, how could this improve relations? The brakes squealed as the truck slid in the gravel to a stop in the circular driveway.

Erik was amazed at the cavalry soldiers' efficiency. With hand motions, the Major instructed the soldiers to encircle the convent, and they completed the task quickly. Fellgeible marched up the stairs with his aids by his side and wrenched open the convent's double doors. Erik joined him.

Soldiers in the black SS uniforms came to attention, recognizing the Major's superior rank.

"What is going on here?" Fellgeible growled. Erik knew the Major was very likely Catholic and would take this as an affront to his faith. Bishof appeared at the top of the stairs. Reaching into his overcoat's lapel, he produced a paper.

"I have my orders," he explained, walking officiously down the steps. He waved the paper in the air. Major Fellgeible snatched it from his hand, glared at the man, and then read it.

"You were ordered to put up flags, to place Hitler's portrait up, and to set 'Mein Kampf' on the altar *alongside* the Bible, but not to do this!" Major Fellgeible gestured by sweeping his hand as if encompassing the disorder and chaos around him.

Their stares locked. Erik felt trepidation racing through him. For a second time, Fellgeible humiliated the Gestapo chief in front of his men.

"I had a report this convent hid Jewish children," Bishof defended his actions.

"And did you find Jewish children here?" Fellgeible demanded, raising an eyebrow. He seemed sure of the answer before he asked the question. Erik looked for Annaleah in the corridor. He found her standing in the Chapel doorway. *Were there Jewish children here?* He tried to read the answer in her expression. But she was a blank page.

Bishof shifted his gaze to the stone floor. "No, sir." All his earlier defiance melted away.

"Gather your men and go," the Major said. "This is my jurisdiction. These are my subordinates. We don't want to inspire an uprising, now do we?"

His lips curved with a false, conciliatory smile. Erik knew Fellgeible walked a fine line. Berlin had issued orders. Bishof had carried them out, but his enthusiasm for violence, power, and control had crossed the line.

Bishof raised his arm in the Nazi Salute. "Heil Hitler." His SS Soldiers mimicked him. Fellgeible returned the gesture but without Bishof's enthusiasm. They watched Bishof and his entourage leave.

Fellgeible turned back and took Mother Superior by both hands, bowing slightly to her. "I am sincerely sorry, your grace, for this unfortunate interference. I will send help to clean up."

He motioned to one of his adjutants, and he hurried off.

"Was anyone injured?" Fellgeible asked. His compassion and wisdom were unmistakable. Here, for the long term, he understood that establishing community with the farmers and common folk was imperative for everyone's survival.

Erik located Annaleah but didn't move toward her. He had never seen her with her hair down, and it was beautiful. She seemed surrounded by a golden glow, but the smile he'd often enjoyed did not welcome him this morning.

"Father Jerzak, Mother Superior, I will leave a guard with you today and assign one for you from now on if you wish."

"I wouldn't want to put you out, Major. We have faced persecution before. But thank you anyway for your offer," Father Jerzak replied. The truth became clear in Erik's mind. *They were hiding Jewish children here and likely planned on helping more.* He glanced at Fellgeible. The Major knew it. Just like Erik knew it. When their eyes met, they made a silent agreement—they would not disclose their suspicions to anyone.

"Please consider a permanent guard. Contact me or Captain Kemperman if you change your mind," Major Fellgeible offered. Affirming his words, Erik dipped his head once. The Major smiled, turned on his heel toward the door, and they walked outside together.

"Bishof is insufferable. A troublemaker and a fool," Fellgeible grumbled. "Violence doesn't make friends, only enemies. You would do well to discontinue any association with him. He will betray you. He is a dishonorable man."

"Yes, sir." Erik lifted both eyebrows and nodded. He watched the Major stroll to his sergeant and gave the orders to set up the temporary guard.

Erik walked down the stone steps to the truck. He turned before climbing in. Looking back, he saw Annaleah standing in the doorway. He wanted to go to her, to take her in his arms, protect and comfort her, but he had to act like a proper German officer. Her lips were parted, and her brow puckered with confusion. When he next saw her at the barn, he would try to explain there was disagreement within the Heer. The Gestapo and Waffen SS were on the side of expansionism, terror, and total war, while many experienced officers in the Wehrmacht feared it would bring Germany to ruin. Nothing would change for Anna, her friends, and the family at the convent and orphanage. The Poles would still be vanquished, and they would not be allowed to smuggle Jewish people to safety. Erik doubted anything could stop them.

Chapter Twenty-Three

ANNALEAH STEPPED BACK INSIDE AND let the doors to the convent close. She stood momentarily lost in her thoughts, supporting her body against the cold stone wall. Once again, Dr. Erik had come to her rescue. So confused by her feelings, she found it hard to dislike or fault him or Major Fellgeible. It might be unreasonable, but she still feared them both. Bishof—he was easy to hate.

She snapped out of her thoughts, went to the kitchen, and collected a spatula. She joined Mother Superior on her hands and knees, cleaning up the broken glass and scraping the solidified wax from the prayer votives off the chapel's stone floor.

"No, Annaleah! Go to your job. Go to the barns and do your work like nothing has happened," Mother Superior whispered as if she believed the Gestapo could hear her. "Don't give the Gestapo a reason to come back. We will permit the painting of Hitler to remain in the corridor. We will display their flags and the book. Maybe they will leave us alone if we pretend to go along."

"They will only get worse. They won't leave us alone," Annaleah replied through clenched teeth.

"Anna," Mother Superior set her hand softly on Annaleah's forearm. "If they think we are with them, we can continue our work. If we fight them, who will care for the children? Be wise, Annaleah. Go now. We will finish cleaning up."

Reluctantly, Annaleah rose and climbed the stairs. She felt defeated when she opened the door to her small room. Her one dresser had been emptied—the drawers pulled out, and her meager possessions dumped on the floor. Her small nightstand suffered the same fate. At least her lamp had been set in the corner and not shattered into pieces. Even the mattress on her bed had been moved aside. *Had they searched for Jewish children under her bed?* She quickly moved the headboard away from the wall. Her diary, full of thoughts and feelings, still hung in the hand-embroidered pouch she'd made and glued to the backboard, keeping her secret thoughts away from spying eyes. She sighed with relief. The diary held nothing about Jewish children, but there was plenty about her confused musings about Dr. Erik. Bishof would use it against the vet if he could. The diary was dangerous in the wrong hands. If Bishof and the Gestapo returned, they would be more thorough the second time through and find it. Hiding it in a new place wouldn't be enough; Annaleah decided to destroy it.

She returned the drawers to the dresser and stuffed them. She'd straighten everything after work at the end of the day. For the first time since she could remember, she dreaded going to the barn, though she longed for the horses. She wanted her nostrils filled with their scent, their lips nuzzling her face, their gentle empathy as if they truly cared for her. What she didn't want was to face Dr. Erik. She needed to thank him, but the way he looked at her left her feeling unbalanced and mystified.

Hesitating at the top of the stone steps, she stuffed the diary into her sweater. She didn't want to answer any of Mother Superior's questions. Her mind made up, she hurriedly turned and descended the stairway into the semi-darkness of the basement. Many times before, she'd sleepily traipsed down these steps to throw wood into the boiler to heat water for the radiators. The amber light from the boiler's fire flickered through the thick glass window in the door. She opened it and tossed the diary in. For a few moments, she watched it catch and burn. The diary was better used to heat water for the steam radiators than to give Bishof a reason to arrest her or Dr. Erik.

Dr. Erik rescued her last night and again this morning. He knew about Jan's midnight visits; if he knew about those, surely he knew about Father

Jerzak's nighttime trips through the woods to deliver the children to the underground. It was treason for him not to report it. Yet he hadn't.

Annaleah buttoned up her coat and wrapped a wool scarf around her neck. It's Christmas red and green reminded her tomorrow was the first of December. The convent's orphans would dream of building a snowman in the yard, making decorations for the two potted evergreens by the doorway, and preparing for the annual Christmas play and carols for the villagers. Annaleah wondered if they would be allowed to do any of it.

She acknowledged one of the soldiers Major Fellgeible left to guard the convent as she walked toward the pasture between the stud farm and the orphanage.

Last night's snow had added at least six inches to the six already on the ground. She trudged through the drifts, staying on the longer forest path to the horse barns. Maybe she could slip unnoticed into work. Annaleah knocked the light, powdery snow from an evergreen branch and watched a breeze catch it, whirl it into the sky, and release the glittering crystals back to the ground in the morning sunlight.

Without warning, she was grabbed from behind. One arm snaked around her waist, and the other covered her mouth before she could scream. Her attacker pulled her deeper into the cover of the trees. She fought, biting his hand in the soft spot between his index finger and thumb as hard as she could. Instead of flesh, she tasted leather. Her attacker was so much bigger and stronger. She went limp, hoping to slide through his grip.

"Ouch! Annaleah, it's me. It's Jan," he whispered.

"Jan?" She twisted toward him and pounded his chest with her fists. "Jan! You scared me!"

"I didn't mean to. But I couldn't get your attention. You just looked at the ground," he chuckled.

"What are you doing here? Jan, Bishof will catch you." She grabbed his hand, and he snatched his rifle, which he'd earlier leaned against a tree. She led him even deeper into the tangle of branches.

"Don't you know we watch over you, Anna?"

"Oh, Jan." She didn't know whether to laugh or cry. "Please. You must stay away. Dr. Erik warned us."

"Dr. Erik?" Jan's eyes darkened and narrowed. "Why must you bring him up?"

"You can't hate him. He didn't have to, but he delivered Caterina's baby. She was in trouble. She could've died. He's a good man," Annaleah argued, anger flushing warmth into her cheeks.

"He's a Nazi. He's the enemy. Don't be fooled."

"I'm not a fool," she pushed her lips forward in a pout, knowing she couldn't expect Jan ever to accept Dr. Erik as anything but a ruthless conqueror. "Bishof is who you should worry about."

"Don't you remember all the years we played in this forest? I know how and where to hide," he grinned, balanced his rifle against a tree, and brought her close, holding her against his shoulder.

"I remember." Her mind filled with memories, and she sighed. She, Jan, and Nelek played 'hide and seek' on their way to the barns after school and rode Janow's horses under the arching branches covering the forest trails. It was a carefree, lovely time, and she wanted it back. Tears began to fill her eyes. She sniffed them back.

Jan pulled off her wool cap and kissed her forehead. It was the first time he'd shown affection since their first kiss months ago at the start of the war. Usually, he scolded her for wanting him to hold her. *It's not the time for this!* He'd say. She snuggled closer. It wasn't exciting, but familiar, comfortable.

She heard the soft crunching of footsteps on the snow, alerted, and dropped to a crouch, pulling Jan down with her. When he started to say something, she hushed him with her index finger to his lips.

"Jan, where are you?" Annaleah recognized Nelek's whisper.

Jan stood momentarily, gesturing for their friend to join their huddle.

"God! Jan! Bishof was just at the convent, destroying artifacts and hanging his hero's flags and pictures on the walls. Don't you understand how dangerous this is? I have to go to work. They will notice I'm not there," Annaleah said, nervous energy making her stomach contract.

"Will you tell us everything you hear? Anything you see?" Nelek asked. He stared into her eyes in all seriousness.

She laughed. "Like which cow had her calf or mare foaled? How do I know what is important?"

"If there are troop movements. Upcoming visits from high officials. Anything, even small details you think are unimportant," Jan said. "Your position as the veterinarian's assistant puts you in places to see and hear things the resistance might be able to use."

"How will I find you to tell you these things?" She frowned. They were asking her to betray the men who had just rescued her. *No one could continue to live under Nazi rule.* She reasoned. Not even Dr. Erik.

"I'll find you," he said.

"But how will you know I learned something important if I can't signal you some way?"

"This box," he reached behind him and took a small wooden box from Nelek's hand. "I will leave it in our oak in the sisters' prayer grotto. Put a message saying "Yes" inside. Then I will come to you at night and wait for you in the trees by the creek."

Annaleah remembered the hollow oak. She, Jan, and Nelek found it when they were twelve and playing hide and seek in the forest near the grotto and the creek. The three had claimed the tree and carved their initials in the rough bark. Jan and Nelek had cleaned the hollow and built a secret compartment out of scrap wood they'd found around their farms. They'd left secret messages for each other there for years as they played their childhood games. She'd completely forgotten it when she was allowed to spend her days riding Janow's horses after classes and during the summers.

"They aren't idiots. Bishof has patrols around the convent and stud farm at all hours," Anna protested.

"If you go consistently to the grotto to pray, they will think it's your routine," Jan beseeched her.

"Or they will suspect I'm doing exactly what I am doing and arrest us both," she answered. These days, every moment was packed full of risk. Despite fear, she must help her compatriots win their country back. Her breath trembled in her throat. "Yes. I'll do it," Annaleah nodded.

Jan grinned and quickly pecked her cheek.

"We must go now," Nelek said, tugging on the back of Jan's jacket.

He picked up his rifle and turned away. Annaleah watched them disappear into the forest.

Chapter Twenty-Four

ANNALEAH SLIPPED INTO LOTNIK'S STALL. He quit eating and came to her, putting his head and neck over her shoulder and pressing her close to his chest. She and the young stallion had a deep connection.

Today was a day full of memories. She remembered the evening Lotnik was born. He was such a strong and happy colt. Within a few minutes of birth, he'd struggled to stand on wobbly legs. At first, he stumbled and fell into the deep, clean straw. Annaleah had helped by bracing his body against hers until he learned to balance. Within a short time, he gained strength and raced circles around her and his mom.

In the early morning, they turned the mare and colt out in the small spring pasture. Lotnik took off and charged around the enclosure at full speed as if fueled by pure joy. Annaleah smiled inside as she remembered his mother chasing after him, trying to keep up, and calling out as if scolding him for his boldness.

That day, Dr. Lesnik and Director Krzytalowicz named him Lotnik, *the flyer*. As they watched him play, they predicted he'd be a winning racehorse one day.

"I love you, my handsome boy," she cooed. He responded by pressing her closer. Those sweet and carefree days were gone now. Sadness returned and weighed on her spirit.

Director Krzytalowicz was gone; he'd escaped just before the Nazis took over the farm. Dr. Lesnik had been reassigned to an advisory position and could no longer deal directly with the horses. She wanted to sink into the straw in the corner of the stall and cry. Bishof had shredded any sense of safety and peace she had in her life. Knowing she could be arrested at any time left her overflowing with dread.

"I knew I'd find you here," Dr. Erik said, sliding the stall door open. Annaleah turned as he walked forward. His smile of greeting faded into worry. He closed the door behind him. He stood on the opposite side of the colt from her, stroked Lotnik's neck, and finally rested his arms lazily on the colt's back. The colt shifted but didn't move away. "Are you all right?" he asked.

She choked back her tears. "Yes. Sir."

"Did Bishof hurt you in any way?" he asked, leaning toward her over the colt's back.

"No. Sir." She backed up a step, and the colt moved away from them and returned to his hay feeder, leaving Erik and her standing face to face.

Erik searched her eyes and dropped his gaze to her lips, making her experience sensations she wasn't sure she understood. *Did he want to kiss her?* Annaleah looked down into the straw. Dr. Erik made her insides feel like a thousand butterflies suddenly took flight. She was afraid of the German. But this wasn't fear.

"So, we're back to Sir?" Disappointment shaded his voice.

She peeked up at him. Confusion pinched his brow into a frown and then softened. She watched his chest rise with breath. She wanted to run out of the stall but didn't dare move.

"No, sir." She couldn't believe she'd just said it and slipped her hand over her mouth.

He stared for a moment, bit his bottom lip, chuckled, and said, "You can call me Erik. You have my permission, Anna." He exhaled. "I don't want you to be afraid of me."

"Yes, sir."

He burst into laughter and shook his head. "Anna. Please. I won't hurt you."

She almost said it again but stopped herself. Embarrassment flooded her cheeks with warmth. His laughter was infectious, and she smiled. "Thank you again. Thank you for rescuing us this morning."

"Ah, yes. You can thank Benit. He told us what Bishof was up to." Erik paused and groaned. "Bishof can be—is a little too zealous in his duties. He was only to help you hang the portrait and flags and ask you to put the book next to the Bible on the altar."

Annaleah stared at him with surprise. "Did you know about the order?"

"No. Not until Bishof showed the directive to Fellgeible at the convent." Erik shook his head. "I'm not privy to communications from Berlin unless they involve my care of the animals here at Janow." He turned, studying the aisleway. Two young women swept the dust and chaff from the hay and straw into a pile.

They immediately looked away. Annaleah knew just by their downcast eyes they'd been listening. Erik scowled, pressing his lips tight together.

"Come, Anna, walk with me. Let's see what trouble the horses have gotten into," he laughed. It was too loud, a show. Erik seemed to suspect they watched and reported everything they saw and heard. *To Bishof?* The ugliness of tyranny reared its beastly head—co-workers snitching on each other in hopes of gaining favors from their masters.

"Ladies," he acknowledged the girls as he passed by. He narrowed his eyes at them, a reprimand no one could miss. Sufficiently warned, they bowed slightly in deference. Annaleah could hear them whispering as she latched the stall door and sprinted a few steps to catch up to Dr. Erik. So, this is what life would be like under Nazi rule—each person isolated by fear and becoming sycophants from necessity. She felt sick.

Erik briskly led her to the apothecary and the door at the far end. He guided her through. Annaleah realized this led to his quarters, where she should never go. She gasped. Looking back at him, she hesitated. Trying to stop the panic pounding her from every angle, she stiffened and pulled her arms tight to her sides. She felt him gently slide his hand on her back and encourage her forward. She stepped across the threshold.

"These are my quarters. We can talk here where no one can hear us," he said. His voice was light, as if he thought the eavesdropping was harmless.

Annaleah wasn't so sure. Erik peeled off his overcoat and helped Anna from hers, hanging both on a coat tree by the door.

"Come in. Sit. I'll make some tea," he gestured to a tan sofa in front of a stone-and-mortar fireplace. The soft light from the waning fire chased away the outdoor chill but was too romantic to chase away her anxiety.

Annaleah sank to the edge of the cushions. Erik strolled to the small kitchen against a windowed wall, filled a kettle with water, and turned on the electric burner. He returned and threw several logs onto the remaining embers glowing in the hearth. He sat in one of the stuffed chairs at the end of the couch nearest her. It relieved some of her apprehension. She felt a little guilty knowing she attributed some of the stories the sisters told her about soldiers to Dr. Erik.

Dr. Erik looked at her as if trying to read her thoughts. "Bishof was wrong to frighten you at the convent. There is some disagreement between the Gestapo, the SS, and the more experienced officers in the Heer." He paused. "There is a German resistance movement."

She nodded and repositioned herself more comfortably in the cushions. "Do *you* hate the Jewish people?"

"No. Anna, I don't hate anyone. I haven't involved myself in politics. I don't understand most of this. The Jews were hardworking citizens in Germany—shopkeepers, professors, doctors, and other businessmen. They kept to themselves, but they never harmed anyone. It's as if the Nazis randomly chose the Jews to be scapegoats for the situation Germany found itself in after the Great War. And here we are again, invading other countries. They make the excuse that the territories used to belong to Germany, and we need living space."

"But Poland never belonged to Germany? Why Poland?"

"They said Poland attacked the Sender Gleiwitz Radio station on the border, and Poland started this war," Erik sucked in a deep breath.

"Do you believe it?"

"No one believes it. Most of us believe it was a false flag operation. An excuse to capture more land," Erik sighed heavily. "Major Fellgeible is certain they wanted the Polish farmlands and cheap labor. I know they wanted the horses." He stood and retrieved a small book from the shelves and brought it to her. It was written in German, but it was all about the Polish Arabian Bloodlines. There were pictures and charts of the prominent horses' family trees. Most charts were complete to at least eight generations, and some traced bloodlines back to the Arabian Desert.

"One of my professors gave this book to me so I'd be prepared before I boarded the train to come here." Erik sat beside her.

"Why would Hitler care about our horses?" Annaleah asked, tipping her head with curiosity.

"The Reich is collecting everything precious, art, sculptures, jewelry, gold, and diamonds. Arabian horses are considered 'living art' and some of Europe's most athletic racehorses. Though I've never seen the Führer on horseback, most world leaders who own horses ride Arabians. Kings have done so throughout history. Hitler wants to declare himself a world leader and a conquering hero. So he wants the Arabian Horses," Erik said.

"Do you think he's a hero?" Anna asked, staring into his eyes. She cringed when she thought of it. She even hated the man's picture.

"All war does is cause ruin and distress to people and animals. It's not heroic."

"Why are you telling me all this?" she asked.

Anna recognized Dr. Erik was in one of those moments of indecision. Should he say the words, or should he not? She knew exactly how he felt.

"I . . . I care for you, Anna. I don't want you to be afraid of me." A fleeting smile crossed his lips. The color flushing into his cheeks made his eyes the deepest turquoise, like the pictures she'd seen in city travel shops of tropical Island waters. She wanted to ask it but didn't dare. *Are you in love with me?* Nervously, she linked her fingers together.

"I need you to understand some things about me," Erik said. "Anna, I'm not a Nazi. I'm just a dairy farmer. My family owns a dairy farm near Bremen. Our nearest veterinarian was hours away, and no help in an emergency. My father and some men from our village collected money and paid for me to attend the university in Munich. I was sent when I was sixteen. As the eldest boy in our family, I was expected to do as my father asked."

"Did you want to be a veterinarian?" she asked, her lips parted as if his story was incredulous.

He sank back into the sofa cushions, resting his head against the back. He turned and gazed at her. "Yes. I have even imagined my life. My father promised to give me some land so I could build my house and clinic. I could help with our farm, marry, raise my children, and serve my neighbors. But the day I graduated, I was handed my conscription papers. My professors went to the Heer Board and convinced them I could better serve the Reich as a Veterinarian than a front-line soldier. My specialty was dairy cattle. They sent me here," Erik chuckled and shook his head.

"Not horses?"

"I learned all about horses and other animals, but my specialty was cattle."

Her feelings toward him softened once again. She understood the war had dashed his dreams, too.

"Do you miss your family?"

"Yes. I only had a few days with them before I had to come here."

"I never had a family. I made the horses my family." She laughed. "The sisters are family, and of course—the other children in the convent's care—but I don't think it's the same as a real mother and father," Anna explained, trying to make conversation.

Dr. Erik stared at her open-mouthed as if he had no words. The silence shattered when the tea kettle began to whistle. He sat forward and rose.

Feeling awkward, like a six-year-old child unsure of what to do, she was too intimidated to move. For a few moments, she watched the red-orange flames in the fireplace dance over the new logs. They crackled and popped in protest.

Annaleah analyzed the room, listening to the soft clatter of the China teacups and saucers being placed on a tray. She read the titles of some of the books of different sizes in the wooden bookcases surrounding the fireplace. They were all about animals and their treatment and care.

After setting the silver tray on the coffee table, Dr. Erik sat beside her again.

"Anna, do you mind if I ask a question?" He scooted to the sofa's edge and began to pour the tea.

"No, I don't mind." She joined him, offering to put a teaspoon of sugar in a cup for him. He had shared aspects of his life with her—maybe she could do the same.

"Do you know what happened to your parents?" He accepted the cup with the sugar in the bottom and filled it with tea, stirring slowly as he gave her his attention.

"Mother Superior said they both died of Influenza. First, my mother, just after giving birth to me. Then my father. Neighbors brought me to the Sisters of Mercy. I've lived here all my life." Anna sipped from the teacup. Looking over the rim, she could see empathy radiating from his eyes. She didn't need his pity. "I've had a very good life, Dr. Erik. You don't need to feel sorry for me," she said softly.

"I don't feel sorry for you," he replied. "I admire you."

"Me? Why?" she laughed.

"You read and speak five languages, have good relationships with the animals we work with, and are a very capable assistant. You seem to anticipate what I will need when treating our patients," he grinned.

"The nuns made us learn the languages. They insisted we'd need them. I hated the classes. My mind didn't want to learn it. I only speak Polish and German well. My French, Russian, and English suffer greatly." She shook her head, scooted to the edge of the sofa, lifted the teapot, and offered a refill to Dr. Erik. He lifted his palm, refusing. She poured herself another cup. The tea and fire had warmed her, and she felt comfortable again.

"Do you have someone waiting for you back home?" After she said it, she wondered why. Did she want there to be someone? The answer was 'no'—even though it was completely unfair.

Dr. Erik smiled and then bit his bottom lip. "No. I used to have a girl before I left for university, but she didn't wait for me to finish my studies. She never would've waited for me through this war."

"But Major Fellgeible has allowed the officers to bring their wives and families here," she said. "Surely—he would let you."

Erik chuckled. "When I find a woman who wants to be my wife, I'm sure he'll let her join me. Now, Anna. I'm going home over Christmas," he announced, all business. He changed the subject so brusquely, Anna was convinced their conversation had strayed to an uncomfortable place. "I'm changing our breeding schedule for the cattle, and I probably should do so for the horses. It is senseless to have babies in the cold winter when there's no pasture. If we breed so the calves and foals come in April and May, the spring grass with all its nutrients will be abundant—no more shivering babies."

"Yes. I always feel sorry for them," she said, and the thought almost brought back the chill.

"Major Fellgeible and I agree. I'm bringing back two yearling bulls for the dairy. My father has bred a line of bulls producing small calves for birthing ease. The calves gain weight quickly and are just as big at sale time as the winter stock," Erik explained.

Dr. Erik described his program, but she was just his assistant. Did he want her to concur with his plan? She nodded absently.

When he was in charge, Dr. Lesnik never asked her to be involved with the dairy operation. He'd hired experienced cattlemen to help him. The Blitzkrieg had changed everything. The Polish men had enlisted in the army to protect the homeland. And just before the Nazis arrived after the surrender, the remaining men went into hiding and joined the resistance. Almost all the work was left to Polish women like Annaleah. At least Major Fellgeible and Dr. Erik were humane. Dark rumors circulated about the labor camps. It was a constant threat hanging over their heads.

Dr. Erik ran the barns with legendary German efficiency. The forage and grain feedings were weighed and tailored to each animal's needs. The bedding straw was meted out and meticulously cleaned twice daily to conserve it. Nothing was wasted.

Carefully, Anna slid her empty teacup onto the table. When she looked up, Dr. Erik stared at her in his unsettling way. Indescribable emotions surged through her like being hit with walls of water from every direction. She liked and hated the feelings all at once.

Dr. Erik set his teacup next to hers, turned, and enclosed both of her hands in his. His skin was warm, slightly calloused, and rough like a man's hands should be. She suddenly felt small and feminine—but protected.

"Come with me, Anna. Help me bring back the bulls. In the meantime, you can meet my family. They would love to meet you. I've written them about how much you help me."

She couldn't speak. The battle inside her head exploded with rights and wrongs. Now, she wished she hadn't promised Jan she'd wait for him. Dr.

Erik was so handsome and considerate—and he made her feel like she was the heroine in a romance novel. The children at the orphanage expected her to help them with the Christmas play. But she could help Dr. Erik with the bulls; he needed her or wouldn't have asked. Lotnik's training could wait a few days.

"Come with me. You'll enjoy it. It will be fun."

Fun. Fun wasn't a word she'd thought about in a while.

Pulling a small book from his shirt pocket, he flipped to a page near the center. "After Christmas, we'll only have a week or two to prepare for foaling. Gisella will be at three-hundred-forty-five days on January 17th."

Once again, Anna was amazed at Dr. Erik's efficiency. He'd calculated the approximate due dates for each of their twenty pregnant mares.

"Am I wrong to ask?" Erik's voice was soft. Surprising her, he stood and gently tugged her to her feet. "Come with me."

Chapter Twenty-Five

GERARD LOOKED UP FROM THE typed pages and glanced at his watch. The three hours he'd allotted were gone. He stared at Karena.

"I don't want to stop reading, but I really must go. I can't expect Dr. Wilson to wait up for me any longer. Can we take this up tomorrow?" he asked.

"If you think I'm going to stop tonight, you're crazy!" Karena laughed.

Gerard shook his head. "I want to know what happens, too."

Karena touched his forearm. "Tomorrow?"

"Shall we go to dinner?"

"Sounds good. But I'm not sure I can get away with not packing this stuff another day. My mother will freak." Karena scooted away from the trunk on the floor, rose, and gestured to all the ribbons and trophies left to put in boxes. "Come on. I'll drive you home."

Gerard closed the binder and stood. He stretched.

"What's your schedule like tomorrow?" Karena asked, grabbing the bundle of letters tied in a blue satin bow he'd promised to translate from German to English.

"We have shots scheduled for a large cattle farm in the morning, but it is like a production line with the Squeeze Chutes. It goes pretty quickly. My only problem is that I never know what other emergencies will crop up. Dr. Wilson has a large practice. There's always something." He shrugged.

Karena dropped her hand to her side and tapped her fingers on her thigh. "I want to keep reading—but with you." She smiled.

"How about I pick you up around five? I'll have a letter or two translated by then. You can catch up reading the letters while I read the manuscript." He grinned. "I know you're going to keep reading tonight."

She pushed her lips forward in a pout, and they laughed. It was a silly conspiracy, but it gave them a reason to connect. She looked at his profile. Tall and handsome, he truly resembled the old, faded picture of his grandfather.

He traded her the manuscript for the bundle of letters.

"Let's put this in my room. I'll grab my car keys," Karena said. They headed for the door. After Gerard passed through, Karena turned to close the door. They were there again. The ghostly apparitions she'd seen the first day she'd entered this room. They were holding hands and gazing into each other's eyes like lovers do.

"Do you see that? Gerard, look!" Karena reached for his hand. He climbed the stairs beside her and peeked through the nearly closed door.

"What am I looking for?" he asked.

"The couple in the chairs by the window."

"I don't see anything." He lifted one corner of his mouth and scowled at her. "It's probably our reflections in the glass."

Karena opened the door all the way. The spirits she thought she'd seen were no longer there—they'd just faded away.

Chapter Twenty-Six

KARENA TOSSED THE CAR KEYS in the green glass bowl on the entry table in her grandmother's foyer. The house was dark. All the relatives had gone to bed. She removed her shoes and set them on the carpet by the door. Still, the wood floorboards in the entryway squeaked as she tiptoed across them.

The fragrance of the freshly baked cinnamon apple pie from dinner lingered in the air, and she breathed more in. Her digestive juices began to flow, so she detoured to the kitchen.

Granny A's kitchen was truly an 'Apple Pie' kitchen. The counters were covered with creamy granite. The white-painted cupboards had window pane-like glass fronts, showing off her neatly stacked Spode Churchill Blue Willow China. A red brick fireplace occupied the room's far end, and a round white farmhouse table and chairs were situated before it. The appliances were all sparkling clean. At least, her mother and the cousins had returned the kitchen to Granny A's pristine condition after cooking tonight's meal.

Karena wondered how Granny A had found living in America after suffering through the war. She was sorry she would never get to ask her questions. She sighed, wishing she'd gotten to know her grandmother more.

Karena opened the fridge and found one slice of pie in the glass plate covered with clear plastic wrap on the middle shelf. Either she ate it or one of the other relatives would.

She removed the pie from the shelf and set it on the kitchen table. "Ice cream. I want ice cream," she said to no one. A gallon tub of vanilla rested sideways on the freezer compartment's top shelf. She grabbed it.

"I'll split the remaining pie with you," her mother said.

She wheeled around to face her mom. *Crap. She's going to want the rundown on my date.*

"Sure, we can share," Karena said.

After heating the pie in the microwave and cutting it into two, Karena placed a slice on each plate. Mom dished out the vanilla ice cream and handed her two forks from a drawer. She placed them beside the plates, and they sat at the small kitchen table.

"Have you heard from Sam?" Mom asked, taking up her fork.

Karena knew the drill: her mother would go around to the back door rather than ask, 'How was your date?' first thing. Why take the easy way? "My date with Gerard was great. He's a really nice guy. And no, I haven't heard from Sam."

"So? Do you like him?" she asked, then ate another bite.

"Gerard? Yes. I like him a lot. He's interesting, has goals, and he's very handsome," Karena said. "But, what's the point? He's up here, and I'm in California when school starts again."

Karena took a bite of her pie. The cinnamon, apple, and vanilla threw a party in her mouth. Savoring the bite, Karena mused, it tasted just like she dreamed it would.

"So. I see you didn't get much of the attic's packing done. What were you and Gerard doing up there?" Mom tipped her head to the side and narrowed her eyes at Karena.

"Mom. Not what you think we were doing! I just met him," Karena protested.

"You were awfully quiet up there. I just want to make sure you're not getting yourself into trouble," Mom said, her brow wrinkled with concern.

Karena contemplated telling her mother the truth. What could it hurt? Maybe she could bargain with her to let her keep the manuscript. She decided against it. "We found some old letters written in German. Gerard was translating them for me."

"What did they say?" Mom asked, looking straight into Karena's eyes and lifting a piece of pie topped with ice cream to her mouth.

"Just stuff about horses and the war." Now, she'd done it. Karena had no idea what the letters would reveal. How would she explain if the letters didn't match her falsehood? And why lie in the first place when she didn't need to? She squirmed in her chair.

"I'd love to see the letters," Mom said.

"He's not done with them. He took them home to translate the rest for me," Karena quickly covered her tracks.

"I'm sure the relatives would love to hear them. It would be very interesting. You know, most of us always thought Granny A was a Nazi."

"Mom. She was Polish, not German. The Nazis hated the Polish people and enslaved them. In my history class, we learned they put two thousand Polish people a day into the concentration camps," Karena argued.

Her mother dropped her fork onto her plate. "Really?"

"Yes. Mom. Look it up. I'm not lying," Karena said with such intensity her mother sat back in her chair like she'd been slapped across the face. Karena thought *I'm not lying—on this point, anyway.* Guilt tickled at her insides. She stood, picked up the empty plates, and rinsed them, refusing to make eye contact with her mother as she worked. She even put the plates and silverware in the dishwasher, circumventing her mother's usual nagging.

"I'm going to bed, and you should too," Mom said, standing from the table. "It's going to be a long day, and we only have two left before the auctioneers arrive to take things to their warehouse."

"Aren't they holding the auction here?" Karena asked, surprised.

"No. The household auction will be next month."

"Do you mean we'll need to come back?" This fact changed things. Maybe she would get to see Gerard again. She smiled.

"I'd like to keep some of Grandpa George's things. So, I thought we could rent a car and drive home. What do you think?" Mom walked over and kissed Karena on the top of her head.

Karena shrugged.

"So yes. We'll come back. You don't have to, though. Dad and I can do it."

"I want to," she said quickly, then paused. "Did you even like Granny A?" Karena asked, turning to stare at her mother.

"I did like her. My brothers didn't. They resented her, even though she was always good to us—never the evil stepmother they pretended she was. And she dearly loved Grandpa George. She taught me to ride horses. When I was young, I was pretty enamored with horses—until high school and boys," She laughed.

Karena parted her lips in shock. "You rode horses?"

"Of course, I rode horses. You couldn't live here and not ride."

"But you never taught me?"

"You were so scared of them. You cried and cried when I took you to the barn." Mom laughed. "And your father didn't like horses or Granny A. He used to hang out with Martin and Ray, and they filled his head with their 'she's horse-crazy' garbage. I think they expected Dad to stay single for the rest of his life after our mother died. They didn't see what a lonely life it would be for him. And you should've seen Granny A when she was young. She stopped traffic. She was so pretty."

Karena bit her bottom lip. "I found the photo album, remember?" She couldn't let them see the manuscript now. They would curse her memory if they knew she'd had a crush on Dr. Erik. Her curiosity was piqued. She had to find out if Granny A and Dr. Erik were lovers. And if they were, what happened?

"Let's get to bed. We have a big day ahead of us," Karena said. She couldn't wait to dig into the manuscript concealed under her pillow.

Chapter Twenty-Seven

KARENA KISSED HER MOTHER'S CHEEK in the hallway and went into her room, locking the door behind her. Mom was getting far too nosey about what she and Gerard were up to. Gerard had followed Karena's wishes, but now she wondered if they should tell her mom the truth. She would eventually find out about Granny A's manuscript.

She flopped on her back across the double bed and reached for her Grandmother's work hidden under the left pillow. She rolled over, opened the binder, flipped to the page she and Gerard marked, and braced herself on her elbows.

December 5, 1939

It was a cold December morning, and Annaleah felt the chill through her layers of winter clothing. She tightened the wool scarf around her nose and mouth. The snow between the convent and barn had developed a crust overnight, and she crunched through to the powder below with each step. The stars twinkled brightly in the clear early morning sky—a contrast to earlier in the year when the smoke from the bombings filled the air. To the east, just on the horizon, a soft pink hue, like a watercolor, hinted at sunrise.

Dr. Erik wouldn't be there this morning. He'd gone with two soldiers to visit his family for the Christmas holidays and to collect the yearling bulls he hoped would upgrade the farm's dairy herd. She had turned down his offer to meet his family, using the orphanage's annual Christmas Pageant as her excuse. She'd explained she couldn't let the children down. They'd looked forward to the play all year, and so had she.

Her mind flashed back to the hours during the Blitz when the Stukas dive-bombed and razed the countryside with their wing-mounted machine guns. She shuddered. She'd kept the children calm by reminding them no matter what, God loved them. They sang hymns in the convent's under-ground basement and created the pageant costumes and props. The whole time, she'd prayed they all would survive.

She slid open the door to the stallion barn. The sweet smell of clean straw filled the air. The body heat from the horses warmed the barn by a couple of degrees compared to the outside, but it was still cold. Annaleah rubbed her gloved hands together, stimulating circulation.

She found herself looking for Dr. Erik. Annaleah hadn't expected to miss him, but she did. It left an unexpected ache in her heart. Over the past months, working with him day to day, she'd watched his compassion and empathy for people and animals in action.

He wasn't like most German soldiers she had the misfortune to encounter. The ones deployed in Biala often mocked and threatened her as she walked to and from the village market. Major Fellgeible wouldn't tolerate it if he knew, but she feared reporting the behavior would bring even worse repercussions.

Earlier, the morning crew fed the horses. Now, they cleaned stalls. Since Dr. Erik was gone, she had been assigned to ride his share of the horses and her own. It was a duty she thoroughly enjoyed.

The morning passed quickly, and she had only one horse left. She led the four-year-old stallion Opal, a beautiful Koheilan I son, to the indoor arena and mounted him for his daily exercise. Distracted, her thoughts constantly strayed to Dr. Erik and her confusion about the right path forward. She cared for Jan. She'd promised to wait for him. But Dr. Erik, not Jan, had been there to rescue her from Bishof and the Gestapo when they came calling. Even thinking it was unfair to Jan. She knew he had to stay on the run if he was to live and eventually free Poland from the grip of the Nazis.

Annaleah cued the stallion into the canter by touching her right leg behind her saddle's girth. She felt Opal shift his weight into his haunches and lift his forehand into a left lead. He was light as a dancer in her hands. She circled him to the left, straightened for only a second and changed leads. The stallion responded perfectly. She wondered if he would be ready to learn the Tempe Canter over the next few weeks. When they reached the far end of the arena, she allowed him to transition into a hand gallop. Opal loved to run, and it was a reward for him—and her. She loved the rhythm of her body moving with his, the cold wind against her cheeks, and the exhilaration of speed.

She collected the colt back to a canter and settled him into a calming walk. When she looked up, Major Fellgeible stood behind the arena's rail with Lieutenant Bishof. Her heart slammed up to her throat. The stallion sensed her fear. He skittered sideways in a half circle, eyeing the men. He bowed his neck and snorted a threat as they passed by the men. Opal started to prance nervously, rolling his tail over his back. Annaleah stroked his neck and softly spoke soothing words to him. He obeyed her but didn't relax. She knew he saw Bishof as she did—a threat.

When she asked him to stop, the stallion danced a few steps, but he allowed her to dismount. Quickly, she unbuckled the saddle's girth, removed it, and hung it over her forearm. She let the horse slip his head out of the bridle. The stallion dashed away, bucking and kicking out at his perceived enemy.

"Good morning, Anna," Major Fellgeible called out and motioned for her to come over to him.

"Good morning, sir." She bowed slightly, but her insides trembled. Had Bishof come to arrest her?

"You remember Lieutenant Bishof?"

A barely perceptible murmur left her lips. "Yes, sir." She couldn't meet Bishof's stare.

"He wondered if you would give him riding lessons," Fellgeible announced. The tone in his voice was harsh, disapproving. When she looked up, his lips were tight. If she read his body language correctly, he wanted her to refuse.

"I must get permission from Dr. Erik, sir," she answered. "Foaling will begin soon, which will mean many late nights for us."

"Ummm, indeed. Perhaps the lessons can start after foaling season." Barely a smile flashed across the Major's lips.

Bishof looked Annaleah up and down. She felt her skin crawl and shuddered in disgust. Dr. Erik had warned her about Bishof. His glower confirmed the warning was true.

"What's wrong with starting today?" Bishof queried. Annaleah forced courage into her spine and straightened from her submissive posture.

"I'm sorry, sir. We've exercised all the horses already this morning. Perhaps, tomorrow?" She walked forward and stood by the exit. Bishof rushed over and opened the gate for her. Forcing herself not to tremble, she stepped through.

Major Fellgeible lifted both eyebrows. "We begin at 6:00 AM," he said, almost as if he knew the hour would discourage Bishof.

"What about him?" Bishof pointed back at the Stallion. "Are you going to just leave him there in the arena?"

"Yes. We'll let him play for a few minutes. I'll put the tack away and come back for him," Annaleah said, adjusting the saddle on her arm.

"Do you mind if I tag along?" Bishof asked, nearly stumbling as he fought to keep up with her.

She glanced at Major Fellgeible, begging for help.

"Lieutenant, I believe you have other work to do? Tomorrow morning, then?" Fellgeible's tone was clear—it wasn't really a question.

Bishof glared, silent anger slipping out of him like sweat. But he had no choice. He was outranked. Finally, Bishof let it go and answered, "Tomorrow, then Fraulein." He turned, snapped the hated salute to Major Fellgeible, and briskly stomped out of the building.

Once through the tack room's door, Annaleah collapsed against the wall. She gasped in several consecutive breaths. Once she had collected herself, she placed the saddle on its designated rack, wiped down the snaffle bit with a cotton cloth, and hung the bridle in its place.

She gathered Opal's halter off its hook by his stall and returned to the arena to catch the colt. Major Fellgeible waited for her by the small man gate, a big grin on his face.

"Anna, which of the riding horses is the meanest, nastiest we have?" he asked.

Annaleah understood exactly where he was headed with his question. "Bruno, I believe, sir. But he's more—exuberant than nasty," she answered, stifling a smile of her own. The thought of Bishof getting dumped gave comic relief, but she dared not show it.

"Bruno. Ah, yes. Perfect."

"Sir?"

"Tomorrow morning, Lieutenant Bishof will begin his riding lessons on Bruno." He turned on his heel and walked toward his office. Annaleah could hear him chuckling all the way to the door.

Chapter Twenty-Nine

THE UNEXPECTED PATTER OF RAIN on the porch roof below her window drew Karena's attention away from her Grandmother's book. She had noticed the storm clouds at sunset, but they'd been predicted to move south and miss the farm. She rose, stretched, and walked over to her window, intending to shut it. The scent of summer rain swirled in the cool breeze whispering through the mesh screen. At first, she thought about sliding the glass closed but changed her mind.

A full moon, a harvest moon, darted in and out of the clouds billowing over the Bitterroots. A faraway flash of lightning branched across the sky, temporarily illuminating the pastures below the house. She heard the horses in the barn call softly to each other and then a distant rumble of thunder.

Karena thought of Gerard. Granny A had arranged for him to come here from Russia. She'd left money for his schooling, which couldn't be cheap—he planned to be a veterinarian—an eight-year degree. She found him a summer working internship with Dr. Wilson, which included a place to stay. Was Gerard the attentive grandson she never had? She chastised herself for being such a brat. There was nothing she could do about it now. Except see to it her book was never destroyed.

Karena turned and stared at the manuscript lying open on her bed. Quickly, she changed into her pajamas. After washing her face and brushing her teeth, she stacked the pillows against the headboard. She slipped beneath the covers and wriggled into a comfortable position. Karena picked up the manuscript and began to read.

December 19, 1939

As evening fell, Annaleah walked through the barn for one last check on the horses. The temperature outside the barns plummeted to below zero, and she wanted to ensure each horse wore the thick winter blankets they had made for them. They were all eating their evening ration of hay. She checked Lotnik by slipping her hand underneath his blanket. His body was toasty warm. Annaleah felt safe leaving him and the other horses.

Sliding the doors to the stallion barn closed, she felt uneasy and carefully scrutinized the landscape around her. The air was cold enough to cause her throat to ache, and her breath condensed into white puffs as they floated away. She wrapped her wool scarf around her head and covered her nose and mouth.

Would Bishof be lurking in the shadows, waiting to follow her wherever she went? Oh, how she wanted the carefree days back again. She pressed her lips tight together and held back tears.

Annaleah remembered her promise to Jan. Was it important to let him know Dr. Erik was away and Bishof would be taking a riding lesson in the morning? Should she walk to the prayer grotto and leave the message in the box in the hollow oak? Would the mundane day-to-day help the resistance in any way? She reached into her jacket pocket and felt the slip of paper she'd put there this morning.

A cold breeze danced through the trees at the edge of the woods, lifting snow from the tree branches. Like a playful child, it whirled the light powder skyward, let it go, and the crystals glittered to the ground like magic dust in the sun's waning rays. Annaleah decided.

She walked toward the grotto, occasionally turning in slow circles, ensuring she wasn't followed. Still not feeling safe, she made one last sweep before pulling the box from its secret place in the gnarly old oak. Annaleah put her 'yes' message inside and returned it. Once more, she observed the grounds around her. Briefly, she stopped and curtsied before the carved stone cross in front of an archway of bare tree branches.

From behind the center of the cross, the setting sun sent shafts of golden light into the sky. It seemed God answered yes to her silent prayer for protection for Jan, Nelek, the children at the convent, and for Dr. Erik. Pray for your enemies filled her mind. But was Dr. Erik really an enemy? She shook her head. She didn't want him to be.

Hurriedly, she walked toward the convent, taking the broader road instead of the deer path through the forest. Vespers would start soon, and she needed to get to the chapel, or Mother Superior would worry about her. She stopped short. In the distance, she could see Bishof's black sedan parked in front of the stone steps to the main door. Annaleah shrank back into the trees, trying to catch her breath. Oh, no. Had he seen her, trailed her, found the message in the tree?

She thought back. Her mind scoured every inch of the grotto, playing back her memories like a slow-motion film. There were no footprints along the road, and only one set, hers, in the forest. She reasoned, but it didn't slow her heartbeat.

Annaleah crept to the back of the dormitories. There was an entry for bringing firewood to the boilers. If the door wasn't locked, she could go through, strip away her outer clothes and pretend she was adding wood to the fire. The sisters would believe it. Would Bishof?

Annaleah stopped at the woodshed, loaded her arms with several logs and made her way to the entry. Taking a deep breath, whispering another silent prayer, she twisted the knob. It turned. She shouldered it open and quickly closed it behind her.

"Where is Annaleah?" Bishof's voice demanded. She heard his boots scuff along the concrete steps to the basement. Wrenching open the fire-box, Annaleah threw a log inside, watching the flames surround it hungrily.

"There you are," Mother Superior said as Annaleah turned. She had to come up with an excuse for not entering by the front door, even though they hadn't asked.

"Oh, yes. It's so cold I thought I'd bring in some extra firewood." She picked up the two remaining logs she'd brought with her and added them to the stack by the boiler. "Lieutenant Bishof, what brings you to our convent? Will you be attending Vespers with us?" Annaleah asked, forcing a fake innocence into her voice.

He looked down to the paver stones. A flush of shame or maybe just embarrassment colored his cheeks. Annaleah felt sick. Though she knew it wasn't reasonable, still she wondered if he knew about the note. But even if he did, how could he decipher the meaning of the word yes. It could mean a yes as an acceptance of God's will—an affirmation of a promise to pray or study the Bible. She could easily explain it away.

"I wanted a moment to talk to you. May we?" He gestured toward the stairs.

"You may use my office," Mother said. Annaleah swallowed her fear. He couldn't know about the messages. He couldn't.

Mother Superior led up the stairs, Annaleah went next, and Bishof followed. They passed by several sisters who were on their way to the chapel. They stared at Annaleah as if she were the one to bring evil upon them.

"You may leave us," Bishof said, addressing Mother. She bowed graciously and seemed to float from the room, the skirts of her habit barely skimming the stone floor. She pulled the door closed, but not all the way.

"Anna, please sit," he said. His tone frightened her. Had something happened to Dr. Erik or to Jan? He turned one of the chairs in front of Mother's desk to face the center of the room and began to pace.

She sank uncomfortably to the edge of the chair. The logs in the fireplace popped, and a shower of sparks hit the stone floor. Bishof rushed to stamp out the glowing embers and used the brass-handled brush from the poker stand beside the fireplace to shove the ashes back inside. He was as jittery as the youngest orphans in a lightning storm.

"How may I help you, sir?" Annaleah asked. She could hear her heart thumping in her chest. She rubbed her hands together to warm them as calmly as she could, then rested them on her thigh.

"I waited for you at the road, hoping to escort you home. Where did you go after you left the barn?" There was no menace in his voice, only concern. It surprised her.

"Oh. I sometimes walk along the creek to pray," she answered, peeking up to see if he bought her story.

He grabbed the other chair, scraped it across the stone, and set it facing her. He reached forward and covered her hands with his. "You mustn't go anywhere without an escort. It isn't safe."

His touch was unwelcome; she straightened but froze, unsure what to do. Annaleah felt her cheeks flush hot. Gently, she removed her hands from under his and stood. She walked over to the fireplace and stared into the flame. Hearing him move up beside her, she sidestepped. She wanted to run but knew it would make things worse.

"I've put a curfew in place, and I wouldn't want my men to assume you are a resistance fighter," he said with a small laugh.

"I understand, sir." The usual harshness left his face, but still, it wasn't a benevolent face. He was tall and strong, but his blue eyes were like ice. A cruel set to his jaw and turn to his mouth spoiled any handsomeness in his features. Dressed all in black, it seemed he wanted to intimidate.

"I thought I could make myself available and see you home in the evenings." He fumbled as he tried to take hold of her hand. She graciously moved away, feigning shyness.

"Oh, No. I couldn't ask you to do that. I'm sure you have more important things to do," she said softly. Every cell in her body wanted to rebel and flee. How could she tell Jan? How could she save her friends if this man accompanied her everywhere?

"It's not a problem, Fraulein. A beautiful young woman like you should be protected." This time, he slipped her hand in his and lifted it to his lips. He thought he flattered her, but she felt trapped. Her life became beyond her control. She fought to keep her face expressionless so he wouldn't see her disgust.

"I will explain our new arrangement to Dr. Erik when he arrives home. I'm sure he'll be grateful. He considers you a valuable assistant. Your safety is important to him." His grin curled only one side of his lips. Studying his face, she realized this wasn't about keeping her from harm. Instead, Bishof competed with Dr. Erik like a stallion fighting over a mare. Dr. Erik was more accomplished, respected by the villagers and farmers, and favored by Major Fellgeible. Perhaps Bishof recognized she and Dr. Erik were becoming friends.

"I will leave you now, Fraulein." He pressed her hand to his lips again. "I'm looking forward to our riding lesson tomorrow morning. "

She couldn't speak, only nodded.

"Good night, dear," he said.

After he left, Annaleah stood by the fire. Her hesitation about giving Bishof his riding lesson on Bruno vanished like a wisp of steam. Bruno wasn't a mean horse; he was just exuberant and liked to run. When he got going, an inexperienced rider couldn't stop him. They would usually fall off humiliated and never want to come back. Perhaps it was what Major Fellgeible wanted. She knew it was what she wanted.

Annaleah heard the tinkle of a pebble cascading against her window's glass. *Jan*, she thought. She had to tell him not to come anymore. Not until the war was over. They would have to find another way to communicate. She pulled her nightgown over her head. She had slipped into bed with it over her clothes to fool the sisters when they came through the dormitories for bed check.

She grabbed her boots and went to signal she was on her way down. The one shadowy figure waved his hand. Annaleah tip-toed down the stairs, through the stone corridor, and out the front door.

After pulling on her riding boots, she dashed down the stairs to the copse of trees by the creek. In the moonlit dark, an icy mist rose and swirled over the water flowing in the center of the stream. Annaleah didn't dare call out. Jan usually came forward to meet her. Instead of waiting for him, she crept deeper into the tangle of bare branches.

"Annaleah, over here." The whisper was throaty and low. Not Jan's voice. Was it a trap set by Bishof to catch her collaborating with the resistance? She hesitated. "Annaleah, it's Nelek."

Her old friend appeared beside a thick oak tree further ahead. Annaleah walked toward him, carefully stepping so she wouldn't snap any branches and call attention to herself.

"Nelek. What are you doing here? Where's Jan?" She asked when they were facing each other. He looked away from her. The moonlight filtering through the tree limbs highlighted the sadness and resolve in his eyes. "Nelek? What is it? What's wrong?" As she whispered the words, she felt dread seeping into her bones like a flood.

He didn't answer; he only reached for her. Pulling her close, he whispered, "Anna, Jan is—"

"Captured? Please. No." Her knees went weak, and she braced herself against his arms.

"No, Anna. Anna—how do I tell you this? How can I?" Nelek moaned.

"Tell me. You must." Deep down, she knew, even though she didn't want to accept it.

"Jan is dead. He has been killed."

She wanted to scream, but her voice left her. She was numb. "How? Where?" The tears began to flow. There was no holding them back. Annaleah's breath was ragged, and she trembled.

"The munitions factory at Lublin. We—we—it's completely destroyed. But Jan was shot. Anna, he didn't make it. He died in my arms." Nelek dropped to his knees in the snow, his whole body racked with sobs. "I couldn't save him. Anna, I—."

"No. Nelek. Not your fault. No." She crouched beside him and petted his hair. Encouraging him so he would stand, she wiped his tears, mixing them with her own. For a long time, they held each other as memories of the years of their childhood together flooded her mind. She remembered the day she promised to wait for Jan as he went off to fight. She remembered his kiss—clumsy, inexperienced, but sweet—her first kiss. "Oh, Jan. Jan," she groaned as helplessness surrounded her in black.

"He asked me to tell you he loved you more than life. Anna, he truly loved you." Nelek tipped her head, forcing her to look into his eyes. "I'm going to kill every Nazi I see," he growled, rage making his jaw tight. "I'll protect you, Anna. I promised."

She nodded. "You must go. Nelek, you must. The Gestapo has increased their patrols. You must stay alive. For Jan, we must survive."

Karena sat for a long time, staring ahead. A teardrop splashed on the page, and she closed the book, setting it beside her on the bed. She tossed back the covers and went to the window. Karena closed her eyes and let the cool breeze dry her tear-stained cheeks.

Granny A's life was hard. She walked on the edge as if jumping from one stone to another in the middle of a raging river. Lightning flashed, piercing the darkness. Karena opened her eyes. She clicked off the lamp by her bed and returned to stand by the window, watching the storm raging in the mountains.

Chapter Thirty

AFTER A FEW MINUTES, KARENA returned to bed. She couldn't stop reading now. She knew her grandmother had survived the war. Obviously. But what happened since Jan was out of the picture? Resuming her comfortable posture, propped up by pillows, she picked up the manuscript, took in a deep breath, and began reading again.

December 20, 1939

Erik removed his duffle from behind the seat of the transport truck, set it on the ground, closed and locked the truck's door. He stuffed the keys in his pants pocket. The new bulls were fed and settling in well, and he felt satisfied. They had survived their train ride and were strong and healthy. He would start his breeding program next August. He was anxious to try the new artificial insemination techniques he'd learned in Vet School. If successful, it would guarantee deliveries in May, avoiding the misery of calving in snow. This year, he wouldn't be so lucky; the calving and the foaling would start in earnest just after the first of the year. He shivered thinking about the cold and the many long nights ahead.

He lifted the duffle bag, positioned the strap over his shoulder, and slid the door to the equipment shed closed. Erik was tired, and his time with family too short to rest sufficiently.

The farm had been exactly as he remembered it. His father's strict attention to detail kept everything in top shape. The buildings and three rail fences were freshly painted white, and the milking parlors sparkling clean and sterile. As he walked with his father to choose the young bulls he'd take back with him to Janow, his father warned him not to talk about the war. Dieter and Bjorin, his younger brothers, were itching to see combat. Erik's father told him their school had demanded all boys join the Hitler Youth. Trying to be a good German, Erik's father allowed it, but not without reservations. His brothers had become Nazis.

While Erik was away at school, they had dutifully worked alongside their father, but maintaining the dairy was hard work and the routine boring. The leaders in the Hitler Youth Group filled their heads with dreams of honor and glory. They paraded in the village in their impeccably tailored uniforms every Saturday. His brothers assumed the war was glamorous.

After seeing the devastation firsthand, Erik knew war was misery. He had seen the Polish people turned into slaves in their own country. The soldiers brought starvation and brutality. Ruin followed in their wake.

His younger sister, Elsa, clung to him and followed him everywhere he went. She insisted on helping choose the bulls to take with him. He smiled at the memory. They had always been close. Elsa wanted to hear all about Anna. Was she pretty? Was she smart? Why didn't she come to meet the family? Did he love her? Were they going to marry? The barrage had started the minute he walked through the front door. His mother had obviously shared his letters.

He'd tried to explain Anna was just his assistant, but Elsa thought she knew better. She claimed his eyes sparkled when he mentioned Anna's name. He laughed it off, but when alone, he admitted to himself, he missed her. Terribly.

Erik had only been gone for ten days., but on his way to his quarters, he noticed the two Gestapo agents who always accompanied Bishof when he came to the stud farm. What was Bishof doing here? *Anna.*

He rushed to his quarters and threw his duffle inside the door. He briskly walked through the barns, searching for her.

Clara, Anna's best friend, stopped sweeping the barn aisle and smiled at him. "Dr. Erik. You're home. Are you looking for Annaleah?"

"Yes. I need her help," he said, squinting at his lie. Clara didn't seem to notice.

"She's giving Lieutenant Bishof a riding lesson in the arena." Clara leaned her weight against the broom.

"Thank you." He turned and jogged to the arena. As he entered, he noticed Major Fellgeible watching from the arena rail. Anna had Bruno on a fifteen-foot lunge line and instructed Bishof on what to do. With his face fixed in a grimace, Bishof looked terrified. Erik had started riding horses as a small boy, so he'd lost his fear. It looked silly on a grown man.

Erik stood next to the Major, saluted him, and breathed out a sigh of relief. "Thank you for being here to protect Anna, sir," he said, keeping his eyes fixed on the lesson.

"I hoped she wouldn't use the lunge line." Fellgeible flashed Erik a grin. Erik knew he detested Bishof. Fellgeible had confided in Erik he wanted to make peace with the Poles. They could easily assimilate into the German culture. He would do his duty. Fellgeible had spent his childhood in military boarding schools. Erik still thought of him as a proper Prussian Officer. But this war rankled him—aspects of it seemed so wrong. The Major didn't elaborate, but Erik silently agreed with him.

"Bruno can be unpredictable, sir." Erik frowned. He feared if Bruno pulled one of his usual stunts, Anna might be blamed for it. Bruno already flicked his ears warily. When Bishof's legs touched his sides, the horse ground the copper bit in his teeth—a clear sign of displeasure.

"I've watched Anna teach. She'll take it slow and easy. Bishof's impatience will get him into trouble." The Major glanced down to his watch. "It's been an hour, far long enough." He opened the man gate and stepped through. Erik knew he'd want Bishof gone as soon as possible.

"Well, Bishof, I think this is enough for a first lesson," Major Fellgeible announced in a commanding voice. "Captain Kemperman is back and needs your help, Anna."

Erik hadn't asked for her help. He couldn't protest; a great excuse to stop the lesson.

Bishof looked as though he wanted to protest, but the Major lowered his gaze, daring him to argue. Erik enjoyed Fellgeible keeping Bishof in line.

Anna glanced his way, and a smile barely curved her lips. Erik wondered. Was he mistaken, or had Anna's eyes lost their sparkle? She seemed sad. He whipped a stare at Bishof. Had the man taken advantage of his absence and threatened her somehow? He turned back to Anna, and when he tried to understand her demeanor, she looked away. His mind wandered to the worst case. Anger began to simmer in his core.

Anna walked to Bruno's head to steady him and exchanged the lunge line for a shorter lead rope, hanging the coiled lunge over her shoulder. She held the horse while Bishof dismounted. Bruno moved sideways as Bishof's right foot touched the ground. It knocked him off balance, and he nearly caught his left foot in the stirrup. Bishof hopped and stumbled away from the horse. He turned aggressively, hurtled toward the horse, and raised his hand to strike. Bruno's ears flattened to his skull.

"Nooo!" Anna raised her voice and shook her head. The horse bared his teeth and charged forward, yanking the lead line from her hands. Bishof staggered, tripped over his own feet, and landed on his back. A puff of dirt exploded into the air, covering Bishof's black clothes in brown dust. Bruno wasn't close enough to even touch him. It would have been comic had it not been so dangerous.

Erik vaulted over the arena railing in one leap, deflecting Bruno's attention from his intended victim. Raising both arms in the air, he chased Bruno away from Bishof. The gelding ran, snorting, bucking, and kicking out as if still fighting an enemy. Bishof wriggled to the fence rail like a snake.

"The horse should be shot!" Bishof yelled, wrestling his body to a stand. He snatched a Ruger from the holster at his waist and fumbled with the safety.

"No horses will be shot in my barn!" Major Fellgeible grabbed Bishof's hand from behind, disarming him before he could load the firing chamber. "Out of my barn. Now!"

Instantly, Fellgeible's adjutants were at the arena gate, ready to show Bishof forcefully out if need be. Erik was ready to remove Bishof from the barn if they hadn't arrived.

Bishof glared but slunk through the gate. Fellgeible released the magazine from the pistol's stock and pulled back the slide, making certain the Ruger's firing chamber was clear. He marched up to the Lieutenant and shoved the pistol at him. Fellgeible kept the magazine.

Erik turned his attention to Anna. She walked to the end of the arena to collect Bruno. He hurried and caught up to her.

"Are you all right, Anna?" She smiled and nodded but kept her gaze lowered to the ground.

"Can you look at me?" he asked, tipping his head toward her to make her look at him. He sighed. Bishof destroyed all civility between citizens and soldiers at every turn.

She lifted her chin, eyes closed, and took in a deep breath. Finally, she focused on Erik's face.

"Something's wrong. What is it, Anna? Can you tell me? Did Bishof do something to you?" The thought made hatred brew in his stomach. He knew how ruthless Bishof was from his school days.

"No." She shrugged. "He wants to *escort* me home in the evenings," she softly snorted an unhappy laugh. "And he insists on these riding lessons."

Her whole body was listless as if she had resigned herself to an ugly fate.

"No. I will escort you home," Erik persisted. "Did he touch you? Did he hurt you?" He tightened his lips.

"No, sir. He didn't touch me." Bruno walked over to her and lowered his head as if apologizing for his bad behavior. Stroking his face, she said, "Ah, Bruno. I know you thought you were protecting me." She took the lead rope dangling from the chin ring in his halter.

Erik looked at the horse and knew Anna was right. When Bishof raised his hand, Bruno thought he would hit her. He marveled at the incredible and deep bond she had with the horses. They walked from the arena in silence. Erik watched as she removed the tack from Bruno and handed it off to Clara. Anna turned Bruno loose in his stall.

She picked up a brush and waited in the doorway for the gelding to roll in the clean straw. Erik stepped beside her.

"Oh, I'm sorry. I forgot you needed me to help you. What do you need me to do, sir?" She turned to face him. Anna looked so vulnerable, helpless.

He wanted to hold her and protect her. He'd promised he wouldn't, but for a moment, he dreamed of tasting her kisses, and desire left him unbalanced and confused.

"Anna, I missed you." He was instantly aware of the other workers in the barn aisle. They almost froze in place and leaned in to hear what he said to her. He imagined them whispering behind their backs.

Erik didn't expect her reaction. She softly caught her breath and braced herself against the door jam like she anticipated his kiss. Maybe even wanted it, leaving him breathless. She shook her head and dashed into the stall, keeping Bruno between them. He followed her, staying on his side of the horse.

She started brushing Bruno's neck, avoiding the inevitable.

"Did you think of me at all?" Erik asked. He needed her to say 'yes.'

"Every day. You are my friend and in my prayers," she answered.

"You seem so sad today. Tell me what's wrong," he pressed.

"Please don't ask. It's just—I'm not feeling well. May I go home?" She seemed to be holding back, fighting through emotion, tearing her to pieces.

He wanted to say, 'no, you can't go.' But he couldn't. "Yes, you may. Clara can finish brushing Bruno. I'll walk with you in case Bishof is waiting." After motioning to Clara, he took the brush from Anna's hand. "Clara, can you finish grooming Bruno? Anna isn't feeling well. I'm sending her home."

Anna made her way past him, turning sideways and tightening her arms to her body so she wouldn't touch him. She stepped out of the stall. At the sliding door at the end of the barn, she grabbed her overcoat from the rack.

Erik started after her, but Clara stopped him, gently touching his arm. He turned. "Yes, Clara?"

"Be nice to her, Dr. Erik. Please," Clara said. "She learned just last night Jan, her betrothed, was killed in the fighting in Lublin."

"Oh, no," Erik groaned. He hesitated for a moment, unsure of what he should do. He knew about Jan. He'd watched him throw pebbles at Anna's window to get her to come down to him late at night. Jan was supposed to have been her lover—the very role Erik wanted to fill. But if Jan was her lover, he didn't play his part very well. Erik had wanted to displace him, just not this way. "Thank you for telling me," he said.

He watched Anna walk outside. He couldn't imagine leaving her to grieve alone. He glanced at Clara, nodded, and turned away.

Anna, he thought. He ran after her.

Chapter Thirty-One

ANNALEAH HEARD FOOTSTEPS CRUNCHING IN the snow behind her. Afraid it was Lieutenant Bishof, she quickly turned. While she waited, Dr. Erik briskly caught up with her as he grappled with his coat and gloves.

"Dr. Erik?" She felt relief flood over her. She had no desire to deal with Bishof anymore today.

"I promised I'd see you home," Erik said. "If you don't mind." His smile was hesitant, his eyes full of pity. Instantly, Anna knew Clara had told him about Jan. Guilt and shame grabbed at her heart with barbed fingers. "Are you okay?" he asked.

"I'm a horrible person. You should stay away from me," she answered. He touched her shoulder, making her want to turn back and face him.

"Well, that may be, but I'll walk with you now." With a soft chuckle, he enveloped her hand gently in his. Anna trudged in the deeper drifts, leading Erik on the deer trail to the prayer grotto.

"Is this a shortcut?" he asked, ducking under tree branches, knocking snow into his blond hair. He brushed it away and off the shoulders of his uniform coat.

"I want to walk by the creek. I do it when I need to pray."

"Because you're a bad person?" He asked it in a light tone, a smile on his face. The sort of smile intended to cheer her. Despite herself, she smiled back. "Clara told me about Jan. I'm so sorry."

"I know." She sighed.

"It's okay to cry." Tenderly, he wrapped his arms around her. Her strength failed, and the dam holding back her grief broke into pieces. Tears welled in her eyes, and she let go in Dr. Erik's strong embrace.

Annaleah let him hold her until she was overwhelmed with shame. She looked up into his eyes. No doubt about it, he made her feel cared for and protected. A new wave of guilt crashed over her. Dr. Erik seemed to read her.

He re-engaged her hand in his and led her through the trees to the bench under the gazebo. After sweeping all the snow away, he encouraged her to sit beside him. "Tell me why you think you are a terrible person."

"Oh, Dr. Erik, I didn't love Jan the way I should have." She dropped her head into her hands. Everything was so muddled. "We'd known each other since our first day at school. When he left for the war, it was such an emotional day. I said I'd wait, and I did wait, but I. . .I was never sure. . . ." she breathed in a ragged sob. "I am a dreadful woman."

"Anna, he died knowing you loved him and waited for him. He died happy," Dr. Erik slipped his arm around her shoulders. She slumped into him.

"You are so kind. You aren't like Bishof and the others." She sat forward. "I must go. I'm taking so much of your time."

He removed a glove and gently caressed her cheeks with his thumb, drying her tears. Dr. Erik stood and helped her to her feet. "I'll walk you the rest of the way. Once you are inside, lock the doors."

They didn't speak. Annaleah assumed Dr. Erik didn't know what to say. She never did either when someone lost a loved one.

The pale yellow winter sun kissed crystals in the snow, and they sparkled. Suddenly, she thought, *Jan is in heaven*. The fear, hatred, and worries of this world were no longer there for him. It was comforting to know.

"Anna, do you see the children?" Erik dropped her hand and dashed to the edge of the tree line along the pathway. She followed him. In the brambles, a small boy shivered with cold. His face was smudged with dirt, his clothes tattered and torn.

Instantly, she knew he was Jewish. Grabbing Erik's hand, she tugged him away. "Oh, let's go. They are just playing," Annaleah said quickly.

Erik frowned at her and resisted. "Come here, come out here, boy."

The boy stood, followed by a small dark-haired girl. Annaleah wanted to cry. They had heard about the convent and orphanage and had come for help. And now they were delivered into the hands of a German. Her heart ached, her mind scrambled for a way to save them.

Erik looked at her. "Anna, are these children from the orphanage?" He offered the means for their escape.

"Henrick, Carolina, what are you doing this far from the convent?" She called them by the first names that flashed into her mind and ushered them from the woods. "We should go back inside. It's too cold to play outside today." She reached for their hands. They were silent, their eyes wide as if intimidated by the German soldier. Annaleah, started to hustle them toward the convent.

She felt the weight of Dr. Erik's hand on her shoulder, stopping her. "Run along ahead, children," she said.

"Wait!" Dr. Erik called after them, and they stopped. "Bishof may be at the junction of the trail and the main road. He wants to walk you home, remember?" Staring at Annaleah, he motioned for the children to come back. "Is there another way to the convent? A back way?"

Annaleah felt her mouth drop open. She couldn't speak, only nodded.

"Come children, this way," he gestured. The girl was weak, and the deep snow hard for her to navigate. Erik crouched, "Here, I'll carry you." He patted his back over his shoulder. Anna watched as the girl did as he asked. "You know the way. Anna, you lead."

She grabbed the boy's hand. His fingers were so cold, she could feel it through her gloves. Ducking under some overarching tree branches, she took them along the creek until they reached the shed, where last night she'd gathered wood trying to escape Bishof's attention.

Two sisters were in the yard and tossed grain to the chickens, who quickly pecked the kernels from the snow. When the sisters saw Annaleah, they whispered to each other and rushed to her and the boy. They stopped when Erik emerged from the trees. He wore the hated German greatcoat. Surely, they were confused by him carrying the little girl piggy-back.

"Here, Sister Margarete, Sister Mary Elizabeta. Can you take Henrick and Carolina inside? It's too cold for them out here today." Annaleah said.

Erik helped the girl from his back, and obediently, both children ran to the nuns. They hustled them inside.

"Thank you for your help, Dr. Erik," Annaleah said, breathlessly. She trembled, but not from the cold. She started to walk away from him, not turning as she said goodbye. Annaleah feared her guilt about lying would give her away, and he would take the children.

Erik stepped in front of her, and she had to confront him. "You think I don't know, Anna. You can't fool me." He reached out and touched her arm. "I know Father Jerzak smuggles Jewish children to safety."

"No. He doesn't—he. . . ."

"Do you think I would turn him in—I would let babies fall into the hands of Bishof or the SS?" He frowned, his disappointment clear.

"But you risk. . . ?"

"Yes. I risk. I play dumb. How could I possibly know which children belong here and which do not?" He licked his lips and grinned. "I'm just a veterinarian. I know breeds of cattle and horses, not people."

"Does Major Fellgeible know?" She stared at him, hoping with all she had the Major remained in the dark.

"No. Not from me."

"But how do you know?"

"I told you, when I can't sleep, sometimes I walk," Erik said softly.

Annaleah considered him. The Norwegian and Dutch families had not reported any of the children Father Jerzak escorted to safety had been killed or captured. She knew he'd seen Jan with her at least once, but was it more? Did Dr. Erik know about the box in the old oak tree's hollow?

"You know I watched you with Jan once."

She did and nodded. She remembered the night he'd told her.

"I need you to understand I had nothing to do with putting down the uprising in Lublin," Erik said.

"How could you, possibly? You were away," she reasoned out loud.

"Jan was a foolish man. I would never have left you," Erik said it so empathically she wondered once again: *Are you in love with me?*

"Even if this was your country?" She pushed a strand of blonde hair back into her long braid. He protected her at his peril.

Erik seemed lost in thought. He looked over her head to the creek and beyond. When he glanced back at her, he smiled. "Anna, take as much time as you need to grieve. We will be fine at the barn. I'll even give Bishof his riding lessons."

Anna nodded, changed direction to walk away, but she paused. "Dr. Erik?"

He stopped and turned back, expectant. Annaleah ran to him, rolled up on her tiptoes, and kissed his cheek. "God will bless you. You are a good man."

She backed away and watched as he touched the back of his fingers to the place she had kissed. Annaleah spun and dashed to the dormitory.

Chapter Thirty-Two

ERIK WATCHED ANNALEAH DROP FROM sight as she descended the steps into the convent's basement. He closed his eyes and relived the rush he felt watching her come to him, standing close, and feeling her warm, velvety lips against his skin. His imagination wandered to a time when he would kiss her with all the passion he barely held in check. From the first day he met Anna, and she was assigned as his assistant, he'd been completely enamored.

Erik walked on the side of the main road. It was a shorter path back to the barn than the deer trail he'd earlier walked with Anna. Once back, he planned to take a quick stroll through the barns, then a light lunch in his quarters, and a much-needed nap.

For a little while, he had peace. There was little warmth in the late morning sun, but a cloudless sky permitted lemon-colored sparkles to dance off ice crystals in the snow on the side of the road as he walked along. The magic filled him with wonder and fueled his thoughts of Anna and love. He touched his cheek where she'd kissed him once again.

As he started through the archway under Janow's slate-tiled roofed clock tower, he saw Bishof waiting for him—an ambush he dreaded. The quiet nap he'd planned flew away like a crow from a barren wheat field. The man paced impatiently. Erik expected an earful. His right eyelid involuntarily twitched when he thought of having to listen to Bishof's complaints about Bruno and demands the horse be euthanized.

"Where have you been? I've been waiting for over an hour," Bishof whined.

Erik greeted him with a dismissive glance and decided to needle him. He knew Bishof was as obsessed with Annaleah as much as he was. "I walked Miss Sabrosky home. She wasn't feeling well. Why are you here? Don't you have better things to do?"

"I'm going to Biala for lunch and thought you'd like to join me. Major Fellgeible's brother is here to visit, and we could casually join them if we go now." Bishof removed his peaked cap and swiped a hand over his greased-down dark hair.

"Ah, I'd like to go, but I have work to do with Anna gone for the day." Erik smiled.

"Yes. Anna. She is a beauty," Bishof stated, then laughed, and poked Erik in the arm. "But a woman brought up by nuns is a cold fish, and there are plenty of hot-blooded fish in the sea." He guffawed, then lowered his brow, looking dark and evil. "We are the conquerors, the master race, and the Polish people belonged to us. They are spoils of war. We are entitled to do whatever we want. If you want Annaleah, take her. Take her, Erik. Major Fellgeible gave her to you."

"Gunther, you can't possibly believe I would rape her." Erik frowned at him. Though there were moments, he'd been tempted to give in to Bishof's endless cajoling. Erik could not. Anna would hate him for it. In his eyes, she wasn't a slave—a spoil of war. He wanted her to give her heart willingly. He wanted Anna to love him. He longed to make her his wife, his lover, his partner, and the mother of his children. She needed time to grieve the loss of Jan. Even if it was nearly impossible to wait, he would wait. And if she never loved him, he would graciously let her go.

"If she were given to me. . . ."

Erik gasped. The thought was too repulsive to allow in his mind. "Is this what you would want for your sister? Your mother?" Erik exclaimed, incredulous. "Anna was assigned to only help with my veterinary work."

"My mother and sister will always be safe." Bishof threw his head back and roared with laughter. "The world will bow to us. They know what we bring. They will submit to the Reich or suffer the consequences." He lowered his glare to Erik's eyes.

"You harm the people even if they submit, Gunther. They live in terror every day."

Bishof snorted, "You were always too soft. Go rescue some kittens."

Erik smiled angrily and straightened to his full height. He stepped forward into Bishof's space. Bishof backed up a step, and his face morphed into an expression of fear. *Intimidation works both ways*, Erik thought. "I would rather rescue kittens than do what you do."

"I will forget you said it because we went to university together. But say it again, and I will remember it all. Every word," Bishof said, but it was weak.

Erik knew the Gestapo wasn't above seizing German citizens, including German Veterinary Officers. He remembered his neighbor who had openly disagreed with the Reich. He was arrested, and his ashes were returned to his family in a wooden box.

Bishof, the sniveling coward, would only come back to arrest him in the middle of the night with force. Erik just wanted to get through this war, do his work here at the farm, and bring Anna home with him when it was all over.

A sly smile crossed Bishof's lips. "We can make a deal. Major Fellgeible's brother is here for a visit. You've met General Fellgeible. The General is in the Führer's inner circle, introduce me. If I get on his good side, no telling where I can go," Bishof said, his eyes glazing over with avarice. "They are having lunch in Biala."

Erik probed him. "A deal? And what do I get in return?" The ultimate brown-noser, Bishof would be lucky if the General even acknowledged him after an introduction.

"I won't bother Annaleah."

Erik sighed, then tipped his head to the side in acquiescence. At least he wouldn't have to listen to his threats, and he'd know Bishof wasn't at the convent, molesting Anna. "All right. Shall we?" He gestured for Bishof to lead the way.

Since Erik's last visit to Biala, The Horseman's Inn had become the army's favorite watering hole. The wooden tables and chairs inside were full of uniformed officers and soldiers. The proprietors, a Polish couple and their two daughters hustled between tables, delivering luncheon orders and foam-topped mugs of beer. It didn't take Erik long to see they were harried and terrified. The soldiers were verbally abusive, demanding, and downright rude. The ever-present threat of the labor camps, or worse, hung over the workers like an evil curse. Erik wished he hadn't agreed to come. He searched the room.

Major Fellgeible and his brother sat in the far corner of the overcrowded dining room by a floor-to-ceiling fireplace constructed of river rocks in varying shades of brown and gray. A robust fire crackled and popped behind an ornate wrought-iron screen. The one cheerful note in the room—the fireplace mantel was decorated with a Christmas garland of fresh pine boughs and garnished with red and green glass ornaments reflecting the firelight.

When the Major noticed Erik, he motioned to him to join them.

Annaleah crossed the colt pasture to the barns. The sun had lowered in the sky, and soon, sunset would color the clouds in coppery pink. She felt bad she'd shirked her duties today to escape Lieutenant Bishof's unwanted attention.

She found Clara and the other women preparing their carts for the evening feeding, and jumped right in to help.

"What are you doing here?" Clara asked in a whisper. "You should stay home while you can."

"I've been assigned to help Dr. Erik and must fulfill my duty. Or he may send me to the labor camps."

"Dr. Erik? Send you to the camps? Oh, Anna, everyone knows he's in love with you." Clara giggled and hushed quickly as several older women entered the feed room. They glared at them with disapproval. "It's written all over his face whenever he looks at you."

"Don't say such things," Anna leaned in so only Clara could hear. She pushed the cart closer to the grain bins and shoveled oats into a big barrel. "If they hear you and believe you, I will be punished for it. I don't encourage his attention. I don't want it." Though she said it emphatically, it wasn't exactly true. What she felt for him was still a mixture of confusion, fear, love, and desire. Too frightened to protest, she kept silent when he took her hand in his. She'd seen what happened to the other barn girls when they refused the advances of German soldiers. At times, like earlier this morning, it felt natural, as if her hand belonged in Erik's.

"He's so handsome, Anna. You're lucky," Clara snickered again, peeled hay flakes from a bale, and set them in a neat stack on the cart.

"He's German, Clara," Annaleah murmured.

"But he's very nice to all of us," Clara reminded her.

"He does love the horses and isn't harsh with them. I think he's a good veterinarian," Anna said. "I don't hate him."

"He's a good doctor! Anna, you've seen how many farmers and villagers come to him for help now." Clara stacked another bundle of hay flakes on their cart. "Even Mrs. Malernoski." Clara stuck her tongue out at the old woman who moved her cart closer to them so she could hear their conversation. She grumbled and waved her hand at them in dismissal.

"Clara, I can't believe you shunned Mrs. Malernoski. You are so bad." Anna quickly rolled the cart out of the feed room into the Mare Barn, laughing.

"Snoopy, old bat! She just wants to hear what's going on with Dr. Erik and you so she can manufacture some gossip," Clara scooped some oats into a bucket and carried it to the first stall in the aisle. They moved to the next stall when she returned.

"She wants to hear about Dr. Erik because he saved Caterina and her baby. He's the only medical help we have anymore." Annaleah felt all the humor of the moment drain away. She wanted to disappear and certainly not to be the subject of the older women's gossip. She put the first flake of hay in a tub and weighed it on the scale Dr. Erik had set up for them.

"I told him about Jan," Clara said. She cringed away from Anna.

"I know," Anna breathed out heavily.

"I didn't mean you any harm."

"Of course you didn't." Jan was gone. He had sacrificed his life for Poland. She was the most selfish woman in the world—wondering about a man she should never love. Jan must be whirling circles in his grave. She shook her head, sighed deeply, and handed the basket of hay to Clara to feed.

As she hung the next basket to weigh, Major Fellgeible slid open the barn doors, joined by his brother. Annaleah, Clara, and the other feeders scurried to form a line for inspection as they were supposed to do.

"At ease, ladies," The Major said. They each took a side step as they were taught. "This is my brother. General Fellgeible. He will be with us for several days. So expect him to be around the horses." As he walked by the women, they curtsied. But a sense of fear rippled like a wave through the line.

Dr. Erik entered the barn, sliding the door closed behind him. He caught up to his superiors, and his presence alone caused the fear to subside. Anna dared to lift her gaze to his face. He gifted her with a small but tender smile. *Did he love her? Did he really?* She couldn't hold on to doubt any longer. It was overwhelming, inappropriate, and much too soon after Jan's passing—but she felt warmth flush all over her body. She thought she loved him, too, and didn't know what to do about it.

The Major and his brother moved on. Dr. Erik stayed behind. The women quickly returned to their chores.

"Anna, are you feeling better?" he asked.

Anna perused each face around her. The women and girls were all listening, studying her, and it seemed dying to be the first with the latest gossip. She bit her bottom lip.

"Yes, sir," she dropped her gaze to the floor. *How do I walk this tightrope? If they've noticed his feelings for me, will they ferret out my feelings for him?*

"I must inspect the feeding, walk with me," he said.

"Yes, sir." She could barely control her feelings. She had fully admitted them to herself. Even walking with him, made her want to blush. She handed Clara the empty hay tub and noted Clara's 'see-I-told-you-smile.'

Anna followed slightly behind him as Erik strolled to the stallion barn. He looked behind him and slowed.

"Looks like they've finished in here," he said. She could see he wanted to say more, but for some reason, he held back. "I'm glad you're feeling better. I wanted to tell you Lieutenant Bishof has given up on his riding lessons." Erik grinned.

The barn was empty, clean-swept, and the only sound was of horses eating their dinner hay.

"Oh, good. Bruno isn't the best lesson horse. I would've chosen Galina." Not knowing what else to say, she pressed her lips tight together.

"You won't have to worry about him anymore," Erik said, walking into Lotnik's stall. He seemed to know she felt safe there. She moved to the opposite side of the horse and began to stroke the horse's silky neck.

Adjusting his winter blanket, she said, "Thank you, again, for saving me, sir."

He breathed out and gazed at her with unmistakable longing. Anna knew she reflected it back to him, as if he looked into a mirror. Inside, she trembled.

"Anna—." He walked to her side of the horse. Staring down into her eyes, he said, "I protect you from Bishof, but who is going to protect you from me?"

She tipped her chin slightly, he bent forward and his lips barely touched hers. So, soft, so tender, so heady, so deliciously exciting. Surrendering to this man's kisses was the next thing to heaven.

Chapter Thirty-Three

ERIK PRESSED HIS FOREHEAD AGAINST Anna's, trying to keep his desire under control. Bishof's words: *You want her, just take her,* flashed in his mind. He stifled it, even though a wave of longing swamped him again, and the temptation was almost more than he could withstand. He kissed her, making a connection he never wanted to break. But Lotnik helped him out of his dilemma. The colt stuck his muzzle against their cheeks as if wanting to get in on the action.

"Hey," Erik laughed, and Anna did too. She held the colt's face by placing a palm on either side of his jowls and kissed him on the tip of his nose. The colt seemed satisfied. Erik understood completely and stroked his neck.

"I guess he's jealous," she said. Erik noticed color race into her skin as she backed away. She'd changed from a woman in love, back to a frightened girl. But she couldn't take it back. He'd seen it. She loved him.

"Anna, I love you," Erik said, softly.

"I think. . . ." She paused, and he anticipated the same words returned. "I think I should go, now," she replied, stepping behind the colt, as if for safety.

"Do you think I would hurt you?" Disappointed, he followed her.

"I don't know. I don't know what I think or what to do." She took in a breath and it caught in her throat.

"Could you love me, Anna? Even a little?" He reached for her, and Lotnik helped. He gently nudged her forward into Erik's arms. "See, Lotnik wants you to love me."

"I do love you. God help me, I shouldn't, but I do love you," she said. He had empathy for her pain, but he could see their future now. It was clear in his mind.

Anna's eyes welled with tears, and he brought her against his chest. "Don't cry. We love each other, it's a good thing, isn't it?" he asked, petting her hair.

"If we had met somewhere else, at another time, not in this war, loving each other would have been good. But here we are. You know we'll be hated by your people and mine?"

Anna was truly a grown woman, a very wise woman. He wished, though, she hadn't thrown reality in his face. He wanted the dream. Sure, he knew it wouldn't be easy. But his friends and family would love her as much as he did. He'd worked hard to make the Polish villagers and farmers more accepting of him. In time, they would.

"Then we won't tell anyone. We can keep it secret." He tipped his head, pleading for a chance.

She quietly laughed as if what he said was ironic. "Clara told me everyone knows you're in love with me. Your secret is already out in the open."

"Ahhh," he groaned. "I must really be in love," he smiled to cheer her, then turned serious. "Anna, I want to marry you and take you home. We could have a good life."

"When I straightened Major Fellgeible's desk several days ago, I read the order from your Führer—German soldiers are not allowed to marry foreign women. I am Polish."

Erik laughed. "He can't control love. God meant for me to love you and for you to love me. I won't obey that order." He shook his head.

Anna gasped. "Dr. Erik, you must. They will arrest you and send you away." She closed her eyes as if trying to shut out the thought. He lifted her chin and pressed his lips against hers again, kissing her deeply.

"No more. No more kisses tonight," Erik blew out a breath, stepped back, gaining control of his body. Anna looked up at him, dreamy-eyed and yet confused. "I don't want to stop, but—I must, I'll go too far. I'll walk you home, now."

She nodded in agreement.

Erik slid the barn door open just enough to squeeze through, keeping Anna behind him. He could see the lights in the main house dining room spilling through the windows, creating square pane shadows across the snow. Occasional raucous laughter erupted from the diners inside. Erik should have been there, but no one had come looking for him. They were safe for now.

The mare and stallion barns were closed and quiet. The Polish workers had gone home.

Erik pulled Anna through the opening, shut it, and crept along in the shadow of the equipment shed. Until he figured out what to do, he would keep their love affair under wraps. He led her past the hay barn to the colt pasture. He quickly climbed the fence and helped her over. They dashed, hand in hand, for the deer trail through the forest.

Once at the prayer grotto, he grabbed her, lifted her from the ground, and spun with her. She felt perfect in his arms. He set her down, but didn't let go.

"No one saw us. We're safe." He laughed. Anna did try, but Erik could tell any happiness she felt was overshadowed. He tried chasing the fear away with kisses. "Is it too soon? I can't help myself."

"No," she whispered. "Erik, I want to love you. I'm just afraid—of everything."

"With time, it will change. I will take care of you. You'll see," he said.

Anna smiled. She reached for his hands and tugged him to walk toward the convent. He resisted. If he could keep her here, he could stay lost in this bliss. Finally, he went along.

A half-moon rose above the Eastern horizon, and the stars began to appear against the darkening sky. They reached the convent and walked to the main door where a brand new snowman stood guard. Through the window panes, warm golden light spread across the snow.

"The children were busy today." Anna smiled. "They do love Christmas."

"I love your smile," he replied. Her shyness returned. He made her uncomfortable. "Too amorous?" he asked, wanting to please her.

"No. I like it," she said. "I should go in. Vespers is starting soon. Good night, Dr. Erik. Sleep well."

He shook his head. "No. You're my love, now. Kiss me."

She stood on her tip-toes, and their lips met. He circled her waist with his arm and pulled her tight. Every cell in his body exploded with passion. Anna was everything he'd ever dreamed of in a woman. He knew he had to let her go. When he did, she backed away from him. He drank in her every move, her every step. They both waited, gazing across the threshold until the door closed completely. Erik turned toward home.

What a day! What started as a disaster had turned into the answer to his prayers. Anna loved him. Nothing could be better.

He chuckled as he remembered Bishof's clumsy riding lesson. And his ridiculous attempt to gain General Fellgeible's favor.

The General clearly saw him as a sniveling sycophant. Perhaps the Major already warned his brother. Every time Bishof spoke or tried to glorify the Führer, the General returned an irritated half-smile, dismissing his comments as drivel. However, the General did let Bishof purchase two bottles of expensive French Champagne—as if he enjoyed taking advantage of a fool.

Erik wondered if the two glasses of champagne had contributed to his behavior with Anna. If it did, it had only whisked away his inhibitions. He'd wanted to kiss her on the first day he met her. He kicked at the powdery snow along the side of the road. He felt like a kid, finding Christmas had come early.

Anna was right to worry. The Führer had issued the order the soldiers were not to get involved with or marry foreign women. In her shyness, she hadn't turned the page. The second page of the order spelled out the exception: If the woman looked as though she were of Aryan descent, Hitler would approve of the union on a case by case basis. Blue-eyed, blonde, Anna exceeded the Aryan ideal. Aryan? No. Anna was Angelic. Erik stopped for a moment and watched the moon rise through the snow-burdened tree branches. He wondered. *Why did he only notice the sky's beauty when he was in love?*

He laughed out loud. *She loves me, too.* Nothing else mattered.

Right then, Erik knew what he must do. He needed to find the Major and tell him he intended to marry Annaleah Sabrosky. It was the right thing, the only thing to do.

Karena sighed. They were in love. Granny A and Dr. Erik were truly in love. Gerard would enjoy reading this tomorrow. She slipped the bookmark between the pages and closed the binder. She tucked the manuscript under the pillow next to her and turned off her small reading lamp.

She closed her eyes, but sleep wouldn't come. She threw back the covers and walked over to her window. Pink and green lights danced across a dark blue sky full of stars. She'd forgotten her weather app had predicted the Aurora Borealis tonight. It was breathtaking. And she could see the whole Milky Way glittering behind it. She'd seen pictures, but this was, WOW. If she were in California, she wouldn't have been able to enjoy it. For a few minutes, she stood transfixed and watched the show.

Thoughts of Granny A intruded. Karena was sure being invaded in a war would make anyone grow up and fast, even if they didn't want to.

What happened? Granny A and Dr. Erik were in love; how and why did she end up here, in America and married to Grandpa George? How did Dr. Erik wind up in Russia?

She laughed to herself. *I've got to find out.* Karena climbed back under the covers, wriggled down to make reading more comfortable, and picked up the manuscript. She wasn't going to be able to sleep anyway. She read on.

Annaleah leaned back against the convent's wooden doors. She admitted to herself and confessed to Dr. Erik she was in love with him. She closed her eyes, reliving his kisses. The light in Mother Superior's office suddenly clicked on, and Mother stood in the doorway. The deep frown on her face let Anna know she was in for a lecture. Dr. Erik told her he loved her, and she wanted instead to enjoy it, even if it was only for a moment.

"Annaleah, please come sit down. I need to talk to you," Mother said. Her voice was soft but stern, letting Anna know she was in trouble.

"Yes, Mother," she bowed in deference and followed her into the office.

"Close the door, will you?"

"Yes, ma'am."

Mother slowly took a seat behind her imposing wooden desk. Anna remembered being sent here once at ten for being disruptive in class. She'd been assigned to scrub the floors in the great dining hall daily for a whole month. She recognized she wouldn't be punished now. She was grown. She was eighteen, but she imagined the lecture.

"I saw you outside with a German soldier, Anna," Mother said. Her expression wasn't anger, more deep concern.

"Yes, Ma'am. It was Dr. Erik. He walked me home," Anna replied, watching her expression change to alarm. Dr. Erik had been here several times to care for their animals when they needed help. All the sisters and orphans loved him.

"Dr. Erik?"

Anna couldn't say anything, she only nodded.

"He kissed you?"

Anna looked to the floor. "Yes, Ma'am."

Mother stood and came around the desk where Anna sat. "Oh, dear child," she slipped her arm around her shoulders. "Don't let him fool you. He is very handsome and charming, but he's still a soldier. They are lonely, away from home, and will seek comfort in a woman's arms. Did it go any further than kisses?"

"No. Ma'am." Annaleah could recite her earlier warning to the girls her age by heart. The soldiers will lie to you. Make promises they will never keep. Make love to you and leave you when you become with child.

"I never expected it of Dr. Erik, but he's a young man," she mumbled and sat in the chair next to Anna. She took hold of her hands. "Anna, you're grown now, and I can't tell you what to do. I can only warn you. Oh, dear. Stay away from the barn. For your own safety, don't go back there."

"I have to go to work. We depend on the money. We need what I earn since most of Biala's shopkeepers have fled or been arrested. There's no one to sell our goods." Anna sighed. "And there's no longer anyone to buy them." Anna remembered delivering their canned goods, lotions, and soaps to shopkeepers at least once a week, but now it was once a month or more.

"We must pray. God will provide another way. We must pray God will protect you." Mother squeezed her hands, and they bowed their heads together. Anna didn't protest. She was afraid of loving Dr. Erik—afraid of what would happen to them both.

Erik walked into the main house and started for the library, where the officers went to smoke cigars and sip brandy after dinner. He knew he'd missed the meal. It wasn't anything new; he often had an animal emergency whose care required him to miss dinner.

Magda, the Polish housekeeper, took his great coat and hat.

"Thank you," Erik said, smiling at her.

"No. Thank you, Dr. Erik. My hen is laying again," she replied. He brightened. He loved hearing his work helped a creature in need—in this case, both the hen and the person relying on her eggs.

"Very good." He held her free hand for a moment. "I better check in."

"I saved some dinner for you. I'll get it for you when you're ready to leave."

"Ahh, you are a jewel," he said as he pointed toward the library.

He opened the door and stepped inside, pushing the door until he heard the latch softly click.

"Captain Kemperman, we missed you at dinner," Major Fellgeible said, tossing the end of his cigar into the fire crackling behind a mesh screen. The four or five officers stood in front of the red brick fireplace, enjoying the warmth along with their brandy. The library was a lovely room. Dark wood bookshelves lined the walls, and the scent of tobacco and leather mingled in the air. Erik wasn't a smoker and found these after-dinner meetings a chore. He usually avoided the cigar and brandy crowd and escaped to his private quarters to read.

"How are all the animals tonight?" Fellgeible continued forward to greet him.

"Happily enjoying their dinner," Erik said. "Sir, may I speak with you—in private?"

Fellgeible tipped his head, raising his eyebrows, and gestured for Erik to lead into the hallway. "What is it, Erik? Not one of our stallions, I hope."

"No. Sir. It's about Annaleah Sabrosky, sir." Erik felt his whole insides go soft just mentioning her name. He smiled.

"Has Annaleah done something wrong? She is such an asset to the barn, but if she's upset you . . . ."

"No. Sir." Erik had to pause. He laughed inside. Yes. She'd upset him, but not in a bad way. "Sir, I—I want your permission to marry her," he said, quickly, dreading the answer.

Fellgeible grinned. "Ah, I wondered if you would become lovers." His smile faded to a frown. "The Führer wants to keep the German race pure. There are rules."

Erik chuckled. "She looks Aryan," he argued.

"She does, son." The Major answered. "But as an orphan, she may not have papers. Don't you know any sweet German girls?"

Erik realized his hopes were fading. He vowed to himself he would marry her anyway. Sanctioned or not. He lifted his chin. He was a man in love. He wanted Anna and no one else. The muscles in his jaw tightened.

Fellgeible must've read his expression. He rubbed a hand over his cheeks to his chin, scrutinizing him. "Lucky for you, my brother is here. He likes Annaleah. Very much. I'm sure he'll sign off on your request." The Major patted Erik on the shoulder, reassuring him. "Come by my office tomorrow after the morning feeding. Bring her with you."

"Yes, sir. Thank you, sir." Erik tried to remain stoic but couldn't keep the joy from igniting his smile.

"Shall we go drink a toast?" The Major asked.

Erik realized he hadn't formally asked Anna to marry him. She might say 'no'. "I still need permission from Father Jerzak."

"Do you want me to go with you in the morning?" Fellgeible asked. The offer was a good one. But the priest might give in out of fear.

"No. I think I should do this on my own," Erik said.

Chapter Thirty-Four

AFTER VESPERS, ANNA SLIPPED QUIETLY back to the prayer grotto. She had taken the long way through the woods bordering the creek, carefully walking in tracks already left in the snow.

General Fellgeible's presence at the barn this week reminded her of meeting him at the racetrack when they picked up Lotnik and the other missing horses from the evacuation. He talked about an enigma machine and rotors. Though she didn't know what it was or how it worked, she thought it might be of value to the resistance.

Guilt and shame fell on her, crushing her heart. Jan was gone. Though she'd never been sure a marriage between them would work, she had promised to wait. She insulted Jan's memory by allowing Dr. Erik to kiss her. But his kisses were so exciting. She melted in his arms and wanted more. When he said he wanted to marry her and take her home with him, she longed for it. She'd never felt this way about Jan. Her feelings were more ambivalent.

Mother Superior's talk had filled her with even more uncertainty. She'd added fear to the guilt and shame. Was Dr. Erik lying to her? Was he only homesick, confused by loneliness, and only wishing for comfort, as Mother said?

The day he delivered Caterina's baby, Dr. Erik changed from a hated occupation soldier to a wonderful one. He didn't betray Jan's midnight visits or Father Jerzak's midnight excursions rescuing Jewish children—he could have. Dr. Erik had always treated all the barn workers with respect. His declaration of love made her want to run from and run to him all at the same time.

Her duty to free her country, to stop the Nazi brutality, and her growing desire for Dr. Erik left her conflicted. Could she help the resistance, respect Jan's memory, and go home with Dr. Erik at the end of the war? Could she have both outcomes? There was no answer to this question.

First, looking carefully around her, she pulled the wooden box from the oak tree. She took the slip of paper reading 'yes' from her pocket and placed it inside. Anna paced back and forth in front of the gnarled trunk and, after a few minutes, returned the box to its place.

So she couldn't change her mind, she ran, stumbling in the snow, back to the convent. She slipped inside through the basement door, removed her boots, and crept to her room.

Annaleah had spent most of the last few hours sleeplessly tossing and turning. When she had finally drifted off, the sound of pebbles softly clattering down her window pane intruded into her dream. *Jan!* She sat up. But it wasn't Jan, he was dead. She squeezed her eyes shut and pulled the covers around her shoulders, but the small rocks tinkling against the glass sounded again.

She rose and crept to the window, trying to convince herself it was nothing. *Just a dream. Just a dream.* Below her, she saw a figure waiting in the shadow of the tree branches. She ducked away from the window, but whoever waited below saw her. A new round of pebbles bounced off the glass.

Quickly, she dressed and carried her boots down the stairs to the door at the end of the corridor. She slipped them on and stepped outside the convent's protection. Ducking through the bare branches, she made her way through the trees beside the creek. Nelek appeared from behind a gnarled oak trunk.

"Nelek, you're here," She huffed out in relief. But fear crept along her shoulders. Dr. Erik had told her about his midnight walks. Would he be walking tonight?

"You left me the message in the tree," he answered, his brow furrowed with confusion. "Now, with Jan gone, I didn't expect it."

"But you checked. I didn't expect you to answer so soon," Anna whispered.

"I have to tell you something, Anna. Don't be sad, okay? Many of us are escaping to Britain. We are going to volunteer to join the Royal Air Force. They are training pilots," Nelek said, his eyes sparkling in the moonlight. Anna knew he'd always dreamed of flying. Just then, she remembered him as the little boy, spreading his arms out and pretending to fly as he ran through the hay fields. "Jan would've wanted to go with me."

"How wonderful. You always wanted to learn to fly. Yes, Jan would've wanted to go, too. . . ," she said, losing her words. She fought to hold back tears.

"What did you want to tell me?" he asked, taking her hand and pulling her deeper into the trees.

She shook her head. "I—oh. The Major's brother, General Fellgeible, is here and I remembered something he said when we rescued Lotnik at the racetrack. I don't even know if it's important. I don't even know what it means. Have you heard of the German Enigma Machine?"

Nelek stepped back from her, shocked. He removed his black knit cap, smoothed his brown hair, and replaced it.

"Have you?" she repeated.

"Yes. It is a cryptography machine. It encodes messages. We've known about it since 1932. Our mathematicians cracked their codes and were able to read their messages early in 1933. We have built copies of their machines, 'Enigma Doubles.' We have promised to deliver them to our allies," Nelek said. "What do you know, Anna?" He grabbed her shoulders, forcing her to look at him.

"He said they added three more rotors." She shrugged.

Nelek gasped. "Oh, Anna." He slowly turned in a circle, then faced her. "Do you know what it means?"

"No." She shook her head and stared at him. "Does this help you?"

"Our calculations must be adjusted," Nelek mumbled.

"You must get this information to the Resistance. They will know what to do." Anna reached for his arm. "Won't they?"

"Anna, you must forget you heard this. Forget you told me. Forget everything. If the Germans find out, they will kill you after they've tortured you." He took both of her hands as if forcing her never to talk. She pulled one hand away and covered her mouth.

"Would it have saved Jan to know this?"

"No. Anna, you weren't responsible for Jan's death," Nelek pulled her into a hug. "I may never see you again, my dearest friend. Promise me, you will tell no one else what you have told me tonight."

"I won't tell anyone," she held back, trying to stifle a sob escaping her throat. "I hate this war."

"No tears, Anna. I can't bear your tears."

She quickly wiped them away and stood tall, pretending to be brave. She didn't feel brave.

Nelek kissed her cheek and, holding her hands, searched her face as if memorizing each contour. "Don't forget me, Anna." He let go, turned, and crossed the creek. From the other side, he waved. Nelek faded into a swirl of freezing mist.

Erik arrived at the convent. Even though it was early and still dark, he knew Father Jerzak, Mother Superior, and many of the sisters would be up and preparing for the day. He reached for the doorknob.

The door opened, and Father Jerzak stood in front of him.

"Dr. Erik, what can we do for you?" Father Jerzak asked, surprised.

"May I speak with you, Father?"

"Yes. Of course, son." The priest stepped back and motioned for Erik to pass through the open door. The long, wide corridor was barely lit by oil lanterns hanging from metal baskets where medieval torches used to go. Scorch marks had permanently blackened the stone behind the lamps. He could see the stairs he'd watched Annaleah ascend to the dormitories above. In the dim light, beautiful tapestries of knights on horseback decorated the walls between the newly placed swastika flags. *A desecration of the holy,* Erik thought and breathed out through clenched teeth.

Mother Superior appeared in the kitchen doorway, her eyes wide with alarm. He knew they had a forbidden radio. He'd heard it when he arrived in the corridor. It saddened him they believed he would or even could report them. But why should they trust him when most soldiers would gladly do them harm?

"I've come to speak with you about Annaleah," Erik said.

Mother stepped forward and ushered him into her office. Father Jerzak followed.

"Sit, please, sit," Father said.

As Erik sat in the spindle-backed wooden chair, the priest stirred the embers in the fireplace and added several logs.

"What has she done?" Mother Superior asked, her face pinched with dread.

"Nothing, nothing wrong," Erik replied, but he recognized his words didn't reassure them.

Mother Superior stepped behind her large wooden desk, and Father Jerzak edged behind her. Erik sat uncomfortably on the edge of his chair. He never meant to frighten them, but it was clear he had.

"I know Anna has no family. I didn't exactly know where to go," Erik fumbled. Father Jerzak and Mother Superior looked at each other. Erik knew his hesitation was being misconstrued. He grimaced, then smiled. "I've come to ask for your blessing. I'm asking you for Anna's hand in marriage."

Reverand Mother and Father Jerzak stared at each other, their mouths hanging open. Erik took in a breath. The sudden hush in the room left him feeling they would turn him away. It was almost as if they didn't dare breathe. "I love her very much," he added, hoping it would help.

"Son, are you Catholic?" Father Jerzak asked.

Erik smiled, relieved. "Yes, Father. I was raised in the church."

Again, the priest and nun shared a silent moment.

"Then you and Anna have agreed to raise your children in the church?" Father pulled a chair around, so the imposing desk loomed between them. He sat tall, as if attempting to assert dominance. Erik worried the Wehrmacht uniform gave him power he didn't have, or want, let alone feel.

Erik realized he hadn't formally asked Anna to marry him. He had imagined their life together; he knew there would be children, but he honestly hadn't thought so far ahead.

"Yes, sir," he answered.

Mother Superior reached forward and unlocked and opened a drawer. She retrieved a cloth pouch and set its contents on the top of the desk—a family Bible and a small blue velvet jewelry box. When Erik picked up the Bible, a stack of folded papers fell to the floor. After rescuing them from the cold stone, he reviewed them. A certificate establishing Anna's birth and baptism and a deed to some land were among them. He smiled. These were the very things he would need to submit to get approval for his marriage.

"Those are Anna's papers. I've kept them all these years for her," Mother said. "She has no money, other than this." She passed the jewelry box across the table to Erik.

He didn't open the box. It was Anna's; he would give it to her.

"Anna's family owned a farm outside of Danzig on the Baltic Sea. Do you know it?" Mother reported, looking up into Erik's eyes.

Did he know it? Yes. He knew it. The Treaty of Versailles gave Danzig free city status and Poland the duty to oversee it. Hitler invaded Poland to acquire the lucrative seaport in addition to taking the rich Polish farmland as Lebensraum and its people as slaves.

"Her cousins have maintained it for her. She was to receive it upon her marriage. But I'm not sure if it belongs to her or to Germany now," Mother said, becoming dour and sad.

Erik nodded. Inside, he felt a slow boil of anger. His homeland confiscated Anna's inheritance. He imagined some preening SS Officer living there now. It seemed so wrong.

"The jewelry inside the box was her mother's, a family heirloom," Mother continued. "She made me promise I would give it to Anna when she married."

Erik opened it. Inside was a delicate gold cross necklace. He looked up at Mother. "How did you keep this from Bishof?"

A sly smile briefly curved her lips. "Give her the necklace on her wedding day. Anna's mother loved her so much. It is her mother's blessing."

Erik nodded. He put the box in the pocket of his great coat.

Morning came too early. Anna stared at herself in the bathroom mirror. Her eyes were swollen and puffy from crying. She splashed more cold water on her face. After repeating it a few times, she looked almost acceptable. Hopefully, the walk to the barn in the cold morning air would take care of the rest. After feeding, she would ride her assigned horses. She could lose herself in the rhythm of their gaits and forget about her friends and the war.

She braided her hair, put on two pairs of long underwear, and doubled her socks. She pulled on her breeches, topping everything off with her thick wool coat and gloves. Planning to sneak by the kitchen, she carried her boots and tiptoed down the stone staircase.

Light from Mother's open office door brightened the end of the long main corridor. Mother was waiting for her. Dread seeped into every pore. She understood. Dr. Erik would make love to her and leave her to raise his child alone. According to Mother Superior, all soldiers were immoral. It was the way of the world.

Anna straightened and walked into the light from the office doorway. She looked inside. Dr. Erik stood from the chair in front of Mother's desk. He seemed surprised to see her but not nearly as surprised as she was to see him. Father Jerzak appeared, took her boots, and set them by the door. He gently reached for her hands and encouraged her into the room. Anna remembered her meeting with Nelek and drew back. Had Dr. Erik found out about her betrayal? Was she going to be arrested? Her whole body wanted her to turn away and run, but she couldn't move. If he recognized her fear, he would know she was guilty.

"Annaleah," Mother Superior's face glowed as if lit by a heavenly light. Confused by last night's lecture, Anna slowly stepped inside.

"Come in, dear girl," Mother said.

Anna looked first to Dr. Erik, then Father Jerzak and finally to Mother Superior for an answer, but found none in their expressions. They were all too happy for this to be an arrest. At least she hoped. She swallowed back her anxiety.

"Good morning," she offered weakly.

"Anna, Dr. Erik has come here to ask for your hand in marriage," Father said.

She stared at Erik. *Marriage?* So, he wasn't going to do what Mother suggested he would. Anna felt relief mixed with trepidation wash over her like a flood. *Is this how marriage was arranged for orphans?* Though she pulled her weight at the orphanage, they were probably happy to give her into someone else's care. Panic gripped her. And yet she knew she couldn't ask for a better husband—a better man. Dr. Erik was young, handsome, and infinitely kind.

"He has agreed to make certain your children are raised in the church," Father Jerzak said.

Children? Anna wasn't sure she was ready for children, especially after attending Caterina's difficult birth.

Erik's love radiated from his eyes. "I want to do this right."

Overwhelmed, Anna nodded.

"It'll be a Christmas wedding. All the children will want to participate. It will be so beautiful," Mother said.

"Christmas?" The holiday was only weeks away. Anna sank into the nearest chair, afraid her legs wouldn't hold her. "I must go feed the horses," she said, dazed.

"Not today." Erik's smile dazzled her. "We need to do some paperwork with Major Fellgeible, and then we are free for the rest of the day."

Father Jerzak placed his hands on her shoulders. "You and Dr. Erik have a lot to talk about. We will leave you."

He and Reverand Mother hurried from the room and closed the door behind them.

Chapter Thirty-Five

KARENA GLANCED AT HER DIGITAL clock on the nightstand by her bed. It was 3:37 AM. Oh, No! She had to try to sleep, or she'd be worthless all day. Mom expected her to help with breakfast by seven. She marked her place in the manuscript and turned to the pictures of Dr. Erik at the beginning of his introduction in the book. *What a handsome man!* She thought. And Gerard looked so much like him, clearly inheriting the best genes.

Karena's thoughts drifted to Gerard. He was tall, strong, and kind—just as Granny A described Dr. Erik. Gerard had real goals, unlike Sam, who only thought about surfing.

She wiggled down into the covers, leaving the book open beside her. She closed her eyes. Karena was furious with Sam. Four days apart and no phone call from him? Today, she'd call her best friend Janie and find out if Sam had been eaten by sharks or died trying to surf a tsunami. It would serve him right if she and Gerard fell in love. She sighed. Gerard falling in love with her, like his grandfather did with Granny A, seemed a much better thought to fall asleep with.

Karena woke to the sound of bird songs outside her window. She glanced at the clock—the bright red numbers read six thirty. With just enough time to shower and get ready for the day, Karena threw back the covers. She sat up to the edge of the bed and stopped. The manuscript was open to Erik's picture, and she couldn't stop staring at it. The gentle doctor, dressed in a white lab coat with a stethoscope hanging around his neck, smiled back at her.

Karena's mind wandered to her experiences here at the farm as a little girl. Granny A and Grandpa George seemed devoted to each other. She remembered them walking along together hand in hand and sharing adoring glances. They were the best of friends.

What happened to Granny A and Erik's love affair? Once again, the persistent question filled her thoughts and made her want to return under the covers and read. Could she pretend to be sick and stay in bed with the manuscript all day? The ruse would spoil her date with Gerard planned for the afternoon. Karena knew she needed to pack the attic. Her mother expected and deserved it.

Karena set her memories aside, quickly showered, and dressed. While looking in the mirror, she braided her long blonde hair. Her mind wandered to Gerard. What would life be like to be married to a hard-working veterinarian? Karena recognized she wasn't an animal lover like her grandmother had been. She found her grandmother's horses big and scary.

She shook her head. Thinking of marriage at this point was silly; she and Gerard hardly knew each other. Karena laughed at herself, slipped into her shoes and headed downstairs to help Mom in the kitchen.

Once outside the kitchen door, she heard Gerard's baritone and slight Russian accent. Luckily, she'd put on a touch of make-up before coming down stairs. She walked through the swinging door.

"Good morning," Mom greeted her. "Gerard is here for you."

Karena could see her mother's delight gleaming from her smile.

"Good morning, Gerard," Karena said, a little perplexed but cheerfully.

"Hi. I thought maybe you'd like to take a morning horseback ride. I don't have to work until tomorrow," Gerard beamed.

Oh, Lord! Didn't he remember how terrified she was of the horses?

"What a great idea," Mom chimed in, flipping the sizzling bacon in the skillet and filling the air with its delicious scent. "Don't worry about helping me with the relatives' breakfast. Aunt Helen will be down in a minute. Go have fun, you two."

"I should finish packing the attic," Karena protested.

"No. It's fine. I've finished my room. I'll do it," Mom said. Karena thought, *If she could shove me out the door, she would.*

"I can saddle a couple of horses, and we can ride in the arena until you're comfortable. You'll enjoy it. You'll see." Gerard tried to reassure her.

"Have you had breakfast? I can fix some eggs and toast real quick," Mom offered.

"Thank you, Mrs. Bradshaw," Gerard said. Mom refilled his coffee and set a clean mug for Karena in front of another chair at the table. Reluctantly, Karena sat down beside him. Mom did everything in her power to shove them together. Karena didn't mind too much, but she disliked how obvious her meddling was. Gerard didn't seem to mind.

As her mother started frying eggs at the stove, Gerard leaned toward Karena, opening up his jacket. Tucked away in an inside pocket, she could see the light blue envelopes of the letters Gerard had taken to translate last night. Karena nodded and grimaced as her mother turned from the stove and brought Gerard a plate of two sunny-side eggs, bacon, and toast.

For a fleeting moment, she wondered if she should tell her mother what they had found. It seemed ridiculous to keep it from her. But for some reason, the secret—their secret—provided her the opportunity to get to know Gerard better rather than pack. Meeting him had made this whole trip worthwhile.

Mom brought Karena her breakfast and sat with them at the table while they ate, sipping coffee.

"Well, we better get going, or we won't get to ride horses. I should help Mom a little today," Karena said, standing and picking up the plates. Gerard grabbed his toast as Karena carried them to the sink. She quickly rinsed the dishes and loaded them in the dishwasher. She couldn't let Gerard think she would leave all the work for her mother.

Gerard stood, his mouth full of the last of his toast wedge.

"I'll see you after your ride. Have fun," Mom said.

Gerard swallowed. "Thank you for breakfast, Mrs. Bradshaw."

"Let's go," Karena said impatiently. She grabbed Gerard's hand and pulled him from the room. The screen door to the porch slammed with a rattle behind them. Karena could only think about the letters. Since Gerard had translated them, she could discover what happened between Granny A and Dr. Erik. The mystery would be revealed.

"So? What do they say?" she asked as they descended the steps.

Gerard slowed and forced her to walk calmly on the path to the barn. "Your mother is watching us through the kitchen window. Besides, I'm not sure you should read them until I catch up to you in the manuscript." He slid open the door to the barn aisle. Karena breathed in the scent of fresh pine shavings. Her grandmother's barn never smelled like a barn.

"Don't tease me. I want to read them now."

"This afternoon, as planned. We trade. I get to read the manuscript while you read the letters." Gerard laughed.

Karena pursed her lips. What could she say? It was the bargain they'd made. "Okay," she said begrudgingly.

The horses were still eating their morning breakfast. Judy and Tammy, the two young ladies her grandmother had hired to care for her horses, were cleaning stalls at the end of the aisleway. They looked up and greeted Gerard with waves and big smiles. Karena realized she wasn't the only girl who found the vet assistant incredibly attractive.

"Morning, Judy, Tammy," Gerard said. He obviously knew them. Karena's stomach tightened with a twinge of jealousy she had no right to feel.

"Karena and I would like to take a horseback ride. I'll ride Aleksander, and I think Karena should start with Jadzia." He smiled. The girls agreed, nodding their consent. Karena wasn't sure she needed their consent and scowled. She was Granny A's granddaughter and one of the current heirs to the horses, at least until they were sold.

Judy handed her pitchfork to Tammy and retrieved a beautiful, satiny white horse from its stall. She led the horse to a grooming bay, and tied it in the cross-ties. Karena followed her.

Gerard brought out a tall, strong, chestnut-colored horse from his stall. Karena assumed he was Aleksander, making the silvery white one Jadzia. Judy brought a tray of brushes and combs from the tack room and set them on the half-wall between the grooming stalls.

"Thank you, Judy," Gerard said. "I'll saddle the horses, so I don't interrupt your work."

After Gerard helped Karena groom her mare, he showed her how to saddle the horse and tighten the cinch. Together, they brought their horses to the arena gate.

Karena felt embarrassed; she had no idea how to ride. Well, she wasn't genetically related to Granny A, after all. So, she wasn't automatically endowed with the horse-crazy gene. But Judy and Tammy didn't know. She noticed them standing on the opposite side of the arena, watching. And likely hoping she'd fall off like a clumsy novice.

Karena reached back into her memories of her grandmother and what she'd observed of her riding style. She climbed on the mounting block on the left side of her horse, lifted her right leg over the mare's back and sat on the saddle. She grabbed the saddle horn when the mare shifted her weight.

Gerard helped adjust the stirrups to fit her, and shortened the reins to the proper length. Karena sat tall, like she remembered her grandmother would. She remembered her light touch on the reins and mimicked it. Gerard mounted his horse and rode up next to her.

Karena asked her mare to walk forward with the softest squeeze on her sides with both legs. Expecting the worst, Karena closed her eyes and grabbed the saddle horn. Calmly, quietly, the mare obeyed her command. Karena breathed out in relief. After making one circle of the arena, she felt her fear subside. She imagined herself as Granny A on the back of her elegant mare. Karena glanced at Gerard riding beside her. He could easily qualify as the handsome and dashing German Captain, Erik Kemperman.

Chapter Thirty-Six

KARENA SAT QUIETLY ON THE porch, waiting for Gerard to arrive for their date. Rocking the white wicker porch swing back and forth, she looked out over the colors of the ranch below. New bright green grass sprouted in the field where, only days ago, the last bales of the second cutting of hay were moved into the storage barn. The pasture abutted a dark green patch of Ponderosa Pine, reaching to the cloudless blue sky. Karena's young cousins rode horses in the freshly tilled brown dirt in the outdoor arena. The fences surrounding each square looked like white stitching on a hand-sewn quilt.

Relaxed and comfortable, Karena breathed in the scent of earth, newly mowed grass, and the hint of pine carried on the warm afternoon breeze. It was beautiful here.

Earlier, she'd finished packing the attic and even helped Mom with the few things left in the empty back bedroom, and she felt good. She could spend time with Gerard and Granny A's book without a shred of guilt.

Karena looked at her watch. It was only 4:00, and she had an hour and a half before Gerard was due to arrive. Looking around, ensuring Mom and the relatives were nowhere near, Karena took the manuscript from under the throw blanket beside her on the swing. She turned to the page she'd bookmarked this morning and began to read.

Dr. Erik dropped to a knee in front of Annaleah's chair. She wanted to marry him but feared it all at the same time. Anna realized her hesitation made his usual confidence falter. It would be best if he didn't ask the question forming nervously on his lips.

"Anna." He gently reached for her hands. "Will you marry me?" His blue eyes were radiant with love. Was she lost in one of the romance novels she'd found at the library? He smiled, and she knew it was real. She wanted to melt into his arms, full of love and desire—but the war. The war made love desperate—impatient. And probably imprudent. She wanted to be swept away—to forget Poland was conquered.

She stood, scooting the chair away, and turned toward the fireplace. A log tumbled forward, and sparks showered and crackled against the backdrop of soot-stained stones. Anna watched until they settled in the ashes.

Erik followed her; she heard his footsteps and felt his hand lightly touch her shoulder.

"Anna, will you consider it?" His voice tensed with hurt. She didn't want to hurt him.

She wheeled to face him. "Maybe we can go to the same concentration camp. I am a forbidden foreign woman. I read the directive on Major Fellgeible's desk." Anna knew she was being unfair. Dr. Erik hadn't asked to be here. His government compelled him. And he didn't ask to love her, he just did, as she loved him. "Yes. I will marry you. I love you." Joy mixed with sadness, and it felt so strange. "I will go down this path with you. But I'm still afraid."

His whole body relaxed, and he pulled her close. She could hear his heartbeat, even through his thick uniform coat. "If they refuse to let us marry, we will run—all the way to America if we must," Erik whispered, his lips brushing softly against her hair. She looked up at him. He tenderly touched her lips with his fingertips and moaned as if overwhelmed with desire. Their lips met, and she surrendered to passion, immersing herself in all the sensations she had always longed to feel from a kiss.

"If we must run, Father Jerzak can help us," she said, softly laughing at the irony of a German soldier fleeing along with Jewish children. Erik picked her up and whirled with her as if they were dancing—his delight igniting hers.

"I adore you," he said. He lowered her easily until her feet touched the ground. He reached into a jacket pocket and took out a ring. "I bought this when I was home. I hope you like it." He reached for her left hand and slipped the ring onto her finger. Surprise swept through her.

Slowly, carefully, she looked at her hand. Now, she wore a ring—Erik's ring—a beautiful diamond centered between two sapphires that sparkled in the firelight. Anna was afraid to wear it. It looked too precious.

"Do you like it? Does it fit? We can resize it. If you don't, we can pick another." Erik smiled.

Anna stared at the ring on her finger. She'd never had anything so pretty. She threw her arms around Erik's neck, and he kissed her again.

"We need to go. We don't want to miss roll call, and we need to see Major Fellgeible," Erik said between kisses.

"We can't tell anyone," Anna said, stepping back, looking at the ring for a moment and then into Erik's eyes.

"Anna," Erik laughed. "We can tell everyone." He turned serious. "Are you so frightened?"

"Bishof will never let us marry." Anna remembered Bishof kissing her hand when he'd come to ask her to give him riding lessons, and she shuddered. Instinctively, she'd understood he wanted something more. Something she would never be able to give him. Everything about Bishof screamed he was jealous of Erik and was a vindictive little man.

"My sweet Anna, you worry too much," Erik said. "But if you'd feel safer, we can wait until we get the Führer's permission."

Anna nodded. "Will we get his permission?"

"The Führer is obsessed with racial purity. You look more Aryan than he does," Erik said with a laugh.

"You must keep this," Anna said pulling the ring off her finger and holding it out to him. "I have nowhere safe to keep it. If the Gestapo sees it, they will take it."

Erik frowned momentarily and then retrieved a small jewelry box from his great coat. "I was supposed to give this to you on our wedding day," he said. "I think it's better you have it now." He took the gold cross from its box. He threaded the chain through the ring. The cross and the ring hung together at the center. "It was your mother's. Mother Superior kept it for you as your mother's blessing."

He walked behind her, fastened the necklace around her neck, and turned her to face him.

"My mother?" Anna stared at the cross and ring together. They were beautiful together, a story of love and sacrifice. She held it against her palm and admired it.

Slowly, Erik unbuttoned the top collar of her blouse. The unexpected sensation of his touch made her flush warm all over, and she sighed.

"You are mine, now, Anna," he whispered. He slipped the necklace underneath the fabric. Anna felt the cool metal against her skin. "Wear my ring next to your heart, and remember I am yours."

The passion in his kiss left her breathless. He pressed his forehead against hers. "I could kiss you all day and all night," he said, briefly closing his eyes. "We need to go." Slipping his arm over her shoulders, he turned them to the door.

Anna felt so comfortable and safe with him. At long last, after these lonely eighteen years, she would have a real family of her own.

Karena closed the book and stood. "Mom!" she shouted. "Mom! Where is Granny A's jewelry box?"

She let the screen door slam behind her. Her mother appeared at the kitchen door, still in her apron. "What?"

"Granny A's jewelry box, where is it?"

"It's in her bedroom. Still on the dresser," Mom scowled at her. "What's this all about?"

Karena sprinted to the bedroom. When she arrived at the door, she scanned the room. The honey-colored light of late afternoon filtered through sheer curtains, giving the room an almost mystical appearance. She hadn't remembered the canopy bed. The gossamer mosquito netting looked like an ethereal mist. The jacquard quilted spread, in reds and golds, made the bed seem like the sleeping chamber of royalty.

She located the wooden jewelry box in the center of the ornate walnut dresser, bathed in a shaft of light as if her Grandmother wanted—no, needed her to find it.

"Karena?" Mom asked, catching up to her.

"Granny had a necklace—a gold cross necklace. Do you remember it? She had a ring—a small diamond with sapphires." Karena headed to the dresser, opened the box, and looked inside. There were a few rings and bracelets, but not the right ones. "Mom, I want her necklace. I don't want anything else of hers."

"I don't remember seeing it, Honey," Mom said. "Are you sure?"

Karena began picking up each piece and looking at it. Was it in the trunk upstairs? She knew she showed desperation.

Exasperated, Mom walked to her and lifted the ring tray portion of the box for her. Whenever Karena or Dad searched for something right in front of them, Mom rolled her eyes at them as she did now.

Underneath the tray, shining in the light, she found a gold cross, the diamond and sapphire ring, and a simple gold band on a delicate gold chain. She looked at her mother's face, took a trembling breath, and fought back tears.

Karena picked it up, threaded the chain through her fingers, and admired the cross and the rings dangling against her palm. She closed her hand around them and hugged them to her heart. "Oh, thank God."

"Karena, what is the matter with you? What's this all about?" Her mother's stern tone demanded. Karena stared hard at her mother. She wasn't ready to give her the answer.

Chapter Thirty-Seven

A GUILT BOMB EXPLODED ALL over Karena's plan to keep the manuscript secret. Looking at her mother's face, she hated herself for keeping Granny A's book from her.

"Karena?" Mom expected an answer and narrowed her eyes at Karena suspiciously.

"Gerard is coming up the driveway. Gotta go," Karena bolted through the screen door to the porch. She intentionally avoided telling her mom the truth.

Aunt Eveline was on the porch swing. She reached for the manuscript binder under the green checked throw blanket.

"Don't touch it! It's Gerard's Veterinary Notes!" Karena yelled.

"Real—ie?" Eveline slurred. *Oh! Boy! She had taken too many nips from her flask!* Karena rushed her and grabbed the binder before Eveline could get her grubby hands on it. But, in her haste, the binder's rings opened. A large chunk of pages plopped to the wooden deck. The last few pages seemed suspended in the air and drifted slowly down as they fluttered to the floor. Karena gasped.

"This isn't a veterinary journal," Eveline said, nearly incoherently. Leaning forward, she picked up some of the pages, straightened, and stood shakily. She lost her balance and sat heavily back down, causing the swing to sway back and forth.

Clutched in Eveline's hand, Granny A's picture with Jan and Nelek and the horses had become a wrinkled mess. And the jig was up. Karena snatched it from her, tearing one of the corners. She scooped up the rest from the deck, stuffing them haphazardly back into the binder.

"What's going on out here?" Mom asked, venturing outside because of the scuffle. Karena sighed and sank to the porch swing beside her tipsy aunt.

Karena watched the white veterinary truck snake up the long driveway to the house. Gerard was right on time, a character trait Sam didn't possess in his repertoire. She laughed out loud. *No hiding the book now.*

Mom stood in front of Karena with her hands on her hips. She shook her head with disappointment.

Karena took a deep breath and exhaled. "While packing the attic, I found this," she held the binder up, pages sticking out on all sides in disarray. "It's Granny A's—about her experience in World War II."

"Oh, who cares?" Eveline said, rising awkwardly from the swing. She exaggerated her disdain with a downward wave of her hand. She reached into her apron pocket, pulled out a silver flask, unscrewed the top, and took an unsteady swig. She wiped her mouth on her sleeve. Mom helped her keep her balance.

"Karena, I'm taking Eveline inside to bed. I want you right here when I come back. And I don't care if you have a date with Gerard. It's off." Mom displayed an angry calm, which Karena had always found terrifying. She secured the book on her lap. When Mom returned, Karena was certain she would be on restriction for the rest of their two weeks here. And maybe for the rest of her life.

As the gorgeous Russian arrived and parked by the porch's front steps, Karena looked at Granny A's necklace, still entwined around her fingers. At least nothing had happened to it in her fray with Aunt Eveline.

As Gerard stepped out of the truck, she smiled. He was one handsome guy. She fastened the necklace around her neck and dropped the cross and the rings down the front of her T-shirt.

The girls at school back home will drool over Gerard. Karena thought. She decided she'd needed to take pictures of him to enhance their jealousy of her *almost* late summer romance. Because after Mom lectured her tonight in front of him, she'd never see him again. He'd know what a terrible person she was.

"Hi," Gerard said cheerfully. She looked up at him and frowned dejectedly. His eyebrows automatically pinched together for a second. He was probably curious about her unhappy mood.

"Good evening, Gerard," Mom said, opening the screen. He stepped over to hold it for her. "Karena won't be able to join you for dinner tonight," Mom said loudly, narrowed her eyes and glared at her daughter. Karena shrank down further in her chair. Gerard glanced her way, his face a total question mark.

Karena shrugged and started to straighten the manuscript's pages.

"Would you like to explain this to Gerard, Karena?" Mom continued.

"I tried to keep Granny A's manuscript a secret because I feared you and the relatives would throw it away," Karena explained. Mom sat down beside her, and Karena handed the binder to her. Gerard pulled up a chair. He leaned forward, his elbows on his knees.

"We were reading it together, Mrs. Bradshaw. We wanted to finish before we told anyone about it," Gerard said. He tried to soften the consequences for her.

"You were in on this?" Mom cast a sideways glance his way, a scowl on her lips.

"Well . . . ." He grimaced.

"No. He wasn't. It was all my idea. I started reading the book and didn't want to share it yet," Karena sighed. "It's all my fault."

"This is what you've been sneaking around and hiding about?" Mom asked, both eyebrows lifted. She laughed. "Karena, Granny A told me about writing a novel years ago. Just after Grandpa George died, so, all your clandestine activities were for nothing."

"Well, not all for nothing. What would Aunt Helen and Aunt Eveline want to do with the book? Throw it in the fire." Karena explored her mother's relaxed face. Karena knew she'd hit her point with precision.

"No. I won't allow it, Honey. Granny A asked me to help her find out if a friend of hers, Erik Kemperman, was dead or alive. She knew your father had government connections." Mom placed her hand on Karena's knee.

"Erik Kemperman was my grandfather," Gerard said, a faraway look clouding his eyes.

"Oh, my goodness. Granny A found him? She sent for you and hooked you up with Dr. Wilson. I understand now. They must've been very good friends," Mom said.

Gerard and Karena shared a glance. Karena shook her head so only Gerard could see. *Don't tell her they were lovers. Don't.* She thought.

"I tell you what. Why don't you two finish reading the book? I'll go back and fix dinner. You'll stay for dinner, won't you, Gerard?"

"Yes, Ma'am."

"Then you can tell me all about it. I'll leave you for now." She smiled. Karena realized, once again, how much her mother disliked Sam and had jumped overboard for Gerard.

Karena stood when her mother did, setting the manuscript on the porch swing. She threw her arms around her mother's neck and hugged her. "Thank you, Mom. It means a lot to me."

"I won't tell the others unless you want me to." Turning, she walked to the screen door and said, "The manuscript is our secret, and your date is back on."

After the screen door closed, Gerard rose and slid over to the porch swing, waiting for Karena to sit. "See how easy things are when you tell the truth?" He took Karena's hand and squeezed it.

Karena wrestled her hand free and pulled the necklace around her neck to the outside of her T-shirt, allowing Gerard to get a look.

"Tell the truth! Gerard, I didn't tell the whole truth," she said, lifting the chain so the necklace sparkled in the pink light of the sunset. "I think Granny A and Dr. Erik were married!"

Chapter Thirty-Eight

KARENA WATCHED GERARD'S CHEST RISE and fall with a big breath. He stood and took hold of her hand.

"Come, let's go somewhere we can talk in private," he said, pulling Karena to her feet.

"Where are you taking me?" She laughed, watching him retrieve the notebook containing Granny A's manuscript.

"Karena, I think they were married, too. But you must understand what happened at the end of the war to learn the whole truth. I don't want to skip any part of their story. Not even a word." He tugged at her, encouraging her down the steps.

"Are you kidnapping me?" she asked, giggling. "You'll miss my mom's great cooking."

"We won't go too far. I don't want to miss dinner."

Under the shade of the large maple tree, two Adirondack chairs and a two-person love seat were arranged around a metal and stone firepit. Gerard led her there. Karena suddenly imagined snuggling together on the love seat, arms touching, fingers entwined, as they read. A blush raced heat into her cheeks. She glanced at him, and his lips parted, exhaling as if he'd shared her thoughts. He paused and then pulled her to the loveseat.

"I think they wanted us to meet. Our grandparents wanted us to find the book," Gerard said. Karena nodded in agreement.

Gerard handed her the manuscript and sat next to her, placing his arm against hers just as she imagined. A fleeting thought crossed her mind. Karena wanted him to kiss her.

"So, give me the pages you read last night. I'll catch up, and we can read the rest together," he said.

"That wasn't our agreement." Karen tipped her head. "You were supposed to give me the letters."

"The letters! I forgot the letters. They are on the nightstand in my room. I was in such a hurry to get here." The way he looked down at his hands made Karena wonder if he told her a lie. A guilty smile stretched across his lips. "Forgive me?"

"It's okay. I can read them later," Karena reassured him, leaning against his side and dropping her head against his shoulder. She opened the binder, handed him the pages she'd read last night, and snapped the rings closed.

Rather than wait for Gerard to catch up, her gaze settled on the print on the next page.

Annaleah and Erik stepped out into the cold afternoon air. The sun hung low in the sky, muted by a frigid haze. As they walked to the barns, dense fog seeped up from the snow and swirled around them. Suddenly, Erik's mood matched the flat gray light. He was overwhelmed by a sense of foreboding. He had rushed her, insisting they marry right away. It had been impulsive, silly, not like him. Still, his second thoughts couldn't extinguish his desire. He had given in to his dreams of holding her and loving her. He acted. Now, he must somehow mitigate the consequences.

Erik turned toward her and took both her hands in his. He stopped. "I want to tell everyone. I want a big celebration—but we can't, Anna."

Fear seemed to ooze from Anna's every pore. Surely, she'd heard the rumors of the brutality, torture, starvation, and murder at the jail in Biala for those who broke the Reich's rules. Gossip was whispered daily through Janow's aisleways, permeating everything like this icy fog through the trees.

Erik didn't fear death. Like Anna, he believed in the Bible's promise of a new life in the presence of God awaited them. But torture and pain? Could he bear knowing he caused her torture and pain? All he wanted was to love her, to belong to her, and for her to belong to him.

"Until our marriage is sanctioned, we can tell no one."

Anna lifted her hand to his lips. "I understand."

Erik's smile collapsed into a frown when she looked at the bouquet Mother Superior had given her. She untied the blue satin bow from the stems and dropped the flowers, one by one, into the snow. Erik groaned. His mother had dried and kept her wedding bouquet in a special wooden box. As a child, he'd watched her open the box and daydream about it. Surely, Anna would've wanted to do the same. His impulsiveness had robbed her of the normal ceremonies and celebrations of marriage.

"When we get to the barn, I'll go into the hay barn and wait a few minutes. Act like nothing has changed. Go to the apothecary and start the autoclave, as usual. When the feeding crew has left for the day, wait for me in my quarters."

"I hate this war," she murmured.

"But I wouldn't have found you if not for the war," Erik said. *What have I done?* He didn't say it out loud. Even if their marriage received the Führer's blessing, it would be disparaged by both the German and the Polish people. Even her best friend, Clara, would hate her. *Could Anna survive being an island, a sanctuary only for each other?* He pulled her close. As he held her, he knew he could never let her go.

Erik held her until only a soft pink glow lingered at the horizon. As darkness settled around them, he released her.

"We'd better get to our chores," he said, knowing they would be completely alone within an hour or two. The thought was deliciously exciting.

Erik watched Anna's silhouette until she entered the mare barn. As he started to turn, in the light of the open barn door, he noticed a shadow against the outside corner of the structure. He squinted, trying to make out if it were a person. Was it a false perception, a symptom of fear, and not real? Erik waited. The shadow confirmed its presence. An orange glow at the end of a cigarette flared in the darkness. Quietly, Erik pressed his body against the wooden siding on the hay barn, melting into the darkness as he watched. The apparition took a long drag, causing the tip of his cigarette to brighten. He dropped it to the ground and crushed it under the sole of his boot in the snow. When the shadow moved, Erik realized he hadn't been seen. The shadow was Bishof.

How much did the Gestapo lieutenant know? Was Anna safe? Urgent thoughts raced through Erik's mind. He had to get to her first, but Bishof had at least a fifteen-yard head start. The barn door softly closed, almost as though Bishof wanted to surprise Anna. Erik bolted around to the back side of the apothecary. He yanked open the door, slamming it against the barn's stone side.

Anna stepped back from the counter, where she loaded needles, syringes, and other instruments onto the autoclave tray. She grabbed at her chest. "You scared me." She smiled.

Erik peeled off his great coat and hung it on a hook by the door. He grabbed his lab coat from the rack and struggled to slip his arms into the sleeves. He glanced around him, searching for Bishof. The man hadn't arrived to look for Anna in the apothecary. He probably searched for her stall by stall, giving Erik time.

Anna had come to help by holding his lab coat steady so he could put his arms through the sleeves. "Are you all right?" she asked.

He briefly smiled at her. "Give me those clamps," Erik held out his hand.

"Are you angry with me? Did I do something wrong?" Erik could see Anna's distress. Bishof could make their wedding day a nightmare. He had to figure a way out of the disaster heading toward them.

Shaking his head, he answered. "No." he slipped his hands into heat-resistant gloves. "No. It's Bishof. He's here at the barn."

Anna gasped. "Does he know?"

"I don't think so. Don't worry. I'll protect you," Erik promised. He turned toward the door connecting the apothecary to the mare barn when he heard the hinges groan. He exhaled, preparing himself for the confrontation.

Erik was startled when Anna dropped a clamp on the autoclave tray, and it clattered noisily, metal against metal.

"Erik?" she whispered, but there was no time for him to explain.

"So, this is where you meet! I knew it!" Bishof growled, standing in the center of the aisleway.

Anna's expression had turned to pure terror. But Erik shook his head once, signaling for her not to say anything. He hoped she understood.

Erik wheeled toward him and gently pushed Anna behind him, positioning his body in front of her. "Of course, we meet here. We must sterilize our instruments after the day's work. We will need them tomorrow," Erik said coldly. Bishof's smirk threatened, making Erik's defenses rise up stronger. It was clear Bishof didn't believe him. They were in a stand-off. Bishof couldn't arrest Erik and Anna for doing their job. The stud farm needed a veterinarian—no one needed the Gestapo chief.

"What can I do for you, Gunther?" Erik asked. He narrowed his eyes, and the muscles along his jaw twitched tight. He returned to removing plungers from syringes and placing them on the autoclave tray, intentionally ignoring Bishof's innuendos.

Bishof took a step back and stared. "I came to walk Miss Sabrosky home. I promised her I would," Bishof said, tipping his head skeptically toward her. "Am I interrupting something, Erik?" Bishof asked in a know-it-all and devious tone. Bishof was aware of how Erik felt about Anna. Erik had admitted it days ago in front of him. Erik wished he hadn't. From the look on his face, Bishof made an assumption—a silent accusation, filling Erik with anxiety and dread.

Erik covered his subterfuge with laughter. "Not everyone is like you, Gunther." It was all bluster. False bravado. "Let's not talk of this here. Step outside." Bishof's face opened with shock. Erik had called him out and wondered: *Is Bishof afraid I will turn violent?* Taller and stronger, Erik could take him down in a second. He shook his head and chuckled as he walked to the door to the outside. He held it open for Bishof to pass through first.

"Haven't you told her you love her? You coward," Bishof roared with laughter before the door closed behind them.

"Gunther, Anna is with the sisters," Erik scolded as if Bishof should perceive her innocence. "She doesn't understand the way the world works. I don't want her to."

"Do you think a woman wouldn't want to be under the protection of a German soldier?" He paused his expression one of disbelief and contempt. "Then you won't mind if I walk her home," Bishof smirked.

"Yes. I mind. I'll walk Anna home when we've finished work. You go do whatever it is you do," Erik said forcefully.

"To protect her from me?" Bishof growled, his eyes narrowing to black slits.

"Yes, to protect her from you, Gunther. You have your women. You don't need to spoil Anna, too."

Bishof threw his head back and laughed. "No? Well, I'll leave that to you, Erik."

Erik bristled inside. Heat rose into his cheeks, and he bit back his anger. His fists clenched at his sides. Bishof had found his weak spot and stabbed him with his words. Erik had no desire to ruin Anna, only to love her. But he feared his impulsiveness had led her into danger he could not control.

Bishof stood straight and examined his face. "I know you want her. Were you intending to make an honest woman out of her? A Polish woman?" He tipped his head in mockery. "The Führer has forbidden marriage with foreign women. You won't be able to marry," Bishof warned. The reminder made Erik's stomach roll. He refused to show it.

Erik pretended to shrug it off. "I'm not a fool, Gunther." Erik laughed. But he was, wasn't he? He adored Anna. He had begged her, no, forced her to marry him against his better judgment and her cautious warnings. And now, he would have to be vigilant to keep their secret and them safe. His thoughts strayed to his new reality. He had to get them out of German-occupied lands and to freedom. Could they make it to Britain? Or America? He would speak with Father Jerzak in the morning. "Gunther, I have work to do. Foaling will start any day now. I don't have time for your silliness."

For a moment, Bishof glared at him. "Join us in Biala. Zena thinks you're a very handsome man."

"These horses are the Führer's now. I must see to their care. It's my duty." Erik scowled at Bishof, hoping to appease him. He even stood taller as he said it.

Bishof clicked the inside of his cheek. "I never took you for the patriotic type."

Erik tipped his head briefly to the side. "You don't know everything. You mischaracterized me."

"Did I? Meet us in Biala at the Corner Tavern tomorrow night." Bishof stood firm, making his point and emphasizing his power.

Erik smiled. He had no intention of meeting them. Bishof turned and started to walk away. "Tomorrow night," he called out, with a laugh.

Chapter Thirty-Nine

ERIK FOLLOWED AND WATCHED BISHOF until he climbed into his car and started the engine. Satisfied when Bishof turned toward Biala and not the convent, Erik strolled back into the apothecary. Anna finished putting the instruments in the autoclave, and as she wiped the counters with an alcohol spray and clean cloth, she turned to look at Erik.

"Does he know?" she asked, her voice weak.

"He suspects something. Let him. He can't prove anything." Erik tenderly took her in his arms. She set the spray and cloth down and slumped heavily against his chest. He expected a barrage of I-told-you-so, but they never came—just ragged breaths full of fear.

"Oh, Erik, what will Bishof do to us when he finds out?"

"He won't find out. If he does, he'll assume you are my mistress. He doesn't love, so he can't imagine others being in love and wanting a life together." Erik paused and tipped her chin so she would look at him. "Remember when we brought Lotnik home, and I told you how I envisioned my life? You are my dream."

She nodded. "What if your government makes you stay in Poland?"

"I want to take you home with me. But if I must stay, when things settle down, we can build our practice here," Erik said, smoothing her hair. He held her gaze until her worried frown softened into a smile. "The Führer will approve our union," Erik said, brushing a strand from her cheek. He decided to talk with Father Jerzak in the morning and make a backup plan in case things didn't go his way. He kissed her forehead.

Erik's reason started to take over, and he sorted through the last months. "Hitler hasn't launched an offensive in weeks. Perhaps his military adventurism is over."

A hesitant smile turned the corners of her mouth. He hadn't reassured her. Erik knew Poland wouldn't stop fighting for their freedom, and the horrible violence would continue. *They shouldn't stop fighting.* Erik thought. If the roles were reversed, he wouldn't. Erik despised this world the Nazis were building—full of hate, full of terror, full of racism and fear.

When he was last at home, he and his father secretly talked about a resistance brewing in the Heer. Though they fought the Führer's battles, many Wehrmacht officers despised the brutality and cruelty of the SS and Gestapo. He knew he was one. Erik suspected Fellgeible might be, too.

"I must meet the Major for our evening inspection," Erik said. "Go to my . . . our quarters and wait for me there." He smiled. "I can't wait for our life together to begin."

Anna walked through the door to Erik's quarters. Neat and clean, nothing was out of place, except for an open book, a pad, and a pencil on the coffee table. The fireplace crackled with new logs. Anna wondered when Erik had time to fuel the fire.

A vase filled with pale pink hot-house roses matching her wedding bouquet graced the small kitchen table. Anna suspected the sisters, but their presence would have caused questions and perhaps given away their marriage.

She walked up the small rise to the bedroom and gasped. Pink rose petals were sprinkled all across the blue quilted bedspread. A white box tied with a satin bow had been placed conspicuously in the center of the bed. With little notice and so much secrecy, the nuns and her brothers and sisters at the orphanage tried to make her wedding night as lovely as possible. She bet they'd sent Benit and Tomas to deliver the flowers. The two ten-year-old boys from the orphanage would relish such happy mischief. She laughed at the thought.

Anna walked to the bed. A folded card tucked under the ribbon seemed to beckon her to read it. Looking around, she felt like a child at Christmas, sneaking to try and guess which gifts were hers under the tree.

Slipping the card carefully from its place under the bow, she read, "Don't wait. Open me."

She untied the ribbon and looked inside. The box held a beautiful gossamer nightgown and robe like she'd seen in movies at the small theater in Biala. Desire and fear mixed in her heart. She loved Erik's touch. His kisses made her feel the overwhelming passion she'd always longed for. But inexperience made her hesitate. Would she be able to please him?

"Erik, walk with me," Major Fellgeible said. Erik briskly caught up to him. Fellgeible's normal inspection was fast-paced but thorough. He wanted a clean, organized barn and, most importantly, the horses in good health. Erik delivered. He wanted the same.

There wasn't a speck of dirt or chaff in the aisleway. The horses munched contentedly in their stalls, looking up only briefly as if to acknowledge the Major. Erik had the respect of his workers, and they hadn't let him down.

Unknown to Fellgeible, Erik and Anna had helped deliver four human babies this month. The gossip had spread like wildfire since Caterina's emergency childbirth. Erik had earned a reputation for helping sick and injured humans and animals. He wasn't sure the Major would approve. But he was the only doctor the villagers had.

After Caterina's incident, he'd taken a soldier and truck and collected the former doctor's abandoned supplies and his medical library before the Gestapo could destroy them.

Erik turned slightly and acknowledged Albrecht, Major Fellgeible's adjutant, as he began to follow at a distance. Out of respect, the young soldier stayed back, giving Erik and the Major privacy.

"Don't mind Albrecht. He knows I may need him for something." Fellgeible grinned. "I saw you speaking to Bishof earlier," the Major started, staring at Erik with a sideways glance. "What did he want?"

Erik took in a breath and slowly exhaled. "He wanted to walk Miss Sabrosky home."

Fellgeible stopped short. "You didn't let him, did you?"

"No, sir." Erik slid open the door so they could complete their rounds.

The Major grunted his approval and walked forward again. "I don't like him coming around. I know I can't stop him. But you must be careful, Erik. I don't trust him around Annaleah. She's a beautiful woman, and he is a very disreputable young man. Like many in the Gestapo services, he's let power go to his head. His arrogance could bring ruin on us all."

"Yes, sir. I agree." Erik nodded.

"Tomorrow, I want you to ride with me in the morning. Will you see to it Danzig is saddled up for me?"

"Yes, sir."

"Albrecht," the Major called to his adjutant. The man who had been trailing after them rushed forward.

He saluted, stiffly. "Yes, sir?" Fellgeible returned an annoyed wave.

"Tell Belvida to deliver dinner for two to Dr. Kemperman's quarters. Go on." The Major didn't speak until Albrecht was gone.

Erik halted and choked back a gasp, trying to gather his composure. He couldn't let the Major have dinner with him. Anna was there, and their secret would be exposed. Fellgeible sent the paperwork requesting approval of their marriage, but he might not be keen to approve of a surreptitious one.

"The young boy Benit and I have become good friends. I like children, so honest," Major Fellgeible chuckled. "He told me you and Annaleah were married today. Is that true, Erik?"

Speechless, Erik stared at the ground. He straightened. The truth was his only option. "I . . . ."

"It might've been better if you'd waited, but I'm not sure I could've at your age," Fellgeible interrupted, laughing softly. "When Elke and I married years ago, ahhh, I remember it well. Your secret is safe with me. And when the Führer approves, we will have a celebration."

"Thank you, sir," Erik said, unsure whether to salute or shake his hand. "I'm so grateful."

"Now, go. Take time with your bride. We will talk more when we ride in the morning."

Erik bowed slightly. He rotated and jogged back through the barn, through the apothecary, and flung open the door to his apartment and stepped inside.

Anna turned to face him, backlit by the orange flames dancing in the fireplace behind her. The blue chiffon gown was more ethereal in real life than he had imagined when he bought it for her. It swirled around her body like mist. She'd let her hair down, cascading in golden curls around her shoulders. Her eyes sparkled, and her full lips parted with longing as if begging for his kisses.

Desire raced through him, and he closed the door, softly leaning into it with his weight, and locked it. His gaze never moved from her. He whispered, "Anna, my Anna. You are so beautiful."

Anticipation overwhelmed him. He went to her and took her into his arms. Erik had never been so in love.

Chapter Forty

KARENA DROPPED HER GRANDMOTHER'S MANUSCRIPT to her lap.

"They were married, Gerard. Dr. Erik and Granny A were married." Karena wiped away a tear from the corner of her right eye.

Gerard grimaced for only a second.

"You knew? You knew!" Karena stood, turned, and placed Granny A's book on the bench. "Why didn't you tell me?" She placed her hands on her hips, disbelief oozing out of every pore like sweat.

"I suspected, just like you did. I didn't know for sure." He rose from the bench, replaced the pages he held into the binder, and faced her. He reached for her hands.

"What could possibly have happened?" Karena lifted her shoulders and let them drop.

"Maybe Hitler didn't approve of their marriage." Gerard bit his bottom lip and furrowed his brow. Karena could see he didn't have the answers. They were going to have to read on. She started to sit, but Gerard pulled her back up. "Come on." He walked backward, leading her toward the barn. She stopped resisting and went along with him.

"Where are you taking me?" she asked, laughing softly.

Dropping her hand, he slid open the door to the barn aisleway. The barn girls had just finished up, and the sweet smell of the grass hay and pine shavings filled the air.

Gerard closed the door behind them.

"What are we doing?" Karena asked.

"You needed a break. You're getting too caught up in our grandparents' story. We have a story of our own to write."

Wow! This was going in an interesting direction. Karena thought. She suspected Gerard wanted to kiss her. The longing in his big blue eyes said so. She felt a wave of excitement rush over her. She'd wondered what it would be like—wanted to find out. She let herself drift in the dream for a moment, but the thought of Sam intruded. She turned away. "Darn it, Gerard. I have a boyfriend."

He laughed. "Well, he's not here to go riding with us. So, I think you're safe."

"Riding?" She stepped back. Gerard knew horses frightened her, even though their earlier ride had been fun. "We can't ride. Mom's almost finished preparing dinner," she reminded him, twisting her body back and forth.

"After dinner? The sun doesn't go down until around seven-thirty. And the arena has lights."

She didn't speak, only let out a nervous whimper.

"You can't get better if you don't try." His infectious smile reminded her how much she wanted him to kiss her. Could she suck it up and ride a horse, hoping to win a kiss and Gerard's affection? You betcha! She'd done it when Sam wanted her to learn to surf and downhill ski.

"Weren't you afraid of horses when you first started to ride?" she asked.

"No. But I was raised at Tersk. My father and grandfather took over as the farm's veterinarians. I couldn't wait to ride." Gerard grinned. "I won't make you ride if you don't want to. I believe, though, that you'll miss out on a lot. Horses are as good a companion animal as dogs. In past times in your country, a person was hung for stealing another's horse. Horses weren't just livestock, farm help, and transportation, but a friend." Gerard took both her hands in his. "Arabian horses are a most loving and people-friendly breed. The nomadic Bedouins used to keep them in their tents at night."

"Granny A told me," Karena said, pondering his words. "My mother never encouraged me to learn about them. They didn't want to have to buy me a horse and pay for the upkeep."

"I understand," he answered her. "My children will be lucky. I'll be a vet. So, we'll have acreage and a farm." He laughed.

"Are you going back to Tersk when you finish your education?" Karena felt a pang of loss. She didn't want Gerard to leave. She wanted to learn all about him, his life, his dreams. Sam never talked about children or even wanting them.

"I'll have to. I only have a student visa," he smiled, tugging her along the barn aisle to Jadzia's stall door. "With the Ukraine war, I could be deported at any time or recalled home to serve."

"What a horrible thought," Karena said, her brow furrowed with worry.

Jadzia's drop-down window was open, and the mare came forward, sticking her head out as if expecting attention or treats.

Karena began stroking her pretty face without her usual fear. She glanced over at Gerard. With his encouragement, she'd learned something new.

"She likes you," he said with a big grin.

"Do you think so?"

"Horses are a good judge of character. Better than we are, I think."

"Gerard, I want to finish reading Granny A's story. It's almost a compulsion." Karena reached through the window and scratched the mare's neck.

"I understand."

"If we continue reading, we might finish tonight. And then we can, as you said, write our own story," Karena rotated to face him. She wondered what he thought of her proposal as he studied her face.

"Your mother expects us for dinner. I can stay a little while, but then I must go home."

Karena bit her lower lip, her mind spinning at thousands of RPMs. "Park at the bottom of the hill. When all the main floor lights go out, come to the kitchen door. I'll wait for you there. We can sneak to my room and read all night."

"Wouldn't your mother be angry if she found me in your bedroom?" Gerard chuckled but tilted his head with intrigue, took a deep breath, and exhaled. "Don't think I don't want to spend time with you. I do. Very much. But Karena, I'm not sure you should risk having me come to your bedroom."

"We'd just be reading."

"Would we?" He let the implication hang in the air. "I must go home. Starting early tomorrow morning, Dr. Wilson and I have several days of work on the Mountain Pine Dairy Farm to prepare their stock for winter. It's hard work, and I need to be sharp. The cows don't understand we're helping them and fight us."

"Of course. I understand," Karena said. She could imagine. She'd seen squeeze chutes on TV. "We can read for an hour or so together after dinner." She stopped petting the mare and faced him. "Come to dinner tomorrow night after you're finished for the day."

"If I can, I will."

"It's okay. I understand you have to work." She caressed his cheek. He grasped her hand and kissed her fingertips. If she could melt, she would've.

"I'm falling for you, Karena. You know, don't you?" he whispered.

"I hope so, because I'm falling for you, too." *Goodbye, Sam—Hello, Gerard.*

Still in dreamland, Karena snuggled down in the covers of her bed. What a fairy tale! Who thought she'd fall in love in Athol, Idaho? She grabbed the pillow next to her and hugged it to her chest. Gerard was right. They had a story to write, and she couldn't wait to start. But their story was entwined with Granny A's. Karena looked at the binder on her bedside table. Though she'd planned to sleep, the pages seemed to call out to her.

"Oh, heck! I have to read. I have to find out what happened," she said out loud. Maybe she appeased her Grandmother's ghost—a gentle breeze stirred the curtains at her open window. Karena giggled, turned the table lamp on, and adjusted the covers over her legs. She reached for the binder and set it on her lap.

January 15, 1940

"We'll meet at the Corner Tavern around one. The lunch crowd should be nearly gone by then," Erik said, leaning across the steering wheel. Anna watched her friend Clara disembark from the car. She slid across the front seat toward the door, wishing she and Erik could kiss like a normal married couple. But their union had to remain secret. The Führer had not yet approved. Anna didn't think he would, but Erik seemed so sure.

She stepped out onto the sidewalk next to Clara. "We'll meet you at one, sir," she said. Anna draped her wool scarf around her neck, nose, and mouth, as much to hide emotion as to keep out the freezing air.

Biala had changed. Many of the shops were empty, their broken windows boarded over. Clara handed her the shopping basket and took her arm. They dashed into the one dry goods store remaining open in the village. The shelves inside were nearly bare. The spices she'd hoped to find were gone. The barrels, usually full of potatoes and beets, were only half full. *The consequences of war—starvation and disease—descended.* She unwound her scarf from her face and let the ends dangle over her shoulders.

Anna blamed Hitler. Why such men wanted war baffled her. Why did they bring this destruction upon their neighbors?

After her barn chores were completed every afternoon, she covertly delivered baskets of canned goods and freshly baked bread to her starving neighbors. But the convent's hidden stores dwindled, and she wondered if they would last through the winter. "God will provide, Anna," Mother Superior always reassured her.

Erik used all his experience and knowledge to increase the dairy's milk production and set aside space in an adjoining building for making butter and cheese. But Anna feared if the SS soldiers or Gestapo discovered their clandestine charities, the food would be confiscated. Erik, Anna, and the sisters would be imprisoned.

Anna looked through the potato barrel and selected a few. Clara brought over a bolt of cheery blue wool cloth.

"What do you think? I could make new riding coats," Clara said. "There's even matching satin for the lining. Mine is so threadbare, and yours is worse."

"It's pretty, but I think we should make coats for the children at the orphanage instead," Anna said, filling her basket with the newly purchased potatoes.

"Are we never to have anything pretty again?" Clara asked with a sigh. Anna put her arm around her friend.

"Things will get better. There is always hope." Anna smiled. She couldn't complain—she had Erik, and he was wonderful. Even if they had to sneak to be together, he was worth every second. For a moment, her heart went out to Clara. The village boys they'd grown up with had fled to become trained pilots for the British Royal Airforce. The only men left were haughty and cruel German soldiers, little boys, and old men.

Clara set the bolt of material on the counter. "For the children," she said to the shop clerk. After she had picked up her change and package, she turned from the counter. Her smile faded into a frown. "Anna, I must tell you something. I don't think you'll like it."

They walked to the outside. "What is it you need to tell me?" Anna dreaded it. Had Nelek been captured? Did Lieutenant Bishof want to restart his riding lesson? The horses seemed fine this morning.

Clara cleared her throat and looked down at the ground. "Dr. Erik has a lover. She's been staying with him at night for the last few weeks."

Anna breathed out and pressed her lips tight together. "Clara, he's a grown man. He's one of the few unmarried officers. Maybe he's found someone to love." She couldn't bring herself to look at Clara. They'd always been so close she feared even a glance would give her secret away. Anna wanted to tell her, even to shout it from the rooftops. Instead, she would need to be more careful and diligent.

"You aren't upset?"

"Why? Should I be?" Anna knew she was a terrible liar. "How did you find out?"

"Belveda told Magda she'd been delivering dinners for two in the evenings. Krystyna said all the curtains across the kitchen windows were drawn shut in the mornings. They had never been before."

"Krystyna?"

"She's been taking him eggs, bread, and cream every morning. Didn't you know? You and Dr. Erik saved her boy when he caught pneumonia, don't you remember?" Clara stepped back, her face twisted into a scowl.

"Oh, yes. I remember. But Dr. Erik told her she didn't have to pay," Anna reported. She remembered watching Dr. Erik studying the bacteria under the microscope and searching the medical books he'd rescued from Biala.

Dr. Erik had given the boy sulphapyridine after determining the infection was pneumococcal pneumonia. The boy had quickly recovered.

"Do you want to wait behind the feed barn tomorrow and see who it is?" Clara's expression changed to mischief.

Anna tried to hold back her gasp. "No! Don't invade his privacy. When he's ready to announce it, he will. Maybe she's a disreputable woman," Anna teased.

"I'm so sorry I led you to believe he loves you, Anna. But even today, he looks at you with such affection—more than if you are just good friends."

"Don't be sorry. Just remember, this is why it's unwise to gossip. Whoever she is could face prison, and Dr. Erik, too. You read the notices Major Fellgeible posted. The Germans don't want their soldiers fraternizing with lesser humans," Anna's voice colored with sarcasm. Still, she felt fear crawling along her spine. Her love affair and marriage were forbidden.

"I'll say no more about it." Clara adjusted her scarf.

"Oh. Look. We have just enough time to make it to the Corner Tavern." Anna pulled Clara along as she picked up her pace. "Clara, please don't say anything to Dr. Erik. He will tell us all when he can. And Dr. Erik is a good man. Warn the others to be careful, too. Everyone could be in trouble. "

March 27, 1940

Despite the war, this year's foal crop was exemplary. Exhausted, Anna stumbled through her morning chores as if in a trance. Yesterday evening, they had moved both mares into side-by-side stalls. Last night, she and Erik delivered their foals. One coming at 2:17 and the second an hour or so later. She smiled at the memory. Stopping momentarily at the corner where the front of the stalls met, she looked inside.

The new dark red-bay filly lay sleeping in the pale golden straw. Her tuft of mane and tail were black, like a maid's feather duster. She had no white markings. The colt next door raced around his mother, his fuzzy chestnut coat accented by a mane and tail as blond as Anna's braid. Bright white socks terminating just above the fetlock joints added flash to his front legs. An almost perfect star was centered on his forehead.

When she toweled them dry last night, she remembered carefully checking for the tell-tale one or two white hairs around their eyes, indicating the horse would be gray in maturity. Both were their final true color and beautiful.

As she watched, the filly stood. Both foals were up on strong, sturdy legs. Anna was always amazed that the newborns would be up and ready to run within an hour of birth. She remembered their first hours and chuckled to herself. She and Erik had finally left the barn at 4:00 AM after making certain both foals nursed and passed the meconium. They waited until the moms had safely delivered the placenta and were content and caring for their newborns.

Now, at 6:00 in the morning, both robust babies dashed around their stalls, testing life outside the womb with an innocent exuberance and filling Anna with laughter and joy. She sighed and wondered what Major Fellgeible would name them.

Anna noticed that Erik had returned from the dairy's milking parlor. He strolled down the barn aisle and caught up with her. Standing behind her, he wrapped his arms around her waist. Without thinking, she leaned against him. He kissed her cheek.

"Someone might see!" Quickly, she stepped forward, looking down the barn aisle in both directions, trepidation oozing like thick poison through her veins. She wished they didn't have to hide their love.

"No one else is here, Anna," he said with a reassuring smile as he turned her to face him. He took in a deep breath and exhaled. "It looks like our last three mares will foal tonight. Elena may foal as early as this afternoon when activity calms down and the workers leave for the midday break." Erik led Anna to the front of Elena's stall. All the signs of imminent foaling were there. But the mare calmly slept. She seemed to be resting up before the hard work of labor began.

"I should ride my horses," she said, studying the mare. "I haven't ridden for days."

"Not today. I told Major Fellgeible you were up until dawn and needed to rest. Tonight, we may be up all night again."

"You were up with me." She tipped her head and raised both eyebrows.

Erik nodded. "That's my job." He laughed. "Help me set up the feed carts. Then we can nap." He rubbed the tension from his neck. "Meet me in the hay storage." He looked around quickly and kissed her cheek again. She watched him walk briskly out of the mare barn. Anna felt she was the luckiest woman alive.

Anna waited a few minutes before following him. She started down the aisleway when the doorway slid open. Lieutenant Bishof entered.

"Oh, you surprised me." Anna felt her heart leap in her chest. Being anywhere alone with Bishof made her skin crawl.

"Here you are. I went by the Convent this morning hoping to walk with you. Sister Margaretta said you'd already gone," he said, narrowing his eyes as if he believed he was told a lie.

"Yes. We had two foals last night. They are beautiful. Come see." She faked cheerfulness and motioned for him to keep up with her. "The Major hasn't named them yet, but see how darling they are. This is my favorite colt of the year so far."

Bishof stared into the stalls and shrugged. "I stopped by to ask if I might walk you home this evening."

Anna could barely breathe. *Did he suspect she stayed with Erik?* Every time he questioned her, she expected he'd try to trip her up. He tried to make her admit to an infraction so he could arrest her. Or Erik. "Oh, thank you for the offer, but Dr. Erik believes our last three colts will come tonight. I will be staying here in case he needs me."

"Dr. Erik. He seems always to need you." Bishof smirked.

"Sir, I am his assistant. He has the horses and the dairy to care for. When we aren't training horses and overseeing the milk production, we are delivering foals and calving. It's spring. Our duties won't slow down until all the mares and cows are rebred."

"Will you be staying in the main house?" Bishof asked. Anna didn't like the look on his face. *Was he watching her, stalking her?* If he thought she boarded in the main house, he would believe he had unfettered access to her.

She didn't answer and turned to leave. He trapped her by slamming his hands against the stall, blocking her escape with his arms. "Answer me, Anna."

The rancid smell of stale tobacco smoke assaulted her nostrils. She pressed her back against the wooden front of the stall. "Sir, please. Dr. Erik is expecting me at the dairy." She could feel her blood pulsing in her carotid artery . If she fought his advances, would he arrest her?

"You are a beautiful and desirable woman, Anna." His glower turned dark with lust. She hugged herself defensively. *Please, Dear God, protect me.* She knew her fear showed through and Bishof fed on fear.

The words of her prayer repeated over and over in her thoughts. She squeezed her eyes shut. Bishof's cold hands brushed against her cheeks and down to her throat. Anna shuddered.

The sliding door at the end of the barn squealed, metal on metal, as it rolled open. The aisleway filled with carefree women's laughter. Bishof quickly stepped aside as if he were only observing the new foals.

"Anna! Dr. Erik said we have two new babies this morning." Clara and Krystyna hustled down the aisleway. They stopped and stared at each other when they noticed Bishof. They both curtsied in deference, not daring to even glance at him. Bishof shot one of the cattlemen because he looked directly at him. Everyone hated Bishof. No one more than Anna.

"Yes. A filly and a colt. Just inside." Anna said, holding sheer panic at bay. "I must go. Dr. Erik needs me." She rotated away from Bishof's trap and bolted down the aisleway. She believed he would chase her. She sprinted to the feed storage once outside. She slipped in through the opening Erik had left for her. Waiting behind the door, she listened for the cadence of jogging footfalls fading into the distance. Bishof believed she'd gone to the dairy on the other side of the farm.

Anna ran to where Erik worked. She collapsed onto a bale of hay.

"What's wrong?" He rushed to her, pulling her into his arms.

"He's. . . going. . . to. . . arrest me." She choked the words out.

"Bishof?" Anna watched as Erik's expression morphed from concern to a cold fury. "Did he hurt you? Did he touch you?" Anna remembered Bishof's hands on her body but couldn't say it. She shook her head. "This stops now." Erik pulled his sidearm from under his coat and pulled the slide, arming his pistol's firing chamber.

"No. No. Erik. They will send you to the camps." Anna could see the muscles in Erik's jaw twitch with anger as he clenched his teeth. She put her hand gently on his arm. "I couldn't endure knowing I caused you to be arrested. I can't live without you."

Anna watched Erik slowly exhale, calming and controlling the boiling rage overwhelming him. Her declaration of love seemed to melt away his immediate impulse. He clicked on the gun's safety and replaced it in his holster.

"Come with me," Erik said, taking her hand. Still, Anna was afraid of what he might do. He led her to Major Fellgeible's office. They entered the anteroom without knocking. The Major's adjutant wasn't at his desk. It made Erik hesitate. Anna could see confusion furrow his brow.

Familiar voices filtered from the Major's office in hushed tones. Erik stopped short and didn't enter. Stepping sideways from the view of those inside, he pulled Anna from the doorway. General Fellgeible was here again visiting his brother; Anna recognized his voice.

"The Führer intends to invade Denmark and Norway. He is bolstered by how easily Austria, Czechoslovakia, and Poland have surrendered. Britain and France declared war but did nothing. He believes they won't fight. They are cowards," the General said.

Anna immediately thought about the message tree in the prayer grotto, but Nelek was in England. She didn't know who to warn and couldn't betray her husband. She looked at Erik. It was clear; he had heard. He slowly let out a quiet groan heavy with sadness. It had been seven months since Hitler sent troops anywhere. Like her, Erik had hoped it was all over. They'd often talked about peace and building a life together. Anna's heart sank. Their dream of the war ending crashed around her like broken glass.

This spring's brilliant crocus, tulips, and daffodils would be met with bombs and bullets.

Chapter Forty-One

April 15, 1941

Anna woke and reached for Erik. He wasn't there beside her. She sat up, rubbing her eyes. In the dim morning light, she saw him in front of the fireplace. She watched him add several small logs to the embers. Instead of returning to bed as usual, he stared into the flames, stirring to life around the new fuel. He reached into a small wooden box on the mantel and retrieved one of the new letters he had stored there. Though he never complained, Anna knew Erik missed his family.

Anna watched him open the letter. He'd done this before. Maybe he was transported home when he reread the words. Her heart ached with empathy. Sometimes, his letters from home made him happy. Other times, morose.

For a moment, she wondered what having a family would be like. Would she ever meet them and belong to them? *Would this war ruin this dream, too?*

Erik lowered his arm, his shoulders slumped, and the letter drifted to the floor like a tree's last autumn leaf. She grabbed the quilt from the bed, went to him, and draped the coverlet around his shoulders. A small smile passed quickly over his lips.

"Shall I make coffee?" she asked. The sadness in his eyes burdened her heart. She feared the words in the letter. She knew Erik would tell her the news from his family in his own time.

"Not yet. Let me hold you." He gently tugged her to the sofa, sat, and relaxed against the armrest, pulling her close into the crook of his arm.

"Good news from your family?"

"Not really. Just more war," Erik sighed. "My brothers have joined the Wehrmacht. Mother says Bjorin might be able to stop by the Stud Farm." Erik's face seemed pinched, and his eyes were full of pain.

"That's good, isn't it?"

"I want to see my brother, of course," Erik's voice was full of distress. "But not because he enlisted and is going to war."

She waited for the rest of his explanation, but it didn't come. "You seem so sad. Can you tell me why?"

"It's nothing. I can't do anything about it, anyway."

Anna snuggled closer and laid her head on his chest, listening to his heartbeat, trying to comfort him with the warmth of her body. She softly pressed her lips against his throat with a reassuring caress.

"Hitler's military adventurism will ruin Germany. I understand reclaiming German lands, but this—no. To steal land and enslave others is wrong-headed." Erik absently petted her hair. "The treatment of the Jews, war, and political prisoners rankles my conscience. God will not let this go unpunished."

"What do you mean?" She sat up, studying his face.

Even though she was his wife, she knew Erik couldn't share everything with her. Surely, he thought he had kept her safe by keeping war details from her. In spite of Erik's attempts to spare her, whispers circulated among Janow's workers. Denmark, Norway, Finland, Belgium, and France had fallen and surrendered to the Nazis. An evil darkness descended on all of Western Europe.

Anna snuggled back down against Erik's shoulder. She remembered yesterday's events. After the morning feeding, a new man had arrived in a sleek black car. From his uniform and the ribbon bars and metals on his chest, she knew he was important. Major Fellgeible introduced him as Major General Henning Von Tresckow.

Anna deduced something had changed. Troops, large armaments, and tanks moved to Poland's eastern border. But didn't Germany and Russia have a non-aggression treaty? She wondered. Without Russia's help, Poland might still be free.

She had gone to set up the feed carts for the evening feeding. The last of the mares would likely foal tonight, and she wanted to help the feeders and rest before her overnight watch. She filled the grain bins from the small storage silos in the back of the barn.

The side door opened quietly. Erik, the Fellgeible brothers, and Major General Von Tresckow slipped inside next to a tall stack of alfalfa. Without thinking it through, she dropped to a crouch behind her cart, a mistake she feared she would regret. Anything, even something as simple as overhearing a conversation, could mean being sent to the camps or being executed on the spot.

Anna knew the storage barn was one of the places the men used when they needed to talk away from prying ears. No one knew who might be a Gestapo informant. Starvation, cruelty, and terror turned even the strongest into cowards and traitors.

She had tried not to listen by squeezing her eyes shut and putting her hands over her ears. But since Bishof and the Gestapo had confiscated all civilian radios, the temptation to listen was too great. When she heard the words 'German Resistance,' she strained to hear more. Anna couldn't stop herself.

She remembered Von Tresckow's urgent throaty whisper. "I'm not alone. Many of us believe Hitler must be stopped and National Socialism destroyed to save Germany and Europe from descending into total barbarism."

"You are right." She heard Major Fellgeible say.

"I agree. Our children will forever be tarnished by his evil." Erik said. Anna's heart soared. Erik proved himself, once again, to be a truly good man. But now, Erik carried the burden of another secret in addition to their forbidden marriage. He joined the German resistance. Though it sounded heroic, Anna knew there was nothing but danger ahead.

After the meeting, Major Fellgeible ordered the cavalry officers not to allow Lieutenant Bishof to enter the stud farm for any reason. Bishof would retaliate.

Later in the morning, Anna had slipped away to the convent. Father Jerzak had hidden a radio in the convent's secret underground. She'd learned from Father Jerzak some of the brighter notes ringing out in this black dirge of human misery. The new British Prime Minister, Winston Churchill, orchestrated the rescue of the British Expeditionary Forces trapped on the beaches at Dunkirk. The British had withstood the Luftwaffe's constant bombardments since July of 1940. Father Jerzak had called both miracles. Maybe, with a German resistance and miracles, this war would end.

Erik shifted his weight, and Anna cuddled closer.

"Are you ready for coffee now? Some breakfast?" she asked, adjusting the quilt around him.

"Hitler is going to attack Russia, Anna. My brother is going to fight there," Erik sighed. "I'm afraid he'll be nothing more than cannon fodder."

Sitting up suddenly, Anna said, "But the British haven't surrendered. And if America enters the war, and with a German resistance. . . ." She watched his expression change with alarm.

"How do you know about a German resistance?" Erik probed her. She shouldn't have said it. His eyes softened, and a small smile barely curved his lips. He nodded and chuckled. "You heard us, didn't you? If America enters the war, I believe the Nazis will be defeated. For the world's sake, I hope they do. But, Anna, in the end, the Americans won't care what happens to a German veterinarian. You must be ready for that."

Chapter Forty-Two

ERIK STOOD BY THE RAILING in the covered arena, waiting for Anna to mount Lotnik. The gentle colt stood patiently and calmly as she climbed and sat on the top rail of the arena fence. Erik marveled at Lotnik's beauty. His dappled grey coat shimmered under the overhead lights like a newly minted silver coin. Lotnik sidestepped near the rail as if offering his back to Anna.

He'd seen several cavalry soldiers get bucked off by their young mounts when ridden for the first time and land on the arena floor in an explosion of dirt. Erik knew Anna had done all the necessary and sometimes tedious work to prepare Lotnik for riding. The young horse trusted her as he should. She had spent days driving him on long lines, lunging him with a saddle on his back. She had leaned across him to get him used to the feeling of weight. Starting two days ago, she stood on the edge of the wooden corner hay feeder and lowered herself onto Lotnik's back. She had rubbed his neck and withers while he ate, making the whole experience pleasurable.

This last step, watching Anna move from the top rail of the arena fence to the colt's back, didn't frighten Lotnik as much as it did Erik. He held his breath, imagining he'd be picking Anna up off the ground. The young stallion seemed expectant, his ears flicking back and forth as he waited for Anna's next command.

She softly tightened the reins to establish contact with his mouth, gently squeezed his sides, and verbally commanded him to walk. The colt took hesitant steps forward, gaining confidence when she praised him and smoothed her right hand along his neck. Erik could see Lotnik's gait become more and more relaxed.

"This is why I let her start the young horses," Major Fellgeible said, stopping beside Erik and watching Anna guiding Lotnik through his beginning paces. "She'll have this colt performing a perfect collected canter by the end of the week."

"He'd probably buck me off," Erik snorted a laugh.

"Many young soldiers have learned the lesson of kindness that way. My father taught me riding a horse is a partnership. They will do anything you ask if treated with love, respect, and gentleness. They must like you enough to get you to the battle, fight by your side, and bring you home again. If you treat them badly, they'll dump you at the battle and leave you to the enemy," Fellgeible said with a chuckle.

Erik nodded. He didn't have the experience training horses like Anna. Fellgeible did. The Major's reputation followed him. He'd prepared and qualified for Olympic competition, but Hitler shut it down after the 1936 games in Berlin.

"We are a mechanized army now. The days of horse battles are over," Fellgeible said. "And now Hitler has shut down horseracing," the Major said, disapproval sharpening his tone. Erik whipped his gaze to Fellgeible's profile. The Major's Prussian stoicism showed through his stiff demeanor.

"Will we be shutting down the horse breeding part of the farm?" Erik's mind scrambled through possibilities. Would Anna be allowed to stay as his assistant if the farm was only a dairy?

"No. Don't worry. When we start racing again, he'll expect us to win. We will need to breed good horses," Fellgeible said.

"What about the Olympics? Will we be fielding an equestrian team?" Erik asked.

"I hope so. But it's frivolous to think of games promoting peace while we engage in war." Fellgeible didn't look at him, but Erik could see the Major's jaw tighten. Finally, he turned and patted Erik on the shoulder and walked away.

Erik watched Anna finish her hour-long ride on Lotnik. *A beautiful woman on a beautiful horse. What a vision.*

Anna beamed. "You're such a good boy. Such a handsome boy," she talked to the horse as she dismounted. She removed his bridle, slipped the halter over his face, and buckled it. She hung the bridle over her shoulder. Lotnik lowered his head and began to snuffle her jacket pocket. She retrieved the carrot and apple pieces she'd wrapped in a handkerchief and offered them to him. Lotnik greedily took them from her flat palm. Her training method was simple and brilliant: make every encounter with humans as enjoyable as possible. Good behavior received a yummy reward and praise. Lotnik seemed to flourish most in her praise.

Erik opened the arena gate for her. "I have to go to Biala for a luncheon meeting. Do you want to go?"

She stepped through the opening, and Lotnik followed. "I should run over to the Convent. I want to buy more of the peaches we canned at harvest."

"I won't argue if you promise to make one of your peach cobblers," Erik laughed. He started to slip his arm around her waist but withdrew and frowned when he noticed Clara standing at the doorway to the stallion barn. The Führer hadn't yet sanctioned their marriage. They were still pretending, and Erik hated it.

"I can't wait to kiss you whenever I want to," Erik whispered. "I'll see you later. Good ride today, Anna." He added the second sentence loud enough for Clara to hear.

"How was Lotnik?" Clara asked. Anna noticed her gaze followed Erik until he disappeared from sight.

"Lotnik is such a good horse," Anna answered.

Clara walked beside her and closed Lotnik's stall door after the three were inside. She unbuckled the cinch while Anna fastened the halter rope to a tie ring. "Anna, I swear Dr. Erik is in love with you. I know he has a secret woman, but he clearly loves you."

Anna chuckled. "Don't be silly." She pressed her lips together, containing her smile and the warmth flooding through her body at the thought. *Erik loves me.* Each evening, when the workers left for the day, she would sneak through the apothecary and into Erik's apartment. They would immerse themselves in their private world away from the secrets and the war.

Picking up a brush, Anna began grooming Lotnik.

"I still think we should hide outside one morning and see who she is," Clara lifted her shoulders. She started for the stall door, opened it, and hung the saddle on the drop-down rack just outside.

"No. We don't want to get him in trouble," Anna protested.

"Do you think it's one of the girls we work with?" Clara asked with a snicker.

Anna huffed. "I don't know. I don't want to know." She removed Lotnik's halter and turned him loose. He stood close to her, nuzzling her hand. "I don't have any more treats, Mister," she said and walked to the stall door. He followed. Anna stroked his face and then closed the stall.

"Why do you protect Dr. Erik, if you think he's just a Nazi?" Clara argued.

"How can you say such a thing? Clara, he's stepped up and is the only doctor our people have. Don't you realize how awful Lieutenant Bishof and his goons are? They will send him to the camps or worse if they find out he has a Polish lover and he helps us," Anna sighed. "Come on. Walk with me to the Convent. I promised I'd bring back some canned peaches before dinner feeding."

Clara pouted. Anna laughed at her as they walked outside. The summer sky was a deep blue, and the trees along the trail were lush with new emerald-green leaves. Branches arching across the road cast cooling shadows. The birds warbled their territorial songs, and a playful breeze brought the delightful scent of roses. It was a lovely day.

Clara finally started to giggle. " I know you're right, Anna. We shouldn't pry. But aren't you even a little bit curious?"

"No. Let's not even think about it. Put it out of your mind." She stared at her friend briefly, then asked, "Are you going to learn to ride this year? I'll teach you." Anna changed the subject as quickly as she could.

"I'm too clumsy," Clara answered. She stopped, put her hands behind her back, and looked at the ground, a sly smile curving her lips.

"What is it?" Anna teased. They knew each other, it was hard to keep secrets.

"I'm seeing someone," she said.

"How nice. Who?"

"You won't approve."

Anna felt a twinge of anxiety. Was it one of the young German soldiers? She had no room to judge. "Do you love him? Then why would you care if I approve?"

"It's Dr. Lesnik's son, Jorges," Clara said.

Anna remembered him from school. He had been chubby and bullied by other boys in their class. But he was very intelligent. These days, Jorges Lesnik was rumored to be one of the resistance's top leaders. Anna always expected him to become a veterinarian and take over for his father. But he'd gone to engineering school instead. The last time she'd seen him, he'd lost his baby face and had matured into a nice-looking man.

"Why wouldn't I approve? I remember him from school," Anna said, shaking her head.

"You thought he was a spoiled brat," Clara said, tipping her head. It was true. In school, he was a brat. But it was defensive because the other boys were so mean to him.

"We all have grown up since school. I'm happy for you." Anna laughed. "When is the wedding?" She skipped forward so Clara wouldn't smack her like they used to when they played as kids. But as she came out to the clearing, she stopped abruptly. "No. Clara. No." She blocked her friend with her body. Clara slid in the gravel on the trail. Anna grabbed her hand and yanked her along until they had cover behind a tree.

"Bishof," Anna moaned. His sleek black car sat in the front circular driveway. Behind it were two empty trucks, the backs covered by green canvas. Two uniformed soldiers with long guns stood at the bottom of the stone stairs in the gravel driveway. Suddenly, Anna couldn't breathe and sank to the base of the tree. She knew the Church had openly protested against the war. "He's arresting them. Oh, Clara. Bishof is arresting Father Jerzak and the sisters. Oh, God, what will become of the orphans?" she murmured.

Clara's face went white. Her eyes widened with fear. Without warning, she stood and bolted to the trail.

"No! No!" Anna cried, but it came out only as a hoarse whisper.

Clara screamed and sprinted in the direction of the stud farm. One of the soldiers wheeled toward the commotion, lowered his rifle, and fired. Three shots shattered the silence. Birds took flight from the treetops like a sudden wind. All time slowed in Anna's world, and she couldn't move. Clara went limp, her arms flailing at the bullets' impact. As if her bones had suddenly turned to water, Clara crumpled to the ground.

The soldier strolled up to Clara and prodded her lifeless body with the toe of his boot. Anna cringed further down into the underbrush. Her heart pounded as loud as a drum in her ears. *Don't see me. Don't see me.*

"This one is dead," the soldier called out to his partner.

"Are there any others?" the second soldier asked.

"I don't see any," the killer said.

Anna heard the sound of hurried footsteps scraping against the convent's stone steps and then crunching in the gravel. They were coming toward her hiding place. She felt every muscle in her body tightening, making her as small and still as possible. She wanted to disappear.

"What is this? What have you done?" Anna recognized the angry tone of Lieutenant Bishof's voice.

"She screamed and tried to run away," the soldier answered.

"All right. Quickly, put her in the trunk of my car. We'll dispose of her later."

"Yes, Sir."

"Carry on with your duties."

From her hiding place, Anna watched the soldier lift Clara and sling her over his shoulder. She saw Bishof turn slowly around, scanning the forest around him as if looking for any of Clara's companions. Anna knew he followed them nightly. She remembered his car creeping along the road behind them as they walked home. Fearing rape, the girls never went anywhere alone.

Anna bit back the wail rising in her throat, but the tears streaming in rivulets down her cheeks—those she could not stop.

Chapter Forty-Three

ANNA HEARD YELLING AND WOMEN and children wailing. From her vantage point in the shadow of a tree, she watched the soldiers walk behind Father Jerzak, the sisters, and the orphans.

"Beeilung! Beeilung!" One soldier shoved Mother Superior with the butt of his rifle. She stumbled forward. He roughly grabbed her, and shoved her into the back of the truck. Even though she slammed her knees on the tailgate, Mother Superior stoically didn't cry out.

Anna gasped. She hated her cowardice. She should rush them, but what good would that do? They would only take her away, too.

"Blonds in this truck. The rest with the nuns." She heard Bishof's command.

Her mind reeled. The rumors were true! They were stealing the children: Polish babies, toddlers, and orphans. Any who looked Aryan were hustled off to Germany. For a moment, she wanted a gun. She wanted to kill all the soldiers—especially Lieutenant Bishof. Frustration made her ball her hands into fists. Fear made her stay hunkered down in the shelter of leaves.

Anna couldn't stand to see anymore and stared deeper into the forest. If she moved, they would kill her like they had Clara.

The underbrush close to her began to move and rustle. *Had they found her?* First, she only noticed shaggy blond hair and a boy's hands. Benit appeared from under the leaves. *Only Benit.* She sighed with relief.

"How did you get out? How did you get away?" Her words spilled between uneven whispers.

"Through the basement boiler room. We need to tell Dr. Erik. I'm going to get Dr. Erik."

Incredulous, Anna thought. *What can he do about this?*

"How did you know about the boiler room door? You weren't allowed. . . ,'" she asked.

"I watched you. I followed you. Lately, you've been coming home, then sneaking back to the stud farm after dark."

"Oh. No. You haven't told anyone, have you?" She stared into his big, blue eyes, trying to discern the truth.

"You're staying with Dr. Erik, and you could get in trouble. I would never tell." Benit grinned, seeming to enjoy sharing their secret. "Besides, I hate the Nazis." He touched her forearm. "Let's go."

"No. Benit. This way." She snatched a handful of Benit's shirt and wrestled him back beside her. "We must go to the Grotto and sneak through the back pasture. Did anyone else escape with you?"

He shook his head. "They hid under the beds and wouldn't come out." His eyes pooled with tears. "I begged them."

Anna hugged him to her. She stroked his hair. "It's okay. It's not your fault." She heard the truck engines grind to a start and grate, metal against metal, as they were forced into gear.

The rumbling noise from the moving trucks leaving the convent's driveway covered their escape. "Go. Go." She pushed Benit ahead of her.

Benit edged on hands and knees through the thick underbrush toward the Grotto. Anna crawled close behind him.

Before crossing the road to the Grotto, she stood, remaining behind the shelter of a large maple tree. She listened for the sound of Bishof's car. Once she felt safe, she took Benit's hand and dashed with him across the road.

The new summer grass in the back pasture had recently been cut and dried in neat windrows. The sun had evaporated the dew, but the scent of new hay still filled the air. The cavalry soldiers would stack the bales and prepare them to be trucked to winter storage. Anna carefully chose a path close to the trees along the fence line. This pasture was not visible from the main road, or the Grotto trail.

Overwhelmed by the image of Clara's murder, she needed to keep Benit and herself as safe as possible as they crossed to the back door to the apothecary. She shuddered at the thought of being shot in the back like Clara and nearly fell to her knees. Fighting her terror with all she had, she pressed on.

Anna led Benit through the apothecary door and laboratory to Erik's apartment.

"Let's go by the fire."

"No. I must find Dr. Erik. He'll save us." Benit straightened to his height, chin up. He was such a brave little man.

"Benit, listen. They may be looking for you. They took all the children. And if they do a roll call, they will know you ran away. They will look for you. Even here," she said grimly. "You must hide." Anna took both of his hands. "Let's pray. God will help us."

Benit scowled at her. She understood.

"Benit, we don't know God's purpose. Remember, God is our creator, and no matter what happens, He loves us. He designed everything; the Earth and all the plants and creatures. He designed the Moon, and the Stars. He knows what's best." She sank to her knees, and Benit reluctantly did, too.

"You sound just like Mother Superior," he said, sarcastically. "Well, He didn't design Herr Hitler and certainly not Lieutenant Bishof!"

Anna smiled softly at Benit. "He did make them. Both of them. We are under the curse of Adam's sin. But God gives us a choice. A person can choose to follow God, accept the gift of grace by believing in Jesus as Savior, or choose to be evil. Father Jerzak says if we choose evil, God gives us over to our corrupt desires."

"Who could desire what Hitler has done to us—to the whole world?"

"I don't know. I'm not perfect, and I need Jesus. I want his gift of salvation. I could never want to hurt people the way Herr Hitler does. Let's pray. Pray for Clara, Father Jerzak, Mother Superior, the sisters, and your friends and family in the orphanage. And pray for our enemies." They held hands, bowed their heads, and silently sent their petitions to God.

When a few moments passed, Anna let go of Benit's hands, crossed herself and stood. She watched as the boy wiped tears from his cheeks, and she fought back her own tears.

"Now, you stay here. I'll go find Dr. Erik and see if there is anything he can do." Anna waited until Benit nodded.

"I will lock the door so no one can get in." Anna stuffed the key from the hook by the door in her pocket.

She backtracked through the apothecary and tested the back door. It was locked. She crossed the room and exited into the mare barn. Remembering Erik had an appointment in Biala, she scanned for the round wall clock over the doorway to the outside. It was one-thirty. He'd be back by now.

Cautiously, she strolled down the aisleway, looking into each empty stall as she passed by. Most of the horses were out in the pastures. Only the stallions were in their barn, waiting to be exercised by the cavalry officers at two in the afternoon. Erik often joined their practices if a medical emergency didn't come calling.

Anna made her way to the stallion barn. The aisleway was full of chatter and laughter as the men groomed and saddled their horses for their afternoon practice. The cavalry soldiers teased each other and made bets on who would complete the Major's list of tasks for the afternoon the fastest and best.

Suddenly, Benit bolted past her, weaving his way through the soldiers.

"Stop! Boy! Slow down! You're spooking the horses!" She heard one of the men lament.

Erik and Major Fellgeible entered the door at the far end. A collision was imminent. The barn aisle unexpectedly went quiet. The soldiers each stood at attention in front of their horse's stall.

"Benit! Benit!" Anna called after the sprinting boy. She briskly walked after him. He had grabbed onto Erik and was babbling so fast, Anna noticed Erik and the Major had to bend down to understand him. She knew the boy told them of the arrests at the convent and Clara's death. Both men straightened, their body language reflecting shock and disbelief.

Anna heard the jarring sound of hurried steps on the concrete walkway outside the barn. The SS soldiers were here for her. And for Benit.

She slipped into the darkness of Lotnik's stall. The colt moved to the front and stuck his head out of the window opening, curious. She wanted to take Benit with her and disappear, but she couldn't reach him. Fear paralyzed her whole body.

The barn door slid open, and she turned, immediately crouching behind Lotnik's body. With Lieutenant Bishof in the lead, four SS Soldiers in their dreaded black uniforms march down the aisleway toward Benit, the Major, and Erik. Erik pushed Benit behind him as Bishof and the SS men confronted them.

Anna peeked through the ironwork on the front of the stall. The storm was here. There was nothing Anna could do.

Major Fellgeible's expression hardened with anger. "What in the hell is going on here? Is what this boy says true?"

Chapter Forty-Four

LIEUTENANT BISHOF WRESTLED A PIECE of paper from inside his jacket and shoved it at Major Fellgeible.

"By order of SS Reichsführer Heinrich Himmler, I have been instructed to arrest the Catholic priest and nuns and to empty the orphanage. We are taking over the convent as our headquarters." Bishof was smug.

"You are arresting children? Why? What have they done?" Erik said, perplexed.

"The blonds—the Aryans will go to Germany and be adopted by German families," Bishof announced.

"And the others?" Erik asked. From times he'd been at the orphanage to help with their animals, he knew most of the children were not blue-eyed blonds.

Bishof didn't answer.

Fellgeible glared at him and handed the paper to Erik. He read it.

"There are two orphans on our list who seem to be missing. The boy, Benit Stanilaw, and the young woman, Annaleah Sabrosky. We believe they are here, and we have come to collect them."

Erik controlled his emotions, letting a practiced calm settle over the rage trembling inside. "The order says you may collect, as you call it, children and non-essential workers. Miss Sabrosky is essential to running this farm," he snarled through clenched teeth. "Gunther, I'm not a fool. You want Annaleah for yourself. She's twenty-one, too old for adoption."

Major Fellgeible's eyes widened. "You will not take her. She is our veterinary assistant and stays here. And the boy stays, too. He's essential. He is our house boy."

"Will you disobey orders?" Bishof lifted an eyebrow. The SS soldiers moved forward as if to take the boy by force. Erik stepped back, pushing Benit further behind him.

The aisle full of cavalry officers moved to defend their Major, shoving Bishof's men back. Shouts of 'stop! back away!' rose in chaotic chorus. Horses danced nervously, pulling against their tie rings.

"Enough!" Major Fellgeible shouted over the noise. "We will not have a brawl here today." He waited until the factions settled down. "Lieutenant Bishof, I have my orders. I am to run this stud farm with the utmost care and efficiency. These are the Reich's horses now. I will keep my essential workers. Lieutenant Bishof, I suggest we retire to my office and call Berlin," Fellgeible's voice threatened.

Erik watched Bishof squirm. The SS soldiers he brought with him seemed confused. They exchanged glances, well aware Fellgeible outranked Bishof. As the Major and Bishof left the barn, the cavalry officers relaxed, but still eyed the SS men with contempt.

Wilhelm, one of the SS men, leaned in toward Erik. "Do you really think he would arrest a woman, just to have her?"

"Do you need to ask? He's a lecherous fool," Erik grabbed Benit's hand and looked at the boy's face, white with fright. Immediately, he was moved to empathy. While he tried to establish a cooperative spirit between the Polish people and their German captors, Bishof ruled by terror.

Erik thought he'd seen Anna earlier in the aisleway and needed to get her away from here. He had decided. They would take Benit with them if they had to run. Mother Superior had given him Anna's birth certificate, but he cursed himself for not pursuing the other papers required to leave. To get them seemed daunting. Bishof would never willingly issue them.

A passport, a certificate of good conduct, proof of permission to travel, and a physical examination certificate would've been easy to get earlier—but not now. As head of the Gestapo police services, Bishof was in charge of it all.

In his mind, Erik mapped their escape. North to Danzig following Father Jerzak's route. He would need papers for Anna and Benit to cross the Black Sea. The Polish Resistance would have to be convinced to help them. Would the Polish people be willing to provide them shelter along the way? Bishof had arrested a priest and nuns in a majority Catholic country, alienating the people even more. Erik was sure their province wasn't the only one.

Two SS soldiers stepped aside as Erik calmly walked hand in hand with Benit down the barn aisle.

"Hey, wait. Halt!" Rolf, another SS man called out. He started after them, but twenty armed cavalry officers stepped forward and blocked his way. Alarmed, Rolf stepped back.

All the Cavalry Officers suddenly snapped to attention when Erik and Benit were halfway down the corridor. Erik wheeled around, clutching the boy to his side. Major Fellgeible and Lieutenant Bishof returned.

Major Fellgeible cleared his throat, waiting until all murmurings quieted. "Berlin has confirmed that Annaleah Sabrosky, our veterinary assistant, and house boy, Benit Stanislaw, are exempt from this new order."

Humiliated once again, Bishof's eyes flashed with anger. Erik wiped his hand across his lips as he breathed a sigh of relief. He knew he had been given a reprieve. Erik would not let this time go to waste. He would get everything in order in case they needed to flee. Gunther Bishof would resent being forced to help him, but was too cowardly to disobey commands from Berlin.

Anna stood. She closed her eyes, and a prayer of thanksgiving filled her thoughts. Lotnik sidestepped close to her. He placed his mouth on her arm, carefully feeling with his lips and only taking a bite of the fabric of her blouse's sleeve. He pulled on it as if trying to entice her into a game. She was moved by his sweet attempt to lift her spirits. But all wouldn't be fine. Clara was dead. Hitler had attacked Russia, opening a new front in the war. And Bishof had shown his hand. He intended to harm her.

Anna threw her arms around Lotnik's neck. Comforted by his warmth and scent, she hugged him. She felt the weight of guilt and sadness, but she had no more tears.

The stall door opened, and she turned. Erik stood quietly in the center of the door, holding Benit's hand. His expression was hard and cold, his jaw tense. He was still the man she loved, but Anna sensed something had significantly changed.

Karena set the manuscript beside her on the bed. She threw back the covers, and walked to the open window. Her heart pounded with fear. She felt every ounce of terror that her grandmother had felt.

She shuddered, trying to imagine what it was like to live every day fearing rape, being arrested and sent to the concentration camps, or shot in the back. How could her grandmother endure losing so many friends and neighbors? Once again, Karena remembered in one of her history classes that over two thousand Poles were arrested each day during the German occupation. Human life meant nothing to the Führer. He and his regime were pure evil.

Karena breathed in the night air, cool against her cheeks. The dark sky was full of stars. She could even see the Milky Way stretching across the horizon. To think of all the stars made her feel incredibly small. Back home, the light pollution prohibited seeing the glory of the nighttime sky. Once again, the aurora created a pink and green spectacle in the north.

For the first time, she felt the wonder of living free. She'd always thought history was a boring subject. Memorizing dates and battles meant little to her, but Granny A made it come alive.

She turned back to the bed. The nightstand clock reminded her it was three in the morning. But sleep was impossible. The swirling questions in her mind needed answers. Karena climbed back into bed, and picked up the manuscript again.

Chapter Forty-Five

February 15, 1942

ANNA BROUGHT MORNING COFFEE TO Erik and set the tray on the table before him. He sat forward on the sofa. Anna noticed he read the chapter on artificial insemination in cattle and its frozen preparation. Her thoughts raced. Maybe he decided to try it. Spring was only weeks away. Erik was always a forward-thinking veterinarian. He would organize and equip the whole venture before trying it. But he'd failed to discuss his plans with her, leaving her on edge. Usually, when he wanted to try something new, he talked to her about it.

Erik inserted a paper bookmark at the page he read, closed the book, and moved the volume to the coffee table. Earlier, he had stirred the embers in the fireplace and added a few logs. Anna could feel the comforting warmth on her back. The sunrise chased the stars back to hiding in the light. Today would be cloudless but a cold day. Winter didn't yet want to let go. She poured him a cup and added fresh cream, preparing his coffee how he liked it. But that didn't seem to please him. He didn't pick up the cup.

"What's wrong, Darling?" Anna asked as she settled on the sofa. She snuggled close to Erik, and he enfolded her in his arms.

"We have been ordered to send some stallions to the German Stud at Mlynow for the breeding season. I found out last night, but I. . ."

"You couldn't tell me?" Anna finished his sentence and sat forward.

"I thought perhaps I could talk them into artificial insemination. But now, I realize we must prepare for that instead." He stared into her eyes.

"Then they are sending Lotnik?" Her voice trembled with disappointment.

"Yes. Lotnik, Witez and others. The stallions will be returned by summer, but that will postpone our breeding season to fall, or we will need to skip this year altogether. I want to see what our young colts will produce their first foal crop." A grimace briefly flashed across his lips.

"Are you going?" she asked, her tone timid. She didn't know what she would do without him. He was the storybook lover she'd always dreamed of. And any trip away was fraught with danger.

Lately, German military supply trains headed for the Russian front were sabotaged and blown to pieces. Even German columns hesitated to take roads through the forests. For safety, they cut the trees back thirty feet on either side of the main supply routes.

"No. I love you so much. I can't leave you. And I'm needed here."

Anna could see all the pain in his eyes.

"The Russian invasion isn't going as planned. Our troops are defeated by the Russian winter, more than bullets and bombs." Erik informed her. "The lessons of history fall on deaf ears."

Anna just nodded, not knowing what to say.

"This is a war we will lose," Erik said with frankness. "They arrest the church leaders, murder innocents, arrest and imprison the Jews. They arrest the Polish people and kidnap their babies from their cradles to send to Germany." His brow pinched with worry. "How much longer can we tolerate this inhuman brutality?" He wrestled free of her and stood. "Anna, it crushes my soul." He paced back and forth in front of the fire.

Anna rose and went to him. She took both of his hands in hers. He stared into her face. "My love, you aren't doing it. You are kind to everyone."

"They make up foolish stories and have resurrected the worship of pagan gods. I can't stand idly by while the Gestapo and SS destroy people's lives, destroy everything," he sighed. Anna could see the invisible weight pressing down on his shoulders.

"What are you going to do?" she asked.

"I don't know what to do, " he whispered, pulling her close. "I don't want to betray my homeland, but I can no longer pretend this insanity and viciousness is not happening. Will God judge me complicit in this evil if I allow it to continue? God! Forgive me for my cowardice."

Erik held her. Her heart was breaking into pieces. He was not a coward. Could she do anything to ease his agony? "We must trust that God will care for us. We must trust that He will show us the way through." In a soft voice, she prayed. Erik didn't resist; he closed his eyes.

"What can I do to help you?" she asked.

"Love me, Anna. Just love me."

She lifted her chin, and he tenderly touched his lips to hers. "I could stay here forever," he said, each word caressing her skin with warm breath. "How do you do it? How do you make me forget the world outside?" He pressed his forehead against hers, and they lingered in the moment, holding on to each other.

"We must dress. We can't be late for the roll call. I must get the Major to approve the equipment I need quickly. I want to be able to breed our mares and keep on schedule," Erik kissed Anna's forehead.

Anna took her place next to Krystyna at Roll Call. Quietly, she studied the line, and counted each face. She remembered Clara used to stand next to her. Consoling herself with the thought, her friend now resided in heaven and no longer had to endure this world of terror created by the Nazis. When the officers entered the courtyard, Bishof was in their number. Several SS Soldiers flanked him. Erik wasn't with them. Anna felt panic squeezing her heart as she searched for his face. Did Bishof know about their unsanctioned marriage? Had the Gestapo Lieutenant arrested Erik? Was she next?

With a smug, self-important sneer on his face, Bishof strolled the line. He carried a riding crop, tapping the leather against his left palm as if mimicking Major Fellgeible. Anna glanced the Major's way, trying to read his body language. The Major's expression was grim, feeding her fears. She caught herself wringing her hands and quickly stuffed them behind her back.

Bishof started down the row of cattlemen from the dairy. Anna knew that many of the men were part of the resistance. By day, they worked in the milking parlors, but by night, they did everything they could to sabotage the German supply trains headed for the Russian front.

As the Lieutenant started back up the column, he selected certain men with his crop. When he did, the SS Soldiers wrenched them out of position and forced them to their knees.

"These men are saboteurs and have committed treason against the Reich!" Bishof shouted, taking a second to glare into each remaining worker's face. Instantly, Anna knew the men were going to be killed. Right here. Right now. In front of the women—some were their wives.

Anna flinched as the first shot rang out. She heard the horses call to each other at the sound. The hot tang of gunpowder and the metallic reek of blood mixed in the air. One by one, the SS executioner shot each man in the back of his head. One by one, they slumped forward to the floor—five in all.

Her stomach rolled and cramped involuntarily. She held back her gag reflex.

Krystyna screamed. Anna stared straight ahead, trembling but refusing to let her tears fall. Several of the barn girls retched, others ran for the doorway to the mare barn. Anna knew Bishof intended to create this terror.

He assumed it would stop the resistance, but it only fueled it. The remaining cattlemen's faces hardened to hatred. Obviously, Bishof didn't understand the tenacity of the Polish people fighting to free their homeland. There would only be more damage and murder.

Someone on the inside had exposed the resistance fighters. Anna looked cautiously at the women down the line, and they stared back at her. A cold blanket of distrust surrounded them all. Since Bishof and his men had taken the convent, they would wonder where Anna stayed. Or did they already know? She and Erik had been so careful not to display any affection for each other away from his apartment. She hadn't told anyone. Would she be accused of collaboration?

Bishof stopped in front of Anna. He slid the end of his riding crop along her neck, catching her braid. She could barely breathe. A devious smile curved his lips. Balancing the braid on the leather end of the crop, he pulled it around to fall across her left shoulder. A nearly silent whimper left her throat. Bishof was going to kill her. She anticipated the soldiers ripping her from the line and forcing her onto her knees. Her thoughts raced to Erik. She wasn't ready to die.

Closing her eyes, she prayed. *Please, God save me!*

The SS men didn't move against her.

"You have already been warned. Annaleah is not to be touched!" Fellgeible growled. Stepping between them, a wave of controlled anger oozed from his every pore. Bishof retreated. Anna reasoned Fellgeible had to tolerate the killing of the cattlemen. Their sabotage was an act of war.

"Do you object to me admiring beauty?" Bishof laughed. "Annaleah is a perfect Aryan Princess. Haven't you noticed?" He looked her up and down. Her body screamed at her to recoil. But to do it would only encourage his sadism. Bishof liked seeing fear in her eyes.

"You heard me. She is off limits to you," Major Fellgeible threatened. "You have done your duty. Now leave us."

"Heil Hitler!" Bishof saluted, his voice full of sarcasm. He waited until Fellgeible returned one to him. Bishof motioned to his men, and they left the courtyard, abandoning the dead for the women to clean up.

Accepting this fate with fear, some of the older women—wives of the assassinated—broke ranks.

"May we help our husbands?" Mrs. Krzytalowicz quietly asked Major Fellgeible.

"No, Go home. The rest of you resume your normal duties. We will take care of this. Go. Feed the horses." The Major ordered. Anna watched as the women hurried away. Motioning to Albrecht, his adjutant, Fellgeible turned his head in disgust. "Get some men to help you. Bury them in the far north pasture. Mark their graves so their families can mourn."

Tentatively, Anna crept up to the Major. "Sir?" she asked quietly. She didn't want to know where Erik was, but she had to know.

"What is it, Anna?" Fellgeible asked, his voice softening.

Even saying the words of her question failed. "Dr. Erik?" His name trembled on her lips.

"Oh, dear girl. Erik is fine. He's gone to Warsaw to collect supplies. He's okay." The Major breathed deeply. "I'm so sorry about this. This is—this brutality is unnecessary."

Anna sighed.

"I want this war over as much as you," he said. He looked away from her as if he bit back words she should never hear him say. But she already had heard them. She knew the disgust he felt for Hitler and the Nazi barbarism. She knew he shared those feelings with Erik, his brother, and a German resistance building bigger and stronger within the Wehrmacht.

Fellgeible took her hand in his and encouraged her away from the carnage. When he spoke again, he lowered his voice. "Erik has told you several stallions will be spending spring at Mlynow. They will return in June." He walked with her to the stallion barn.

"Yes, sir." It took all the strength she had inside to stand. Her mind kept replaying the murders over and over. She could barely concentrate.

"What do you think of his artificial insemination scheme?" he asked.

Five men were dead. Thinking about breeding horses seemed so trivial. "I don't—I don't know," she sighed. " We won't need it if the stallions return in June. But it's a good backup plan. Erik always has the farm's success in mind," she answered. "Will you tell the wives of the men who died today?"

"Yes. I will see to it, Anna. Those men incapacitated our troops, forcing them to go without much-needed supplies. War is an ugly business." He justified Bishof's actions with hollow words, but his expression said he hated what had happened.

She looked at the ground and kept him from guessing her true feelings. Her thoughts raced, but she held back, pressing her lips tight. *We didn't ask for this war. Your Führer stole our homeland, bombed our cities, enslaved us, and kidnapped our children; what did you expect?*

"Yes, sir," Anna said. Deep sadness and defeat made her listless. Everything in her life was beyond her control. She longed for the only comfort she knew. "I should ride Lotnik."

Fellgeible nodded his consent. She turned to go. "Anna," he said. "Don't hate me. Don't hate Erik. We are doing what we can."

Chapter Forty–Six

November 1, 1942

ERIK PULLED THE STALL DOOR closed. "That's the last one." He smiled at Anna and slipped his arm along her back. Anna and Erik watched, side by side, as the two fillies explored their new home. The first day away from mom would be stressful. They rustled around in the clean, fresh straw as they circled the inside of the large stall but never became frantic. The fillies recognized they had each other and settled.

After a few minutes, the fillies found the hay in a shallow feeder along the front wall of the stall. Both buried their faces in it. At six months of age, they could easily succeed on their own.

"All the new foals have been eating well for almost two months. I don't think they care that their moms aren't here," Erik said.

"Weaning is hard, but mostly for the mares," Anna replied.

During their first foaling season together, Anna explained to Erik that it would be easier on the weanlings if they stalled two together. It made sense. He instituted it as a farm practice.

So far his experiment with artificial insemination was a success. He'd Employed A.I. with the stallions that were delayed. All the farm's mares were pregnant. The stallions had only arrived home a week ago, too late to have a successful breeding season without it. Cavalry horses weren't a priority to a mechanized army. The trains supposed to bring the stallions home had been delayed. Most rail traffic had been commandeered to supply the troops on the eastern front.

This year's spring foaling had gone off without a hitch. All the new babies were healthy and strong in time for weaning and ready to weather the coming winter.

"What's next?" Anna asked, looking up into Erik's face. He wanted to kiss her. However, they still hadn't received permission to marry. It was becoming a hard burden to bear. He remembered he shouldn't even have his arm around her and dropped it to his side.

"I need to walk through the cattle barns and make sure milking went well. And then Fellgeible wants me to meet with some men from the territories of Bohemia and Moravia—Hostau, I believe. He will want you to show off some of the horses," Erik said.

"Will we have to send our stallions away again?" Anna asked. Erik knew she dreamed of riding Lotnik, and another trip away for breeding would be a setback.

"I'm hoping I can talk them into A.I.," Erik lifted his eyebrows and grinned.

"Is that why you tried it this spring?" she asked, cautiously touching his hand with hers. He gently intertwined his fingers with hers.

"Yes. I wanted to experiment. I wanted to see if we could successfully do it with our horses," he chuckled. "It changes everything. No more trips away. No more injured mares or stallions. We've been doing it in cattle for years."

"Ummm, just injured people?" she laughed.

"Good thing our stallions are so good-natured and trusting," he answered. "It's because of you, you know that, don't you? All those nights, attending each foaling, establishing yourself as part of their lives—their herd. You have been the first person they see, smell, touch. I've learned a lot from you, Anna," he said.

She squeezed his hand. "I can't count the things I've learned from you."

Erik heard the tack room door open. Anna immediately dropped his hand. "Which filly do you think is best?" she asked loudly. Erik understood. They pretended to stand side by side to evaluate the weanlings, not because they were in love.

He turned. Krystyna stepped into the aisleway. In his mind, Erik quickly reviewed his and Anna's conversation, making certain he hadn't said anything that would jeopardize their future. He resented having to watch every word and deed. How could anyone be expected to live under this darkness and not rebel?

"Ah, Krystyna, come. Tell us which of the fillies you like best." Erik relocated, leaving space between Anna and him. Krystyna didn't look at him but stood on Anna's far side.

"I like the bay one. She's my favorite of all this year's foals," Krystyna said, glaring at him with distrust. He had been careless. It seemed so natural to put his arm around Anna's shoulders, to hold her hand.

"I like her, too," Erik said. "Krystyna, will you stay this afternoon and help Anna with the stallions? Some important men are coming to look at them, and I want them to be groomed perfectly."

"Yes, sir," Krystyna answered.

"Well, I'm off to do a walk-through of the cattle barns. I'll leave you ladies to it." He left them, hoping his wariness was unjustified.

In the afternoon, Erik stood along the outdoor arena fence with Major Fellgeible, Major Gustav Rau, and his entourage. With breathtaking precision, the cavalry soldiers presented a mounted drill with the six-year-old stallions. Rau meticulously noted each stallion on forms attached to a clipboard.

The soldiers removed the saddles and, one by one, led their mounts for inspection. Erik feared this was an audition. He hoped they didn't plan to take their best horses and would accept his breeding recommendations instead. The soldiers were dismissed from the arena.

The autumn air and gray sky suggested coming snow. Erik noticed a drop in the temperature on his cheeks and fingertips. He retrieved a pair of gloves from his pocket and put them on.

"You have done a wonderful job. These are the finest horses I've seen in the Reich," Rau said.

"We continued with the established Polish breeding program. Now, we'll show you some of the younger stallions." Fellgeible motioned with a wave, and Anna rode Lotnik into the arena at a trot. Erik glanced at Rau. The man's mouth had dropped open in surprise, and he studied Lotnik and Anna as she took the horse through his paces.

"You allow women to ride?" Rau asked as he leaned in toward Fellgeible.

"This one, yes. She's one of the best trainers we have. The horses love her and willingly obey," Erik smiled. He was proud of her. "She is very skilled."

"And very beautiful," Rau added, putting Erik on edge.

"Very," Fellgeible commented. "She was here when we arrived. She's an orphan from the convent next door—well, that is when it was still a convent. The previous director allowed the neighboring children to come to see the horses after school and in the summer. He allowed them to groom and clean. He even allowed those with aptitude to ride."

With an imperceptible signal, Anna asked Lotnik to canter, and he immediately shifted to the three-beat gait.

"Nice!" Rau smiled. "How old is this horse?" he asked.

"Three," Erik answered.

"Have her bring him here," Rau said.

Major Fellgeible gestured, and Anna brought the horse to the fence line and stopped. She dismounted so Rau could see the horse's conformation. But Erik noticed his interest drifted to Anna instead. Erik couldn't blame him. He knew exactly how it felt to see Anna for the first time. His first reaction was to step in to protect her. He stifled the impulse.

Rau opened the man gate and strolled into the arena. Erik followed as he walked around the horse, marking boxes on his form. "How long have you been riding this horse?" he asked, shifting his gaze to Anna.

"For about six months, sir. His training was interrupted for a few months when we were asked to send him to Mlynow for the breeding season. But he's remembered everything he's been taught and gets better every day." Anna smiled.

"May I?" Gustav Rau asked, but it really wasn't a question that required an answer. He traded his clipboard for the reins. Anna stepped back as Rau adjusted the stirrup length on the English saddle and checked the girth.

"I mount from the fence, sir," Anna said.

"Ah, thank you, young lady." He repositioned the horse close to the fence, stepped on the bottom slat, then swung a leg over the horse's back. Lotnik stood quietly for him, only shifting to balance this new heavier weight. Rau gathered the reins. Erik could see he was an experienced and confident horseman.

Erik retreated back through the man gate to stand next to Major Fellgeible. Nervously, Anna went to the center of the arena to watch. Erik was sure she hoped the colt would behave.

Rau skillfully engaged Lotnik through his repertoire and rode back to where Erik and the Major stood.

"This is truly a horseman's horse!" Rau exclaimed. Erik felt dread creeping along his spine like a spider. Anna's training might've just sealed Lotnik's fate. Anna had done her job to the best of her ability. If he could, Erik needed to talk Major Rau into artificial insemination instead of taking Anna's favorite horse from her.

After the sumptuous lunch Fellgeible ordered prepared for his guests, the men walked through the weanling barn. Then, they went to the pastures to inspect the mares and the yearling colts.

The colt pasture was bordered on the west by the narrow gravel road that meandered along the creek from the convent and ended at the prayer grotto. Earlier, he had watched Anna walking that way. She still maintained the custom of quiet afternoon prayers she'd learned from the sisters. He strained to see her through the nearly bare branches of the maples and oaks growing along the fence line. He couldn't see her. Since the Gestapo and some SS troops had taken the convent, he'd been wary of letting her go to the grotto at all.

"Exceptional colts," Rau commented. "Especially that one." He pointed to a tall gray. He was one of Lotnik's first sons and had been blessed with his father's beauty, balance, and symmetry.

Out of the corner of his eye, Erik noticed four or five men in black uniforms creeping along the road, followed by Bishof's black car.

Anna!

"Excuse me," he said, as he bolted through the pasture, remembering the shortcut trail he and Anna had taken many times to be alone in the grotto. Erik nearly vaulted the fence. He caught a glimpse of the soldiers jogging down the road. He didn't wait but crossed quickly, disappearing into the brambles and underbrush. Bare branches grabbed his clothes, and exposed tree roots clawed at his boots to trip him.

He reached the grotto only seconds before the SS soldiers.

Anna knelt in the grass before the concrete bench where they'd talked and read to each other on quiet summer afternoons. Without warning, Erik grabbed her arm under her elbow and lifted her to her feet. He whirled her to face him and into his arms. He could hear Bishof's car engine and tires.

"Kiss me. Don't talk. Trust me. Just kiss me, Anna," Erik whispered against her cheek. Confused, she studied him, her mouth open in surprise. "Trust me," he said again. She immediately obeyed and yielded to his embrace. He kissed her deeply, and she returned his passion with passion. He heard Bishof's car door open and his footfalls crunching in the gravel.

"So, this is where you meet," Bishof growled. "You and your Polish whore." He gestured, and his SS Soldiers spread out in a semi-circle around them. "Foreign women are forbidden."

Erik immediately shielded Anna behind him. He could feel her fingers dig at his waist, even through his uniform jacket.

"Take what you want. Isn't that what you said, Gunther? Major Fellgeible gave her to you. We are the master race; the women belong to us. Those are your words. Have you changed your mind?"

He could see the blood race into Bishof's cheeks. He'd been caught by his own callous words. Seconds ticked by as they locked in a stare like two bull elk readying for battle. Erik knew Bishof could easily have his soldiers arrest or kill him.

"Let Anna return to the barns. This is between you and me," Erik said icily.

Frustration left Bishof sputtering. He dismissed his soldiers with a wave of his hand. "Leave us!" he commanded.

Hesitantly, the soldiers turned toward the convent and walked down the road, turning back as if they weren't sure they should go. Erik glared after them until they were out of sight.

"You may go, Anna." Anna held on to Erik's hand as long as she could before he insisted she leave with a tip of his head. Erik kept an eye on Anna as she disappeared into the forest. He didn't observe her cross the pasture but hoped for her safety, she did as he asked.

"I will send you both to the camps!" Bishof screamed.

"You can take advantage of the Polish women, but I can't? Is that your new rule?" Erik laughed, moving forward, almost daring Bishof to fight. Erik was taller and stronger than Bishof. Without his soldiers as support, Bishof cowed. "I did what you told me to do. You have no right to complain."

"I said I won't allow you to be with her!" Bishof threatened, his voice becoming high-pitched and childish.

"I don't need your permission," Erik scoffed. He turned and strolled toward the pasture.

"Anna is mine," Bishof yelled at his back.

Erik heard the click-snap of Bishof pulling the slide, arming his Ruger sidearm.

He gritted his teeth and spun around. "Do you plan to shoot me, Gunther? Over a woman? I am the stud farm's veterinarian and the only man with enough medical experience to care for Biala's people. Who is going to treat the sick, injured, and dying people and animals? You?" He snorted in disgust.

Erik stood his ground. He and Bishof were locked in a face-off. A bully but ultimately a coward, Bishof backed away. Erik lifted his hands and continued forward. "You arrested nuns, priests, and orphaned children. You shot unarmed men and women. Why wouldn't you shoot me?"

The closer Erik got to him, the more he read panic on Bishof's face. "Go ahead, shoot," Erik closed the distance, his stare fixed to Bishof's eyes. Bishof dropped his arm to his side, defeated. Erik took hold of his arm, slid his hand down to the gun, and removed it from Bishof's fingers.

"I could've done it. You know I could!" Bishof backed up, tripped, and fell over a log marking the side of the road. Erik disengaged the gun's magazine and put it in his pocket. Pulling back the slide, he cleared the firing chamber. When finished, he reached for Bishof's hand and helped the Lieutenant to his feet.

"Stop it, Gunther, you aren't the monster you try so hard to be," Erik breathed out. He returned the empty pistol to him. "Be better than this," he scolded.

"You understand I had my orders." Bishof brushed some dried leaves from his jacket.

For a moment, Erik felt like they were back at university and roommates. Once more, Bishof was indefensible. But he'd defended Bishof then, and he repeated it now. He pitied the wretched man.

"I understand orders." Erik directed his glare to Bishof's eyes. "But don't ever threaten Anna or call her a whore. She is a victim of this war—an innocent. And if you ever point a gun at me again, you'd better pull the trigger—because if you don't, I'll bury your body where they'll never find it."

Bishof could no longer look at him. "You always had it so easy. Everyone always admired you," Bishof grumbled.

"Umm." Erik knew his schoolmates hadn't liked Bishof then and would surely despise him if they could see him now. "You and Fellgeible are in charge of this district. You would have better control if you ruled with kindness."

"That's the animal lover in you talking, Erik. You aren't a soldier. These people hate us."

"Can you blame them?" Erik asked, waiting for a concession that never came. "Come on. I'll buy you a beer."

The men walked the deer trail through the forest and climbed the fence to the empty pasture. Once on the other side, they headed for the officer's dining room and bar. Erik opened the door and stood aside to let Bishof enter.

"I still won't let you have Anna without a fight."

Erik shook his head and laughed.

It had been a while since he'd spent any time here. Major Fellgeible had converted the main house's dining room into a bar where the cavalry officers could rest and relax at the day's conclusion. Flames blazed behind an ornate brass screen in the substantial stone fireplace at the back wall of the large room. At this hour, only a few of the tables were occupied.

In the corner, a man played a soothing melody on the piano. That would change when the rest of the men finished grooming their horses when drill practice ended. With a few beers down, the soldiers would become boisterous.

Erik lifted two fingers toward the bartender, indicating they wanted beer. Bishof took a table on the left side of the fireplace. Erik picked up the foaming mugs and delivered them to the table.

Major Fellgeible and Major Rau entered just as Erik sat down. "There you are," he said, walking briskly to the table. Erik stood in deference to his commanding officer. Reluctantly, Bishof rose, too. "May we join you?"

"Yes, sir."

"Good afternoon, Lieutenant Bishof," Fellgeible said, like he endured a headache and nausea all at once while having to offer the greeting. The Lieutenant is our local Gestapo Chief. Lieutenant, this is Major Rau from Hostau in our Sudetenland territories." They sat down.

"Where's Annaleah?" Fellgeible scanned the patrons in the bar. "I have good news." He motioned to the barkeeper to bring two more beers.

"I'm sure she's with Lotnik, sir. His stall is where I find her most after-noons. Unless we have some work," Erik said.

"I've come to a decision," Rau announced. "We are taking the stallions, Lotnik and Witez II, to Hostau."

The bartender brought the additional full beer mugs and a large pitcher for refills.

Rau smiled. Erik returned a tentative one to him. Anna would be devastated.

"You are reassigned, Erik. You'll be going to Hostau with the stallions," Major Fellgeible announced and then took a sip of beer.

Erik looked into his glass and watched small golden bubbles rise to the surface. *How could he leave Anna? How could he stop them from taking her favorite horse?*

"I've asked Major Fellgeible if he would consider parting with Anna. I've never seen a woman with such skill with horses," Rau said. "What do you think?"

"Oh, yes, sir. I've been working with her for these years. She's very good with horses and a very competent assistant," Erik said, relief flooding over him like warm ocean waves. He glanced at Bishof, his brow contracted into a scowl. He sat up, rod straight. Erik knew he wouldn't protest. He couldn't. Both Majors outranked him. Erik forced down his smile.

"I almost forgot," Fellgeible said, reaching into the inside pocket of his jacket. "This is for you." He handed a folded paper across the table to Erik. "The Führer, Herr Hitler, has personally approved of your marriage to Annaleah. See, at the bottom, it has both his signature and seal." Fellgeible sat deep into his chair, satisfied.

Bishof dramatically scooted his chair from the table, scraping the rounded ends against the hardwood floor. He stood. "I must go now. Thank you for the beer."

"Major Fellgeible and I would like to take you and Anna to dinner in Biala to celebrate," Rau said, a large smile beaming across his face.

Bishof grunted loudly, turned, and marched from the room.

"Thank you for this, sir," Erik said.

"Well, go on. Go tell your bride. Tonight we celebrate, and tomorrow it's back to work. You'll need to pack your things and what you need for the horses. We will transport the stallions next week," Fellgeible said.

Erik could hardly speak. He rose from the table, nodded to both men, and strode briskly for the door. He couldn't wait to find Anna. He couldn't wait to tell her all her prayers had been answered.

Chapter Forty-Seven

KARENA SANK BACK INTO HER pillows. For a moment, she savored the feeling of relief that washed over her. Granny A and Dr. Erik were going to Hostau together. They would be free from the evil Bishof. But, still, they didn't end up together. At the end of the war, had America refused Dr. Erik entry? She measured the final pages of the manuscript with her fingers and glanced at the clock on the bedside table. The illuminated red numbers announced the time: one-thirty-four in the morning. Funny. She wasn't tired.

Karena had announced she would finish reading Granny's book even if it took all night. She could feign illness in the morning and sleep in. God knows she'd done it enough growing up whenever she wanted to ditch school. Karena sighed. *I'm such a brat.* For the first time, she didn't like the feeling.

Granny A's book made her realize life was serious business. Childish games were deceitful and lies were wrong. She vowed to tell her mom the truth in the morning. But for now, it was back to Granny A's story, the horses, and Dr. Erik.

March 7, 1943

The clickity-clack and gentle side-to-side sway of the train was almost hypnotic. Anna listened to Erik's deep breathing as he slept. She snuggled up to Erik's side. The small sleeping berth in their compartment didn't seem cramped when she was in his arms. He stirred and pulled her closer.

"Can't sleep?" he asked, kissing the top of her head.

"I didn't mean to wake you. I am just so excited to be going with you," she answered. "Warsaw is the furthest from Biala and the convent I've ever been ."

"I'll take you everywhere. We'll see the world together," Erik whispered.

"Do you think this war will ever end?"

"Wars always end. I guess the question is, what will the world be after?" He petted her hair.

"I'm so afraid." She nestled against his side.

"So am I, Anna. What I hear from the Russian front is bad. The SS is brutal, but the Russians are equally so. All human decency is lost, and vengeance is king. We can't live like this forever. One day, we will have to make peace."

"What makes men do this?"

"I don't know. A lust for power, avarice, arrogance?" Erik sighed. "Fellgeible informed me that the commander of the territory around Hostau is a hardline Nazi and in charge of the concentration camp in the area. Our only saving grace is that Rau is not and has never been a member of the party. He's supposed to be as horse crazy as you." He chuckled and kissed her forehead. "Rau is more of an opportunist. He has a dream of making equestrian sport great in Germany and wants to breed a special horse to achieve it. He sold his idea to Hitler and the high command. The stud farm is almost a haven. It is located in the Sudety Mountains."

"Does that mean we are safe?" Anna said. She softly touched her lips to his throat.

"Maybe, for a while. We are safe to be married now. I can hold your hand and kiss you whenever I want. Now, try to sleep. We stop at Prague in a few hours, and we need to be rested to load the horses into trucks for the trip to the farm."

Anna pressed her body against Erik's warmth and felt the delight of loving him. A prayer of thanksgiving filled her mind as she drifted off to sleep.

Other than in photographs, Anna had never seen mountains. She sat between the German driver, Rolf, and Erik in the center of the bench seat. The truck bumped along the gravel road through rolling grass-covered hills, tracts of towering pine forests, and high mountain meadows, all nestled against the backdrop of snow-covered peaks. Lotnik and Witez were going to like it here. She felt her whole body relax.

They finally rolled through the small village of Hostau. Typical of the area, quaint brick and stone houses and shops lined the main street, their gray slate roofs glinting in the sunlight. Pedestrians on the sidewalks stopped to stare as the convoy rumbled by. Anna heard the horses call out as they neared the stud farm on the outskirts of the town.

She couldn't wait to see the new accommodations. She hoped for spacious stalls and lush pastures. When they pulled to a stop in front of the barns, she realized it was a much larger structure than Janow. The mares and foals were housed on one side and the stallions on the other side of the U-shaped structure. The administration, veterinary offices, and apothecary formed the bottom.

Rau stood in front of the main doorway, a big smile stretching across his face. He adjusted the Fedora he always wore and rolled his cigar between his thumb and index finger.

"Erik, come meet the director. This is Lieutenant Colonel Hubert Rudofsky, the director of this operation. Colonel, this is Captain Erik Kemperman, the young veterinarian I've been telling you about. And we mustn't forget his beautiful wife, Anna." Rau flicked ashes from the end of his cigar. "She has inspired me to consider starting a women's equestrian team for the next Olympics. You'll agree, Hubert, once you've seen her ride."

They shook hands. "Let me show you where to put your horses." Rau carefully snuffed out the end of his cigar and dropped the rest into his shirt pocket.

They walked through the main doors to the left corridor. On each side of a long aisleway were spacious stalls with mortared stone walls topped with ornate wrought iron scrollwork. Inside were lovely, well-fed, shiny Thoroughbred, Lipizzaner, and Trakehner stallions. Witez and Lotnik were to take their place in this barn of Europe's finest horses. Anna was awestruck.

"What do you think, Anna?" Rau took her hand and threaded her arm through his. Rau glanced back at Erik and winked. Anna tried her best not to recoil. Was she in the company of another Bishof?

"They're all so beautiful." She smiled while carefully withdrawing her arm from his grip. She waited a step for Erik to catch up and took his hand. All she could do was hope she hadn't offended her new boss. He waited for her and Erik to catch up and didn't seem insulted.

"The British have the Thoroughbred, the Austrian the Lipizzaner, so I'm thinking of crossing Lotnik with some of the Lipizzaner mares. As you may know, I want to create a horse breed that's strictly recognized as German."

Anna nodded. "Yes, sir. My husband told me. I was taught that the Thoroughbred's foundation sires were three Arabians, and that the Lipizzaner's also have Arabian blood." Her thoughts raced back to what Erik had told her. Rau wanted to breed the Aryan horse for the Aryan race.

"The Trakehner breed has Arab blood, too. I believe all breeds are improved by Arab blood," Rau looked at her with approval. He motioned to one of the grooms in the barn, and the man opened a new bale of straw and spread it on the floor of the clean stalls prepared for Lotnik and Witez.

"May I bring our horses in? They've been traveling for days," she asked.

Rau snapped his fingers, and the two men bedding the stalls came to attention.

"Go unload the stallions and bring them in," Rau commanded. "Now, Dr. Erik, may I show you and your lovely bride your new quarters?"

Anna started to go with the men to unload the horses, but Erik gently tugged her to his side. He shook his head so only she could see. As Erik and Anna followed Rau to their newly assigned living space, she stared at the back of Rau's Fedora-covered head. Inside, she trembled. She and Dr. Erik would still be forced to participate in this insanity. There was no peace here. Briefly, she closed her eyes. They were becoming a part of breeding the superhorse for the super race.

Erik left Anna to familiarize herself with their new apartment. The housing was located at the end of the main building near the long row of stalls at the beginning of the stallion barn. He followed Rudofsky and Rau to the main office. As they walked through the door, Erik noticed the two men waiting inside.

"Erik, meet Captain Rudolf Lessing. He's my adjutant and our head veterinarian. Rudolf, this is Captain Erik Kemperman." Erik reached out and shook his hand. Lessing matched Erik in his Cavalry Captain's uniform. He was tall, close to Erik's six-foot-two. Erik speculated he was a good veterinarian and a good horseman. Rau wouldn't allow anything else. Lessing matched the Nazi ideal—blond and blue-eyed. But he seemed stiff and uncomfortable, as if he didn't like being in charge. Erik understood. He'd happily relinquished that duty when he left Janow. He turned his attention to the second man.

"This is Wilhelm Dressler—we call him Willi. He has been assigned to care for the breeding stallions. You will work with him. I will have you oversee the mares and foaling. Major Fellgeible said you were very conscientious in that department," Rau said.

Dressler enthusiastically pumped Erik's hand when he shook it.

Willi Dressler smiled, showing all his teeth. Erik immediately liked him. Willi's friendly personality was bright and winning compared to Lessing's reserve. Willi's strawberry blond hair, the smattering of reddish freckles over his cheeks and nose, brought out a sparkle of mischief in the deep blue in his eyes.

"Willi, take Erik through the facility and show him around. We will expect you and Anna at dinner," Rau added.

Erik nodded. He gestured for Willi to lead the way.

June 7, 1944

Anna and Erik had settled into life at Hostau without difficulty. Anna set the plates and mugs on the small kitchen table in their apartment. She reflected on her life over the last year. The 1944 foaling mares had all finished delivering last week. Tirelessly, the three veterinarians and Anna had worked many late nights, ending up in Erik's apartment in the early mornings to unwind. At first, Captain Lessing didn't want Anna to assist with the foaling. His wife wasn't a horse person, and Anna's desire to help was unexpected. He changed his mind when he watched Erik and Anna work as a delivery team.

Finally, they'd all caught up on the lack of sleep. Working together over the past months helped them to become very good friends. However, news from the war always seemed to be bad news for Germany. British General Montgomery had overpowered the Axis forces at El Alamein, and Rommel had surrendered in North Africa. The Allied powers had invaded Sicily, and Italy surrendered on September 3, 1943. In January of 1944, the German siege of Leningrad ended, and on the fifth of June, Rome was liberated.

Yesterday, the radio the Lessings had given Anna and Erik as a welcome gift declared that Allied forces had landed at Normandy rather than Calais as anticipated by Hitler. The Allies had fooled Berlin. Each Allied victory left Anna in a terrible quandary. She adored her husband but secretly longed for Poland and all of Europe to be released from the Nazis' grip.

Here at Hostau, in the shelter of the surrounding mountains, they lived in a protected bubble. Anna's mornings were filled with riding mature horses, and her afternoons were consumed by the early training of the new foals. Within days of birth, she had them in halters and taught them to lead.

Director Rudofsky often watched her work. He and Rau hinted at a women's Olympic team when they talked to her. The daydreams of riding Lotnik in a Dressage Competition she'd entertained all those years ago at Janow almost seemed possible.

Erik and the other veterinarians had just finished rebreeding the mares for the season. But Anna sensed Erik worried more and more each day about the war.

"We won't be left unscathed," he said, sinking into the chair across from her at their small kitchen table. He tuned the radio dial away from Gobbel's propaganda to music. "This man speaks nothing but lies."

Anna's thoughts snapped back to reality from the misty thoughts of Olympic gold. "You don't say these things to Willi and Captain Lessing, do you?"

"Of course not. Only to you. But one of these days we must face reality. Germany will not, nor can it, prevail. The world cannot live under this brutality." Willi's familiar rap on the door broke into his whispered rant.

Each morning lately, both Willi and Captain Lessing joined Erik and Anna for coffee and breakfast. While the horses enjoyed their morning meal, the men would discuss their chores for the day. Anna hated that now their conversations included agonizing over the war.

Erik rose, opened the door, and Lessing and Dressler entered. They briskly walked to the small table and sat in their usual seats. Anna had already set coffee mugs, plates, and silverware at their spots, anticipating their arrival.

"Morning, Anna," Lessing said, lifting his mug so she could easily fill it with coffee. "I smell cinnamon. What have you baked for us this morning?"

Willi was not his usual cheery self. Anna could feel his unhappy vibe as if it were transmitted through the coffee cup. "Cinnamon rolls," she answered, hoping to cheer everyone.

"Erik, we've got to make a plan for the horses," Willi said as Erik returned to his seat at the table. "We can't let Ivan take them."

"Stop the defeatist talk," Lessing interjected. But it was without conviction. His eyes flicked to Anna's. He attempted to reassure her. The Red Army advanced from the East, the Americans from the West, and they all knew it. "The Wehrmacht will make a stand. I hear Hitler has a new weapon that will turn the tide." He lowered his voice as he stirred cream into his mug. "I spoke with Director Rudofsky. He wants to save the horses. But the Commandant is adamant he will not surrender. He will order us to fight to the last man."

Erik groaned. "We will have to make a plan without him. The horses are the finest in all of Europe. They are irreplaceable. We can't let them be slaughtered in battle or end up as Russian stew."

Anna's imagination filled with scenes of horror: machine-gunned horses falling in the pastures. She caught her breath.

"What choice do you think we have?" Lessing asked, his brow pinched with worry.

"If we say we won't fight, we will be shot," Willi warned and nervously stood, circling in place behind his chair. He sat down heavily. Lessing raked his fingers through his blond hair.

"We all agree the Russians won't understand the value of the horses. Right?" Erik waited for Lessing and Dressler to nod. "We must have a plan to evacuate West, no matter what. If that time comes, we must have a place to go. It's not defeatist to be prepared. It's common sense."

Anna brought fresh cinnamon rolls from the oven and set them in the center of the small kitchen table. She decided not to sit with the men. Part of her didn't want to hear anymore, and another part couldn't turn away. She stood behind Erik softly, placing her left hand on his shoulder.

"Sit, Anna," Lessing said. "Tell us what you think."

Erik took her hand and encouraged her to sit beside him. He kissed her fingers as she sat down. He smiled at her with so much love that her cheeks flushed, reflecting his feelings. They must escape, survive, and save the horses.

"Erik is right. We must make a plan to evacuate the horses. You have to think of your wife and daughters, Captain Lessing. The Americans don't have the same reputation as the Russians. And they won't slaughter the horses for meat," Anna reasoned. "We go West. We surrender to the Americans."

"The Americans won't kill you or Sasha Lessing and her children, but they will shoot us," Willi said, sweeping his hand and pointing to the men at the table.

"It all depends on who gets here first. Either way, we may be killed," Lessing murmured. "If not by Russians or Americans, by our own soldiers."

"No. I don't accept that." Anna sat back in her chair. She remembered what Mother Superior and the Sisters did when confronting a crisis. "We must pray. God will help us." She reached for Erik's hand to her right and Captain Lessing's to her left. One by one, the men all looked at each other.

Finally, they joined hands and bowed their heads. At that moment, Anna believed with all her heart that God had heard their prayer.

July 21, 1944

"Yesterday, there was an unsuccessful attempt on our Führer's life. The perpetrators of this heinous crime have all been arrested," The voice on the radio announced. Anna felt sick as the details of the bomb planted underneath the meeting table at the Wolfsschanze (Wolf's Lair) in East Prussia were reported. Hitler survived.

She twisted the dial until the radio clicked off. If only they'd succeeded, the war would be over. Instead, there would be retribution. The plotters would be killed if they weren't already dead. Anna started to slip into her riding boots but stopped, leaning against the spindles at the back of her chair.

Outside the window of the apartment, the sun shone brightly. The sky was brilliant blue, cloudless, and beautiful. It belied the human world of chaos on the ground. Hostau was still untouched. For only a few seconds, she hoped it never would be. They could be sheltered here, encircled by the mountains' protective arms.

She heard the door to the apartment slam. Erik appeared and reached for her. "Baby, they have arrested Major Fellgeible."

"What?"

"His brother, the General, was involved in the assassination attempt yesterday."

"But the Major wasn't. He was at Janow. How could he be involved?" As the words left her lips, she knew in her heart the Major was guilty. She remembered all the conversations she'd overheard. "Are we implicated?"

Erik shook his head. "I don't think so. We didn't do anything. Besides, we were here with the horses." He sat in the chair next to her and positioned her boots so she could easily step into them. "Go about your day. The Führer is alive. Pretend to be happy, even though it is a lie."

"Erik, do we know who we can trust?"

"Willi. I think Lessing, sometimes. Willi and I have discussed giving the horses to the Americans. But the logistics of moving 250 mares, many pregnant, some with new foals at their sides, is overwhelming. The stallions we can ride out. But we don't have the staff to accomplish it. We can't do that in secret. Someone will notice," Erik brushed his hand through his hair. "Where will we go? We need feed, water, bedding, and the means to transport it. Speaking of staffing, Anna, we don't have enough soldiers to defend the farm. Can we defend against the Red Army or Patton's Third Army if they won't help us?" Erik breathed out heavily through his mouth. "We have to convince Rudofsky, but he's afraid to make a decision." Erik sighed again. Anna could see the desperation in his eyes. "What if the Germans turn the war around? What if the Russians get here first? Will Patton save the horses if we go to him? Or will he shoot us before we can ask or explain? None of us speak English." Erik's chest shook with a small burst of laughter. "I understand Rudofsky's fear. It's just that we have to try. These horses are priceless."

Anna took both his hands in hers.

"I know what you're going to say. God will help us. No one said trusting Him for help would be easy. Especially since I am on the wrong side. Even though I was forced, conscripted, I didn't stand up for what is right."

"Darling, you did what was right. Don't you see that? You did everything you could for us." Anna lifted his hands to her lips. Standing up, she slipped into her riding boots. Erik stood facing her. He wrapped his arms around her. She remembered all the times he had treated the sickness and injuries of the Polish people and animals around Biala. He'd taken on the duties of a doctor when there wasn't one.

"Everything is going to be okay. We will escape, even if we must steal Lotnik and Witez and ride out of here."

"When I was a child, Dr. Lesnik used to tell us that Arabian horses could fly you away from danger. How I wish that were true. We could flee to America and freedom on the wings of flying horses," Anna said.

"Yes." Erik held her closer, caressing her cheek with his fingertips. "No matter what, my love, I will protect you." It was a promise she knew he wanted to keep.

She slipped her hand in his, and they walked out to the stallion barn.

Colonel Rudofsky stood in the center of the outdoor riding arena, barking out the gait changes he wanted as Anna rode along the rail on Lotnik and Erik on Witez. As soon as the command left his lips, the horses seamlessly executed the change. The horses performed perfectly. Rudofsky usually had corrections. *Tighten your reins, Anna. Sit up taller, Anna.* Those instructions did not come. The look on his face was that of distracted worry. These days, everyone at the barn shared the same expression, except the prisoners of war who cleaned the stalls and swept the aisleways. Anna heard them whispering joyfully, knowing their liberation was near. They kept track—Patton's Third Army was on the outskirts of Paris. The Red Army had liberated Warsaw.

"That's enough for today," Rudofsky said. "Cool out your horses. I'm not feeling well. I'm going home." He left the arena; his shoulders dropped as if defeat sat on them like a black raven.

"Follow me," Erik said as soon as he heard Rudofsky's car engine start.

Erik dismounted and opened the end gate. He sprung lightly back into the saddle after she'd passed through on Lotnik. Erik and Anna often rode on trails through the forest to relax and settle their horses after their workout. Witez and Lotnik were still energetic and seemed to prance down the shaded trail. Erik turned Witez off the main road and led Anna and Lotnik deeper into the forest on a new path they hadn't ridden before.

"Where are we going?" Anna asked, catching up so they could ride side by side.

"You'll see."

Anna laughed. "Lead on, Captain."

After half an hour, they rounded a small hill, and the forest opened into a beautiful westward-sloping meadow. "Why aren't there horses grazing here?" she asked. The tall grass reached almost to the bottom of her stirrup. The grain heads rippled in the slight breeze like waves on water.

"We will cut and bale it soon for hay, then we'll turn horses out on it," Erik explained.

Anna realized she had been so afraid lately she hadn't explored her surroundings, nor had she enjoyed the beauty of the outdoors as she would at home.

Erik skirted along the edge of the hay field, leading them to another patch of forest. When the forest yielded this time, it opened to a spectacular view of rolling hills and a misty valley beyond. Erik pulled Witez to a stop at the beginning of a long, grassy incline.

"There—see Anna, in that valley is where I expect the Americans will camp when they arrive," he said. "It's perfect."

"General Patton?" she asked.

Erik nodded. "When they get here. I will ride down and ask them to rescue the horses."

Anna studied the landscape. From here, the rolling hills before them gave the illusion of an easy ride. Anna worried, since the weather usually came from the west. The front range could have washouts and ravines they couldn't see.

Erik laughed when he saw her face. "Don't worry. There is a narrow road. It winds around the hills and along a creek. I've walked it and timed it. It takes three hours to reach the valley on foot—maybe one on horseback. It takes longer to get back. It's all uphill," Erik paused. "I don't know why, but we have no soldiers in this area," Erik reported. He steadied Witez and stroked his neck. "See, there, if you look carefully, you can see the remnants of the trail." He pointed to the north. Anna strained and finally saw it. She whipped her gaze to his eyes.

"You walked this?"

He nodded. "If it comes to it, if it looks like we cannot save all the horses, we can ride out," he continued. "We can save Witez and Lotnik."

"I hope we never have to make that choice," she answered. Lotnik pawed the ground. "He wants to go."

Erik looked at his watch. "Let's ride this further. I want you to be familiar with this path in case."

"In case of—what?" Anna asked.

The way the breath filled and left his lungs, the way his eyes turned dark and serious, told her all he wanted to say. Without words, he reminded her that the world outside the stud farm was dangerous.

"Erik. In case?" Anna insisted. She had to make him say the words, or it wouldn't feel true or possible unless he said the words.

"There's an old barn off this trail. It's deep in the forest, hidden from view. It's on the German side of the border. That's where we will meet if we get separated or where you can hide if you need to escape without me. I'll show you." He turned Witez down the trail and started to walk ahead. Anna squeezed Lotnik's sides, and he trotted to catch up. When she was beside Erik, she asked Lotnik to walk.

He slowed Witez, matching Lotnik's rhythm, and they rode side by side. "I'm not trying to scare you, Anna. We have to be realistic. I am a German officer. I may be killed—not by the Russians or Americans, but by Germans. By turning over the horses, I'm committing treason."

Anna pressed her lips tight. Her eyes welled with tears. "I can't—don't want to be without you."

"Trust me, Baby. I don't want to be without you either. I will do everything I can to save us, and to save the horses."

April 24, 1945

In the mare barn, Erik and Willi sat on clean bales of straw across from each other. Through the open barn door, they watched the rising moon backlight billowing clouds in gold and silver. The evening stars seemed to turn on one by one as the sunset slowly faded to darkness. It had been a surprisingly warm day, but now a chill crept into the air.

Anna appeared from their apartment. She carried a tray. Fragrant steam rose from the hot coffee in swirling wisps. She offered a cup to each and kept one for herself. Erik warmed his hands by wrapping them around the mug. Anna smiled, pulled a pair of gloves out of a pocket, and handed them to him as she sat beside him.

"What do you think? Will Fonzella foal tonight?" she asked.

"Yes. She's ready. She is waiting for dark and quiet," Erik said, lowering his voice.

Willi leaned back, bracing himself against the stall wall. "Paris is liberated, and the bombings continue even with the Führer releasing his so-called wonder weapon. It's too late for his V-2 rockets to make a difference. Last month, the Americans crossed the Rhine. Where are they? What's keeping them?" Willie sighed. "We are going to lose this war. The Russians are advancing. Fast."

"Willi," Erik scolded, slightly tipping his head toward Anna.

"Do you want me to lie to her? Prepare yourself, Anna. Don't listen to Erik." Willi laughed.

"We have over 300 horses here. When the Americans get closer. . . ." Anna started.

"You heard what the British and Americans did to Dresden. They leveled it in three days. What would happen to the horses if they bomb Hostau?" Willi grumbled.

"Willi, if you want to defect, I'll cover for you with Lessing," Erik said. "No one will blame you."

"The Russians are just over sixty miles away. If I go, I'll take you with me, Anna," Willi teased, a big grin on his face. Then he became serious. "I've heard the Russians are exacting revenge in horrible ways on German citizens as they roll through," Willi said.

Erik ground his teeth and scowled as a warning. He wanted to spare Anna from this information, but he'd heard the reports, too. Unthinkable brutality had been unleashed against women and children who were innocent survivors of the war. Daily, refugees trickled through Hostau as they fled in front of the Red Army. Erik had expected the Americans to arrive or for the Wehrmacht to make a stand. Neither happened, and the German Army was conquered from all directions. The Russians were nearing the gates of Berlin.

"I won't wait much longer. Captain Lessing is very concerned about the horses, but Rudofsky is still afraid to make a decision," Erik said. "It will be nearly impossible to move the pregnant mares, and those that have given birth have young foals at their sides. We have no trucks or transports. The newborns may not survive if we have to herd them to safety. If only the Americans were closer."

"So, you're undecided, too?" Willi asked.

"No. I want to give the horses a chance. I'm not thrilled about committing treason," Erik said. He stood and set his mug on the tray. "Do you still have that German to English dictionary you showed me last month?"

Willi tapped his shirt pocket. "I do."

"They are further away than I wanted, and it will take longer than you expect, Willi. But we go to the Americans tonight," Erik said.

Chapter Forty-Eight

KARENA SET THE BINDER ON the bed beside her. Her heart pounded out an adrenaline-fueled rhythm. *It's not real, it's history—the past,* she told herself, though she felt like she was living this war with Erik and Anna. Karena rolled to her side on the bed and glanced through her window. The sky outside slowly lightened. But she didn't want to quit reading. She couldn't.

Karena threw back the covers, stood, and fluffed her pillows. She climbed back in and wriggled her body into a comfortable position, settling into the pillows behind her back. She reached for the manuscript and spread the pages across her lap.

April 24, 1945

Fonzella foaled. The perfect chestnut filly struggled to stand but fell nose-first into the deep, clean straw. Immediately, she tried again. Her front legs were splayed out wide, wobbling precariously, but she managed to get all four legs under her. Erik watched and chuckled. This filly was tenacious and strong. Whether she reasoned it through or acted by instinct, the little one quickly learned that to stay upright, she needed to move forward when she started to fall. Within minutes, the little fräulein dashed around the stall, testing and strengthening her muscles and balance.

"If we are going to go, we should go," Willi cautioned. Erik nodded and slipped out of the stall. He glanced at his watch. It was already one in the morning. Much later than he'd intended to go.

"Anna will stay and care for the mare and foal, making sure all systems are go. You will, won't you, Anna?" Erik asked. He knew she would. Anxiety had made him jittery. Anna came and stood close to Erik's side, and he put his arm over her shoulder. "If the mare is unable to pass the afterbirth, or the filly gets in trouble, go wake Dr. Lessing."

"And if he asks where you are?" Anna tightened her grip around his waist.

Willi seemed to first look to Erik for direction, then blurted out, "Tell him—tell him one of the villagers woke us to help him with a colicky horse."

"No. Anna. Tell him the truth. Tell him we have gone to ask the Americans to rescue the horses. Tell him we can't let the animals go to slaughter to feed Russian troops. We have to try to save them," Erik said, overriding his fear and choosing to do what was right. Still, he dreaded the firing squad that awaited him if this ill-conceived plan didn't work. He had been warned.

He retrieved the small cloth bag he'd brought from the apartment. Erik had walked this mountain trail several times. The last time was yesterday. But he'd never walked it at night. Darkness had joined his list of potential enemies. They could use flashlights very sparingly. Any light at all could make them easy targets. Still, he brought one with him, hanging it by a ring on its handle to his belt. He unbuttoned his shirt and placed his hand-drawn map of the village, which included the German Command headquarters, the prisoner-of-war barracks, the stud farm, and the surrounding trails and roads he remembered from his daily horseback excursions with Anna. Being a veterinarian and not a war tactician, he hoped he hadn't forgotten anything important. He stuffed the paper inside his undershirt next to his skin and buttoned up. If they were taken prisoner by any side other than the Americans, they would find the map. It was a chance he'd have to take.

It wasn't really treachery or disloyalty to save these magnificent horses, was it? He sighed. He'd never believed in Hitler's Reich. Even when still in college, he'd viewed it with a healthy dose of skepticism. His time spent at

Janow had solidified his rebellious views. He would've died for those views had he not fallen in love with Anna. Since then, he'd only wanted to live and share life with her. Now, the time for sacrifice had come.

Quickly, he continued preparing. He removed binoculars from the bag and hung them by the leather strap around his neck. They would be nearly useless in darkness, but when they were closer to the Allied camp, he and Willi might be able to discern the person best to accept their surrender.

He kissed Anna and wrestled into his jacket. He patted his right pocket, reassuring himself the remnant of the torn white shirt was there. He would use it to signal submission and cease-fire to the first reasonable American they met in the valley. As dangerous as it seemed, they chose to cede unarmed. If their own soldiers caught them, they could say they were returning from a villager's veterinary emergency. And if the Americans didn't shoot them first, they could demonstrate their sincerity.

Anna handed each man a full canteen, some freshly baked biscuits, and ham wrapped in cloth napkins. Erik and Willie stuffed their jacket pockets.

"Do you have that dictionary?" Erik asked. "I don't even know how to give up in English." He laughed sarcastically. *A half-baked plan was an understatement.*

"I do," Willi said. "I've even been practicing. We kommen to give you pferde," Willi shook his head and growled. "Horses. Güt horses. Sehr güt horses." A big smile opened his face.

Erik returned a hesitant one. *God, I hope the Americans have an interpreter.* He thought. "You are brave, Willi. Personally, I'm scared to death," Erik said.

"I'm scared, too. I'm just faking it." Willi grinned.

If all went well, they would be outside the Allied camp just as dawn broke on the horizon.

"Anna, I love you." He reached for her and held her close for a few more seconds. "Time to go."

He turned and strolled with determination to the open door. Erik took a long look at Anna, etching a rich memory of her in his mind as he closed the barn.

For a few moments, Erik and Willi stood, allowing their eyes to adjust to the darkness. A whisper of cool night air, laden with the scent of pine, brushed against Erik's cheeks. Billions of stars glimmered against a black velvet sky. To the west, a half-moon hung close to the horizon. Its light wasn't any help. Erik would have to lead from memory.

"Shall we?" Erik asked.

Willi laughed. "Are we fools?

Erik nodded. "Probably. But someone has to do it."

They started down the trail when the silence was interrupted by raucous, slurred singing. Erik quickly pulled Willi into the forest behind some trees. He dropped to a crouch, forcing Willi down beside him. He took in only shallow breaths and turned to Willi with an index finger to his lips. From behind the tree's tangled branches, he peeked out toward the road. Several SS Soldiers dressed in the dreaded black uniforms laughed, stumbled, and braced themselves against each other. They headed up the road to their barracks on the south side of the stud farm. They would sober up quickly if they found them. Erik waited for several minutes after they passed by to stand. He looked both ways before stepping back onto the roadway.

"I thought you said there were never patrols along this road!" Willi grumbled an accusatory whisper.

"They were drunk, not a patrol," Erik replied. "Be ready, Willi. There will be more surprises. There are always surprises."

"I wish I were drunk," Willie complained.

"Ummm. Do you want to go back?" Erik asked. "Give me your dictionary, and I will go alone."

Willi shook his head. "No. We do this together."

"Let's go this way," Erik motioned as he turned off the main road to the meadow trail.

Anna ran to Lotnik's stall when Erik slid the door closed to the mare barn. The stallion slept comfortably in the straw, with his legs stretched toward the center. When she turned the latch to his door, he rolled up on his belly and stared at her, his ears pricked forward. He recognized her and knew she wasn't a threat. He stayed down. She slid the barn door closed, crossed the distance, and went to him. Since she had started training him, Lotnik had always let her climb on him, hug his neck, and stroke him. Anna could get him to lie down when she wanted to mount and ride bareback. He seemed to know how much she loved him and reveled in her soft, familiar touch. He would practically do anything for her.

Lotnik closed his eyes while she gently stroked his neck. "Erik has gone to get help to save us, sweet boy." The horse groaned softly as if he acknowledged her words. "I don't know if I can live without him. I love him," she whispered as she petted his satiny coat behind his ears.

Anna leaned forward against his neck and closed her eyes. But she couldn't rest. She could only imagine the horrors Erik would face if caught and not understood or believed. All she could do was pray.

After a few minutes, she climbed from Lotnik's back. She returned to look at Fonzella and the new filly. Anna discovered there, at least, everything was proceeding perfectly. Anna smiled.

Riding this trail was much easier than walking it, Erik thought. He'd considered riding to the camp but had discarded the idea. Even the sound of a horse's footfalls would alert soldiers. They might take it as a threat, shoot first, and ask questions after.

They had reached the creek—the halfway mark. They were close to the German-Czech border. If there were patrols, they would be around the next bend. Erik turned off the trail and guided Willi toward the abandoned barn. This detour in the forest would skirt around the checkpoint across the overgrown path. In Erik's scouting walks, the small post had never been manned. Tonight, Erik decided to be extra careful. If they were caught, he feared for Anna. Who would protect her? And the horses would be lost, and this trek would count for nothing.

"Proceed carefully, Willi. There is a checkpoint ahead," Erik whispered. "Follow me."

Willi nodded.

They moved like cats hunting prey, soundlessly placing each step so not even a leaf rustled or a twig snapped in the darkness. The frogs and crickets went silent as they passed, sending a chill down Erik's spine.

They reached the abandoned barn. Erik studied the woods around them and finally sat on one of the two tree stumps the owner had once used as firewood chopping blocks and rested. He gestured for Willi to take the other.

Erik wanted to stay outside the barn, prepared to hide if a guard unit suddenly appeared. The recent troop movements changed the dynamics hour by hour. He opened his canteen and took a cautious sip. Listening intently, he noticed that the night creatures had resumed their chatter.

Willi unwrapped a biscuit and slowly ate. It was good to keep up strength. From here, the trail steepened and became dangerous in places.

Erik watched the sky. The Eastern stars had shifted, some ducking behind the Western horizon since they started their journey.

"Finish up, Willi. We must go. I want to get to the Allied camp before sunrise. Then we will deal with fewer soldiers," Erik said, tossing the rest of the biscuit he'd started to eat into the forest for the animals. He folded his cloth napkin over the remaining one and put it back in his pocket. Willi gobbled the rest of his food and swigged water to wash it down. He stood, brushing the crumbs away from his uniform.

Erik led the way. They emerged from the forest to the west and well away from the empty checkpoint.

A star-studded darkness still ruled as they approached the last and steepest part of the trail. The narrow road meandered precariously along the side of a rocky ravine. Erik could see dots of light at the bottom of the hill. He stopped, retreated behind a boulder beside the road, and tried the binoculars, focusing in on the light. Several soldiers stood around a burn barrel, warming their hands and drinking what Erik guessed to be coffee from tin mugs.

Erik didn't know what he had expected. *Giants, maybe?* But aside from their military fatigues, they looked like other men, just like him. He glanced at his watch. It was early, four in the morning. He and Willi had made good time.

Pulling the white shirt from his pocket, he tied it to a stick he found at the side of the road. He motioned for Willi. He took in a deep breath and stood.

Willi raced ahead of him. Before he could admonish him to be careful, he saw Willi's ankle turn as he slipped on a rounded stone in the road. Willi tumbled over the edge. Erik increased his grip on his makeshift flag and raced to his friend. Willi was about six feet down against a bush in the ravine. Erik slid down the embankment, causing a small but noisy cascade of dirt and pebbles to clatter down the hillside. When he stopped to help Willi, he heard it. Someone nearby racked a round into the firing chamber of his rifle.

"Halt! Stand up and make yourself known! Hands up."

Erik braced Willi as he stood. "Nein! Nicht schieBen! Don't shoot! Nein Waffen! Wir haben keine Waffen!" Willi yelled. "We are kommen to give to you pferde—horses, finest horses!" He stumbled when he tried to put weight on his ankle. Erik noticed Willi's foot wasn't exactly positioned right. Damn! His ankle was broken.

"Hands up! Hände hoch!" The voice commanded.

"Put your hands up, Erik. Do you want them to shoot you?" Willi wriggled away and held his hands up. Erik waved the white cloth in the air. Slowly, he turned in a circle. Seemingly, out of nowhere, American soldiers surrounded them. Were these men *The Ghosts of Patton's Army?* He'd heard the term from soldiers passing through Hostau who had encountered them. They were famous and feared for their deep, devastating strikes into enemy territories. No wonder he and Willi had been unaware of their presence, even though they'd been cautious. Or thought they were.

"Nicht schieBen!" Erik repeated. "Horses. Ergeben. Surrender. We give...um...horses to you?" He mimicked what he'd heard Willi say. "Nein Waffen. No weapons."

A soldier stepped forward, took his surrender flag, and threw it to the ground, immediately establishing dominance. He quickly frisked Erik and then Willi.

"They're unarmed. This one is hurt," pointing to Willi, the American reported.

The senior officer came forward. He was a young man, his face rough with the stubble of a day-old beard. His blue eyes were kind for a ghost. "You want to surrender horses to us?"

"Ha! Here's two more who would prefer American to Russian cooking!" Erik heard the words behind him, and laughter. He didn't understand, but he knew they mocked him by the tone. *Fine. Make fun, just save the horses and don't kill me,* he thought, smiling sheepishly.

"Ja," Willi said. "Güt horses. Finest horses."

"Viele Pferde," Erik said.

"Many horses? Come on, then. We need to go see the Colonel." The man in charge motioned for them to follow. Two other soldiers prodded them along with the barrels of their rifles. When they noticed Willi dragging his left leg, they helped him.

Erik breathed easier when he saw the Jeep only a few feet ahead. Another soldier, the driver, patted them down once again.

"Gentlemen," the soldier in charge said, gesturing for them to step into the Jeep. "I'm Lieutenant Quinlivan." He pointed to his chest.

"Rittmeister—Captain Erik Kemperman." Erik pointed to himself, then to Willi. "Captain Willi Dressler," Erik said stiffly, trying to contain his fear.

Quinlivan jumped agilely into the Jeep. The driver started the engine and drove rather recklessly down the ravine. Willi groaned as they bumped along. When they made it to the valley, the driver turned right, avoiding the tent city the Americans had built. He pulled to a stop in front of a farmhouse Erik assumed they had commandeered to function as headquarters.

"Come, come," he said, motioning the Germans to follow.

Erik helped Willi hobble up the porch stairs and into the building. He wasn't sure what to expect. Had they understood they wanted help rescuing the horses? Were they going to be interrogated and then hustled off to a prison?

In the center of the well-lit room, a dining table large enough to seat eight had been placed in front of a stone fireplace. The surface of the table was covered with maps and charts. Three pressed and polished men in uniform poured over the papers. They seemed to be discussing a route.

"Colonel Reed, sir?"

"Yes? What is it, Quin?" The Colonel looked up. He was tall, fit, and obviously in charge.

"These men are Germans, sir. Captain Kemperman and Captain Dressler, they say they have come to surrender horses to us. Really fine horses."

Hank Reed studied the men. "Horses?"

"Ja. Arabs, Lipizzaner, Trakehner, Thoroughbreds." Willi reached in his pocket, thumbing frantically through his German to English book. "Hostau." He pointed east.

"Quin, go get Captain Baker. Wake him up if you have to," Reed ordered. "And get this injured man to medical."

Two soldiers appeared to take Willi to have his ankle looked at. Willi quickly handed Erik his dictionary. Erik felt helpless. He wished he'd taken the time to learn more English. Stifled by the language barrier, Erik and Reed smiled awkwardly at each other.

"Coffee?" Reed asked.

That word Erik understood. "Danke, sir."

Reed motioned for an assistant to bring coffee. He arrived with two mugs, just as Captain Baker entered the room. "This is Captain Kemperman. He doesn't speak English. He says he wants to surrender horses to us."

Baker chuckled. "He's come to the right place. We are the 42nd Cavalry Reconnaissance Squadron of the 2nd Cavalry Group, after all. Most of us know horses."

Reed laughed. Baker repeated it to Erik in German.

"Cavalry?" Erik repeated. He shook his head in wonder. Anna's prayers were answered. Amazed, he whispered 'Thank you, Almighty God of Miracles,' in his mind.

He remembered the map he'd drawn and retrieved it from under his shirt. He handed it to Colonel Reed. The Colonel unfolded and studied it, and smoothed the creases out on the table.

"Tell me about these horses," George Baker said in perfect German.

Erik felt his whole body relax and breathed out in relief. "At Hostau I am a veterinarian. We have a big farm where we breed Arabs, Lipizzaners, Trakehners, and Thoroughbreds. We have collected the best horses in all of Europe. The Russians are close. We don't believe they will respect their value. Priceless horses. Can you help us save them?"

Baker repeated Erik's flood of words into English.

Reed said. "Baker, ask him if he is in charge at Hostau?"

Baker accommodated.

"No. The Director, Lieutenant Colonel Herbert Rudofsky, is in charge of the farm. He agrees with us but is frightened to act. We want to rescue the horses, the German Reich's Commander for the area does not. I am committing treason coming to you for help, but the Russians killed the whole Royal Hungarian Lipizzaner collection when they marched through. Hostau is in their path. They will surely slaughter the horses. Purebred bloodlines will be lost forever." Erik's plea was impassioned.

Baker translated. Reed's stern expression changed to worry.

"Jimmy," Reed called out to his secretary. "Get me General Patton on the phone. Is this map correct?" He looked intently at Erik's face.

"Yes. It's right," Erik answered.

Jimmy looked up from the battered wooden desk at the far end of the room. "I have General Patton on the line."

Reed rushed over and picked up the phone. "General, sir. I have a German veterinarian here. He wants to surrender Hostau and the stud farm there to us. He says they've collected the best horses in Europe at this farm. They fear the Russians will get there first and slaughter the horses for food."

There was a brief pause, and everyone in the whole room seemed to be holding their breath. Erik was.

The reply came from the other end loud enough for everyone to hear. "GO GET THEM. MAKE IT FAST."

Chapter Forty-Nine

April 25, 1945

ANNA STRETCHED AS THE MARE barn doors slid open. Precisely at six in the morning, with German efficiency, SS guards marched four prisoners of war into the building to start the morning feeding and cleaning. They didn't look at her but stared at the ground. They were thin and dirty, and Anna's heart filled with pity. Early every morning, she snuck food to them. She left freshly baked bread and hard-boiled eggs wrapped in cloth napkins in the brush box near the tack room. The SS guards never looked there.

Anna didn't know their names, only their faces. They weren't allowed to speak to her. But they knew her name. How patient they were. They waited until their SS jailers left before searching the box for their breakfast. Anna worried it was their only daily meal.

Erik knew she did this, and as time passed, he helped. He never scolded her. He'd only warned her to be careful.

Dr. Lessing and Director Rudofsky entered the barn after the men. Anna stood erect in front of Fonzella's stall. She knew they'd come to inspect the new arrival.

"She's beautiful," Lessing said, a broad smile on his face.

"Have you named her?" Rudofsky asked.

"I thought, 'Cinnamon Spice,' sir. She will be a chestnut with a flaxen mane and tail." Anna grinned. "And her personality is quite spicy. She's already kicked out at her mother."

"Where's Erik this morning? I've looked all over for him and Willi?" Lessing asked.

Anna's smile faded, and a dark cloud of dread engulfed her. She began to rub her palms together nervously. Unable to hold back the truth, she let her shoulders drop in submission. "They have gone to ask the Americans to help evacuate the horses before the Russians arrive and kill them all."

Both Lessing and Rudofsky audibly groaned. Anna saw the prisoners cautiously look at each other with eyebrows raised. They immediately put their heads down and continued to work. They swept and cleaned at a noticeably accelerated pace as if that would bring their rescue sooner.

Lessing grabbed Anna's hand. "Not here," he warned just above a whisper. "Anna, do you have coffee on the stove? I sure could use some. How about you, Hubert?"

Rudofsky nodded.

"Shall we go to your apartment?" Lessing asked, but it really wasn't a question.

"Of course. I have baked fresh bread."

Anna had barely closed the door when Lessing raised his voice at her. "Anna! Anna! How could you let them go? What were they thinking?"

Anna glared at him. She wanted to retort. If she were in charge of the world, there would've been no war in the first place! She breathed out heavily. Lessing and Rudofsky didn't know Anna was Polish. She was only here, married to Erik because she *looked* Aryan—whatever that was.

"I'm sorry, Anna." Lessing softened.

She recognized he yelled out of frustration. "Erik and Willi have done what they thought was right. We all knew this day would come." Pretending it wouldn't was intentional blindness, she thought, but held her tongue. "When that intelligence officer— Colonel Holters was forced here because of the fuel shortage, he told us the war was essentially lost. Didn't you hear him?" His warning to get out now and save the horses was clear.

"Sit at the table. I'll pour you some coffee," Anna said as graciously as she could.

"How many horses are we talking about?" Hank Reed asked, and Baker translated.

"Three hundred mares, some pregnant, some with foals at their sides. Fifty Stallions," Erik replied.

Reed whistled and ran a hand over his hair. Erik understood. They would need at least sixty trucks and trailers, plus transportation for feed, bedding, and equipment. They could ride the stallions out. Maybe they could get by with less, but many of the mares were pregnant, and herding them would be dangerous. It should be used only as a last resort. Erik wanted to evacuate all the horses and get them all to safety.

"Quin, I want you to gather a team, do a SITREP (situation report), and get back here fast. Take Captain Kemperman to guide you to the farm," Reed commanded. He leveled his gaze at Erik as if he expected him to balk at going back to the farm. Erik would show him how wrong he was.

"Sir, may I?" Erik asked, walking to the table of maps. He found his hand-drawn one. He looked to Captain Baker to translate for him. "I suggest we go by Jeep to here." He pointed to a location on the map. "There is a trail that bypasses the checkpoint at the border. It terminates at an abandoned barn. We could leave the Jeeps there. . . ."

". . . And walk the rest of the way on foot. I think, sir, we should dress as civilians. We can get a sneak peek. See what we're up against," Quin said enthusiastically.

After Baker translated it, Erik said, "Most Wehrmacht soldiers have been redeployed north to defend Berlin. There is only a small attachment of SS soldiers left guarding the prison camp north of the stud farm. No one really guards the stud farm. We have been mostly hidden until now. The city has a civilian patrol, not particularly loyal to the Nazis, and mostly little boys and old men."

"Well, little boys and old men can be very dangerous when forced to protect their homes and families. How many soldiers are usually at the checkpoint?" Reed asked.

"None. It's been unmanned for months," Erik answered. "The way into Hostau was impassible because of winter snow. It's free now, but mountain storms are unpredictable. The SS will fight to the last man. They are your biggest problem."

"All right. Get going. Report back as soon as you can."

Lessing set his coffee mug down on the table. Deep in thought, he pulled the soft center of the warm bread away from the crust and ate it. "I'll go to Obersturmbannführer Höss and ask for his permission to surrender the horses to the Americans, again. Erik and Willi have forced our hand. They are right, you know. We should've done it long ago."

Rudofsky nodded, saying nothing. Anna filled their coffee cups. She went back to the sink and pretended to wash dishes, all the while listening to their conversation.

"It might be stronger if you go, too." Lessing stared hard at Rudofsky.

"He'll just say 'no.' He believes we can still win. He intends to fight. And that we shouldn't bring it up again. He warned he'd shoot us for treason. You remember he said fighting to the death is the only honorable thing to do."

Lessing laughed. "From the man gassing millions of prisoners? What a skewed sense of honor."

Anna dropped a coffee mug to the floor, and it shattered into pieces. *Gassing prisoners? Millions of them?* A cold chill suddenly ran throughout her body as if she'd been touched by pure evil. She'd known there were prison camps and labor camps. But this? Genocide and murder? She crossed herself.

Rudofsky sighed.

Lessing stood and went to Anna, helping to pick up the pieces. "You didn't know? Anna, I'm so sorry you had to find out this way."

"Does Erik know Höss is gassing prisoners?" she asked. "Does he?" Her eyes brimmed with tears.

"No. Not many people do. I am sure Berlin is aware that the civilian population would rise against them if they did know."

"Then we need the Americans to rescue people, not just the animals," she said strongly.

"Hubert, Anna's right. We must surrender all of Hostau, people and animals. It's time—long past time."

Near the Czeck border, at the abandoned barn, Erik, Lieutenant Quinlivan, George Baker, and twelve 2nd Cavalry soldiers waited impatiently for sunset. In their peasant garb, they should blend in pretty well. Hostau was a small village where everyone knew everyone else. They decided to wait to enter after dark.

Erik remembered how upset Willi had been when Reed wouldn't let him go along. But his broken ankle would've slowed the reconnaissance squad down.

Quinlivan divided the men into small groups of four. All twelve men stood in a semi-circle near their commander. "We will go one group at a time into the barn at Hostau. When it's safe, the next group goes." He instructed. "Erik's apartment is at the far end and will serve as our base of operation. From there, we will disburse and assess our enemy's locations and capabilities. I want you all back at Erik's apartment by midnight. Are you ready?"

There were affirmative nods all around.

The men left three Jeeps at the abandoned barn. Cautiously, they made their way through the forest, rifles at the ready at all times. With Erik as their guide, they crept through the last meadow and the forest that edged the road to the horse barns.

Erik halted the group at his usual entry point to the road. He looked and listened for danger. He remembered when he and Willi started this adventure; they'd almost stumbled into a group of drunken SS officers. From the open windows of the beer hall at the north end of the stud farm's pasture, piano music and German patriotic songs mixed and spilled into the air. He didn't want to repeat his earlier experience, so he led the Americans south, staying in the forest.

When they were across the road from the mare barn, he led them forward. Quickly, quietly, Erik edged the sliding door at the end of the barn open. The mare in the last stall neighed a greeting. Erik heard other horses scrambling to their feet, expecting treats. This wouldn't alert anyone as out of the ordinary. The vets took turns patrolling the barn at night. It was their job to make sure the horses were secure.

Erik closed the door once all twelve men were assembled in the aisle-way. As he took the lead, he realized Anna had no idea what was headed her way. Good thing she was so spontaneous and pleasant-natured.

He rapped twice on the door, softly, before opening it.

Anna turned from the fireplace when she heard the door open. Erik caught his breath. He'd only been away for a few hours, yet she struck him just like she had the first day he'd met her at Janow.

"You're home," she said, a beautiful smile radiating from her face.

"I'm home." Erik motioned the recon team through the door. They silently filed into the room. Lieutenant Quinlivan moved forward.

"Mrs. Kemperman, we're sorry to disturb you, but we are here to rescue your horses," he said. George Baker tripped as he rushed forward to interpret.

"Oh, thank you," she answered before any words came from Baker. "I speak English. Not perfectly, but hopefully well enough."

Erik smiled. Her convent education was welcome tonight. He wished he'd taken advantage of her offer to help him learn the language.

"I will be sending reconnaissance teams out and using your apartment as a base. We will be out of your way by midnight." Quinlivan explained.

"Then you've agreed to save the horses?" Anna asked.

"Yes, ma'am."

"There are prisoners of war—they are starving. Can you save them, too?"

Quinlivan was speechless for a few seconds. "We will liberate everyone who wants to be freed."

"You are welcome here, sir. How can I help?"

Erik had never been more proud of her.

The last of 'the ghosts of Patton's Army' returned from their reconnaissance missions. Anna served them hot coffee and freshly baked shortbread, and they prepared to go.

Lieutenant Quinlivan waited with Captain Baker until the last.

"Erik, don't worry. We can find our way back to the Jeeps. I'll leave you this communication device." He handed Erik an SRC-536 Handie-Talkie radio. "Colonel Reed will want to meet with your Captain Lessing and Colonel Rudofsky to negotiate the terms of surrender of the horses. Tomorrow. Let them know it's urgent."

Erik nodded his agreement. Would his German superiors agree? Erik had to do his best to make them.

"We will come to get the horses anyway. Without an agreement, we'll come with guns blazing. It won't be easy. Czechoslovakia is posted in the Soviet area of influence according to the Yalta Conference agreement. But I'm not letting prize horseflesh get into Russian hands if I can help it."

Erik couldn't hold back his surprise. "They've divided Europe already?"

"That's war, Erik. We're just pawns in this game," Quinlivan answered. "You just want to end up with your lady and your horses on the American side." He nodded toward Anna. "Keep the radio with you. We will tell you when we are on the way. Pack light, get the horses ready to go."

"Will it be a week?" Erik asked.

"Days, buddy. The Red Army is nearly at the door. They may not appreciate being relieved of horses in their sphere before they can get their hands on them." Quinlivan paused as if to make sure Erik understood and was still on board. Before he turned, he saluted with a nod. "Come on, Baker. You can flirt with the ladies later." He chuckled.

Erik hadn't noticed before, but Captain Baker stared at Anna, almost transfixed. Erik went to her, slipped his arm around her waist, and she nestled against his side. With that gesture, he let everyone know Anna was his.

Baker acknowledged him and said. "Sorry, Cap. I didn't know."

Erik smiled. *Captain Baker was going to be a problem, he mused.* Erik hoped he wouldn't have to see him again. Or at the very least, Anna wouldn't.

Chapter Fifty

April 26, 1945

ERIK SOUGHT LESSING BEFORE THEIR morning briefing and found him in front of Rudofsky's office door. "Sir, I must speak with you," he insisted. Erik displayed a confident and urgent attitude.

Lessing sighed. "What is it, Erik?"

"Yesterday, Willi and I went to the Americans." Lessing's mouth opened and closed. He uttered no words. Erik waited stoically for the consequences—a dressing down, a stripping away of rank, immediate imprisonment, a firing squad. What he'd done was treason. "They are ready to negotiate the rescue of the horses," he continued. Whether the leadership wanted it or not, Erik had left them no choice.

"Anna told us. I didn't want to believe it. But, you told her not to lie. So, she didn't." Lessing shook his head. "Erik, you need to understand that Colonel Rudofsky and I agree we must get help for the horses from the Americans. We should've gone to them days ago when we learned they had crossed the Rhine. This task should never have fallen on your shoulders." Lessing's cheeks colored. Erik wasn't sure if it was out of anger or shame. Lessing didn't excoriate him for acting, and Erik was surprised. "Where is Willi?" Lessing asked.

"He fell and broke his ankle. He is being cared for by the Americans. He is in a cast and isn't fit to travel," Erik explained. "Sir, the Americans need to meet with someone from our side today. Their intelligence indicates the Russians are rapidly approaching Hostau from the East. With your permission, I will ride down to their camp today. We may need a written letter of intent," Erik offered. "If we wait any longer, it will be too late."

"I'm the lead veterinarian here. It's my duty to go," Lessing said. "When we found out you'd gone to them, Rudofsky put me in charge of all negotiations. You and Willi forced our hand, but someone had to. We were dithering. So many German Officers are living in a fantasy land. They believe the radio propaganda and not their eyes—even while they are losing a battle."

"It is hard to face being on the losing side, sir."

"Are you a party member?" Lessing asked. Erik wondered if it mattered.

"No. I've never been. I was forced to exchange my graduation certificate for conscription papers. I was assigned to Janow," Erik said. His mind wandered to his plan to open a private practice. He put it aside. Dreams had no place in war.

"We deserve to lose. All these years, I've closed my eyes, lowered my head, and worked for the horses. I've seen enough. I've heard enough lies," Lessing said, his expression filled with sadness. "I changed my mind about the Nazis while I was Rau's adjutant. We were on a train on our way to choose—no steal—horses for this farm. As we waited for our train to depart Brest, the Nazi Party Officers drank champagne and toasted each other over the latest victories as if they'd fought the battles.

"A converted cattle train arrived at the station carrying the broken, wounded bodies of our soldiers from the Russian front. I saw them, and they could see us through the windows. They were in appalling conditions. We were in luxury. Did the Nazi Officers stop to honor them, salute them, thank them? No. Erik. They pulled down the window shades. They pulled the shades on all those hurt and injured boys—our troops—who now had ruined lives."

Erik had never seen this side of Lessing before. His stoic and emotionless demeanor belied an empathetic heart. Like Erik, seeing the end to this war and saving the horses had become more than a passion. It had become a calling.

"Captain, we've got to get our wives and your daughter out of here. Negotiate, if you can, that our families will be safely quartered behind American lines," Erik said, his chest tightening with worry. "The Americans will liberate the horses, whether or not our commander agrees. If they come with guns blazing, horses and people will die. I can't have my Anna in the middle of a battle. I know you don't want Sasha and your daughter, Karen, there either."

Lessing closed his eyes, his lungs filling with breath. He didn't speak. It was as if he couldn't speak. He just nodded.

If Lessing was successful, all they had to do was wait for the American Cavalry to arrive. Erik's thoughts strayed to a film he'd seen in the theater before the war. "Send in the cavalry!" were the hero's last words. Then, a scene shifted to galloping horsemen riding in a cloud of dust to save the day. They'll be coming in tanks instead this time, but. . .*Send in the cavalry.*

Erik walked with Lessing and Klaus, a groom from the barn. Lessing planned to ride his black thoroughbred "Indigo," and Klaus would ride a white Lipizzaner Stallion rescued from the Russians with a defecting Yugoslav Cavalry Unit.

"Take the small trail opposite the beer hall. If anyone sees you, they'll think you're just out for a morning ride." Erik explained the route he and Willi had followed to get down to the American camp in the valley. He gently held Indigo's bridle, steadying him while Captain Lessing mounted. "Ask for Colonel Hank Reed." Erik squinted his eyes. "Sir, are you sure you don't want me to go with you?"

Lessing sat tall on the back of his black thoroughbred. "No. I need you to stay here. No one else has your level head and common sense. They are likely to panic and jeopardize everything."

"Good luck, sir. And go with God," Erik said, watching Lessing and Klaus walk their horses casually down the road. If any SS officers saw them, they would believe they were on their way to help a villager with a veterinary emergency. After they turned onto the forest trail, Erik heard the horses take up the three-beat rhythm of a gallop.

Erik went to work packing boxes with medical supplies in the apothecary. He'd sent Anna to pack tack boxes full of brushes, combs, and horse blankets. He ordered the farm's farrier to trim, reset, or replace any of the stallions' worn horseshoes. As it stood, the pregnant mares and mare and foal pairs would be transported by truck to safety behind American lines. If there weren't enough trucks, the stallions could be ridden out. The only problem would be if there weren't enough horsemen to ride them. Surely, they could recruit men from the 2nd Cavalry unit. Erik had quietly introduced them to the prize horses when they'd walked through the barn last night on their clandestine tour.

Outside the apothecary's window, Erik heard car tires crunching on gravel. He looked outside. A big, black Mercedes pulled up before the farm's entry doors. A young boy raced around the front of the car and opened the back door.

What now? Erik wondered. As he watched, Rudofsky raced to greet the man who stepped out. Erik quickly stuffed the half-packed box into a broom closet. He had to intervene to keep this man from inspecting the laboratory. By his uniform alone, Erik could tell that Rudofsky ranked lower in the hierarchy than he did. Medals, ribbons, and an Iron Cross decorated the man's left side above the pocket.

"Captain Kemperman?" Erik heard Rudofsky call out.

Erik scrambled into his uniform coat and stepped out into the hall as he buttoned it. "Here, sir," he answered. "I was organizing supplies, sir." He pulled the door to the apothecary closed behind him.

"Erik, this is General Schulze. He's replacing Obersturmbannführer Höss." Rudofsky's face had drained of color. "He's the new commander for the area. He says he's heard about our horses and would like a tour."

Erik's energy slipped away, replaced by an overwhelming sense of dread.

Schulze was a big man. And by big, Erik meant fat. Beads of sweat formed on his forehead, and he constantly dabbed it away with a wadded handkerchief. His cheeks were red, but not with a healthy glow. Schulze's dark eyes held contempt for everyone around him. His breathing was labored, and no wonder. He was overweight and a smoker. The tip of a cellophane-wrapped cigar held his button-down front right pocket flap askew.

Erik saluted. "You'll have to forgive our mess today, sir. We are in the middle of spring cleaning and reorganizing." He hoped his story would cover for any of the workers still packing up tack boxes. Especially Anna. The thought sent a chill down his bones. He had to get her to safety.

"Shall we start with the stallions?" Rudofsky asked. It was clear to Erik he had no idea what to do or say.

The workers should be finished on the stallion side of the barn. Erik had them start packing there, even before he'd spoken with Lessing this morning. Erik opened the door from the office hall to the long stallion row. He breathed easier seeing the clean center aisle and the tack boxes neatly arranged in front of the stalls.

"Let me know if you'd like me to take any of the horses out for a closer look." Erik smiled, but it was strained. A new general was a new problem. The old commander had been adamant: absolutely no surrender, not to the Russians, and not to the Americans. Negotiating for that, perhaps at this exact moment, was an act of betrayal.

At the start, their attempt to save the horses stood on a paper-thin ledge, ready to crumble. *Where did this new general fall? Would he let them evacuate the horses?* If not, the Americans would roll in without an agreement, and people and animals would die. Rudofsky could no longer guarantee the peaceful surrender of the horses.

All fifty stallions were eating their morning hay. It didn't take long for Erik to recognize Schulze was no horseman. When a horse moved forward to greet him, the rotund General backed away.

The General did not comment to Rudofsky for good or bad when the tour ended. Erik realized this man couldn't care less about their precious horses.

"I'm here to defend Hostau with my militia of Volkssturm," Schulze announced. "We are here to fight to the last man."

Volkssturm? Erik knew what that meant. Germany had reached the bottom of the barrel. The General was in charge of the civilian army, mostly made up of untrained young boys. They were no match for the organized and battled-hardened American Army. All Erik could see ahead was death. And the farm? It could muster maybe ten soldiers. The mistreated prisoners of war would be no help. A battle would give them a chance to flee.

Rudofsky exhaled a trembling breath. Being assigned to care for the Reich's horses was a far cry from fighting with tanks, bullets, and grenades. They were sheltered here. Not one of the veterinarians had fired a weapon since target practice in basic training. They were trained to save life, not to destroy it.

"I've got to reach Captain Lessing," Erik said.

When Rudofsky started to protest, Erik lifted both hands, shook his head, and walked away. He slipped into the quiet of his apartment and retrieved the small radio Quinlivan had left with him last night. For a moment, he hesitated, fearing his message could be intercepted. He decided he had to risk it.

Anna arose from bed. She found Erik pacing in front of the fire. At first, she didn't want to disturb, knowing she had no power to console him. Erik hid any bits of information that he thought would scare her. The horse evacuation must not be going as they hoped. Assuming he was a bundle of nerves, she went to him and took both of his hands in hers.

"Sit with me," she said, tugging him to follow her. She led him to the sofa. He sat, but immediately scooted to the very edge of the cushion.

"What is it, love?" she asked.

"I tried to notify Lessing by radio that General Schulze is now the commanding official of the area, but he is already on his way here with an emissary from the Americans. Any attempt by Schulze to fight the Americans will end in catastrophe. His soldiers are children, just boys. They will lose. Anna, you, the farm, and the horses will be in the direct line of fire."

She lifted his hands to her lips.

"If there was a time to pray, it is now." Erik stood.

"If Captain Lessing has arranged for safe passage for us, Sasha, Karen, and I can ride to the American camp first thing in the morning," Anna said, standing to face him. "Sasha can ride one of the trained Arabian mares. Captain Lessing's daughter has a pony. We can slip out just as dawn breaks. Then you would have one worry off your mind," Anna soothed him.

"Oh, Anna. I can no longer guarantee safe passage. The SS still has patrols in the forest. They would hear the horses," Erik said. He tipped his head slightly, his brow puckering with concern.

She grinned at him. "My love. You and Willi made it to the American camp. Captain Lessing made it. No one knows what your plans are. We can make it. We can pretend we are out for a morning ride."

"I know you can," he smiled, but it was insincere.

Anna rolled up on her tiptoes and tenderly touched her lips to his cheek.

"This has got to work. It has to," Erik said.

Anna knew he didn't only mean her risky ride to the American camp, but also the horse rescue.

Erik stood tall. The sound of horse hooves clattering against the cobblestone barn aisle alerted him. "Captain Lessing," he said. He took hold of her shoulders, pulled her close, and kissed her—a rough kiss, a desperate kiss, unlike his usual tenderness. He veered around her and dashed for the apartment door.

Erik found Captain Lessing and the American in the stallion barn. The two men dismounted and tied their horses. Erik could see the exhaustion in their eyes. And he had more bad news to impart.

"Captain Kemperman, this is Captain Tom Stewart, the American emissary. He will present a letter of agreement from General Patton to Obersturmbannführer Höss in the morning."

Erik shook Stewart's hand.

"I'd like to get Captain Stewart fed and settled for the night," Lessing said. But he stared at Erik, picking up on his anxious vibe. It was two in the morning, and Erik knew his appearance had to be unsettling. "Wait for me."

Erik unsaddled Indigo and then the Lipizzaner, hanging their saddles on the fold-down racks at the front of each stall door. He untied the horses and put them away. He added a large flake of grass hay to each horse's feeder.

When Lessing returned, Erik started speaking. "Sir, Höss has been replaced by General Schulze. He oversees a militia of Volkssturm—boys, really. We can no longer guarantee the peaceful delivery of the horses."

Lessing sank onto the tack trunk in front of Indigo's stall, covering his face with his hands.

"We must go and talk them into the bargain. This can't become a shoot-out. Anna, Sasha, and Karen will ride down to the American camp in the morning. They will be protected there."

Lessing stood, his stature straightening with resolve. "I must speak with Rudofsky tonight. Erik, you will go with me to see Schulze first thing in the morning. Captain Stewart has letters of agreement from Patton. We must get his consent."

"Yes, sir," Erik said. He would get Anna, Sasha, and Karen on their way and then support Lessing in every way he could.

Chapter Fifty-One

KARENA DROPPED BOTH HANDS ON the manuscript. One roadblock after another hit the German veterinarians, but they persisted. Their dedication to saving the horses amazed her a little. What was it about those horses that had captured their hearts? Karena wished her Granny A was still here to explain it to her.

In their world, overwhelmed by everything wrong and evil, perhaps they were motivated by the desire to do something right. Would rescuing the horses appease their consciences and remove the burden of guilt they surely had to bear? It made her think.

More than anything, though, she wanted to know what happened—what separated Granny A and Dr. Erik? They seemed to be so in love. She had to read on.

April 27, 1945

Through a soft grey mist, Erik looked out of his apartment's kitchen window at the rolling green pastures. He sipped his coffee. Anna still slept. She finished packing only two hours ago, and he insisted that she rest for a few hours.

This was a beautiful place to raise horses, he thought. He understood why Gustav Rau had chosen it. Even now, as the dying gasps of the Third Reich plunged his world into chaos, its beauty promised a return to peace and tranquility.

Captain Lessing would be here any minute with the American, Captain Stewart. They needed to come up with a strategy for saving the horses, a plan B, in case the Nazi commandant insisted on a fight. They had to ask General Schulze to let them evacuate the horses. They had to convince him that giving the animals to the Americans was the only chance the horses had of survival.

Erik heard the familiar rap on his door. He set his mug on the table, smoothed his hand down his clean and pressed uniform coat, and prepared himself for his day. General Schulze had left Erik with the impression that he was unreasonable yesterday. Erik and Lessing had to face him early this morning.

He opened the door. Lessing and Stewart stepped inside.

"Are you ready?" Lessing asked.

"Yes, sir," Erik said, noticing Stewart sniffing the air like a hungry dog.

"Is that fresh coffee I smell?" Stewart asked in broken German.

"There's no time," Lessing said, impatient to get his confrontation with Schulze over with. "I have to see to it Captain Stewart is returned to the Americans by noon, or they will come get him."

Erik knew that the stud farm would be in the crosshairs. As stubborn and recalcitrant as Schulze's demeanor was, noon bordered on wishful thinking. Erik turned and retrieved a mug and filled it with coffee.

"Black, please. That's perfect." Stewart took the mug and savored a sip.

"Bring it with you," Lessing said, his face stern. "You don't understand. General Schulze may arrest us, imprison us, or just shoot us."

"Sure, I do," Stewart retorted. "That makes this coffee all the more delicious. It may be my last." He laughed. Erik made note of the amiable nature of the Americans. They were aware of the possible outcomes and bravely faced their duty anyway.

The men walked briskly out the door, down the hallway, and exited the main entrance. The morning mist clinging to ridges and folds in the mountains turned to pink and gold in the rising sunlight. A rooster crowed, announcing daybreak. The men quickly made their way toward the General's quarters. It was early, and Erik feared Schulze wouldn't be pleased if they woke him. But the clock was ticking, and they only had six hours until the noon deadline.

"Captain Stewart, will you take our wives and children with you when you go?" Erik asked. "I'd rather they be in your camp when the time comes."

He started to say more, but Stewart interrupted. "Of course. If we make it, I'll get them to safety."

Lessing grimaced. Erik knew he hadn't had time to make provisions for his family. "Anna helped them pack yesterday," Erik said, watching Lessing let out a grateful sigh.

The men walked up the cobblestone street, past the manicured yard of St. James's Church. The stone steeple reached skyward as if reaching for God's hand. Erik was filled with hope.

They arrived at the General's quarters. No guards were posted this early at the front entry, as if Schulze didn't fear the approaching Russians or Americans. Obviously, the General had bought into the Nazi propaganda.

Erik opened the door for Captain Lessing and entered after him. The General sat in front of an oak desk. His eyes narrowed. He seemed to know who they were and why they were here. Before the door finished closing, the general's face flushed with anger. He pounded his fist on the small desk and stood, shoving the table forward with his belly.

"How dare you betray Germany!" he yelled. "I should shoot you right here and now!"

Erik expected him to do just that, but stood his ground.

"You had no right to go to the Americans. No right!"

Lessing surprised Erik with his unflappable demeanor. He took the browbeating in silence. Schulze could've called in his guards, but didn't.

"You are going to die, and the American is my prisoner," Schulze's eyes flashed.

"Sir, we are in charge of the Reich's horses. They will be captured by one side or the other. Stop living in a fantasy. Your teenage boys can't fight off battle-hardened soldiers and their bombs and tanks," Erik argued. "The Americans have agreed to protect the horses—the Russians will kill them."

Lessing glared at Schulze. "The Americans must have their emissary back by noon, unharmed, or Hostau and the stud farm will be attacked full force."

"You choose, General. Let us move the horses to safety, or let them become Russian stew," Erik growled. He could see the General considered his plight. If, by miracle, Germany ultimately prevailed, how would he explain that he let the horses feed Russian troops? His lips tightened to a thin line. It became a stare-down—a game of chicken. Erik silently prayed that reason would win out.

"I won't be held responsible for this. You need to go to Generalmajor Weisenberger." Schulze retorted. "His headquarters are in Klattau. You will have my permission if he gives his."

"Thank you, sir. Your dedication and loyalty are honorable, as is our desire to save Hitler's horses," Lessing said. He saluted. Erik did not.

They left. As they walked toward the farm, Lessing turned to Erik and said, "Klattau is twenty-five miles away." His voice trembled. "I can never make that by horseback and return Captain Stewart to the Americans by noon."

Erik stopped in his tracks. The minute they jumped one hurdle, another appeared. "You must try. Take Captain Stewart by motorcycle. There's one in the feed barn with a sidecar. Go as fast as you can," Erik said, breathing deeply. "I will ride to the American camp and tell them Stewart will be late." The men started walking briskly down the lane. "Sir, I will take Anna, Sasha, and Karen to the Americans. If this goes wrong, our women and children need to be safe. They are innocent in all this. Anna is Polish. She can't be punished for being married to me."

"Polish?" Lessing seemed shocked, but then his eyes lit up with terror. "Sasha fed and housed Stewart overnight because of me. That's treason."

The men briefly looked at each other and ran for the farm.

Erik found Anna brushing Lotnik as if she were prepared to go about her usual morning chores.

He stepped through the open stall door and took the brush from her hand. "Saddle up Gazella Two and Madera. You, Sasha, and Karen are riding with me to the American camp immediately."

Erik undid the clasp on Lotnik's halter and let him free in his stall. Anna was momentarily stunned but quickly followed his orders. She pulled the stall closed as she left.

"Go, quickly. I'll tell Mrs. Lessing. Pack only the things you'll need overnight," Erik instructed.

"What's happened?" Anna asked, trotting alongside him.

"I'll explain on the trail. Go. Go." His voice was desperate. "Wait. Anna. I love you."

She turned back and smiled at him. "I love you, too."

Within fifteen minutes, three Arabian mares and Lessing's daughter's pony were saddled, packed, and on the main road. Erik noticed several peasants turning to stare as they rode by. He couldn't give them any clues about what was coming their way, not yet anyway. The villagers loyal to the Reich would interfere, perhaps believing saving the horses was treachery, not heroism. Erik feared they would set up an ambush.

The sun overhead was bright and warm. It was a perfect day for a jaunt through the woods and a picnic. Erik waved to the villagers and smiled, even though he wanted to tell them to flee Hostau. If Generalmajor Weisenberger decided to take a stand against the Americans, there would be chaos.

Erik led his refugees off the road to the meadow trail. They rode to the border, and Erik went ahead, scouting for small SS bands patrolling the forest. The way was clear, and they reached the outskirts of the camp within the hour. When they entered the camp, they were immediately arrested. They were taken at gunpoint to Colonel Reed.

When Erik looked at the round clock above the Colonel's desk, he understood the sudden distrust. The noon hour had passed. It was two.

Captain Baker stood beside Colonel Reed.

"We ran into difficulty securing a ceasefire and peaceful transfer of the horses," Erik said, and Baker translated. "Captain Lessing and Captain Stewart had to go to Klattau, twenty-five miles north of the farm, to negotiate with the area commandant. They couldn't complete their mission before your deadline, but they are trying to secure the agreement now. Please allow them more time."

"Captain, I want to help you save your horses. We have our orders. With or without permission, we are going in." Reed was clear.

"I understand, sir," Erik felt defeated. He wished he and Anna had ridden Lotnik and Witez. He could surrender the Polish stallions and ask the Americans for asylum. He understood from Captain Stewart that hundreds of German soldiers and refugees were turning themselves over to the Americans every day. Everyone seemed to know the war was lost, except the Germans in charge at Hostau.

"May I ride back and see if I can help Captain Stewart?" Erik asked.

"Are you here alone?" Reed studied him.

"No, sir," Erik said.

Two soldiers brought the women and girl into the room. Reed stood shocked.

"I have no delusions about where Germany stands. I am asking you to shelter my wife and Captain Lessing's wife and daughter."

Reed smiled. "You do believe you can secure Captain Stewart's return." He nodded. "All right. You may go. I expect you to contact me as soon as you secure Stewart's release, and he's on his way to us."

"Yes, sir," Erik said. "When you come, we will have the horses ready to evacuate. One way or the other." He turned and took both of Anna's hands. She was scared, but said nothing. Her smile said it without words; she trusted him completely. He had to be worthy of that trust.

Erik met up with Lessing and Stewart on the trail at the border. It was such a relief, he lost his words.

"It's clear all the way to camp," Erik finally said.

"See you boys in the morning," Stewart said, a big grin on his face. "I'll leave you here." He pivoted his horse to face down the canyon toward the valley and took off at a hand-gallop.

"It went well?" Erik hesitated. They could still be in for a battle. He knew how much Lessing wanted to save all the horses.

"Weisenberger told me, 'Do whatever you want.'" Lessing laughed. "As we left, I noticed some of his men were packing up. I didn't know if they were deserting or the whole unit was moving. Everything seemed to be in turmoil."

"Anna and Sasha are safe," Erik reported.

"Let's make sure Stewart is," Lessing said.

The two men rode behind him to the rocky cliff face. They saw the trail winding down through the draw and ending at the camp. In a few minutes, Stewart came into view, riding the white Lipizzaner stallion. When he met with the perimeter patrol, he stopped for a second and then resumed his gallop to Colonel Reed's quarters.

With Stewart home and the women and children safe, Erik's mind calmed enough that he noticed the camp. In the last two days, the Americans had fenced in several large pastures and built smaller paddocks for the stallions out of logs they'd harvested from the forest. Yankee ingenuity. He heard about it, but now he'd seen it in action.

Erik smiled. They had accomplished the first part of their mission.

After putting the horses away. Erik and Lessing retired to Erik's apartment. He found the delicious stew Anna had left in the refrigerator for them. He dumped it into a pan and turned on the electric stove.

Lessing took down two glasses. He poured a finger of Jägermeister in each. The two men stood in front of the stove, waiting for the stew to bubble. They turned toward each other, smiled, and clinked their glasses together in a heartfelt toast.

Chapter Fifty-Two

April 28, 1945

ERIK AWOKE TO THE DISTANT rumbling of diesel engines, occasional sporadic machine gun fire, and small explosions from tanks. *The Americans!* He leaped out of bed and quickly dressed. They had promised Reed there would be no resistance when the American troops arrived to take charge of the stud farm. Erik had warned, however, that the veterinarians could not control what they might encounter on the way to the farm.

A part of Erik smiled, imagining their rescue would soon be here. Another part still clung to fear. Something could always go wrong. Erik strolled to the farm's front entrance and studied the horizon. Rudofsky and Lessing arrived, pressed and polished. They stood side by side, watching for the appearance of the trucks and tanks.

None of the leaders of this horse breeding experiment were members of the Nazi party. Yet they had assembled this unique collection of the finest horses in Europe under the guise of breeding an Aryan horse unique to Germany. A horse that could not be defeated on the racetrack, in any sport competition, or in war. The Super Horse for the Super Race.

As he watched in silence, Erik ruminated over his feelings about the war from as far back as his college days. He had never believed in the eugenics and racism of the Nazis. Instead, he believed that, under the pretense of superiority, they justified savagery and the plunder of their neighbors. Not one of the Nazi leaders lived up to the strong, stoic, blond ideal they touted. He'd often wanted to ask: *Do you even have mirrors?* Where did fat, unhealthy, drunkards like Schulze get the idea that they were the elite? The violence they'd sown would reap the whirlwind.

"Anna," he whispered to himself. Would he and Anna be swept up in the retribution that loomed like storm clouds on the horizon? By loving her, by pleading for her hand in marriage, had he condemned her? As a German officer, would he face retribution for the crimes he allowed to be committed in his country's name? After the evacuation, he would beg Colonel Reed to help Anna escape to America. She had nothing to do with this war. For a fleeting moment, he wondered if he could ask if they both could go free.

Erik glanced at the village's main street. A black limo arrived in front of General Schulze's headquarters. The driver quickly opened the back passenger door and the trunk. Young boys in uniform hurried boxes from the building and threw them haphazardly into the car. The pudgy General hastily climbed inside. The limo sped away in a cloud of blue exhaust smoke and dust. Erik laughed to himself. For all his bluster, the General fled Hostau at the first signs of trouble. But he headed east. Instead of landing in American hands, he may find himself captured by the Russians.

Within minutes, Erik noticed General Schulze's young, confused, and disorganized militia filing out of town with their horse-drawn artillery heading in the same eastern direction. Briefly, Erik wondered what orders the General had given to the Volkssturm. Was it to fight to the last man? Or with their cowardly General gone, would they disband and go home? He hoped for the boys' sake that they would choose the latter.

"Well, I will go down in history as the man who gave away Hitler's horses," Rudofsky sighed, looking at Erik.

Erik shook his head. "Sir, you chose to save their lives. History will portray you as a hero," Erik said.

"Keep watch. I'm going inside to remove Hitler's portrait and all Nazi emblems and flags." He laughed. "Viva America!"

Rudofsky was an Austrian by birth but, most of all, a devoted horse-man. Erik knew Rudofsky and Lessing were not members of the Nazi party. Delivering the horses to the Americans was the right choice. The only choice.

As Erik and Lessing watched and waited, Erik saw the first American M8 Scout car cresting the small rise in the road in front of the beerhall. It was followed by several M8 Howitzer Motor Carriages and two M24 Chaffee light tanks. Small American stars and stripes flags fluttered from brackets mounted on both front sides. Though dangerous, the local Nazis would not be able to stand against this modest American force. Erik prayed the Nazis wouldn't try.

Quinlivan had explained his plan to Erik when he'd left Anna in the Americans' care. Reed would divide his available troops into three parts. One unit would advance from the north, a second one from the south, and Quinlivan's would return to Hostau up the forest trail they had traveled the night of their original reconnaissance.

Erik heard Lessing breathe out in relief and smiled inside. A soldier jumped out from the right side of the first Jeep in the convoy with a folded flag. He pulled down the Nazi flag and raised the American flag, letting it fly over the stud farm.

The Cavalry had arrived to do what they do best. They were here to save the day.

Anna looked out the window of the cottage Colonel Reed had given her and the Lessings to use. She was afraid to open the door. She realized the man who knocked was one she'd met before, a Captain Baker. He stood at the front door with several soldiers, with trays covered by cloth napkins. Anna recognized the scent of ham and freshly brewed coffee. She knew Sasha and Karen Lessing were as famished as she was. Earlier, Karen and Sasha had scoured the cabinets for food and found them empty, so this was a blessing. Anna cautiously opened the door.

She stepped aside, and the soldiers practically danced in, setting the trays on the dining table. Captain Baker delivered a Mason jar filled with meadow wildflowers. Anna smiled at the gift, but still had misgivings about the gesture. She suddenly remembered the Russian soldiers pillaging the convent as they withdrew from Poland at the beginning of the war, and backed away in fear. Anna studied the men, wary of their motives.

"How lovely," Sasha said. "Thank you, Captain Baker." She sat when another soldier held a chair for her and then for Karen. Sasha seemed to trust them.

"At your service, ladies," Baker said cheerfully. He pulled out a chair for Anna, gesturing for her to sit. *Was this the way the Americans treated their prisoners?* Anna appreciated it but still viewed it with skepticism.

Willi hobbled through the door on crutches, his lower leg encased in a plaster cast. Anna knew this wasn't the way the POWs were treated in Hostau by the Germans. They were starving and filthy, and the injured were left to die of infection. She and Erik had secretly fed and treated them whenever they could. Willi wore clean clothes, and his face was freshly shaven. His cheerful personality had returned. He was like he was when they first arrived at Hostau.

"Anna, you are here. Safe." He lumbered toward her as if seeking a hug. She smiled at him, but embracing him was unwieldy. The wooden crutches were in the way.

"Sit down, Mrs. Kemperman. Enjoy your breakfast while it's hot," Captain Baker said, grinning. Anna relaxed a little because the captain respectfully acknowledged her by her married name. She sat, and Baker took the chair beside her. With a flourish, like a magician completing a magic trick, he removed the napkin covering her plate. She couldn't help but smile. Baker set his elbows on the table, resting his chin on his folded hands. A big grin cracked his face open, and his eyes sparkled. He had revealed a plate with a generous helping of scrambled eggs, ham, hash-browned potatoes, and toasted bread. A veritable feast. All the same, he made her uncomfortable, and if she weren't so hungry, she'd have difficulty eating.

"Will they be bringing the horses down today?" Willi asked, taking the chair on Anna's other side.

"Tomorrow, I believe," Baker said, replying to Willi's broken English. "We have to evaluate how many trucks we need. Three hundred horses are a lot of horses."

"But you will get them all out, won't you?" Anna asked.

"Yes, Ma'am," Baker said. "Once the farm is secured, my unit will move in to load the pregnant mares and mares with foals. I understand we may be riding the stallions out."

"I should go back with you. I can help. I can ride," Anna said, thinking of Lotnik. He'd been on the mountain trail before, but only with her. She wasn't sure how he'd react to a new rider.

"I'm afraid we won't be able to allow that, Missus. There are reports of rogue bands of SS soldiers roaming the forests," Captain Baker reported. "Captain Kemperman went to a lot of trouble to ensure you ladies were safe."

Anna took in a deep breath, her hunger suddenly replaced by uneasiness. "Oh, God! I want the war to be over!"

Erik stood beside Captain Stewart, watching as trucks and trailers pulled into a convoy line along the back of the barn. Evacuation would start first thing in the morning.

In a surprising twist, many of the newly American-freed prisoners of war had volunteered to help load the horses. They counted it as an act of revenge against their German captors. Many of the prisoners declared Hitler would never get the prize horses, no matter the outcome of the war. It became a mission to them. To Erik's amazement, he, Lessing, Rudofsky, and the few German cavalry officers working the farm were not counted among the enemy, even though they wore the Wehrmacht uniform. As the last of the trucks rumbled to a stop in line, Erik felt a sense of relief. Tomorrow, this part of their journey to safety would be finished. They would beat the arrival of the starving Russian troops, and the horses would be in the American sector.

Major Andrews had quickly set up perimeters around the pastures nearest the barn, preparing to defend the horses and the farm if need be.

Armed with rifles, Erik patrolled with Lieutenant Quinlivan, his second-in-command, Major Robert Andrews, and Captain Stewart, reassured themselves they could successfully defend the horses with their small unit of seventy soldiers and equipment. Erik was grateful the Americans trusted the veterinarians. They knew the Germans betrayed their home country and risked life and limb to secure the horses. And if their heroic mission failed, they would face a firing squad.

In the woods, beyond the pastures, Erik thought he saw shadows rush between the trees. "Soldaten," he whispered to Stewart, who understood rudimentary German.

"Soldiers?"

"Soldiers." Erik pointed to the trees. "Shutzstaffel. Waffen SS."

The men saw a muzzle flash, heard the snap of gunfire and dropped low, taking cover behind one of the Chaffee tanks. The Americans returned fire. A 75 mm Howitzer launched a round in a blaze of fire, and it exploded in the trees, smashing and raining branches and leaves on the enemy. The ratta-tat-tat-tat of a machine gun barrage followed, pinning the SS soldiers down. Unable to return fire, some retreated, others emerged from the woods, waving white flags, arms raised in surrender. Erik, Quinlivan, and Stewart dashed for safety inside the stone walls of the barns. With rifles ready, they positioned themselves in the stalls nearest the action.

The horses became restless and panicky when gunfire erupted. Erik and Lessing raced to administer tranquilizer injections to calm the most frightened animals between skirmishes.

For the next five hours, clashes breached the silence, and when the German small arms fire met American brute strength, the soldiers slunk away or surrendered. Finally, peace settled around the farm as the sun disappeared below the western horizon.

Erik sank to a straw bale in front of Lotnik's stall. Lessing sat across the barn aisle from him on another bale, clutching his rifle.

"Do you think that's it? Are they finished?" Lessing asked, wiping his brow with his sleeve.

"Who knows? Don't they see the war is essentially over?" Erik complained.

"They believe the propaganda," Lessing sighed.

Lieutenant Quinlivan joined them, smiling like Alice in Wonderland's Cheshire Cat. "Gentlemen, our troops from the North and South are converging on the farm. The Germans have retreated, and we're evacuating the horses as soon as possible."

Chapter Fifty-Three

April 30, 1945

ERIK FELT THE MUSCLES IN his back cramp and ache. He rolled his shoulders and stretched side-to-side to relieve the pain. The final truck pulled forward to be loaded. This one should be easy. They'd saved it for last. The three mares had recently foaled, and they could easily coax the mares to follow their babies into the truck bed.

Erik shoved the last reluctant colt up the loading ramp and hoisted him into the truck bed. He corralled him against the makeshift side railings with outstretched arms while Lessing led Mom up the ramp. When the pair was reunited, soldiers quickly slid the wooden slats into place across the back. They left just enough room for Erik and Lessing to inch through and then locked them in place.

Erik jumped down, helped the soldiers remove the ramp, and loaded it into the back of the equipment truck. He stood back and thought, By the grace of God, they'd accomplished this part without incident.

"Good news," Quinlivan said, walking up to Erik. "The hay, straw, and grain supplies have just crossed the border into Germany." He showed Erik his hand-held radio. "When we arrive, we can at least feed the herd." He laughed.

Erik was always surprised by the Americans' lighthearted demeanor. They had seen real combat. Erik had only seen the aftermath when he'd had to treat the injured. The skirmishes of yesterday were the only times he'd fired a weapon. Quinlivan and Stewart likened it to swatting a mosquito.

"Was there resistance?" Erik asked, and Stewart translated. Though Erik felt they routed all resistance yesterday, he couldn't be sure. There were rumors of pockets of German troops throughout the mountain forests, fighting to the end.

"All quiet," Quinlivan replied, lifting his hand and displaying crossed fingers. The loading was complete, and the horses were secure. The lieutenant signaled to the truck driver. Soldiers guided the trucks around the barns and onto the main road.

It was a beautiful April day. The sun overhead provided them with a perfect temperature—neither too hot nor too cold. The sky was crystal blue and cloudless.

Quinlivan assembled the riders. Erik studied the group crowded in the outdoor arena for instructions and horse assignments. It was an interesting milieu. Poles, Brits, Czechs, Yugoslavs, and German resistance fighters, freed from the labor camps—volunteered to ride the stallions and geldings, and to herd the small band of remaining mares to safety.

Lessing and Stewart would lead the remaining twenty-five pregnant mares, assisted by five soldiers riding geldings, ensuring the herd stayed together. The band would be protected by some M8 Scout cars.

A half-hour later, Erik, Quinlivan, and the hodgepodge of riders, American soldiers, German cavalry from the farm, and newly released prisoners of war, would follow down the meadow trail.

The men went to their assigned horses. Erik mounted Witez, and Quinlivan sat astride Lotnik to ride in sweep position, in case more inexperienced riders needed help. They followed the unlikely caravan of Europe's finest horses down the road past the beerhall, taking the trail through the forest to the border.

Erik stopped and turned back to look at the stud farm that had been home for the last two years. His spirit was filled with hope. He briefly envisioned home, his father's dairy, and the veterinary clinic dream that awaited him. With Anna by his side, it all seemed within reach. He was sure this war was over. For a moment, Hostau was quiet as if the whole village held its breath.

Erik heard a distant rumble. He could see a brownish cloud rising from the road on the far eastern end of the main street. He focused on the sound. Was it German reinforcements? The Russians? His heart pounded in his chest. Both possibilities were terrifying.

Like an olive-green monster materializing out of the dust, the first T-34 Russian Tank lumbered down the rise in the road. It was the first of many. A long column of tanks snaked down the last mountain curves to the village.

Erik wheeled Witez west toward the forest trail, squeezed the horse's sides, and galloped toward the American camp.

Anna paced back and forth in the main room of the small farmhouse. When the trucks with feed supplies arrived, she quickly raced out and pitched in, readying the temporary paddocks for the arrival of the horses. She filled feeders with hay, and the make-shift troughs with fresh water. As soon as the horses reached the valley, she wanted to get them settled. But more than anything, she wanted to know Erik was safe.

While eavesdropping on Erik and Dr. Lessing's earlier conversations, Anna had learned that rogue bands of Nazi soldiers roamed the forests. So she didn't dare walk to the tree line to pray.

Anna told herself that saving the horses was a mission blessed by God. Who would expect the Twelfth Cavalry to occupy the valley just miles from the secret breeding farm at Hostau? There were many military divisions, but this one was packed with horsemen. Who would believe Erik and Willi would stumble on men who knew and loved horses when they left to ask the Americans for rescue? It was truly a miracle from God. With eyes closed, she whispered, *Thank you*.

The first horse transports should arrive two to three hours behind the supplies, but Anna had no sense of time. She realized worrying didn't make time pass faster; it just made waiting insufferable.

Anna feared Captain Baker was following her. Whenever she emerged onto the front porch to look toward the mountain trail, he would materialize as if from nowhere and want to talk. She wondered if Colonel Reed had assigned him to watch her. Did the Americans believe she was dangerous or a spy?

Anna stopped pacing and listened. She heard the mares she and Sasha had ridden to the camp begin to call out. She rushed to the porch to look. The mares came forward in the pasture, ears pricked, and nostrils flared. They knew their herd mates were arriving. Though she couldn't see the trucks yet, she could hear the engines.

Erik slowed Witez and rode to Lotnik and Quinlivan's side. "The Russians are at Hostau."

"We'd better hustle," Quinlivan said, spurring Lotnik into a trot. Their action cued the other riders to pick up their pace.

Suddenly, several rifle shots rang out from the wood line. Snipers! Controlling Witez as he danced around in place, Erik looked toward the forest and noticed familiar boys—General Schulze's Volksstrum. He spurred Witez to get out of the line of fire.

The forward stallions began to spook and panic. The American soldiers were able to manage the frightened horses and push them into a hand gallop. Within minutes, the pounding of charging horses replaced the sound of gunfire. They crossed the border, and the rifle fire stopped. The excited animals pranced and danced nervously the rest of the way down to the valley.

After he entered the protection of the American camp, Erik watched as the American patrols emerged from everywhere, surrounding and providing protection for the escaping soldiers and horses. He dismounted and held Witez by his bridle reins. He looked back toward the forest. A handful of German soldiers—boys—emerged from the trees waving white flags. They surrendered to the American forces. Erik recognized one of the young men. These were the very soldiers who, only moments ago, had fired on them.

Erik led Witez to one of the empty paddocks next to Lotnik. He couldn't help but smile. The beautiful gray was already being groomed and coddled by Anna.

"Darling," she whispered. She opened the gate and ran to him. He dropped Witez's reins and held her close. She felt wonderful in his arms, her soft cheek against his. Witez, not one to miss out on hugs, nuzzled his way between their faces to get his share of love. Erik and Anna both laughed.

"Not one man or animal was injured. Can you believe it?" Erik said, holding Anna's hand as they walked quietly around the paddocks. They reached the large pastures the Americans had built for the mares and foals. Erik leaned against the top log rail of the fence, watching a group of three colts racing around their grazing mothers.

"They've all settled in so well," Anna mused.

Erik rubbed his brow. "This is only temporary. We rest them here for a few days, and then we move west to a farm in Mansbach. Lieutenant Quinlivan says it's an elaborate stud farm with everything we need. Plus, it is in the solidly American-controlled sector. Depending on how things go, we will be safe there for a while."

"Safe. What a wonderful word. But I already feel secure because you're here." Her voice was tender, and the words caressed him with their softness. He slid his arm along her shoulders, but knew they weren't out of harm's way.

As dusk darkened the sky, stars began to appear above the pink glow on the horizon. "Shall we go in?" he asked.

"Of course. You must be exhausted," Anna said. "If you'd like, I'll give you a back rub until you fall asleep."

She reminded him once again why he loved her so much. Erik couldn't think of anything better.

May 1, 1945

Through the veil of sleep, noise filtered into the bedroom's open window. Erik woke and listened carefully for a threat. Instead, the delicious smell of food—onions and garlic caramelizing in butter, potatoes, and beef—stirred his hunger. He looked out the window. It was dark, and stars still glittered in the sky. Anna rested against his shoulder, and he closed his eyes, savoring the warmth and comfort of her body against his.

"Baby," he whispered. "It's time for me to get up and feed the horses." He kissed the top of her head. She snuggled up tighter to his side.

"Must we? You feel so good. I don't want to move," she said softly.

"Neither do I. But. . . ."

"Duty calls." She finished his sentence for him. "Just a few minutes longer?"

He wrapped his arms around her. "When this is over, we'll go somewhere and be alone. Just the two of us. I promise." Erik realized they had never had a honeymoon, like traditional couples in peacetime used to do. The simple things he remembered and expected to happen since childhood had been destroyed by war. He had to make it up to her somehow.

Anna playfully pulled back the covers, rose, and tossed his clothes on top of him. He laughed and watched her dress. He quickly dressed, too.

Hand in hand, Anna and Erik went outside the cottage. Erik stood on the porch looking out over the serene pastures. The Lipizzaner mares' slick white coats shimmered in the full moon's light. Their black foals raced and played as they followed their moms to the hay the soldiers spread in a long row from the back of a truck.

"The Americans—so efficient. They've done our job for us," Erik commented, squeezing Anna's hand. He saw Captain Baker approaching the cottage with a steaming kettle, hopefully of coffee. "Get some mugs for us, Anna," Erik asked. But he noticed she'd stiffened, and her mouth tightened into a frown.

"Guten Morgen," Baker called out cheerfully. "I brought coffee when I noticed you were up."

Erik nodded his thanks with a smile. Anna brought out a small tray with mugs, spoons, a pitcher of milk, and a sugar bowl. She set them on the small table between two chairs and quickly moved to Erik's side, linking her arm with his. A goofy grin creased Baker's face when he looked at Anna, like a schoolboy with a crush on his sixth-grade teacher.

"Colonel Reed needs to meet with you and Captain Lessing this morning. He thinks we must start moving the horses to Mansbach early tomorrow morning." Baker poured coffee into each of the cups. "Cream?" He doctored a mug and handed it to Erik.

"Thank you," Erik said.

"Anna?" Baker asked.

"Yes, cream please," Anna said. Erik studied her. Baker made her uncomfortable. She took the mug of coffee Baker offered cautiously, intentionally making sure they didn't touch. Her fear or distaste was subtle. Did she consider the Americans as enemies, even after they had helped evacuate the horses? Or had Baker been too forward around her on the one night Erik had been required to be away?

"Will you sit?" Erik asked, gesturing to the chairs on the porch.

Baker lowered himself into a chair. Erik pulled another chair over for Anna, keeping her next to him and on the opposite side of the table from Baker.

"Mansbach is two hundred kilometers. Do you think we can make that in one day?" Baker asked.

"If the trucks can go thirty-five miles per hour, the transported horses should take about four hours. We would have to allow time for unforeseen hazards. So, four to six hours might be reasonable. Six to eight days for the horses we ride and herd," Erik said. "I'm worried for the horses that aren't shod. Their hooves will be worn to the quick, even if we pack them with mud. They could be irreparably damaged." He sighed.

After an exasperated pause, Baker said, "We need to find more trucks." He stood, setting his empty on the tray. "Well, Dr. Kemperman, let's go see Colonel Reed. We have work to do."

Erik rose from his chair and swigged down his last swallow of coffee. He reached for Anna, offering her his hand. She shook her head.

"I'll clean up," she said. Erik tried to read her. It was clear she didn't like Baker.

"We'll talk when I get back," he whispered as he kissed her cheek.

As the men started down the stairs, a sliver of gray light brightened the eastern horizon.

"Hey! Baker! Did you hear?" A soldier turned and jogged backwards, slowing as he passed the men. "Hitler is dead! Hitler killed himself!"

"Is the war over?" Baker yelled back.

The soldier shrugged.

Baker started to translate, but Erik understood. "Tot?" He let out a small laugh.

"Der Fuhrer ist tot."

Chapter Fifty-Four

August 20, 1945

THE SUMMER MORNING WAS CLEAR and bright. The sun would soon rise over the mountaintops and bathe the pasture grasses with light. The young foals would frolic and play together while their mothers grazed in the warmth. Anna dressed in clean, tan Jodphurs and a crisp white blouse. She braided her long, blonde hair. She slipped into her riding boots and rambled to the kitchen, pulled on her apron, and began to fix breakfast.

Looking out her kitchen window, Anna saw Erik, Captain Lessing, and Lieutenant Quinlivan returning from their early morning ride as she prepared an apple strudel. Their ride had become a tradition. Smiling, she realized they had left exercising Lotnik for her to do after breakfast. She slipped her pastry into the oven.

The past weeks had raced by. The journey to Mansbach had been exhausting for men and horses. Anna and Erik had settled into their new accommodations. It was a small apartment like Erik's had been at Janow, but Anna was comfortable here. Through the summer, life had been blissful. They foaled out the remaining pregnant mares. They rode horses through the grassy meadows without the threat of bullets, bombs, and hostile soldiers.

On May 7, 1945, Germany surrendered unconditionally. The war in Europe was officially over. To Anna's surprise, the Americans had accepted the German cavalry officers as if they were old friends and not prisoners of war. The Nazi leaders, on the other hand, were justifiably rounded up and jailed. There were unconfirmed whispers of Russian atrocities in the Soviet sector, but they paled in comparison to the reality of the German extermination camps. Every time she thought of it, Anna shuddered.

At the end of the horse evacuation, it was rumored that Colonel Rudofsky had hung up his Wehrmacht uniform, dressed in civilian clothes, and walked home to his family. It was like that everywhere. A letter from Nelek told her the news from Poland. Major Fellgeible was rescued when his prison camp was freed. But Father Jerzak, Mother Superior, and the convent's sisters had all died in the squalor of the Majdanek labor camp near Lublin. She had learned that Benit escaped his Nazi captors and fled along Father Jerzak's secret route to Holland, where he'd joined a group of resistance fighters.

Colonel Reed had asked Erik to stay and help with the horses until their ownership was adjudicated. Though Reed's unit was called a Cavalry Group, they were mechanized and didn't have a veterinary staff to help care for the horses now in their charge. Erik agreed to stay, but Anna feared it was more for her than self-preservation. Horses had always been part of her life. He would never ask her to give them up.

After arriving at Mansbach, Colonel Reed contacted the Austrian, Alois Podhajsky, director of Vienna's famous Spanish Riding School, to return the 219 purebred Lipizzaner mares to their home. Though Anna was Polish, she was just an orphan from the convent next door to Janow Podlaski. She had no authority to take ownership of Janow's Arabian horses for Poland. Poland had fallen under the Soviet fist, and no one could come to claim the horses, even if they wanted to. The Polish Arabians became 'spoils of war' and possessions of the U.S. Army.

Anna looked out the window again at the beautiful green pastures below. She knew her future was uncertain. She feared Erik could be arrested as an officer of the Reich at any time. Europe demanded retribution. Russia was already taking theirs. The stories told by refugees about the treatment of German men, women, and children were frightening. Erik only walked free because the Americans lacked veterinarians. Anna closed her eyes and praised God for that.

She filled the coffee pot with water and placed it on the stove to percolate. The scent of baked apples and browning pastry filled the air before the small round kitchen timer buzzed, and Anna removed the strudel from the oven.

Erik, Lessing, and Quinlivan would soon gravitate to her kitchen for breakfast. The men seemed to have become great friends, and Erik had learned to speak and understand some English. Lately, he'd insisted they only speak English, even privately. He believed he would need to know the language when he finally returned home and opened his veterinary clinic. Still, they were unsure what being conquered by the Americans would look like.

"Ooh, Anna, it smells heavenly in here," Quinlivan said as the men entered the apartment.

Erik stepped behind Anna, wrapped his arms around her waist, and kissed her neck. "Thank you for this. You are such a good cook; I'll never be able to get rid of these guys." He laughed.

"That's right. Why would I trade Anna's cooking for the slop served at the mess tent?" Quinlivan replied.

The men took their regular seats around the table. As Anna set plates and silverware in front of each man, she mused on how easily and quickly they had given up hostilities. They were bound together by a common love—horses. She filled mugs with coffee. Erik sliced and served the pastry.

"Later this morning, Colonel Fred Hamilton from the States will inspect the horses. I think he plans to choose horses to take back to the remount stations," Quinlivan announced, then took a bite of strudel. He closed his eyes as if savoring the buttery sweet pastry. "Oh, this is heavenly, Anna."

"Will you ask this man if they are returning Lotnik and Witez to Janow?" Anna asked, filling his cup with coffee. "Your generals gave the Lipizzaners back to Austria. Surely, they will give the Arabians back to Poland," Anna said, not meaning to be disrespectful, though they could take it that way.

"Anna, Poland is now in the Soviet Sector. Stalin is the same as Hitler, just a Russian version. Maybe even worse," Lessing said. "You surely don't want to go back to that."

"Rudolf is right, Anna," Quinlivan said. His face screwed into a frown. "Like Patton, I believe we shouldn't stop at Berlin. We should press on to Moscow. Kick the commies out." He took a sip of coffee and then looked over the rim of his mug. "Don't repeat that. It's not very popular."

"I've had enough of war," Erik said. "Do you think the command will let us buy Lotnik? He's Anna's favorite, and I can care for him at my father's dairy," Erik said. Anna smiled at him. He was such a good-hearted husband. *But, pay for him with what money?* she wondered. Germany was in ruins. Even if Erik could establish his clinic, who would be able to pay for his services? It might be months or even years before the farms were restored to their before-the-war profitability. Owning Lotnik was a dream she believed would go unfulfilled.

"I don't know. I don't control that part of it," Quinlivan answered. As he looked down into his coffee cup, Anna saw the desperation in his eyes. "I can ask."

George Baker and Willi announced their arrival with a soft knock on the door. They didn't ride with the group. Willi was still on crutches, though his broken ankle was healing well. Captain Baker usually spent early mornings translating communications from German to English for Colonel Reed.

Anna quickly retrieved mugs for them as they took their usual seats. After filling their cups, she started another pot of coffee on the stove.

"Anna, Colonel Reed asked if you would ride Lotnik for Colonel Hamilton when he arrives later this morning," Baker said sunnily.

She felt her heart sink. She knew it was the best outcome for Lotnik— going to America. He would be well-treated. Could she stand never seeing Janow's horses again? The thought hurt her heart.

Once the men returned to work, Anna slowly walked to Lotnik's stall. She removed a brush from the tack trunk in front.

"My beautiful boy, an American is coming this morning to decide your fate," she whispered as she opened his stall and went inside. He lifted his head, greeting her with a soft nicker. She began brushing away the remnants of overnight straw clinging to his coat. "How can he look at you and not want to take you to America? Huh?" She brushed his coat to a satiny shine. All the travel of these last years should've taken a toll, but the good-natured colt took it in stride. Lotnik had always trusted her and the humans around him.

"I'll see to it you get him, Anna. Or that you come to America with him," Captain Baker's voice made her turn. She smiled at him.

"Do you have that power?" she asked, tipping her head in disbelief. He had brought her saddle and carried it over his right arm. He stepped into the stall.

Captain Baker was a nice man, a good man. But when he was around her, he stared at her wistfully. Other women would use this vulnerability to their advantage. Anna could not.

"I do," he said in a self-assured tone. "Both you and Erik. I have a ranch in America. I can sponsor you."

"Captain Baker, you should talk to my husband about this. I let him make those decisions. He has plans for a veterinary clinic in his home village." Anna said cheerfully, trying her best not to offend him but letting him know she was married.

She heard brisk steps coming down the aisleway. "Anna, they are ready for you," Erik said. When he stepped into the doorway, his smile faded into a frown. Baker's face turned bright red, revealing his motives weren't as wholesome as he pretended.

At least Baker had the intelligence to stay on Lotnik's opposite side. Anna slipped Lotnik's bridle into place and led the horse out of the stall. Erik said nothing as he walked alongside her toward the arena. At the end of the barn row, Erik placed his hand on her shoulder before she could step into the arena.

"Be careful, Anna. Captain Baker is in love with you." His eyes pleaded for reassurance.

Anna nodded. "I am sorry for him." She smiled. "Because I'm hopelessly in love—with you." She stepped close to him and kissed his cheek. For a moment, she held his gaze, turned, and led Lotnik into the arena at a jog. When she reached the row of men at the rail who would determine Lotnik's fate, she mounted the horse.

Erik joined the men along the arena rail, waiting and watching as Anna rode Lotnik through his gaits.

October 12, 1945

Six long years ago, Hitler invaded Poland. Anna stood on the balcony of her hotel room, watching the sun burn away the light mist in Bremerhaven harbor. Erik strolled out and stood beside her. She dropped her head against his shoulder. Parting crushed her heart.

The Americans had chosen one hundred fifty-one horses for the remount stations. In the mix were Janow's Arabians, Europe's finest Thoroughbreds, Lipizanner mares from the Caucasus. In a terrible twist, the Russians demanded their share of the Polish Arabians, settling for twenty mares in the peace negotiations. They had stolen six-year-old Ofir in 1939 when they withdrew from Poland. They wanted the purebred Polish-Arabian mares for their breeding program. Erik and Willi had been recruited to take the Russians their mares. It made Anna seethe.

Both Anna and Erik had suffered such losses in this war. Erik's father and mother died in an Allied bombing that razed the dairy to the ground. His brothers perished on the Russian front, and his younger sister was lost—rumored to have married and moved away to God knows where.

Erik had no reason to stay in Germany. He bore up stoically. What could they do about it all now?

"Are you ready to go?" he asked.

"No. Erik, I'll stay with you," she said, choking back her tears. She had promised him she wouldn't cry, and here she was crying.

"It's only for a short time. My love, I'll join you in New York in a little while," Erik kissed her forehead. "The horses will be more comfortable if you are with them."

"I could wait for you here. Then we can cross to America together."

Erik sighed. "And let Lotnik cross alone? I need you to go to America. You'll be safe there. Germany is in chaos. It's not safe."

"Can't they find someone else to go for you?"

"I know the horses. I speak Russian. Willi and I can do this quickly. It's a four-day train ride to Tersk. We unload the mares and turn around. I'll be back in Bremerhaven in less than two weeks. I'll meet you in New York within a month." Erik pulled the tickets out of his pocket to show her. She carefully read the train tickets, one to Tersk through Moscow and one tracing back over the same route from Tersk to Bremerhaven. Carefully, she slipped them into the folder he kept in the left inside pocket of his brown tweed jacket. Before returning the envelope, she found the ticket for *RMS Queen Mary*, the ship that would bring Erik to the States. Colonel Reed had called it *Operation Magic Carpet*. The Americans had such fun names for military operations. They'd called the horse rescue *Operation Cowboy*. Anna laughed at the memory.

"I just worry about you," Anna said.

"I'll be traveling with Willi. And then, with many of the soldiers we've met from the Second Cavalry aboard the ship. I will be in good company." Erik reassured her. "We'll meet in New York and join Captain Baker at his ranch. He's agreed to put us up until I get my veterinary practice going."

Anna could visualize it. Even the hard work. She couldn't wait to have a home.

"Come on. Let's get you settled in your cabin." Erik hugged her and took her hand.

Once at the dock, they watched as the horses were led into slated wooden crates and lifted by a hoist onto the deck of the Liberty ship *Stephen F. Austin*. In the ship's hold, the crew had built individual box stalls for the stallions, standing stalls for the mares, and small pens for groups of foals.

After inspecting the accommodations for both Anna and the horses, Erik walked with Anna to the ship's deck. The ship's loud warning blast announced it was time to depart.

Anna grabbed a trembling breath. She didn't want to let him go.

"It's only a month," Erik reminded her. "A short month, and we'll be together. No more war. No more separation." After a sweet, lingering kiss, he said, "Goodbye."

Anna leaned against the deck railing and watched Erik, waving until the ship pulled away. When she could no longer see him, she retired to her cabin and wept.

November 1, 1945

It was a cold morning. An icy fog hugged the buildings and docks at New York Harbor. The scent of diesel fuel, iodine, and salt mixed in the air. The dark gray ripples against the dock shimmered with rainbows of oil. *The RMS Queen Mary* was arriving soon, and Anna stood, bundled up against the chill with Captain Baker. He had offered Erik and Anna a new start. He'd even procured Erik's travel papers, the train and ship passage. Anna knew it was for her, but she also hoped once Erik was home, Baker's crush would fade away. They watched the massive ship slowly navigate the dock.

The *Stephen F. Austin* had only pulled into dock in Newport News, Virginia, three days ago after a harrowing trip across the Atlantic. They had encountered a storm that wreaked havoc. An eight-day trip had turned into sixteen. Some horses were injured, but not seriously. Despite the chaos, all thirty of Janow's Arabians had survived, including the foal born en route.

This morning, anxious and hopeful, Anna watched as the *Queen Mary* docked at Cunard's Pier 90 in New York City, and the crew lowered the covered gangplank. Soldiers disembarked, grabbed by wives and sweethearts. She scanned the railings along the decks for Erik.

"George. I don't see him," she cried frantically. "Do you see Erik?" She grabbed his arm, eyes wild.

"Wait here," he said, heading for the ship's steward.

Anna had expected to receive a telegram, but they arrived with the horses eight days late, and everything was a ball of confusion. Erik's itinerary said he would arrive today.

The crowd disbursed joyfully reunited with loved ones. The dock became unexpectedly quiet. Captain Baker returned, his face grim. He had news she didn't want to hear. Dread overwhelmed her.

"Anna, he never boarded the ship. He hasn't tried to redeem his ticket."

She closed her eyes and let the words wash over her. She was too shocked to react. Her heart pounded against the crushing worry that overtook her. Was Erik dead? She didn't want to believe it.

Captain Baker put his arm around her shoulder. "Come on, Anna. Let's go to the hotel, and I'll make some calls. He just missed this crossing. Everything will be okay. He's fine."

Anna knew it wasn't fine, and nothing would ever be fine. Anna feared—no, she knew at that moment she would never see Erik again.

Chapter Fifty-Five

KARENA SAT, HER BACK AGAINST her pillows. She fingered the page, making sure it was the last one. When a tear splashed and darkened the white paper of the manuscript, she snapped out of her shock. She set the binder beside her, folded back the covers, and rose from bed.

The clock on the bedside table read eight-thirty. She snorted a laugh. She'd read all night, and she wasn't even tired. Karena set out clean jeans, a t-shirt, undies, and socks on the end of the bed.

After padding quietly to the bathroom, she turned on the shower and adjusted the temperature.

"Okay. Slow down. Think this through. Dr. Erik wasn't dead, silly," she said out loud to herself. "Gerard wouldn't be here if he was, dummy." She tipped her head side to side and rolled her eyes. "Oh, No!" Karena squeezed her eyes shut. "They really never saw each other again. She never knew he was alive. Did he fall in love with a Russian woman and decide not to come back?" She tested the water; it was her preferred temperature. She stepped inside.

Karena poured a dollop of shampoo into her hand. "Wait—the letters. I have to get hold of the letters Gerard translated for me. Ooh! He knows what they say. He didn't want to tell me." She lathered her hair and stood under the warm shower until all the soap was rinsed away and swirled down the drain.

Quickly, she finished bathing. She toweled dry, combed the tangles from her hair, and brushed her teeth. As she dressed, she knew she had to find Gerard. Even if he was working. She knew she wouldn't rest until she read those letters.

When she opened the door to her bedroom, she could smell breakfast—coffee, bacon, and homemade cinnamon rolls were on the menu. Walking down the stairs, she wondered how she'd find Gerard. She could call the veterinary clinic, but then they'd all think she was a forward girl chasing him. Actually, she was, but not for the reason they would surmise.

She walked through the living room but was stopped by the view through the large bay window. It was incomparable. Late August, and the meadows and pastures were still emerald green. The Bitterroots rose up, covered with stands of Ponderosa Pine and Douglas Fir. It was no wonder Granny A loved it here.

Karena heard voices in the kitchen. *Darn it!* The relatives were up, but it was too early for them. They usually straggled out of bed around nine-thirty. Hesitantly, she walked forward into the doorway.

Gerard sat at the kitchen table, the morning newspaper spread out in front of him and a steaming mug of coffee in his right hand. *Just the guy she wanted to see.* He and Mom were talking about the weather.

Karena narrowed her eyes, lowered her head, and walked into the room.

"Good morning," she said, walking over to her mom and kissing her cheek. "Oh, Gerard. Good morning," Karena wanted to blurt out, *'Tell me what was in the letters!'*

Gerard was so polite. He stood and pulled out a chair for her. That took the impulsive wind out of her sails. She was a little miffed that he made her wait to find out about the contents of the translated letters. *Okay, so Granny A and Dr. Erik didn't end up together—but why?* That question swallowed her whole like an Anaconda!

She sat in the chair, staring at him. Mom filled two plates with breakfast.

"Why don't you two have breakfast on the porch? The relatives will be down in a minute, and you won't have to put up with them if you're outside."

What a great suggestion. Once she got Gerard alone, she was going to find out. Karena picked up her plate and mug of coffee, walked to the front porch door, and shouldered her way through. Gerard followed. They sat at the small two-person table by the deck railing. The morning air was cool, like a harbinger of colder weather to come. The leaves on the large maple tree across the lawn had a golden tinge to some of the leaves. In a few days, Karena would have to go home. She wasn't sure she wanted to leave.

"I finished the manuscript overnight." She leaned forward across the table. "What happened? Did the letters explain?"

Gerard nodded. He reached into the inside pocket of his jacket and set them on the table in front of him. "I thought you'd finish, so I brought them."

"Well? What do they say?" She lifted both palms toward him, begging him to explain.

"Karena, most of the world isn't like America," Gerard started. "Not as civilized."

"Okay. I know that. Especially at the end of a war. . . ."

"Stalin was paranoid. It was clear by the time World War II broke out that he was insane. He was so crazy, he killed many of his best military generals when they disagreed with his battle plans. He sent unarmed soldiers to fight Panzer Divisions. And Communism was not the answer it promised to be. The people didn't cheerfully donate their possessions to the State. He had to take the farms and businesses by force. The Communists had just replaced the Czar with a new, more terrifying dictatorship. Stalin had become more murderous than the Czar."

"I read that in my history classes," Karena said, motioning for him to continue.

"After unloading the mares at the farm at Tersk, Grandpa Erik and Willi went to the train station to leave Russia. They were arrested and returned to Tersk. The authorities knew they were veterinarians, and they needed veterinarians."

"So they just took them? How could they justify. . . ?"

"They were Germans, and Hitler and the Germans were anti-communists—enemies. Hitler's Germany caused World War II, so I guess they felt Willi and Erik owed them. They knew the German government was in disarray and wouldn't have the resources to look for them. They guessed the Allies wouldn't either. You know, two German guys, who cares?" Gerard picked up his mug of coffee and sipped. He continued, "My Grandfather tried to contact Anna, but all his letters were confiscated. He and Willi were jailed at night and brought to the stud farm by armed guards during the day to work." Gerard stirred his scrambled eggs with his fork and took a bite.

"Then Anna didn't know if he was still alive?" Karena asked. She felt sadness, imagining losing contact with a loved one and being left in limbo. But then she remembered Sam hadn't returned her calls, and he had no excuse like Dr. Erik. Unless a shark had eaten him, Sam was just a coward who didn't want to face breaking up with her.

"Your grandmother did everything she could to find him. She contacted the German, American, Polish, and Russian embassies, and the Red Cross, begging for help locating him. But the director at Tersk didn't want to lose his most competent veterinarian, so he lied and told them all Erik had died. He even produced a death certificate.

"Your Granny A returned to Europe three times. She didn't want to believe Erik was dead. At the time, Russia closed its doors to Americans, and it had taken over Poland. They were so afraid the Americans would conquer them, they would've jailed her as a spy," Gerard said, sadness in his voice.

Karena dropped her fork on her plate. "And we were terrified the Russians would nuke us. Still are." Karena picked up her fork and ate a strawberry. "Then they never saw each other again?"

"No, they didn't. Before Grandpa Erik passed, he gave me these letters in a wooden box. He begged me to take the letters to Anna. Without my parents' knowledge, he had squirreled away money for my flight and expenses. He had enrolled me in an exchange student program. When I arrived two years ago, I came to the farm, introduced myself, and gave her Grandpa Erik's letters."

"You didn't read them?" Karena asked, incredulity in her voice.

"They weren't addressed to me. They were private. If I had, I might not have done as he asked." Gerard frowned. "I loved my grandmother. But she betrayed Erik. Her father lied and told the authorities Erik died. He kept him from going home. When the Russian government finally released the surviving German prisoners of war in 1956, they wouldn't allow him to leave."

"If someone did that to me, I'd hate them. I'd hate them forever!" Karena said, scrunching her face into a grimace. "How could he stand it?"

"I think he did what he had to—to survive. You are blessed here in America. The Soviet Government back then killed anyone it considered undesirable. They murdered thousands of Kulak farmers because they owned a couple of cows and maybe as much as five acres," Gerard snorted a sarcastic laugh and shook his head. "They starved millions of Ukrainians to death when they collectivized their farms. They killed millions in their Gulag labor camps. They committed more genocide by their policies trying to establish the communist Utopia than Hitler. Erik had already been declared dead. What would stop them from killing him if he tried to run? In the 1990s, Russia finally westernized a little. It's much better now.

"After I read the letters to translate them for you, I realized Grandpa Erik was always kind to my Grandmother, but he never loved her. Not the way he loved Anna." Gerard pressed his lips together tightly. He sorted through the stack of envelopes and pushed one across the table to her. Karena hesitantly picked it up, never letting her gaze drop from Gerard's. She opened it. Inside, with the letter, she found Hitler's permission letter for Erik and Anna's marriage, Erik's return train ticket to Bremerhaven, and his ticket for passage to America on the Queen Mary. Never used. Karena looked up at Gerard, unable to keep the sadness from closing in, surrounding her. She clutched Granny A's wedding rings that hung on the gold chain around her neck. She would never take them off. Never!

Carefully, as if she unfolded an ancient treasure, Karena opened the letter. Below the German words, Gerard's printed translation stood out in red ink.

"My dearest Anna,

I write this letter with the hope that my grandson, Gerard, has found you and life has gone well for you. I have written to you many times, nearly every day, but my letters were intercepted and confiscated. If you are reading this, Gerard has risked much to bring it to you.

I pray that your fond memories of me will persuade you to help him remain in America to complete his education. Leaving you was never my choice. My love for you has remained unchanged, even to this day, as I reach my ninety-fifth birthday.

Willi and I were arrested and imprisoned by the Soviet Communist Government after we delivered the Arabian mares. As German officers, we were seen as enemies. Unlike the other German prisoners released in 1956, I was kept at Tersk and forced to serve as their veterinarian. I was constantly reminded I owed them my life, as repayment for the atrocities committed by Germany during the war.

Only weeks ago, I learned you were told I was dead when I failed to meet you in America as we had planned. For decades, I was denied any contact with the outside world. The director of the farm informed me that you and the horses we'd worked so hard to save perished when the "Steven F. Austin" sank in a storm at sea. But in my heart, I could never let myself believe you were gone. My hope was rekindled when American horse breeders visited Tersk, and I learned you were alive. All these years, we were kept apart by deception and lies. My heart breaks in two as I write these words—as I imagine the life we were denied.

Now, I am old and frail. As I near the end of my days, my mind is full of you, full of memories of the years we shared. I relive those days whenever I close my eyes and dream. I have never stopped loving you, my most precious Anna. In heaven, I pray we find each other.

With all my heart, Erik."

Karena couldn't hold back the tears streaming down her cheeks. "Gerard, it's so sad. Granny A didn't get the love of her life, nor the horse she'd adored, raised, and trained. I was so standoffish around Granny A. I listened to my relatives and their disparaging remarks. I see it now. I know she loved Erik, too. There was always a quiet melancholy about her. A brokenheartedness, a spirit of longing. I'm such a bad person," Karena said. "I didn't understand her."

"No." He laughed. "How could you know? How can we know what war does to its victims without living through it?" He sighed. "One good thing—together, they changed horse breeding in America and Europe by saving the priceless horses. Grandpa Erik always said it was worth the sacrifice."

"So, do you think the Russians would've killed the horses? Eaten them?" she asked.

"Yes. They might've done that. Stalin couldn't feed his troops like the Allies did. But I think people were wrong to think they wouldn't value the horses. They have a pretty good breeding program these days."

"Yeah. With the stolen Polish horses." Karena's eyes welled with tears, but she didn't let them fall. "Granny A told me she tried to buy her favorite horse, Lotnik. But months before she and George could come up with the money, and the remount stations closed, the Colonel in charge sold him to one of his friends as his private riding horse. Witez II was sold at auction a year or so later to a breeder named Earle Hurlbutt and Calarabia Farms. His family loved the horse, and under their care, he became a very famous stallion and show horse. His offspring garnered many national championships."

Gerard reached across the table for her hands. "Do you think Granny A loved George?"

"I think so. She was always good to him. Maybe, like Dr. Erik, she did what she had to—to survive," Karena said, sorrow in her voice.

"She bred a fine herd of horses. They were her comfort." He finished his coffee, and after setting his mug down, he said, "In her heart, Granny A never believed Erik was dead. She told me she went to the "Pride of Poland" horse sale several times, hoping he'd be there. Grandpa Erik told me if he'd seen her, he feared he would have run away with her."

"I hope they are together in Heaven," Karena said.

Gerard nodded. "Let's not stay in this mood. Let's go do something else, something happy."

"Should we go for a horseback ride?" Karena felt her breath catch after she said it. She was still afraid of them. But there were lots of things she'd been afraid of in life. She decided to face her fear head-on. "All right. I'll clear the dishes and meet you at the barn."

Karena rinsed the plates and loaded them in the dishwasher. Mom stood from the table and walked over.

"Did you and Gerard have a nice talk?" she asked, peaking both eyebrows. *Snoopy to the last*, Karena thought. But she had her best interests at heart.

"Yes. I really like him. Now, I wish we didn't have to leave on Saturday."

"I know. I love it here. I'd forgotten how simple and relaxing ranch life can be. Dad has decided to fly up and drive back with us," Mom said. "Maybe we can convince him to keep this place."

"I'd love that. Well, I'm going riding with Gerard. See you in a couple of hours," she said. Before passing through the kitchen door, she stopped, turned back, and hugged her mother.

A smile passed slowly over her mother's lips, like a secret.

Karena walked up to the barn. Gerard brushed the mare he intended to ride. But he came out of the stall and set the brush on the tack trunk. He took hold of her hands and pulled her into his arms.

"Karena, will you think about coming to Idaho for college?" he asked. "This week with you—I really want to get to know you better. A lot better." A blush colored his cheeks. He stared into her eyes and then studied her lips as if determining how best to kiss her. She nearly melted. She knew she sighed. His lips touched hers, as soft as a breeze stirring through the flowers in a garden. They lingered there, lost in a moment so tender yet so electrifying. Karena yielded to a more passionate kiss. She could easily fall in love with Gerard. No. She already had.

"I knew your lips would feel like this, taste like this," he whispered.

Too fast. Too impulsive. No matter the stop signs her brain held up, Karena knew it was too late to prevent it now. *If Granny A were here, what would she advise her to do?*

Follow your heart and fall in love. Write your own story. The words were as clear as if Granny A were standing beside her. Karena couldn't help but smile.

Author's Notes

This novel is a work of fiction, but it is inspired by historical events. When writing this book, I followed history, but where there were small conflicts between historical accounts, I chose the version that best served my plot. The main characters in my story are fictional.

A brief history:

From the 1600s, the Polish Aristocracy acquired and bred some of the finest Arabian Horses in the world. On the First of September 1939, Hitler invaded Poland and started World War II. Russia entered the conquest of Poland on the Seventeenth of September, and the Polish government surrendered later that month. The nation was divided at the Bug River, with Germany controlling the western half and Russia controlling the country's eastern half. As the Russians withdrew from Poland, they stole nearly all of the stud farm at Janow Podlaski's mature Arabian bloodstock. The stud farm fell to the brutal Nazis. It has been asserted that 21.4% or six million of Poland's civilian population was killed during the Nazi occupation.

During the occupation, the stud farm was under the leadership of Wehrmacht Major Hans Fellgeible, a consummate horseman. The farm reclaimed many horses lost during the initial evacuation at the start of the war. In 1943, specially chosen horses from Janow were sent to Hostau,

Czechoslovakia. The breeding farm located there was tasked with breeding a superhorse that would be forever associated with the Nazi Aryan Super Race. Major Fellgeible efficiently managed the Farm until July of 1944, when he was arrested and accused of being a player in the Valkyrie Plot to overthrow Hitler.

In the closing days of World War II, knowing and perhaps hoping the war was over, the clear-eyed veterinarians at the secret breeding farm feared that the collection of Europe's finest horses would be lost to starving Russian troops advancing from the East. To the West, at the border between Germany and Czechoslovakia, a division of Patton's battle-hardened Third Army impatiently awaited new orders.

Committing treason against the Reich, the veterinarians scrambled through the mountains, armed only with a German-to-English dictionary and a white shirt as a surrender flag. They hoped to reach the American camp and beg for help to rescue the priceless horses. Without knowing who they'd meet, the vets stumbled onto the Twelfth Cavalry Second Reconnaissance Unit jam-packed with experienced American horsemen.

The Unit's commander, Colonel Hank Reed, contacted General George Patton and presented the German veterinarians' request for help. Patton replied with a resounding "Go get them, make it fast!"

With that, "Operation Cowboy" became one of the great rescue stories of the war. The Americans rescued over five hundred horses, including Janow Podlaski's Arabians, Austria's Lipizzaner, and famous European Thoroughbred Race Horses. The Second Cavalry also liberated the prisoners of war, Jewish concentration camp detainees, dissenters, and resistance fighters imprisoned near Hostau. Instead of leaving and going home, many of the newly released captives joined with the German Veterinarians and helped with the horse evacuation. The last horses to leave Hostau, fifty stallions, were ridden to safety just as the first Russian tanks appeared on the village's eastern edge. The final skirmishes that occurred during "Operation Cowboy" were the final battles of the war in Europe.

The Arabian Stallions Witez II and Lotnik were taken as *spoils of war* and imported to the American Cavalry Remount Stations. With the arrival of the Polish stallions, Arabian Horse Breeding in the U.S. was changed forever. In the years following the war, beautiful and athletic Polish Arabian horses were imported and were introduced into many private Arabian Horse breeding programs.

World War II European Time Line

- January 30, 1933, Hitler becomes Chancellor of Germany
- March 15,1938, German Anschluss with Austria
- November 9, 1938, Kristallnacht
- September 30, 1938, The annexation of the Sudetenland under the Munich Agreement
- March 1939, Hitler invades Czechoslovakia Britain rearms and reassures Poland
- August 23,1939, The Molotov-Ribbentrop Pact (Russian-German non-aggression pact)
- September 1, 1939, Hitler invades Poland
- September 3, 1939, Britian and France declare war on Germany
- September 17, 1939 Russia attacks Poland
- September 27, 1939 Warsaw surrenders, Russia withdraws from Poland
- September 1939, to May 1940 the Phony War
- April/May 1940, Hitler invades Denmark and Norway
- May 10, 1940, Blitzkrieg and Chamberlain resigns, Churchill becomes Prime Minister
- May 26, 1940, Dunkirk (Operation Dynamo)
- June 11, 1940, Italy enters war
- June 22, 1940, France signs armistice with Germany
- July 10 to 31 October 1940, Battle of Britain
- September 22, 1940, Tri partied Pact

- December 1940, British rout Italians in N. Africa
- April 6, 1941, Italy and Germany attack Yugoslavia (Operation 45)
- June 22, 1941, Hitler attacks Russia (Operation Barbarossa)
- August 1942, Allies invade N. Africa
- October 23, 1942, Battle of El Alamein
- November 1942, Battle of Stalingrad, Allies push into N. Africa
- May 12, 1943, Axis surrenders in N. Africa
- July 1943, Allies invade Sicily
- August 1943, Allies take Sicily
- September 3, 1943, Italy surrenders
- November 1943, Allies meet at Tehran
- January 1944, German siege of Leningrad ends
- June 5, 1944, Rome liberated
- June 6, 1944, D-Day in Normandy
- August 25, 1944, Paris liberated
- September 8, 1944, V2 Flying Bombs
- December 16, 1944, Battle of the Bulge
- March 1945, Allies cross the Rhine
- April 1945, Russians reach Berlin
- April 28, 1945, Mussolini captured and executed
- April 30, 1945, Hitler commits suicide
- May 7, 1945, Germany unconditionally surrenders
- May 8, 1945, V.E. Day

If you enjoyed this book, please leave a review
at Amazon.com or Goodreads.

Sarah Vail
Author

Sarah Vail spent forty years in private industry before retiring to Coeur d'Alene, Idaho to write mystery-suspense fiction. She has always enjoyed writing. To enhance her fiction novels, she has continued her education by taking classes in Creative Writing, Criminal Justice, Forensic Science, Criminology, Criminal Interrogation, Weapons Handling, and World History through the years. Miss Vail is an award-winning Author. Throughout her life, she admits to being a little horse-crazy. Her current novels include: James Street, Snow Country Lane, Old Schoolhouse Road, Lightning Ridge Road, and The Legend of Flying Horses. All are available in eBook, softcover, hardcover, and audiobook formats.

Judy Parker
Horse Illustrations

Judy Parker has dabbled in art since childhood. She started tattooing in 1978 and expanded her creative talent to fine art, freehand drawing, and painting around 2010. Judy owns Judy Parker's Pacific Tattoo Studio in San Diego. Her clients and customers find her artwork beautiful, imaginative, and stunning, whether in black and white or beautiful, rich colors. Her tattoo artwork and paintings can be viewed on Facebook, Instagram, and other social media platforms. For art or tattoo inquiries, you may email Judy at: Tattoojudils@yahoo.com.

John Stahr
Airplane Illustrations

Artist, aviator, creative dynamo, John Stahr lives
for flight and anything that relates to flying cre-
ativity. His 50 years in the custom painting field
transforming all modes of transportation into
creative motion. Since 2001 he has focused on
aircraft and all things flying. Not only custom

painting everything from BizJets to biplanes, in his "back of the hangar"
art studio, John creates fine art, textile design, aviation themed graphics
and sculptural elements. He hand built the sport plane of which he flies
for fun and sharing the joy of flight with others.

www.ingramcontent.com/pod-product-compliance
Lightning Source LLC
Chambersburg PA
CBHW020836030726
47496CB00001B/253